APOCALYPSE MEOW MEOW

James Proimos III

illustrated by
James Proimos Jr.

BLOOMSBURY
NEW YORK LONDON OXFORD NEW DELHI SYDNEY

To the Maryland SPCA for taking good care of Brownie before he found a home with us —James Proimos III

For Bugga —James Proimos Jr.

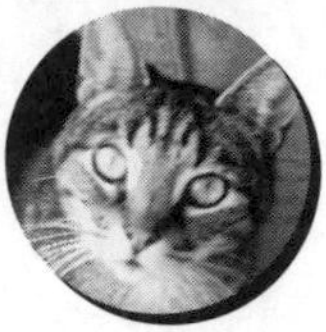

First published in the United States of America in November 2015
by Bloomsbury Children's Books
www.bloomsbury.com

Bloomsbury is a registered trademark of Bloomsbury Publishing Plc

For information about permission to reproduce selections from this book, write to Permissions, Bloomsbury Children's Books, 1385 Broadway, New York, New York 10018
Bloomsbury books may be purchased for business or promotional use. For information on bulk purchases please contact Macmillan Corporate and Premium Sales Department at specialmarkets@macmillan.com

Library of Congress Cataloging-in-Publication Data
Proimos, James, III.
Apocalypse meow meow / by James Proimos III ; illustrations by James Proimos Jr.
pages cm
Summary: Brownie, Apollo, and their ragtag group of strays are delighted when the rat shows them a nearby Twonkies factory that could provide a lifetime supply of food, but to reach the treats, Apollo will have to have a duel with the very large, very sophisticated "cat" that guards the factory.
ISBN 978-1-61963-472-5 (hardcover) • ISBN 978-1-61963-713-9 (e-book)
1. Graphic novels. [1. Graphic novels. 2. Dogs—Fiction. 3. Lion—Fiction. 4. Survival—Fiction. 5. Humorous stories.] I. Proimos, James, illustrator. II. Title.
PZ7.7.P76Apt 2015 741.5'973—dc23 2014042883

Book design by John Candell
Printed and bound in the U.S.A. by Thomson-Shore Inc., Dexter, Michigan
2 4 6 8 10 9 7 5 3 1

All papers used by Bloomsbury Publishing, Inc., are natural, recyclable products made from wood grown in well-managed forests. The manufacturing processes conform to the environmental regulations of the country of origin.

The Prologue

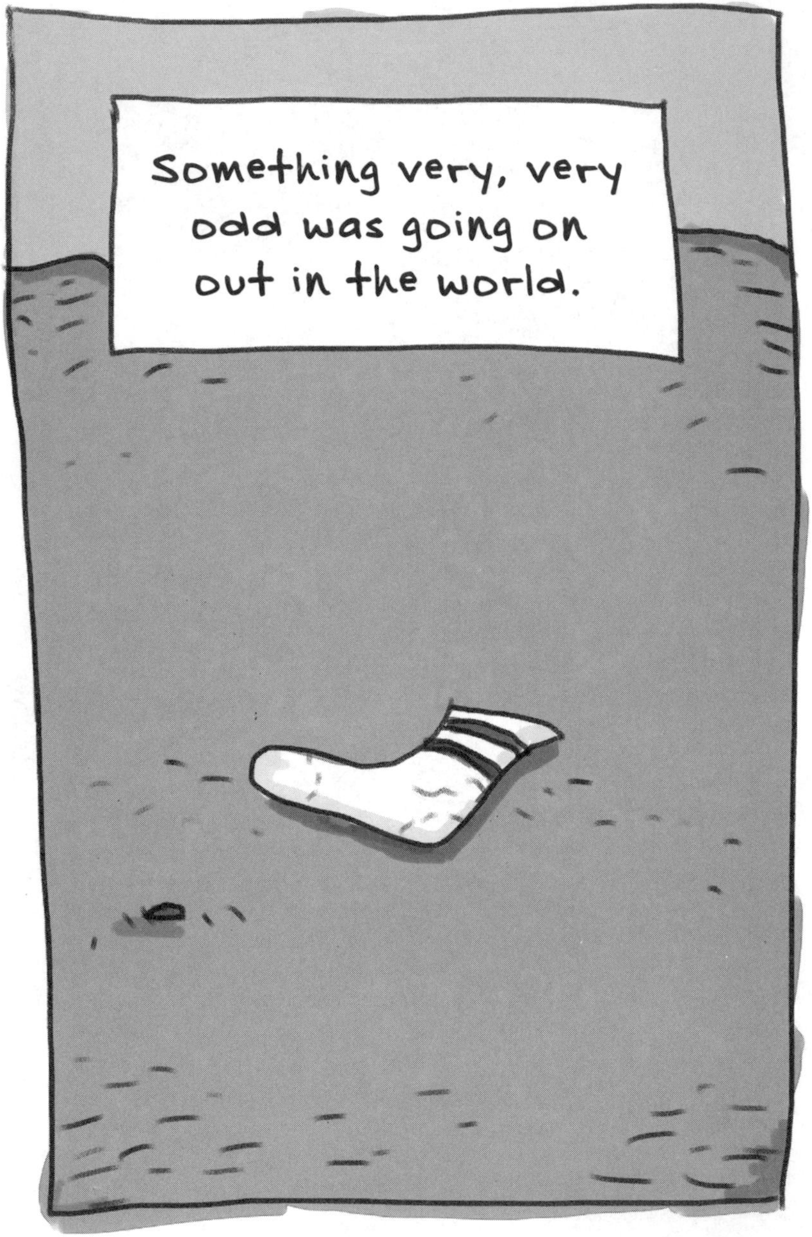
Something very, very odd was going on out in the world.

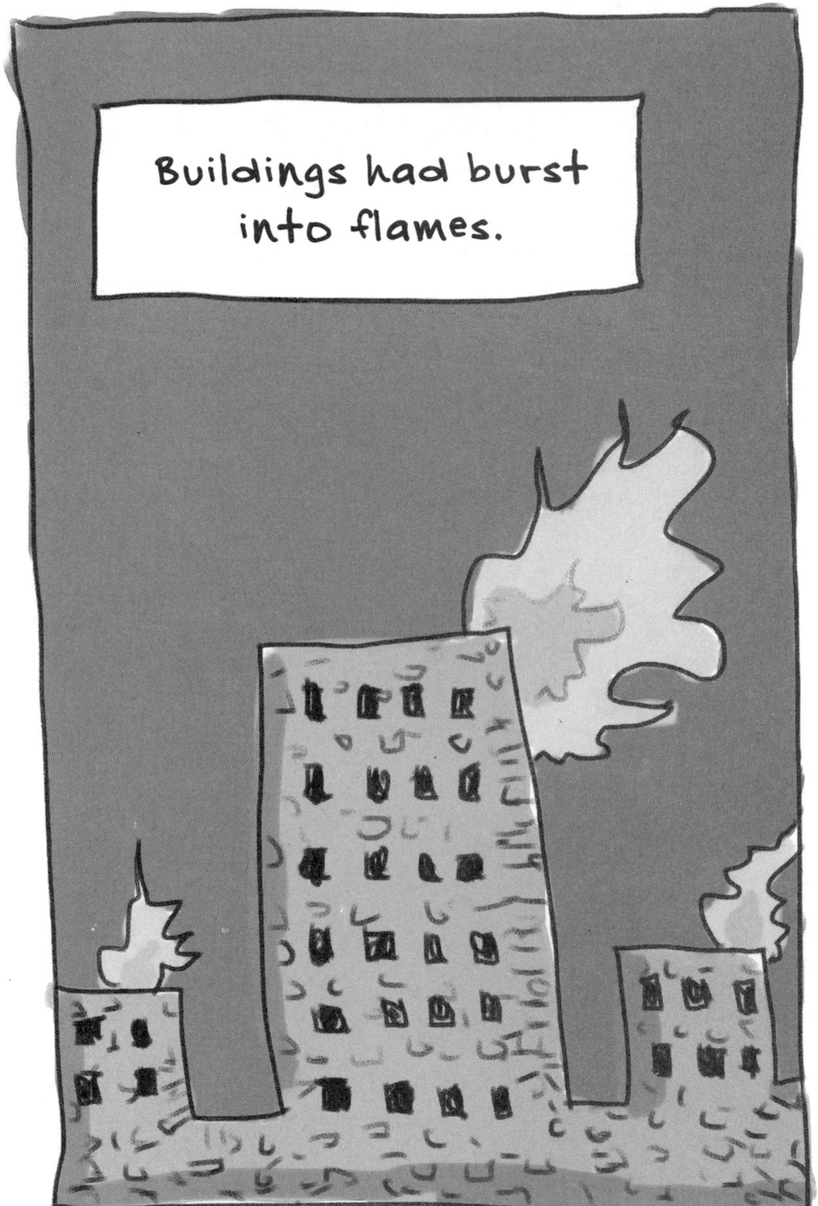
Buildings had burst into flames.

The kooks who made outlandish predictions suddenly seemed far less kooky.
THE END IS NEAR!

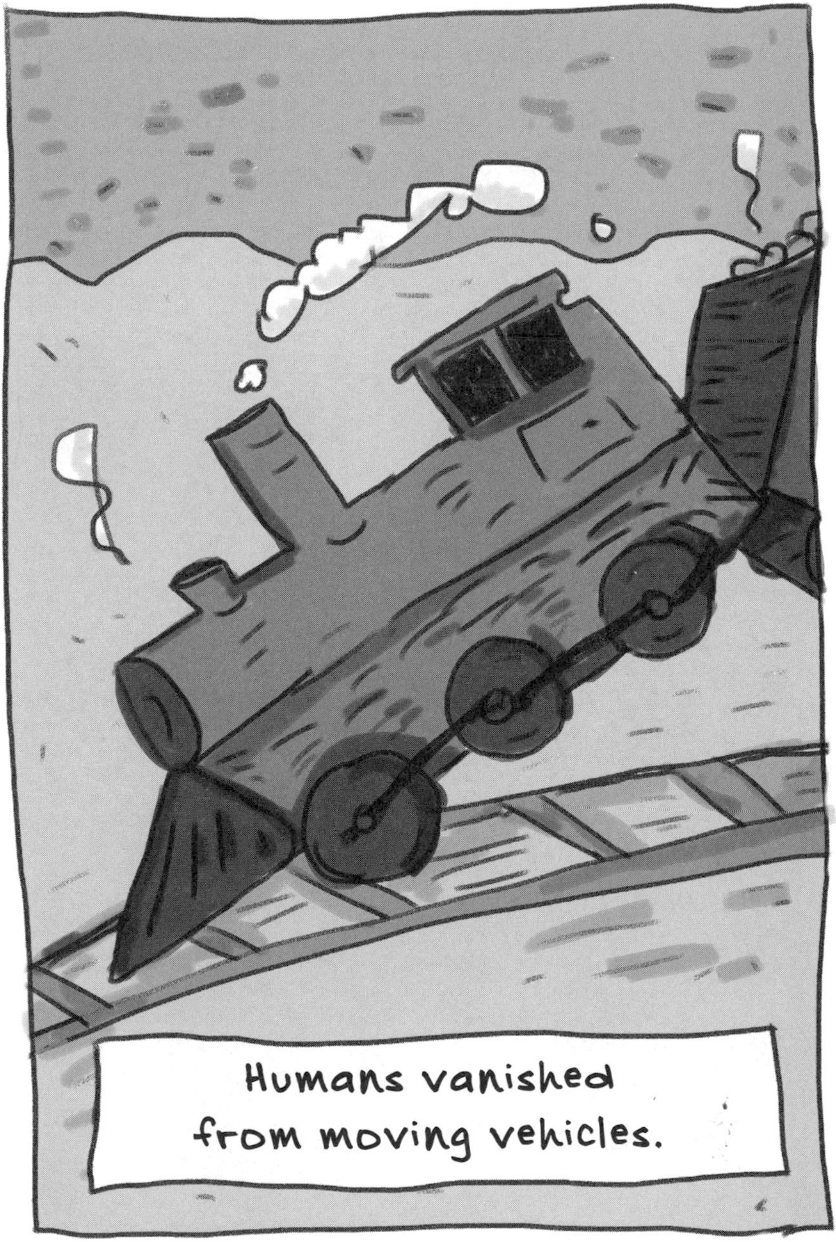
Humans vanished
from moving vehicles.

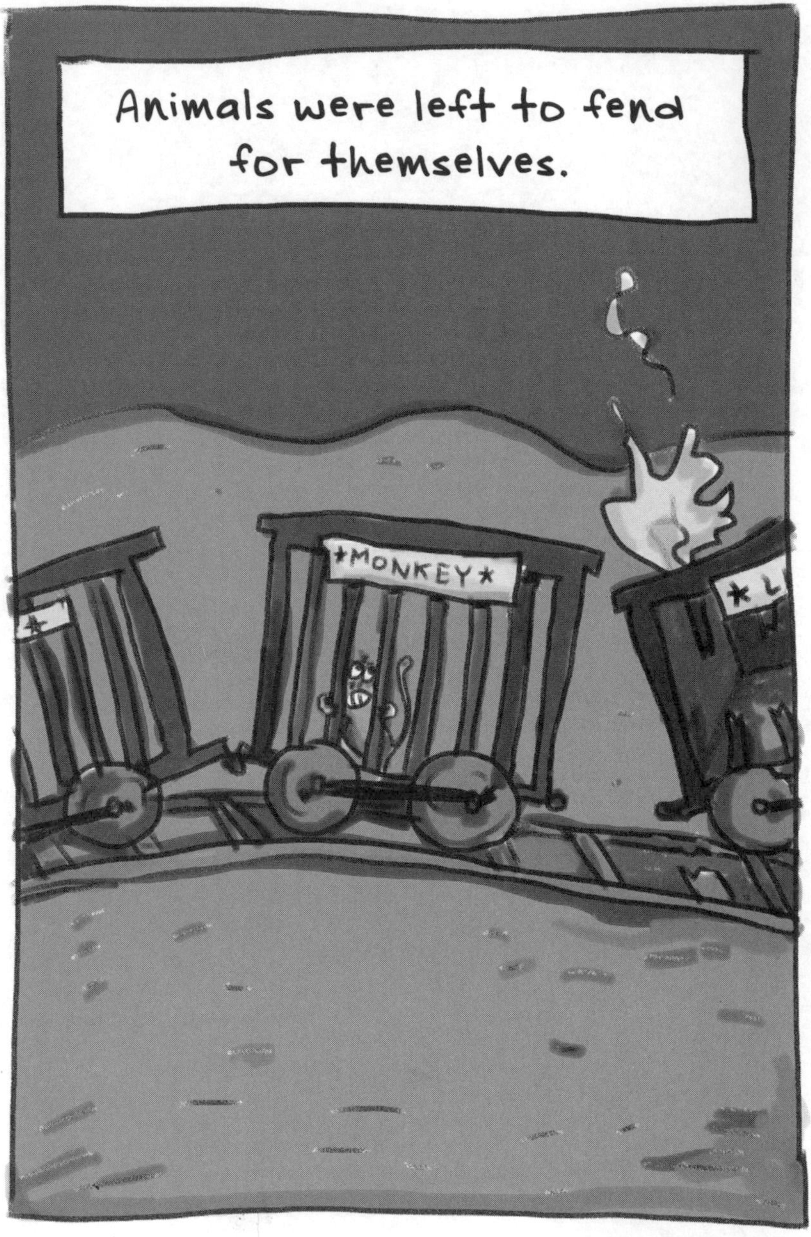
Animals were left to fend for themselves.
MONKEY

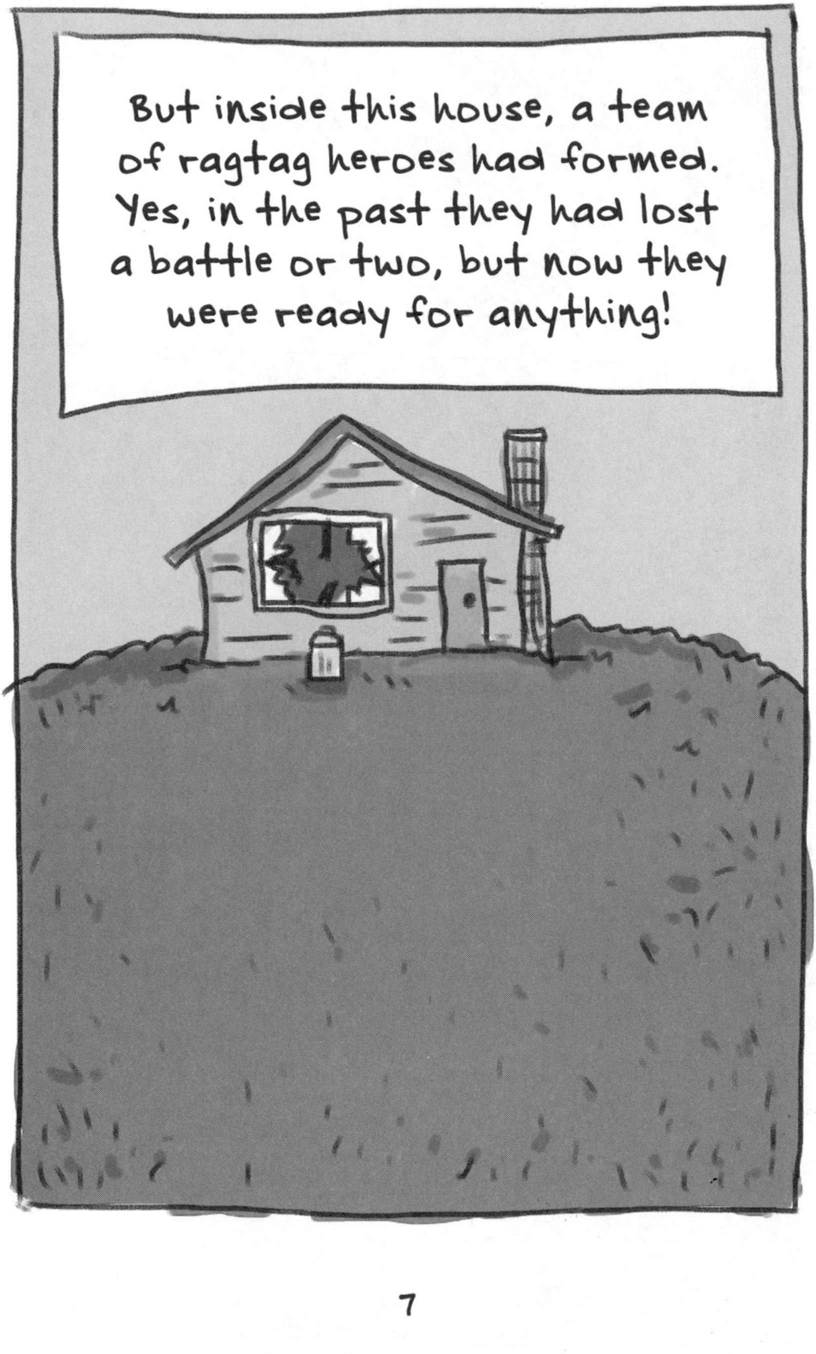
But inside this house, a team of ragtag heroes had formed. Yes, in the past they had lost a battle or two, but now they were ready for anything!

Scene
One

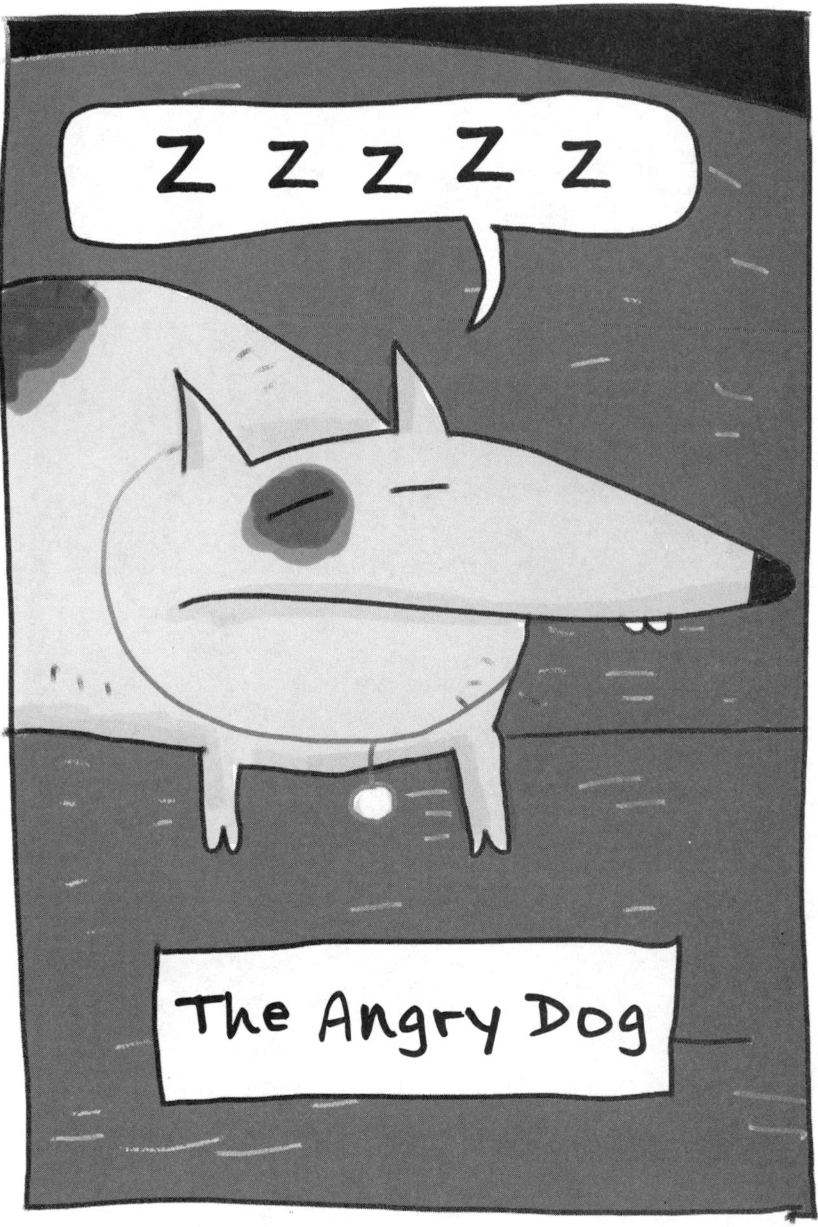
Z Z Z Z Z
The Angry Dog

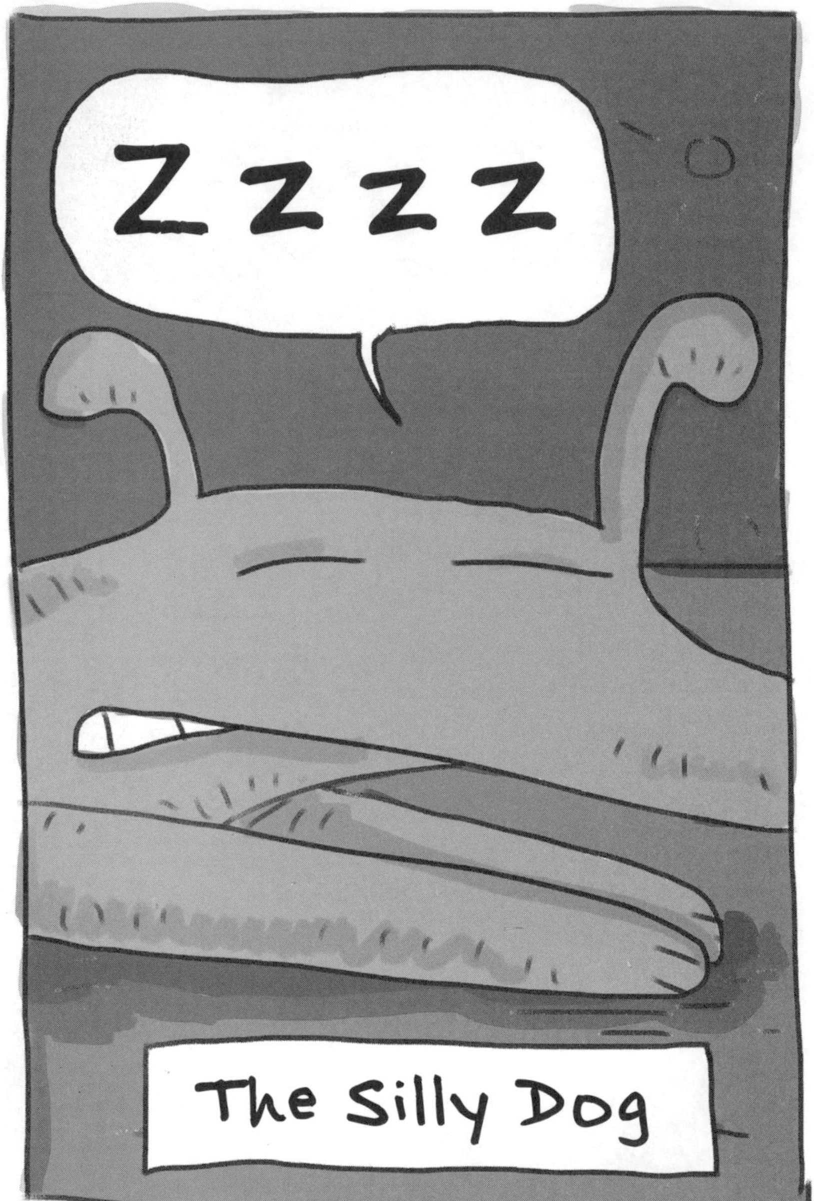
Zzzz
The Silly Dog

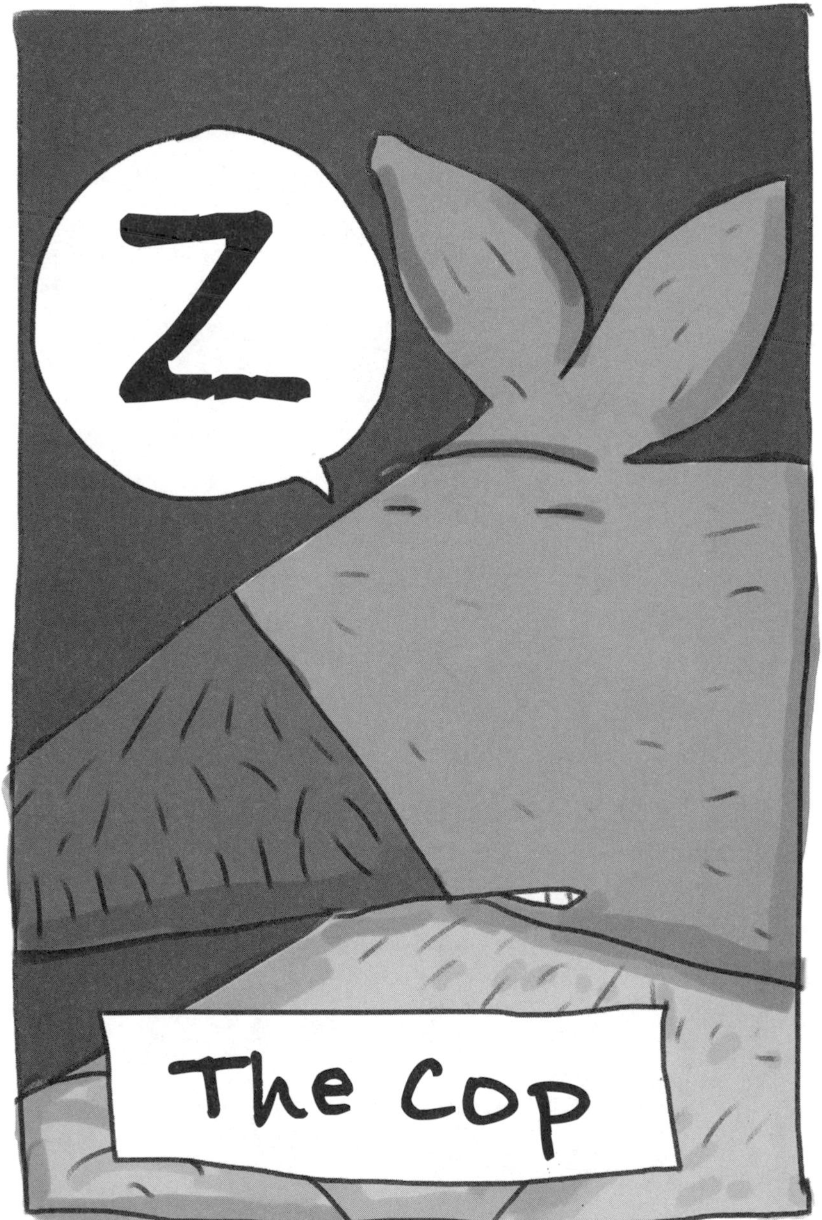
Z
The Cop

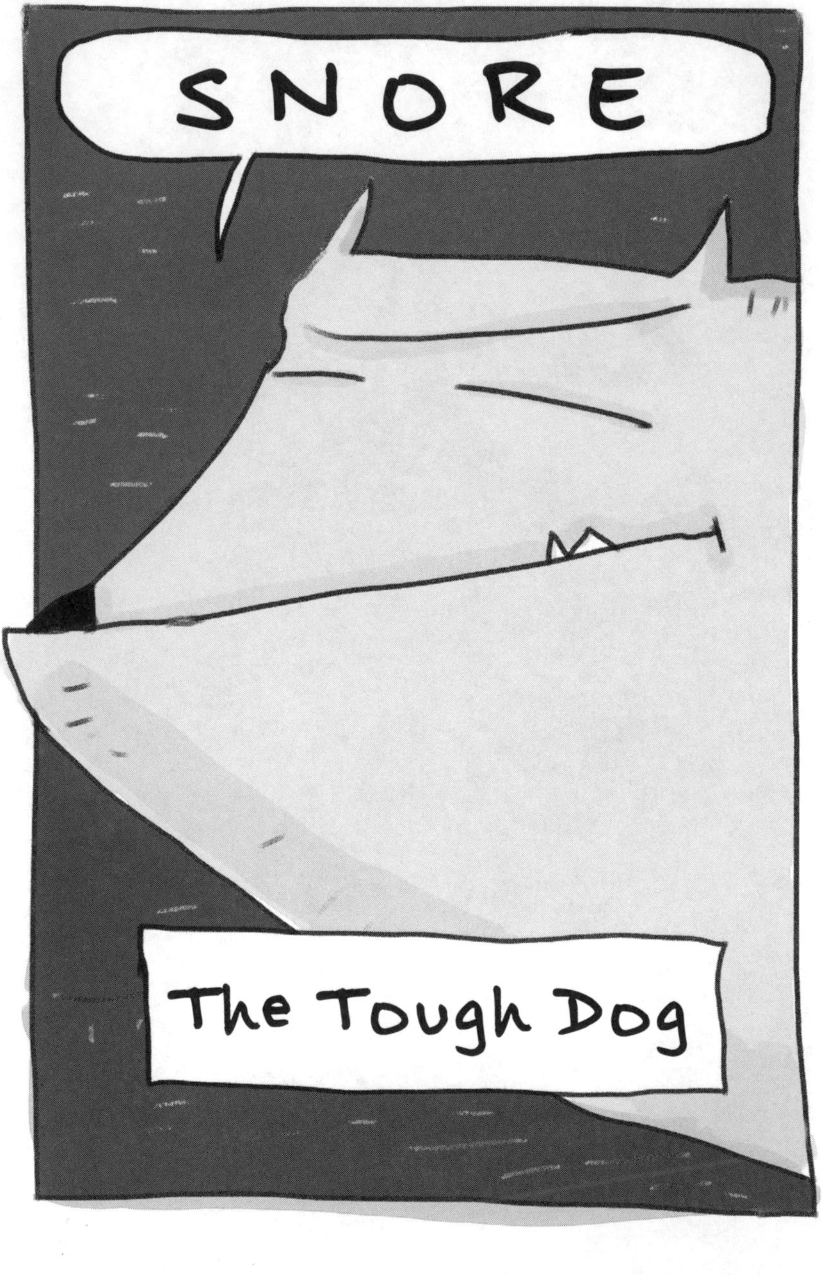
SNORE
The Tough Dog

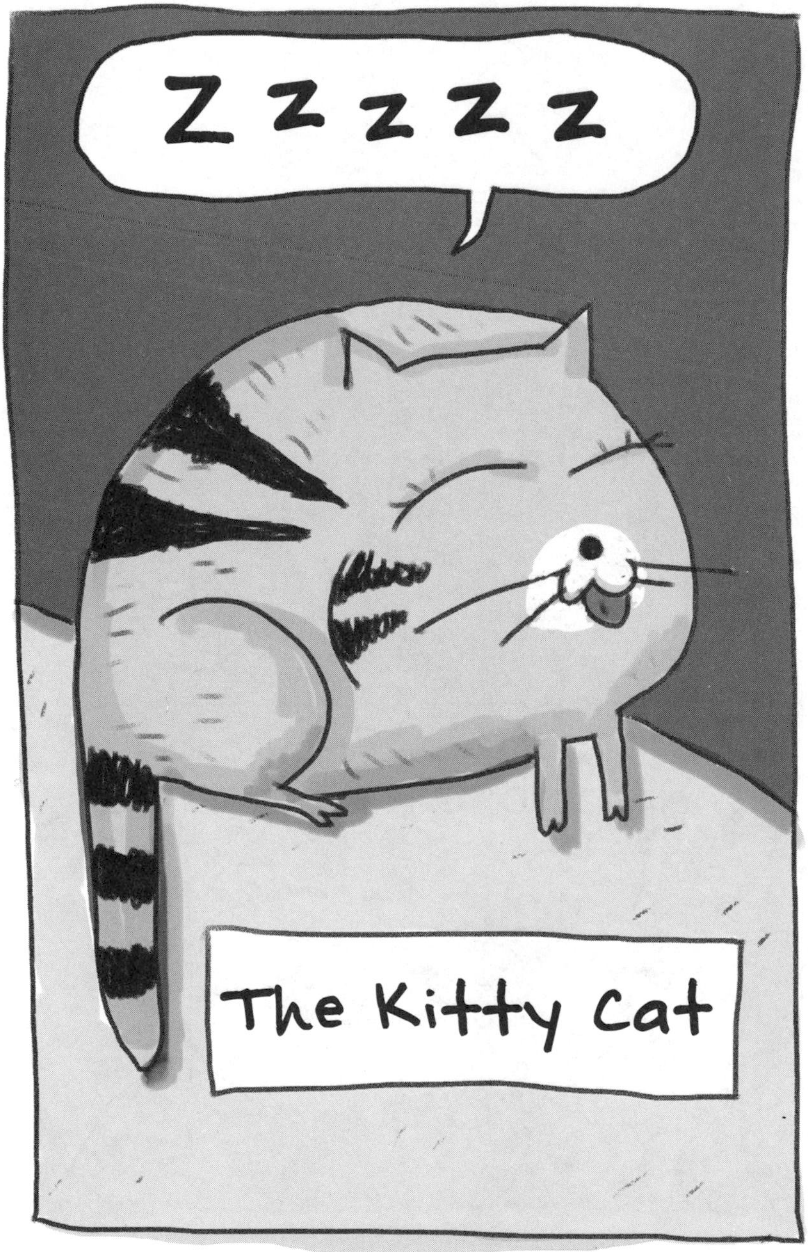
Z Z Z Z Z
The Kitty Cat

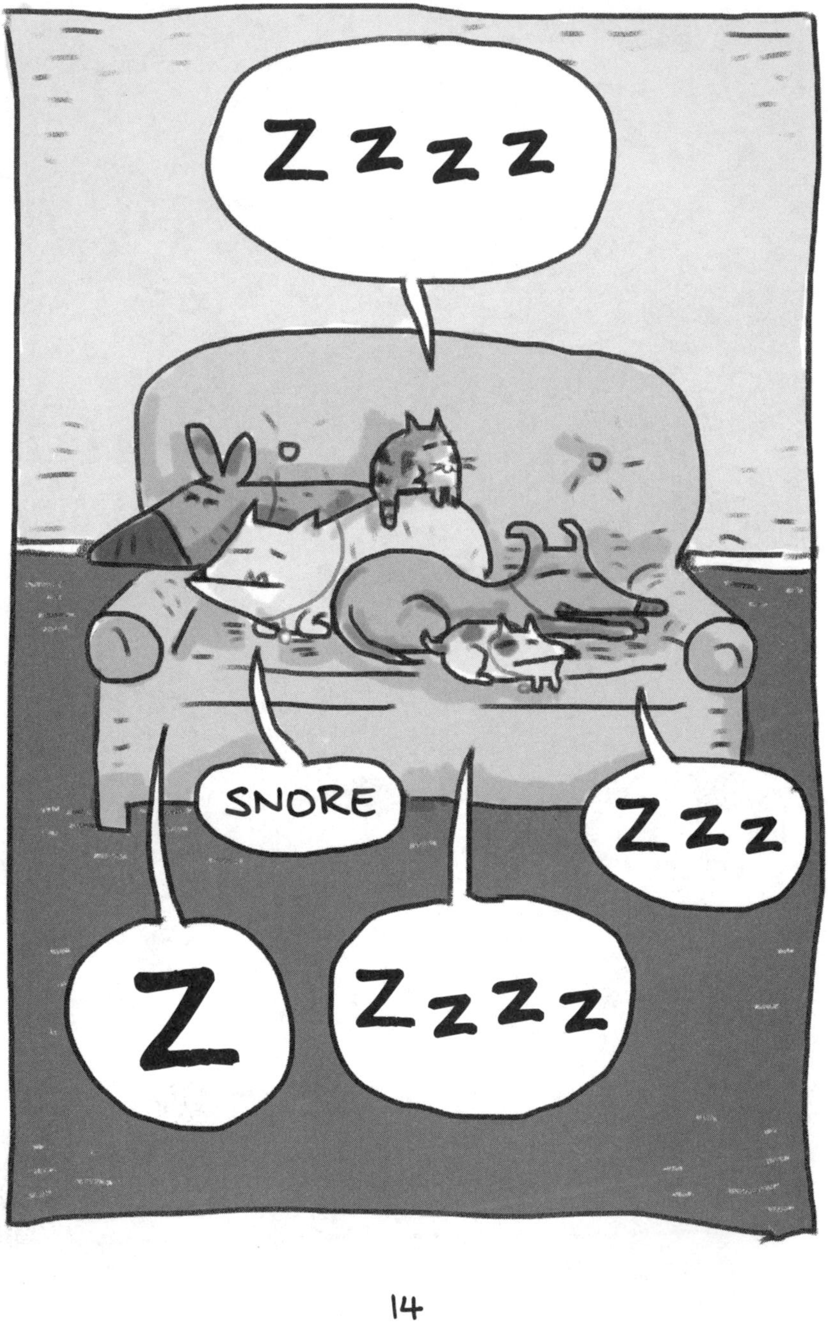
Zzzz
SNORE
Zzz
Z
Zzzz

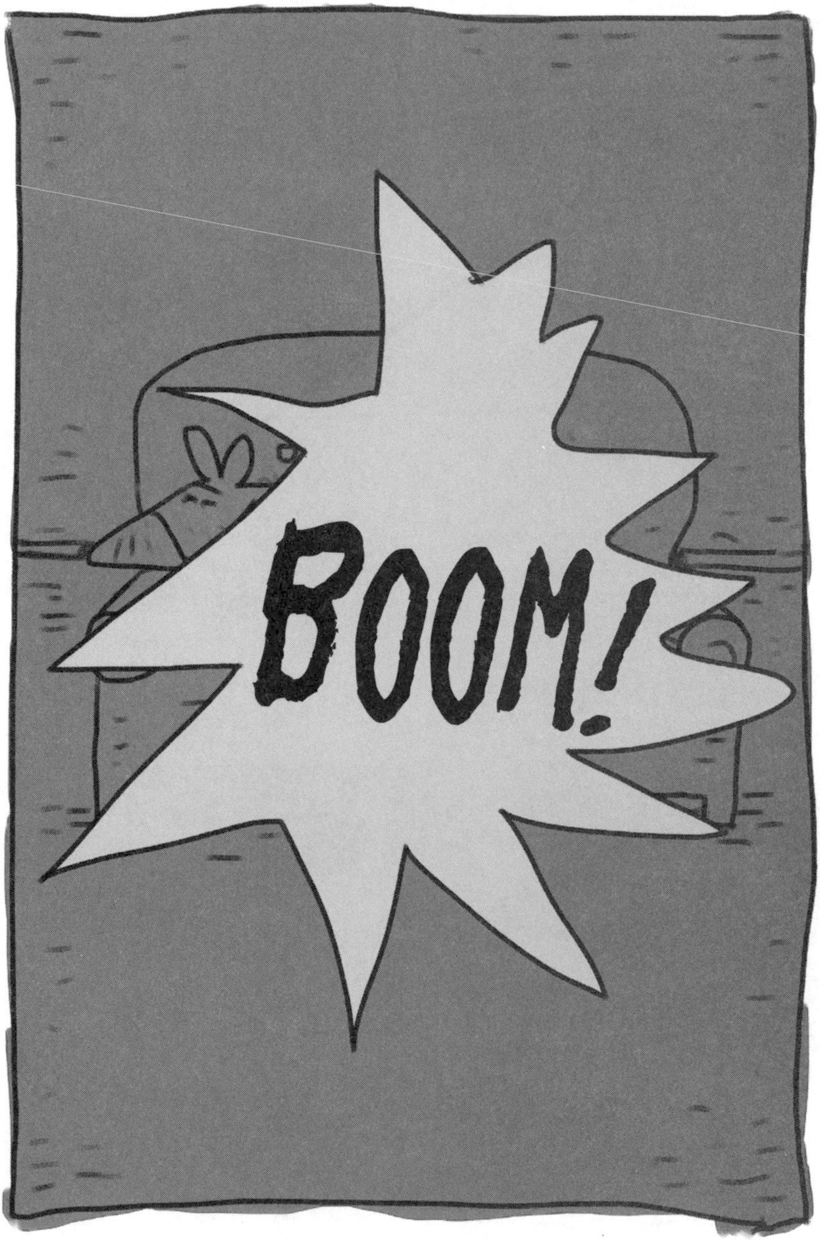
BOOM!

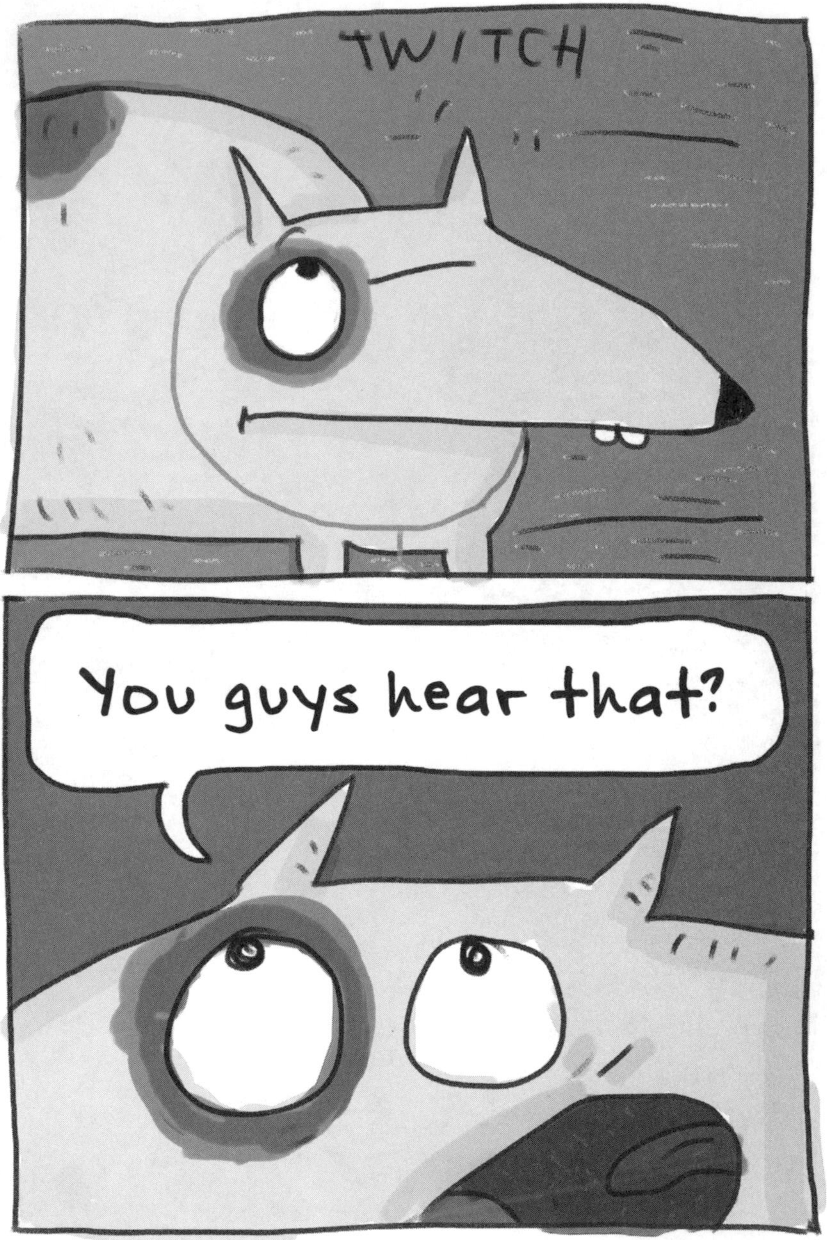
TWITCH
You guys hear that?

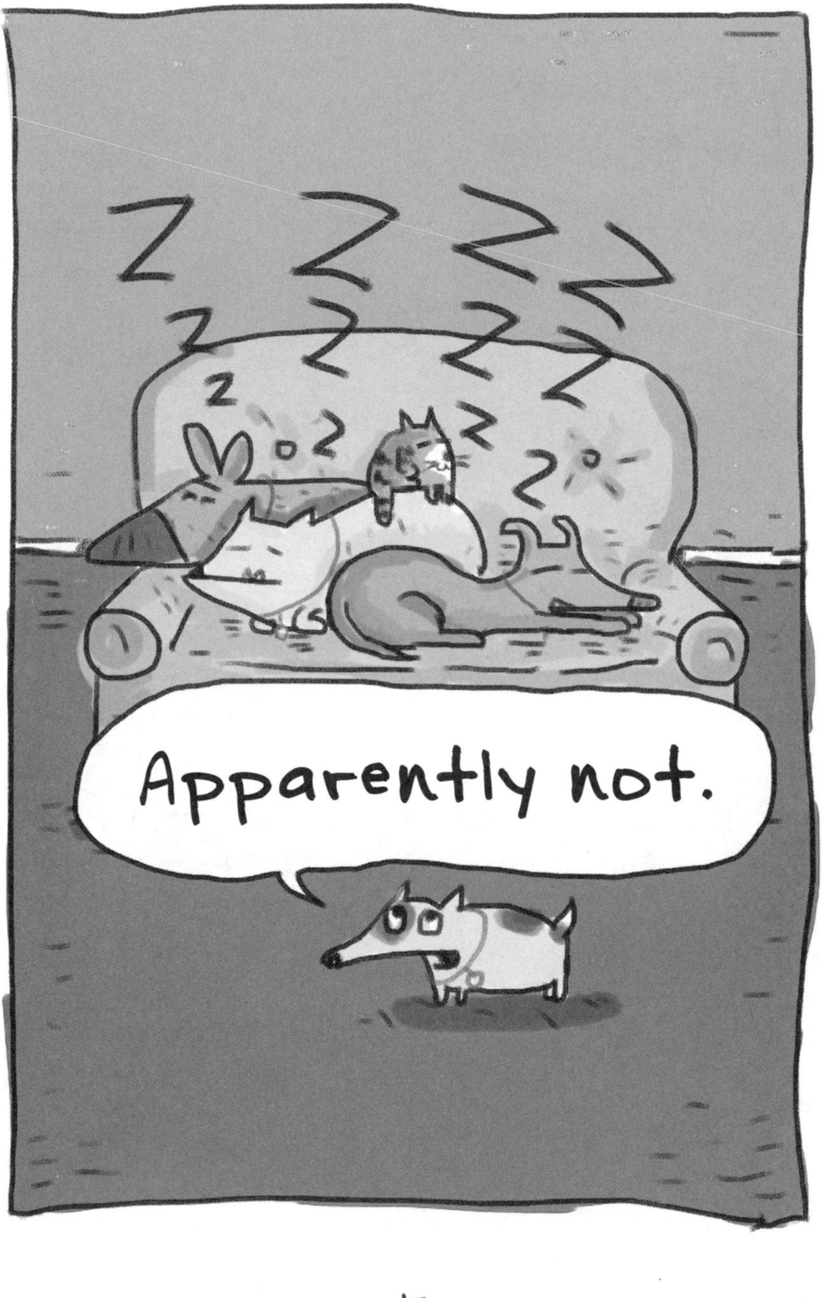
Apparently not.

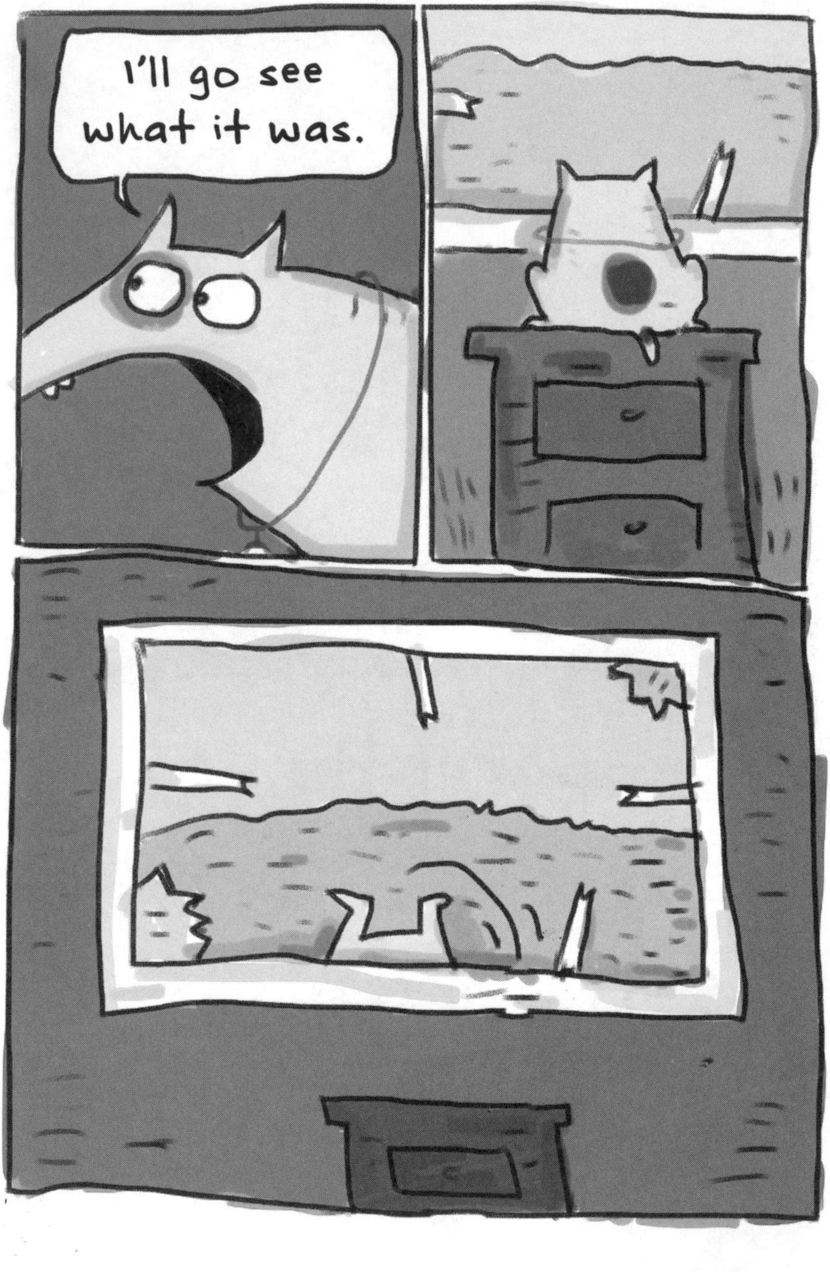
I'll go see what it was.

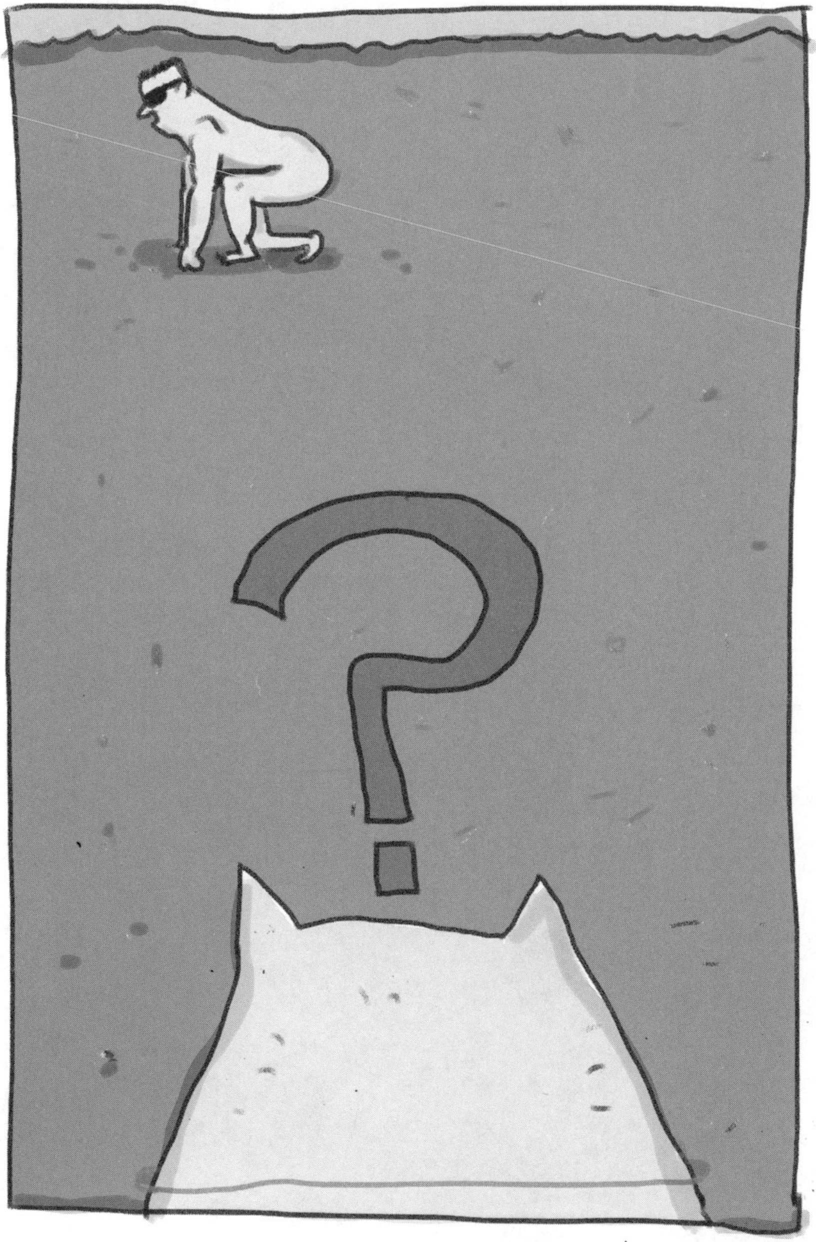

Scene
Two

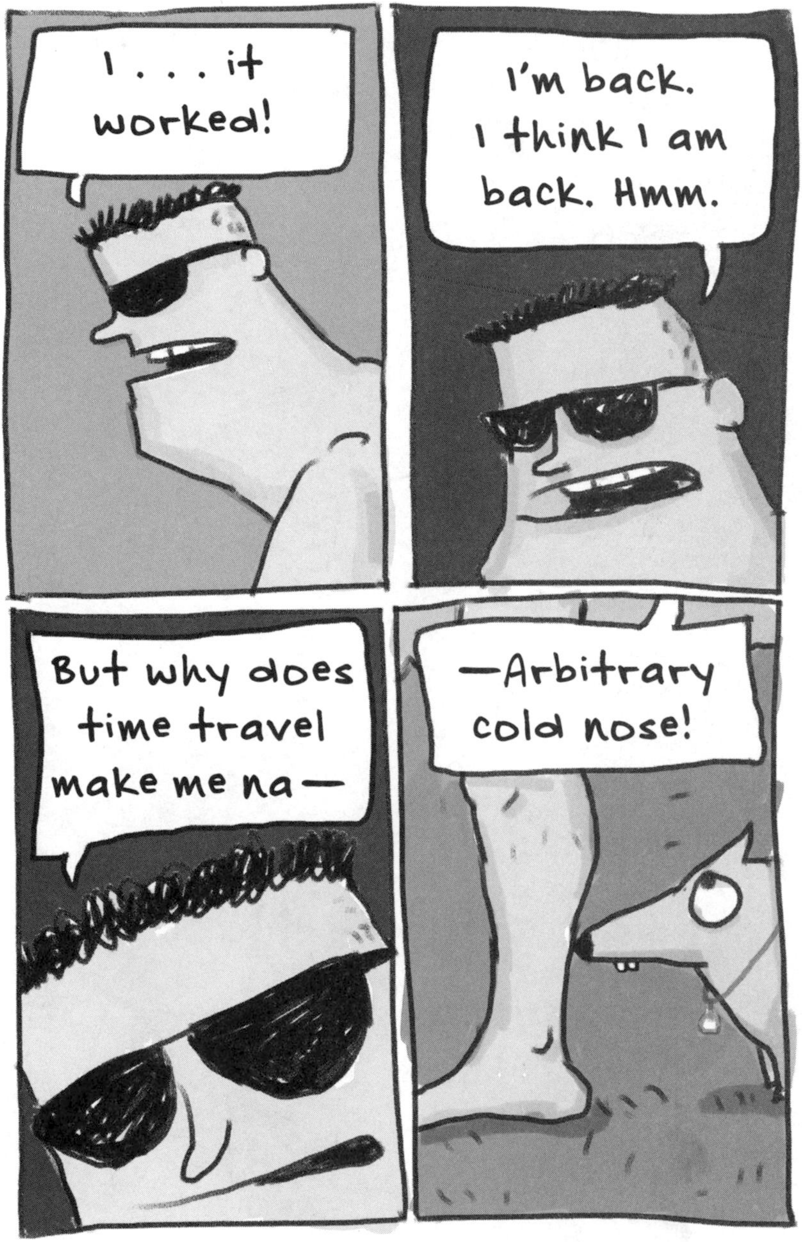
I . . . it worked!
I'm back. I think I am back. Hmm.
But why does time travel make me na—
—Arbitrary cold nose!

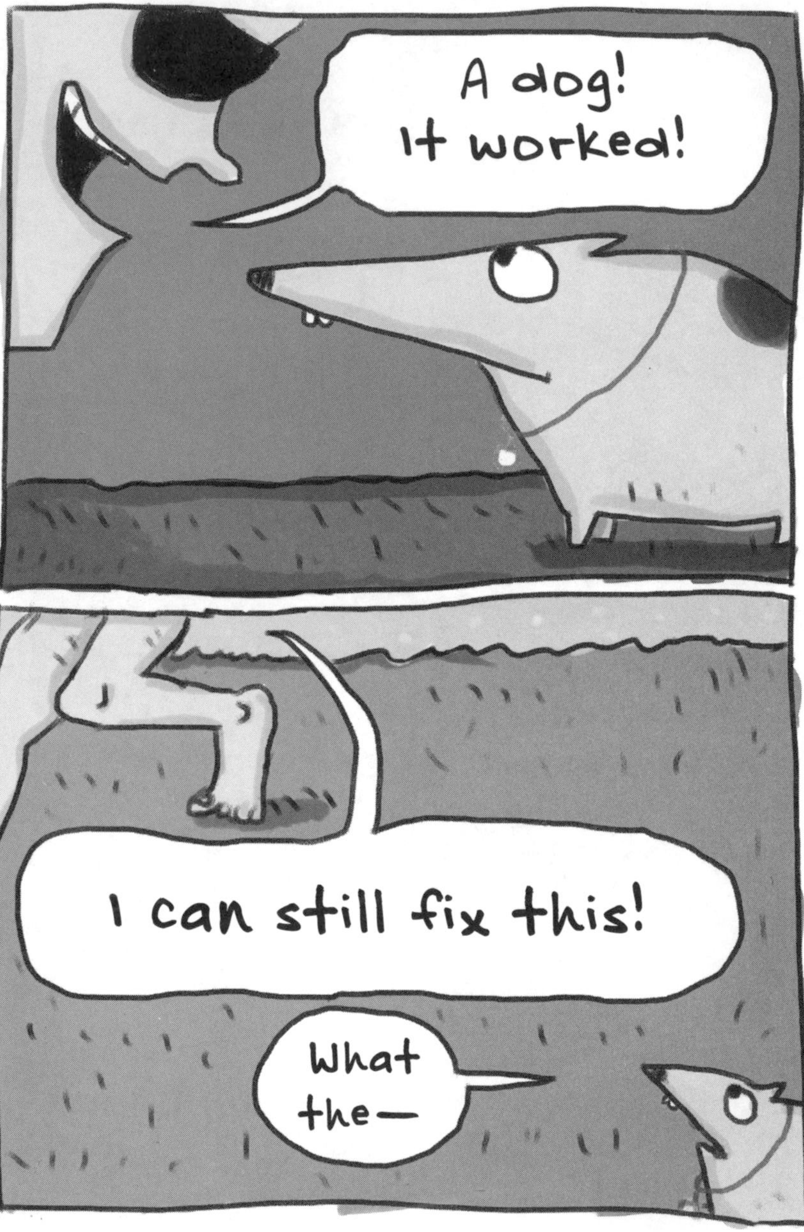
A dog!
It worked!
I can still fix this!
What the—

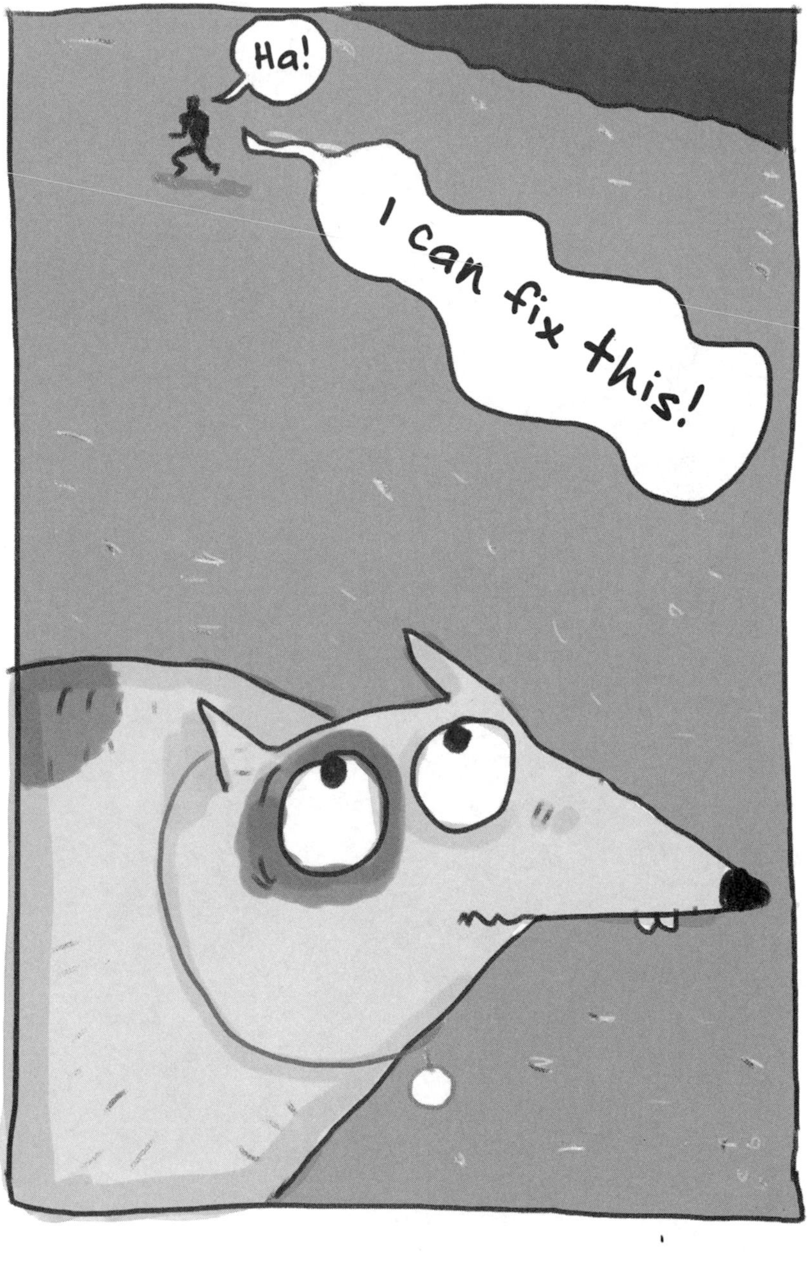
Ha!
I can fix this!

Scene
Three

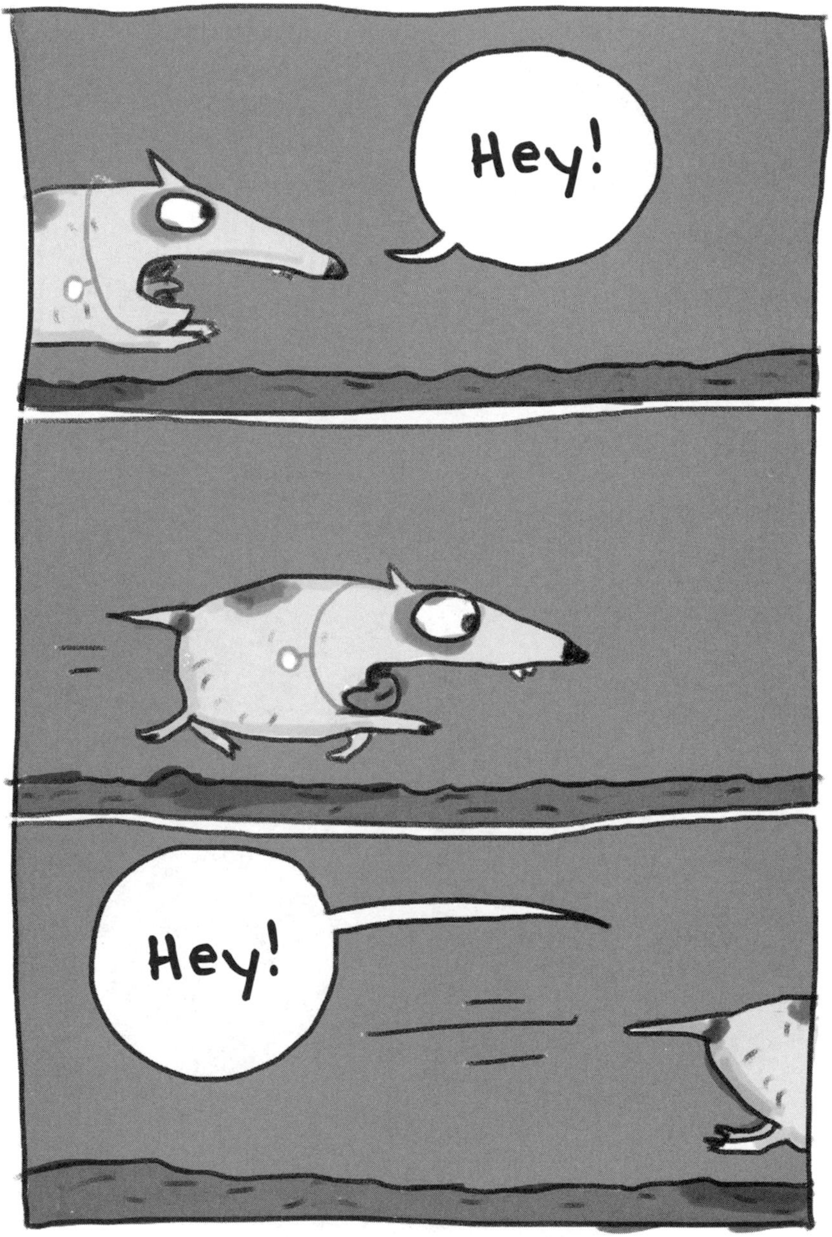
Hey!
Hey!

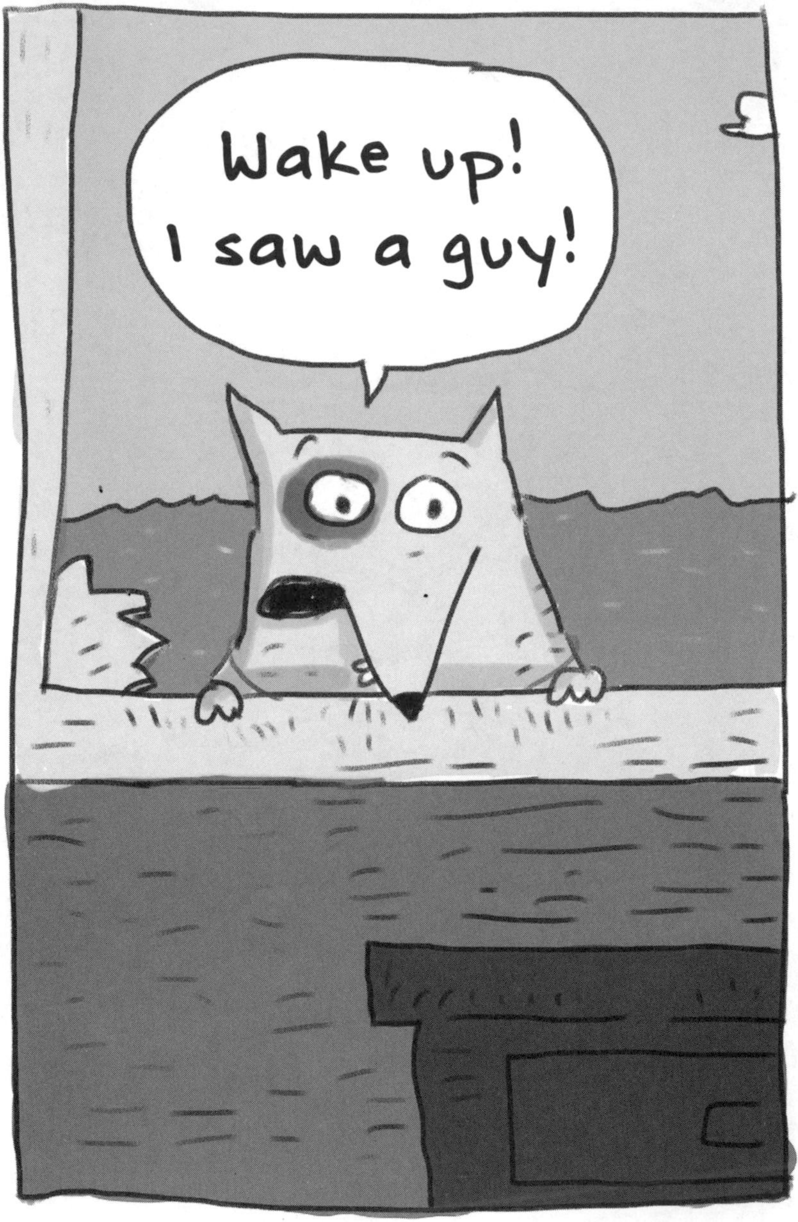
Wake up!
I saw a guy!

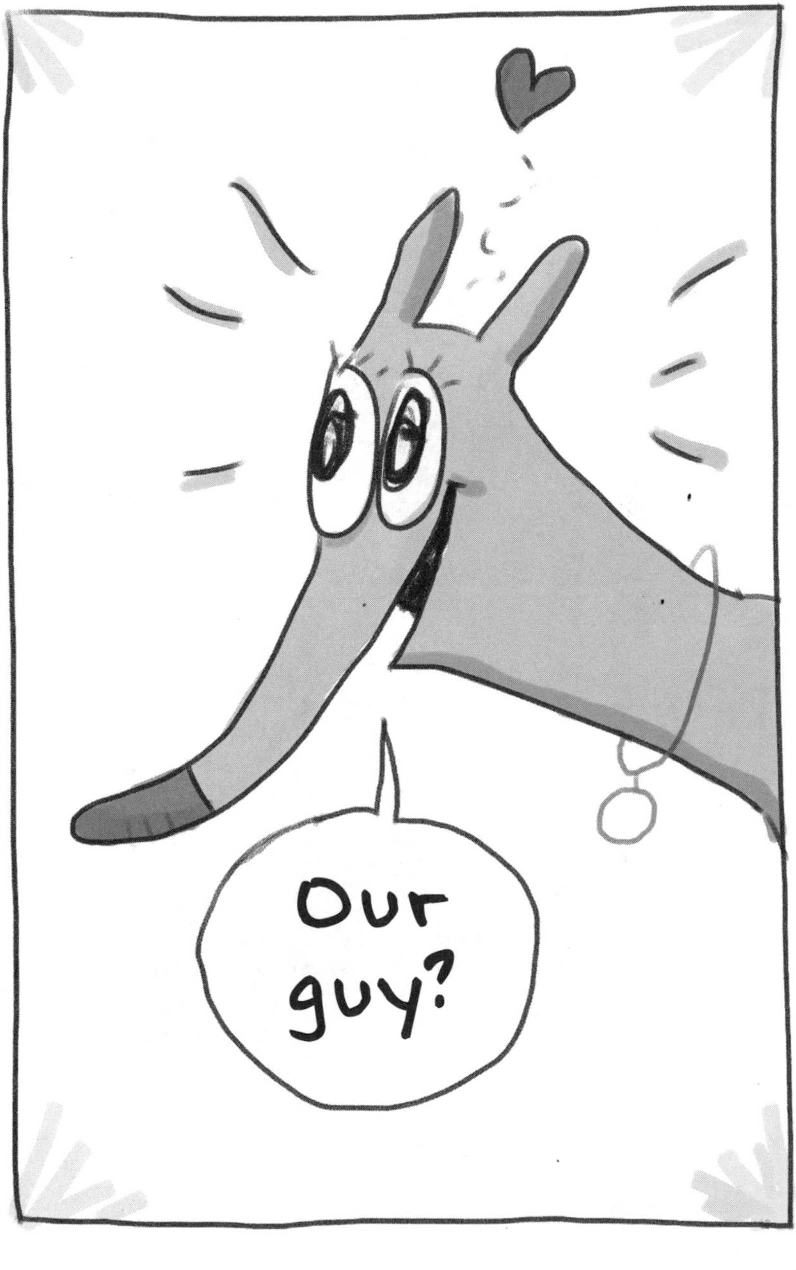
Our guy?

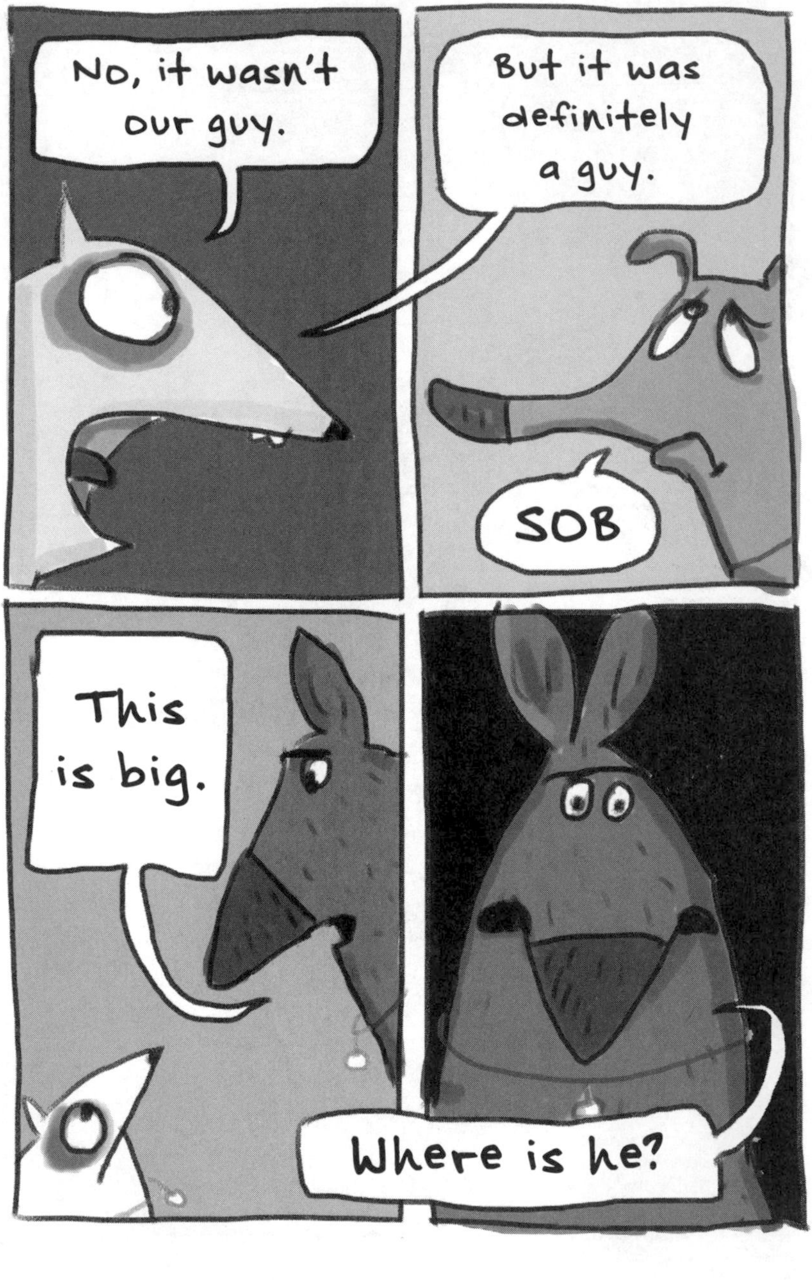
No, it wasn't our guy.
But it was definitely a guy.
SOB
This is big.
Where is he?

He sorta ran off.

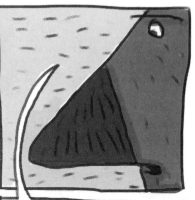

He don't see so good. I bet it was our person.

He may know what's going on. He may know where all the other people are.

And where more food is.

We are all out!

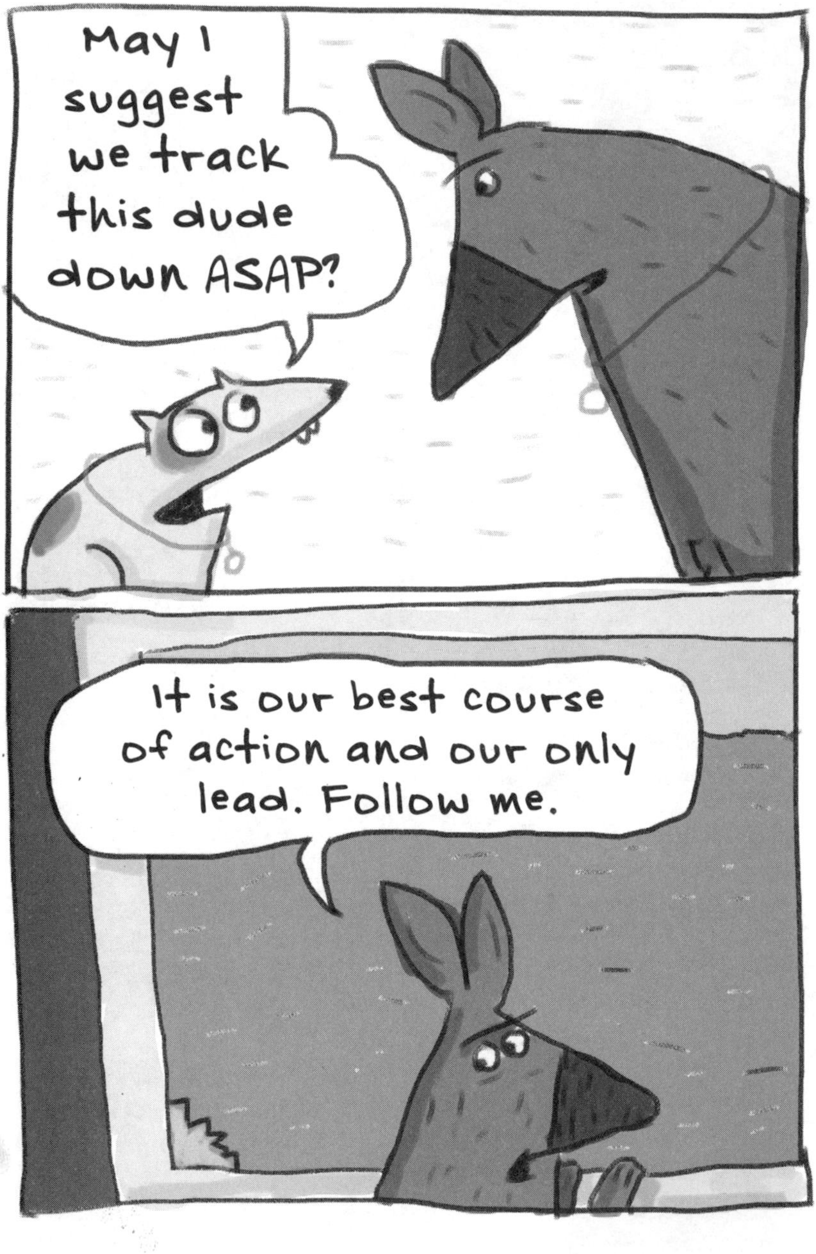
May I suggest we track this dude down ASAP?
It is our best course of action and our only lead. Follow me.

Scene
Four

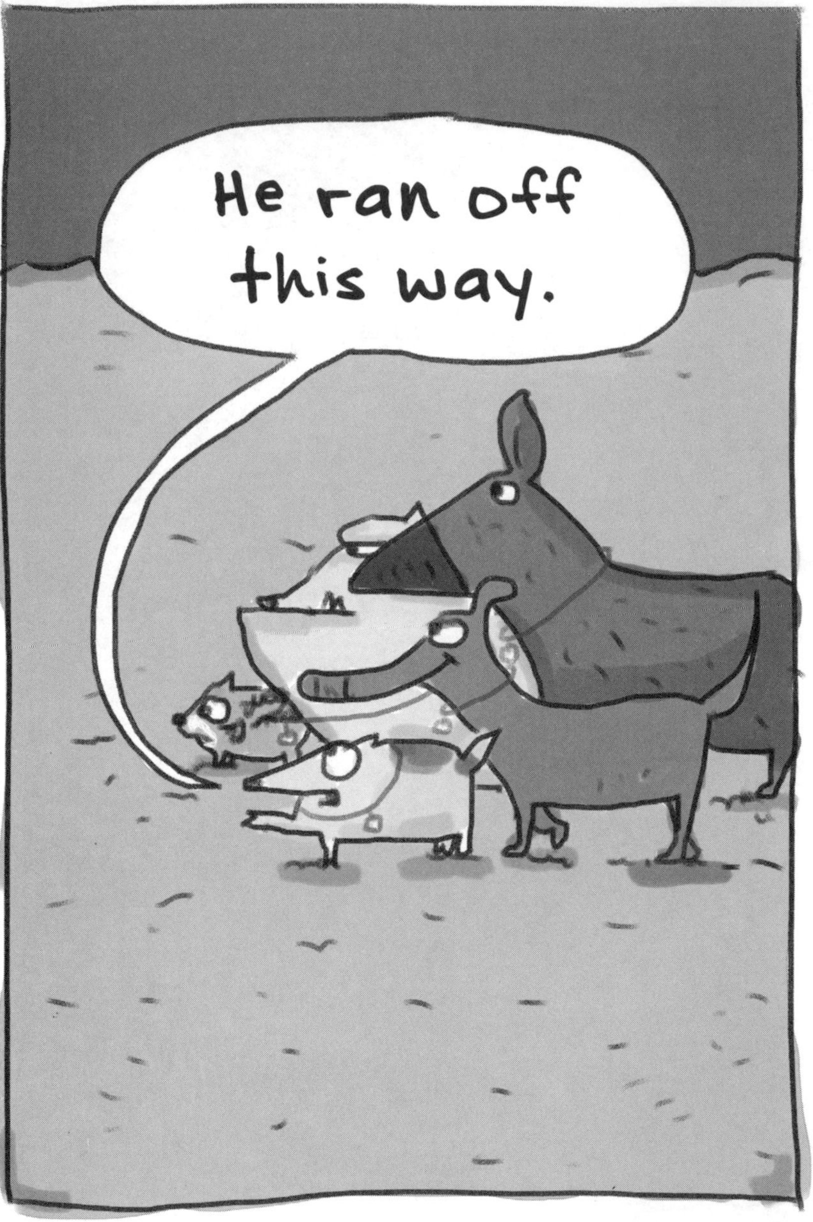
He ran off this way.

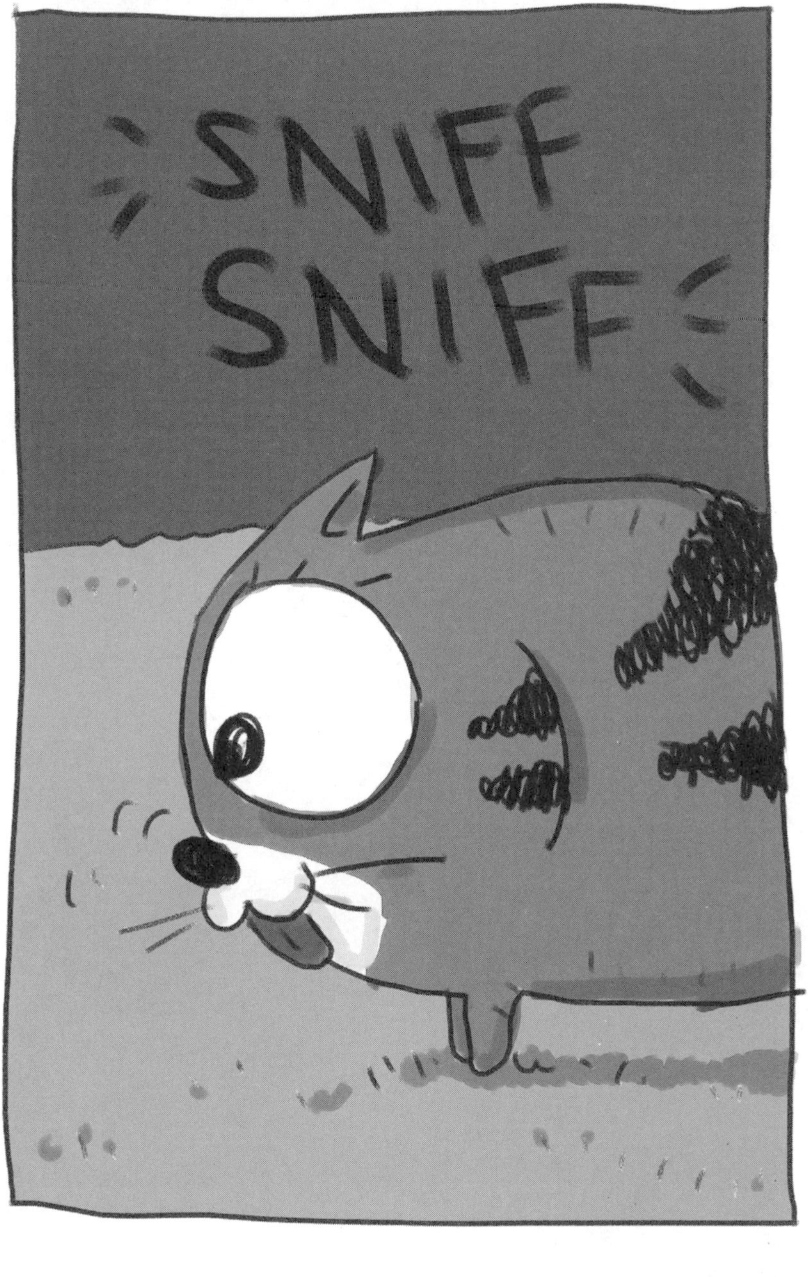
SNIFF
SNIFF

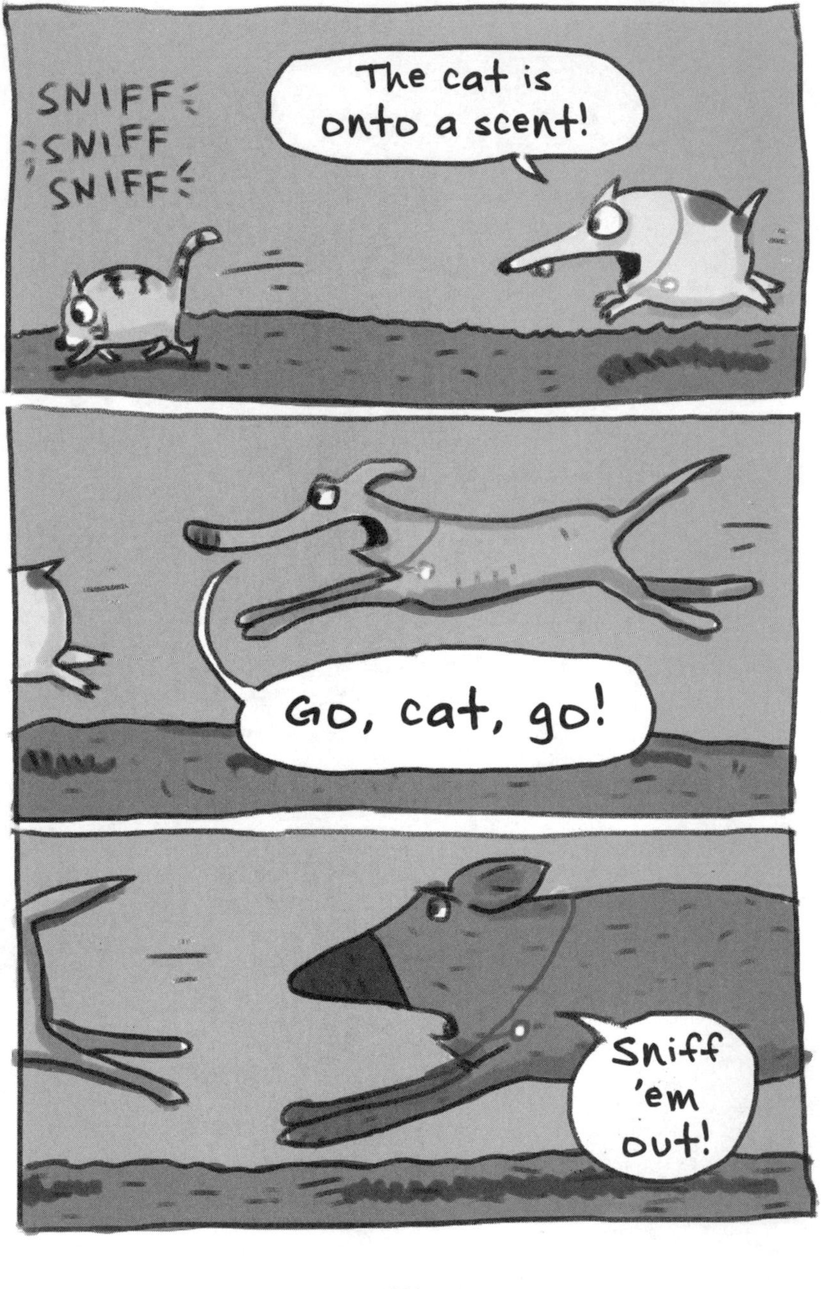
SNIFF
SNIFF
SNIFF
The cat is onto a scent!
Go, cat, go!
Sniff 'em out!

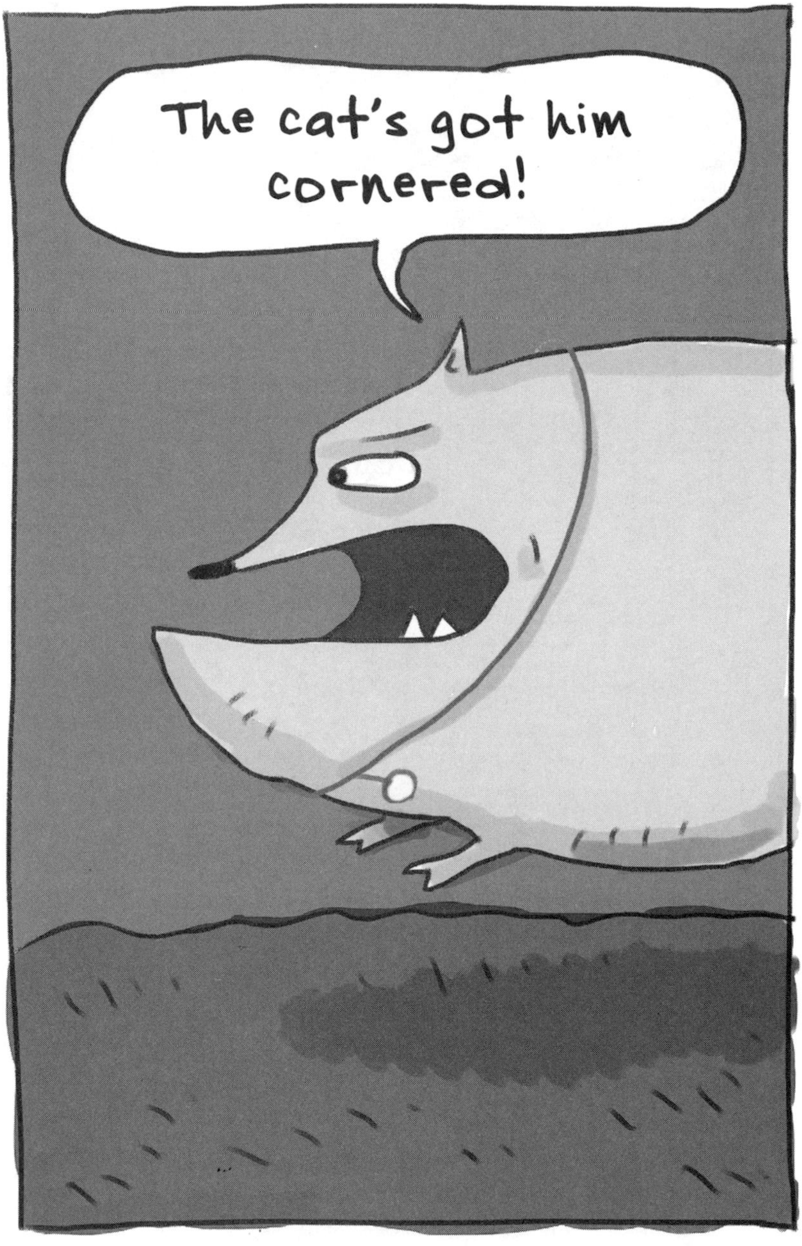
The cat's got him cornered!

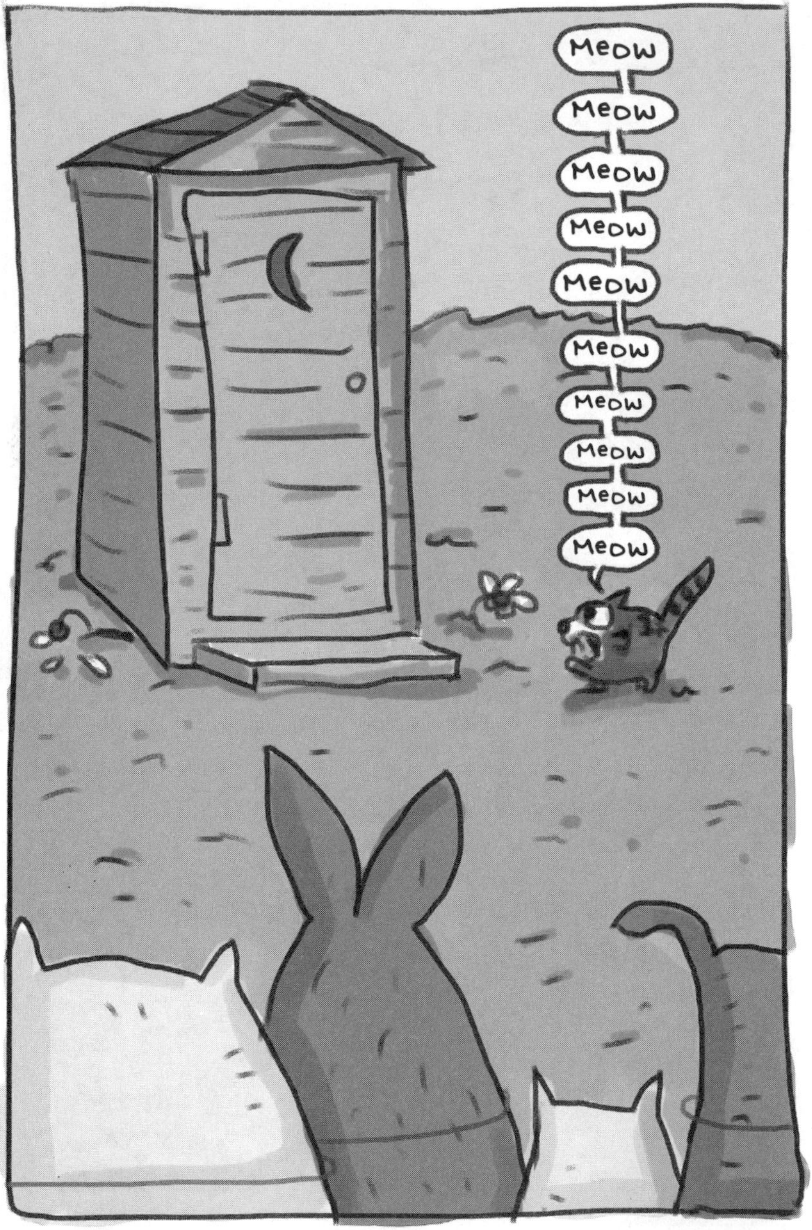
MEOW
MEOW
MEOW
MEOW
MEOW
MEOW
MEOW
MEOW
MEOW
MEOW

Scene
Five

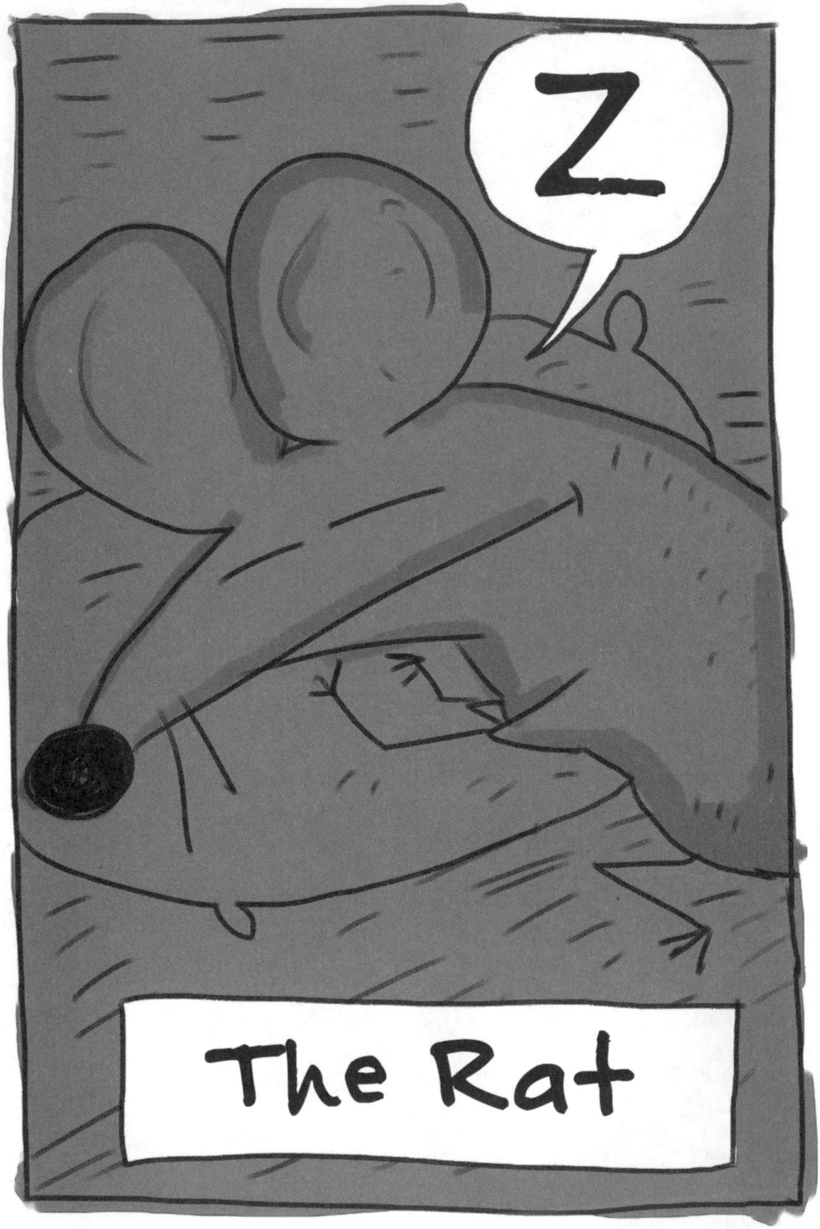
Z
The Rat

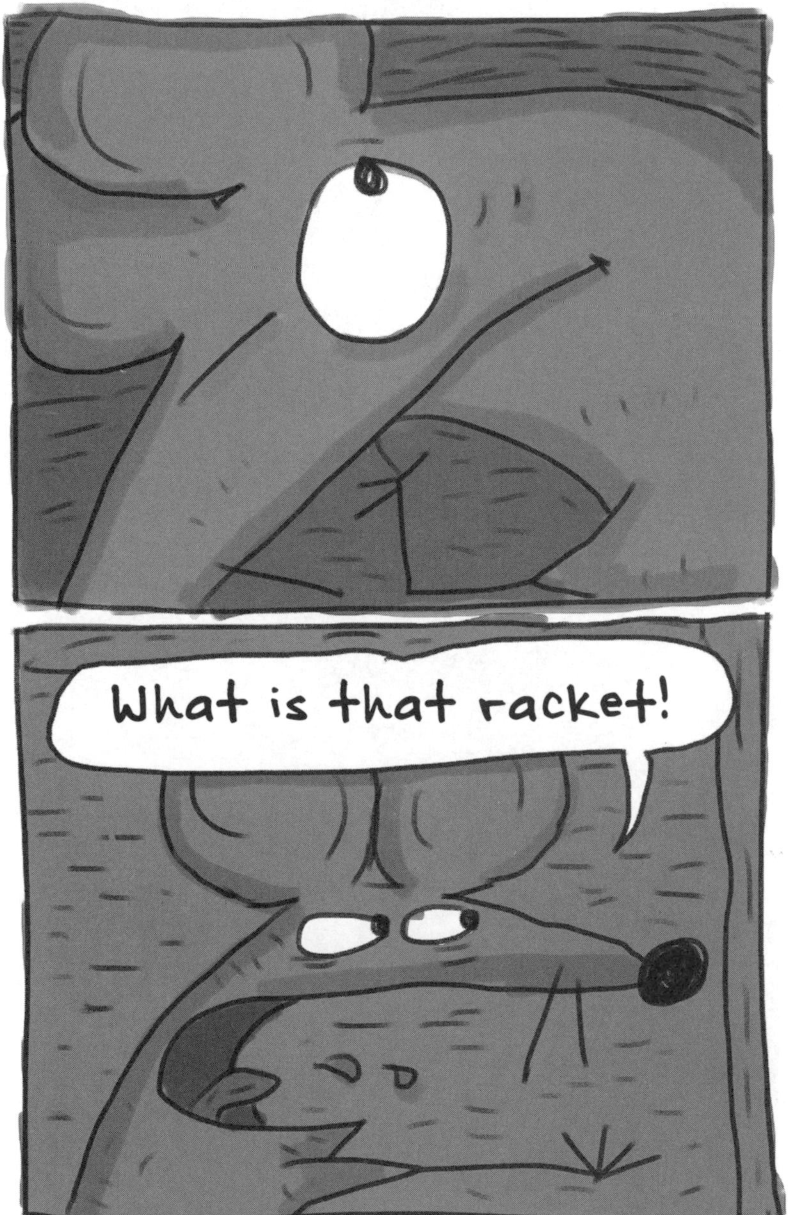
What is that racket!

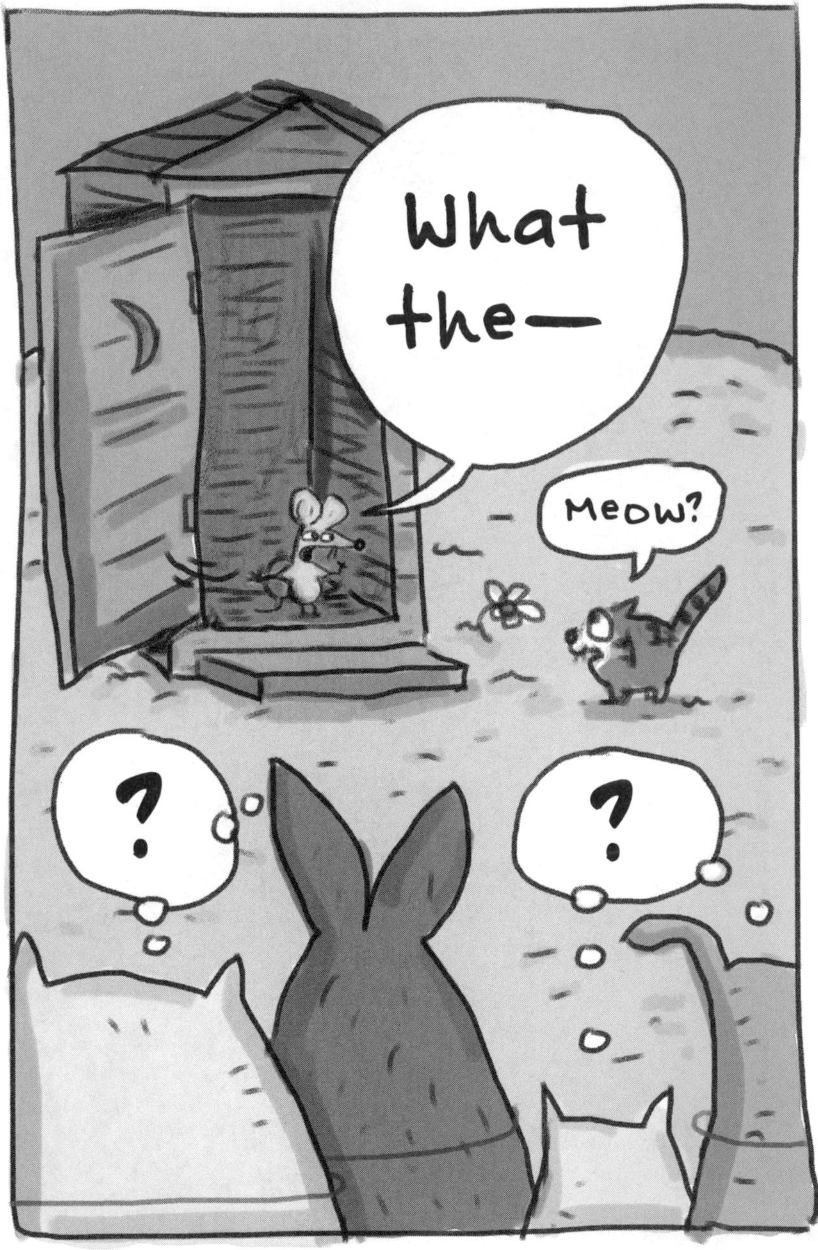
What the—
MEOW?
?
?

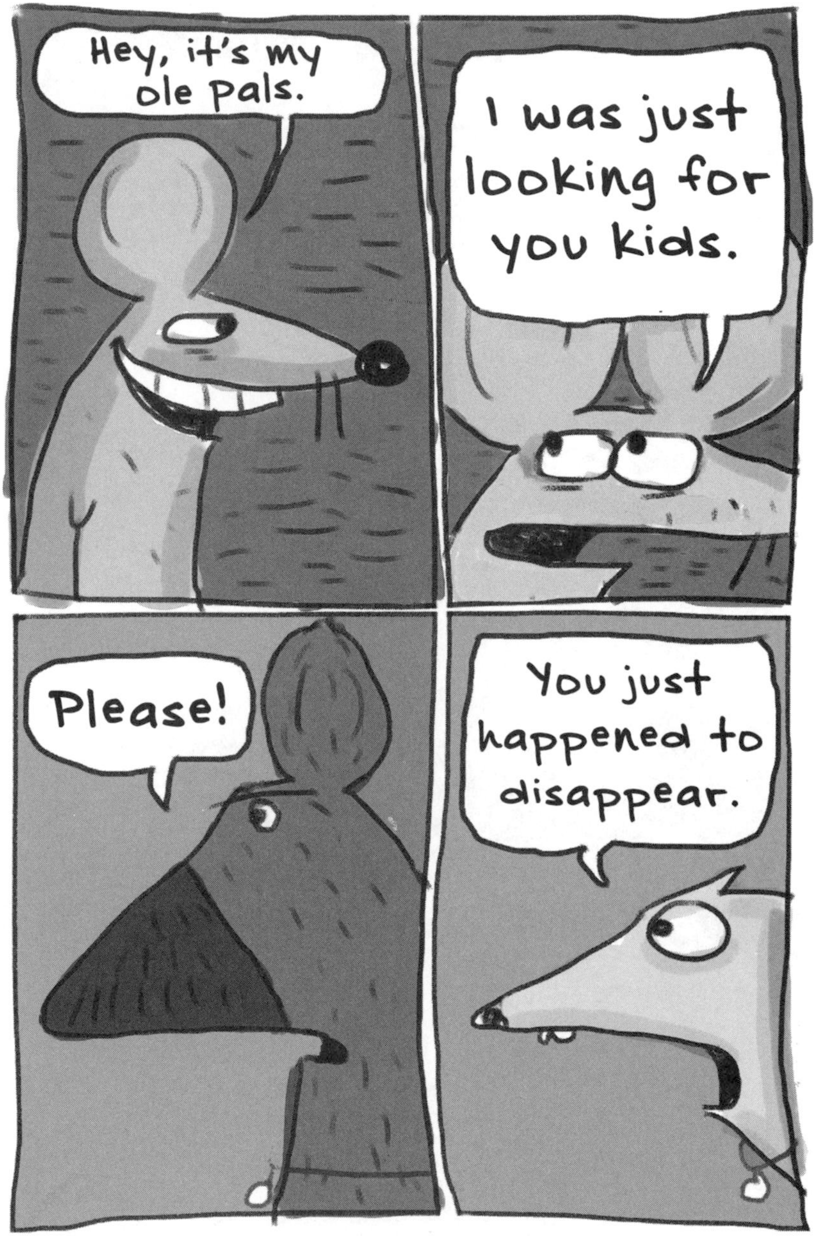
Hey, it's my ole pals.
I was just looking for you kids.
Please!
You just happened to disappear.

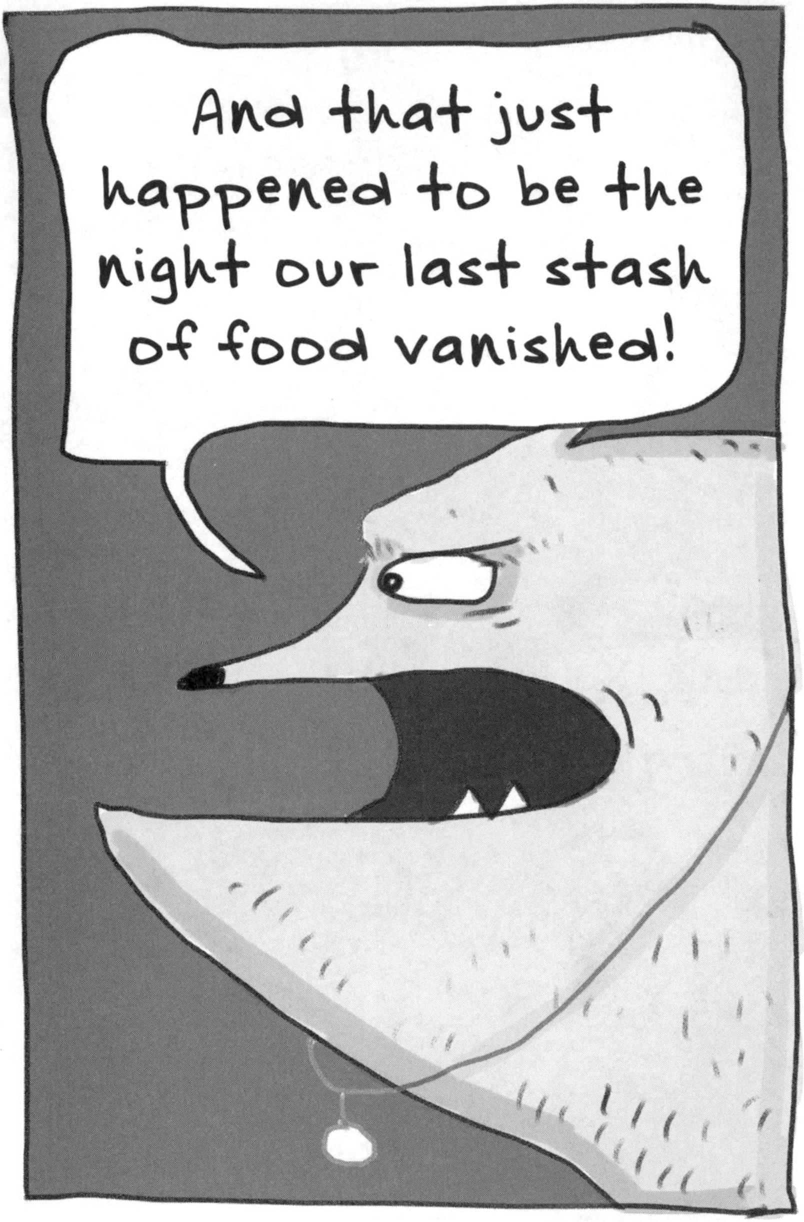
And that just happened to be the night our last stash of food vanished!

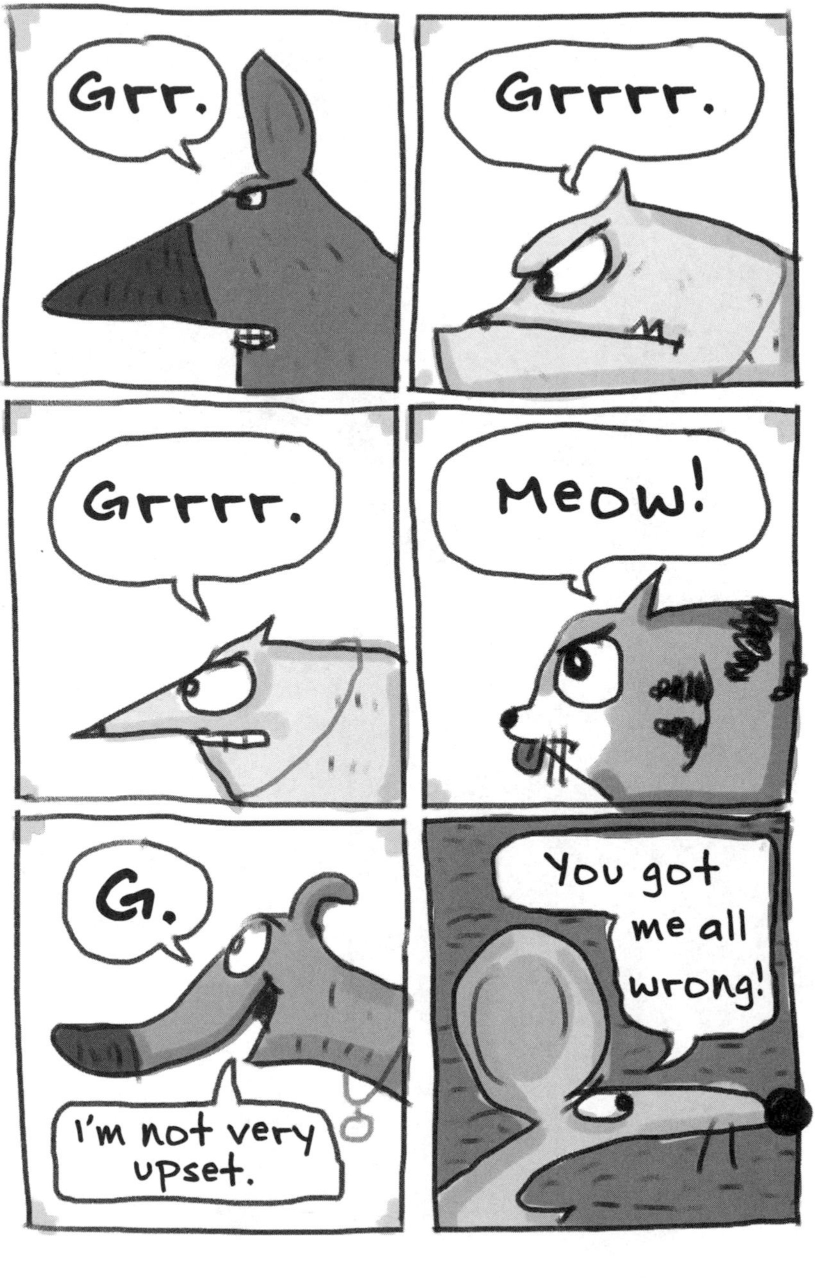
Grr.
Grrrr.
Grrrr.
Meow!
G.
I'm not very upset.
You got me all wrong!

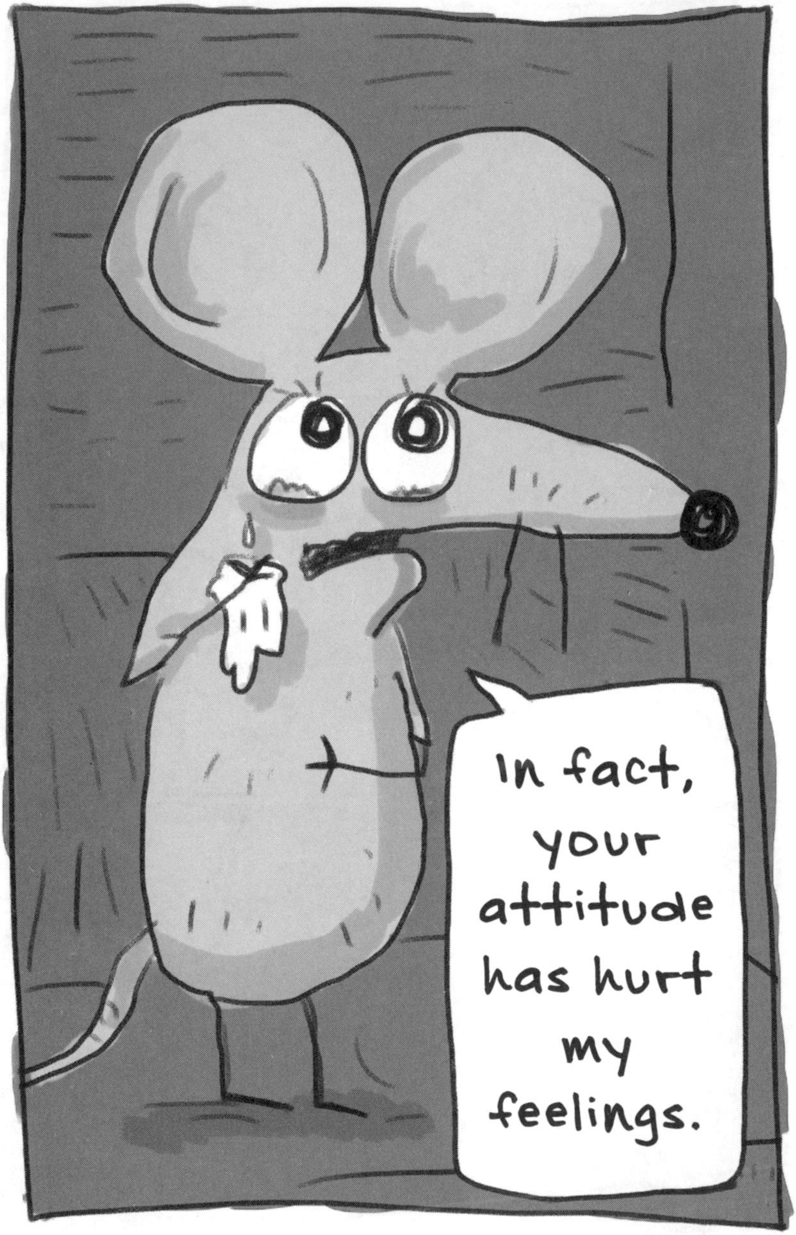
In fact, your attitude has hurt my feelings.

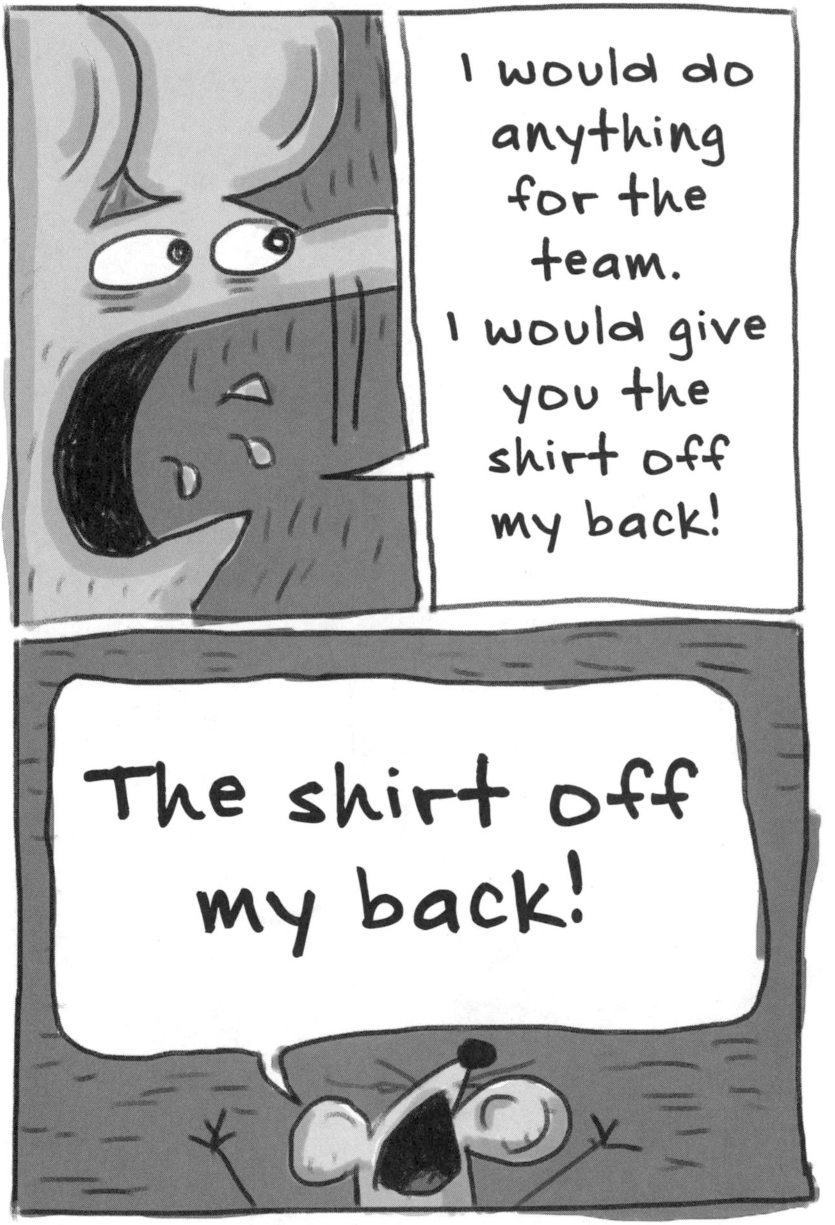
I would do anything for the team. I would give you the shirt off my back!
The shirt off my back!

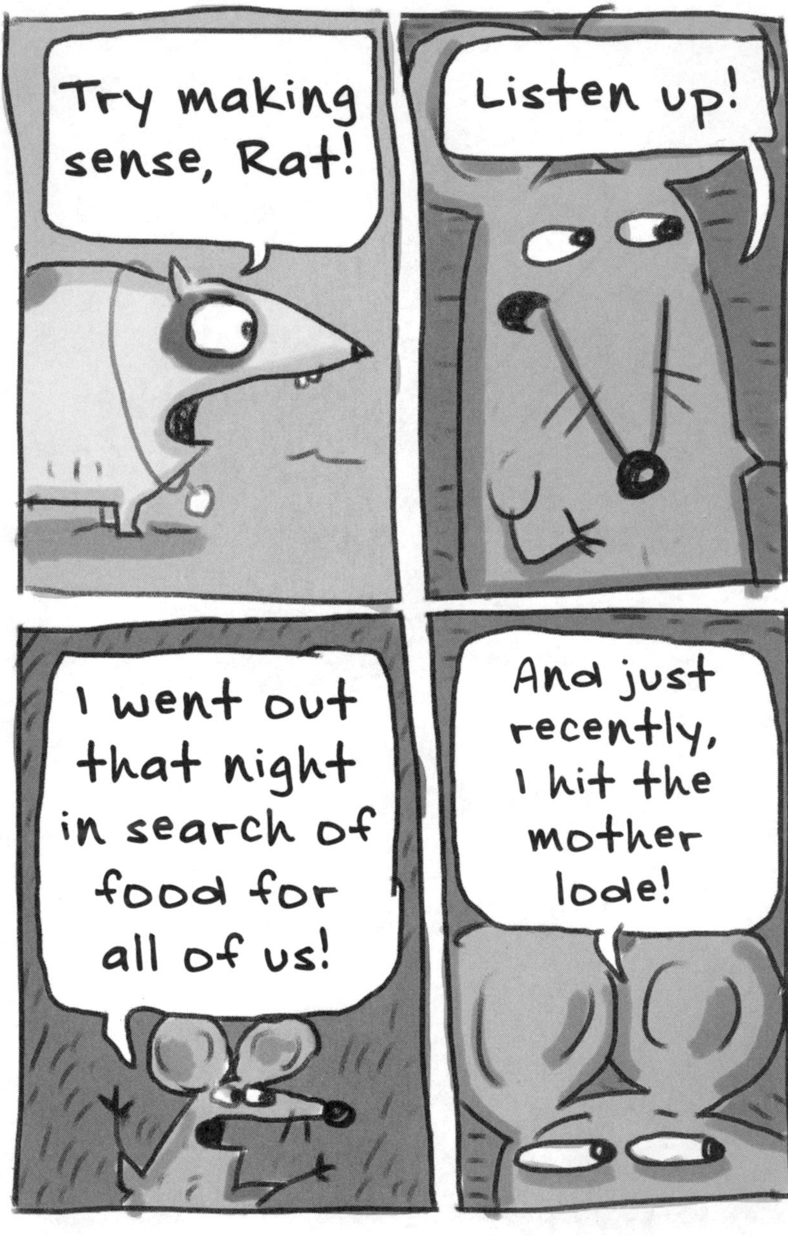
Try making sense, Rat!
Listen up!
I went out that night in search of food for all of us!
And just recently, I hit the mother lode!

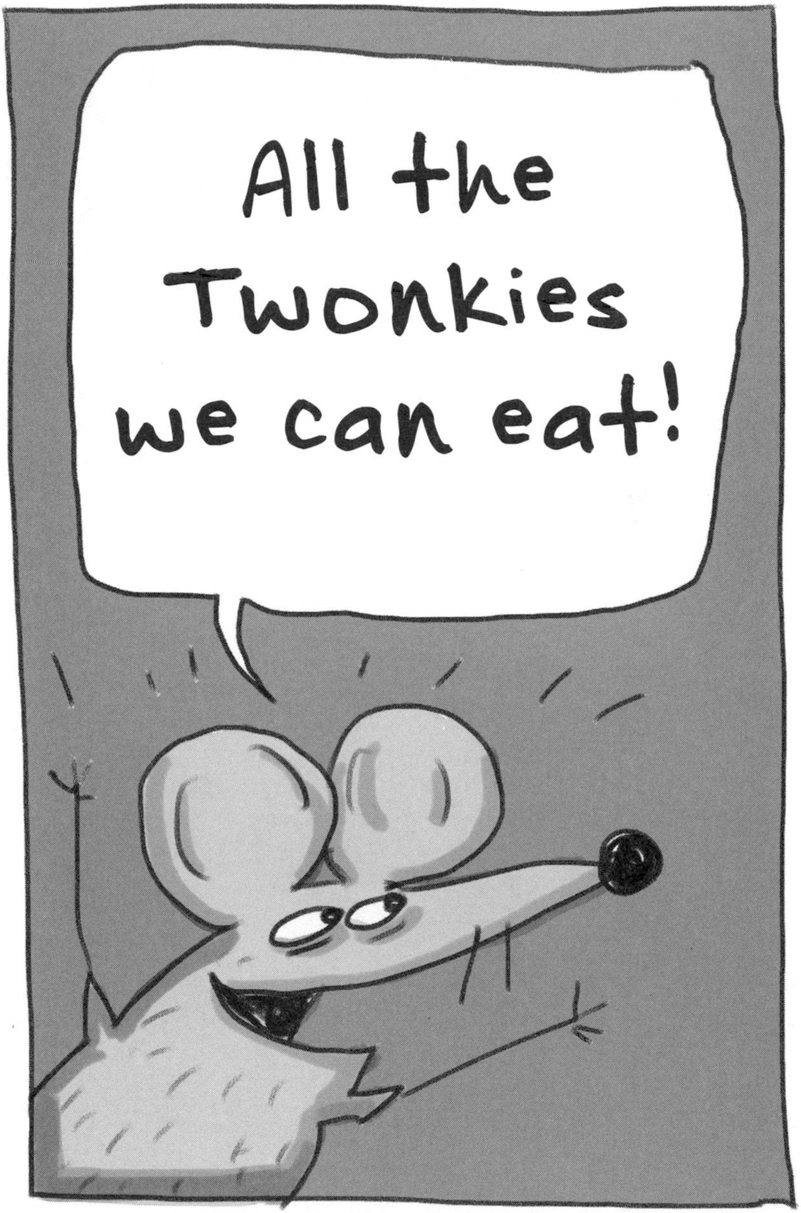
All the Twonkies we can eat!

For those of you not in the know, a Twonkie is a tiny snack cake filled with sugary goo.

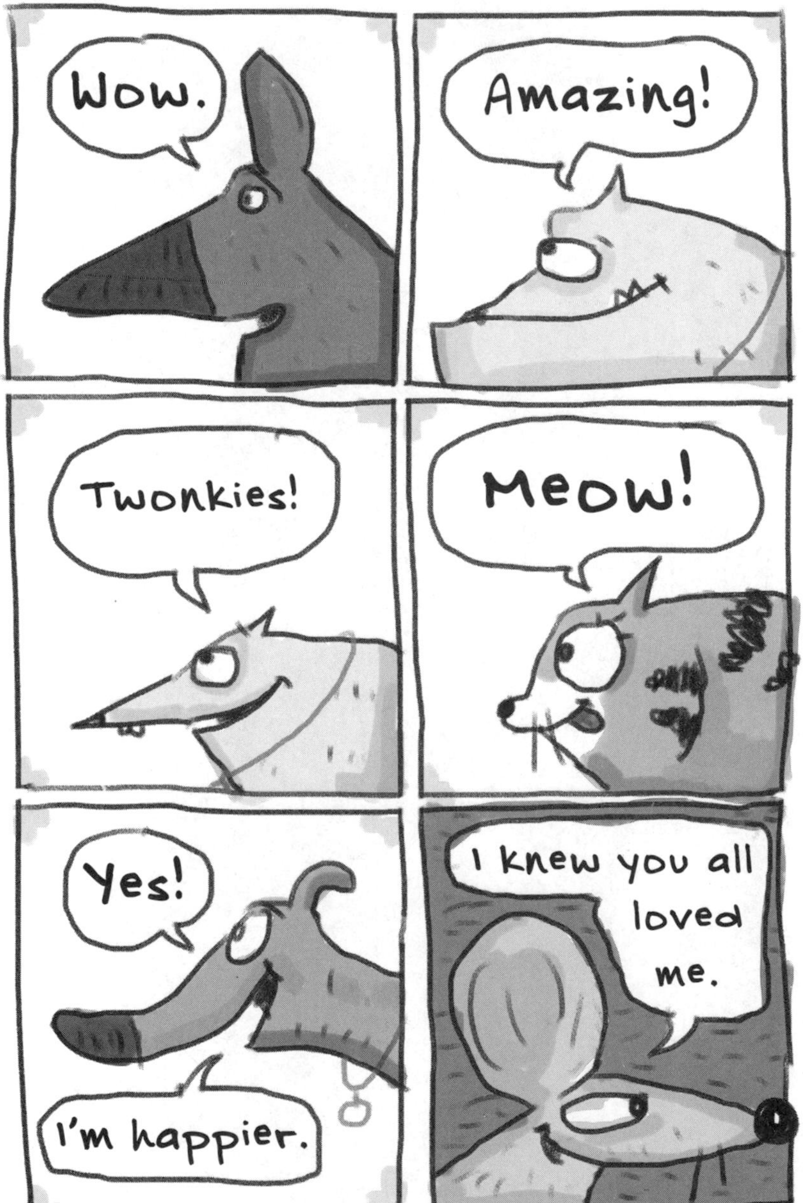
Wow.
Amazing!
Twonkies!
Meow!
Yes!
I'm happier.
I knew you all loved me.

Scene
Six

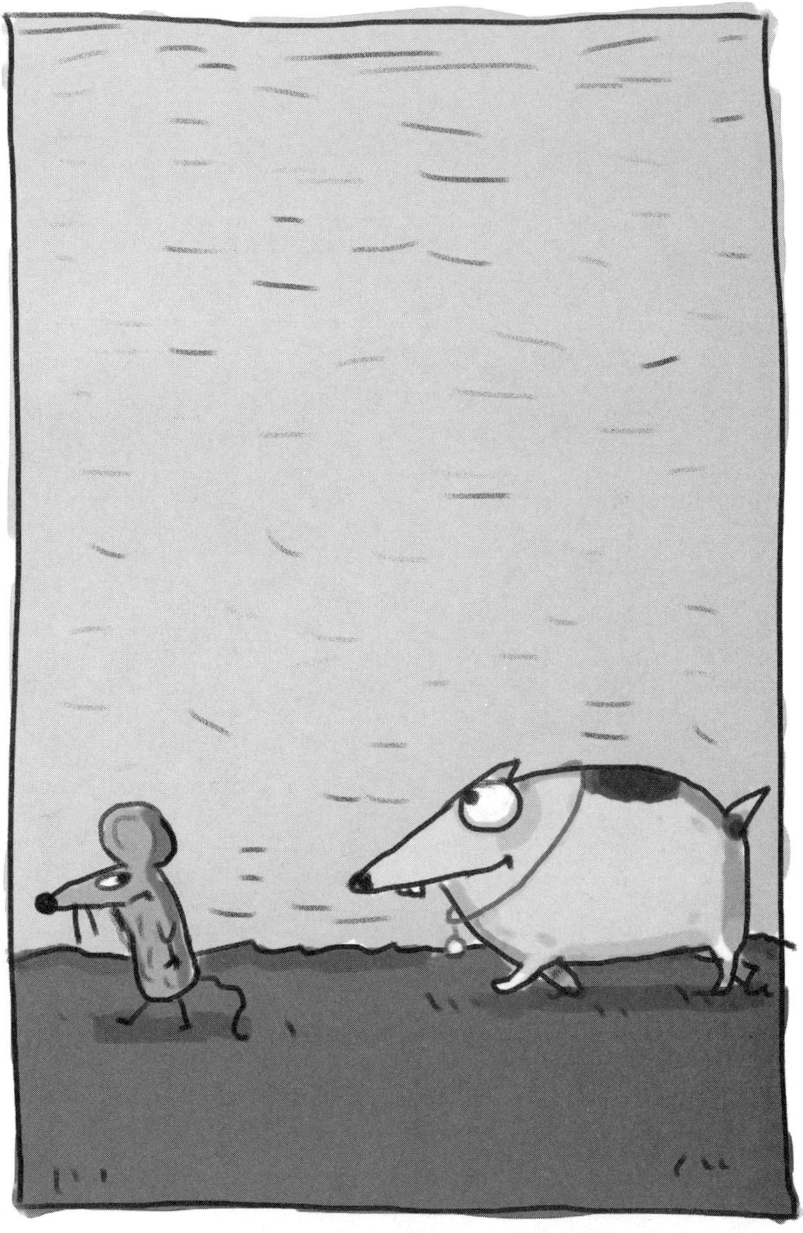

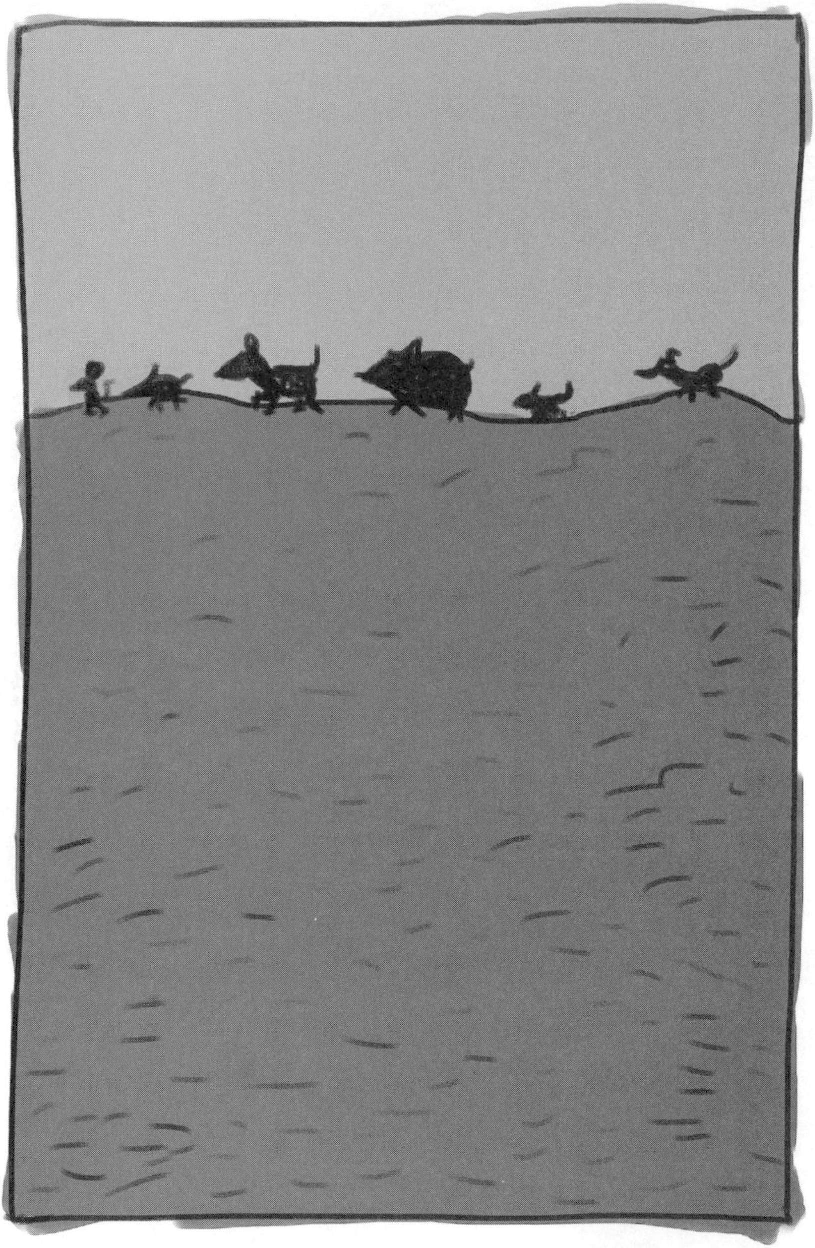

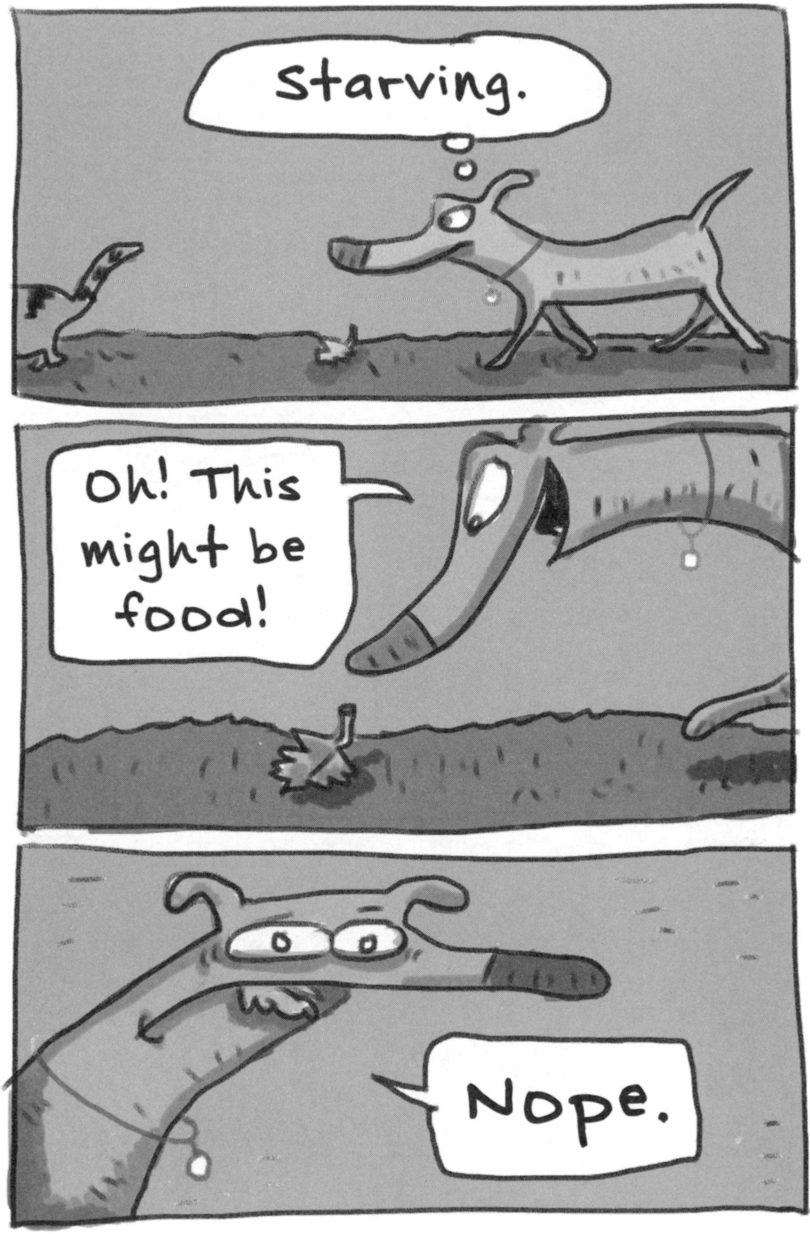
Starving.
Oh! This might be food!
Nope.

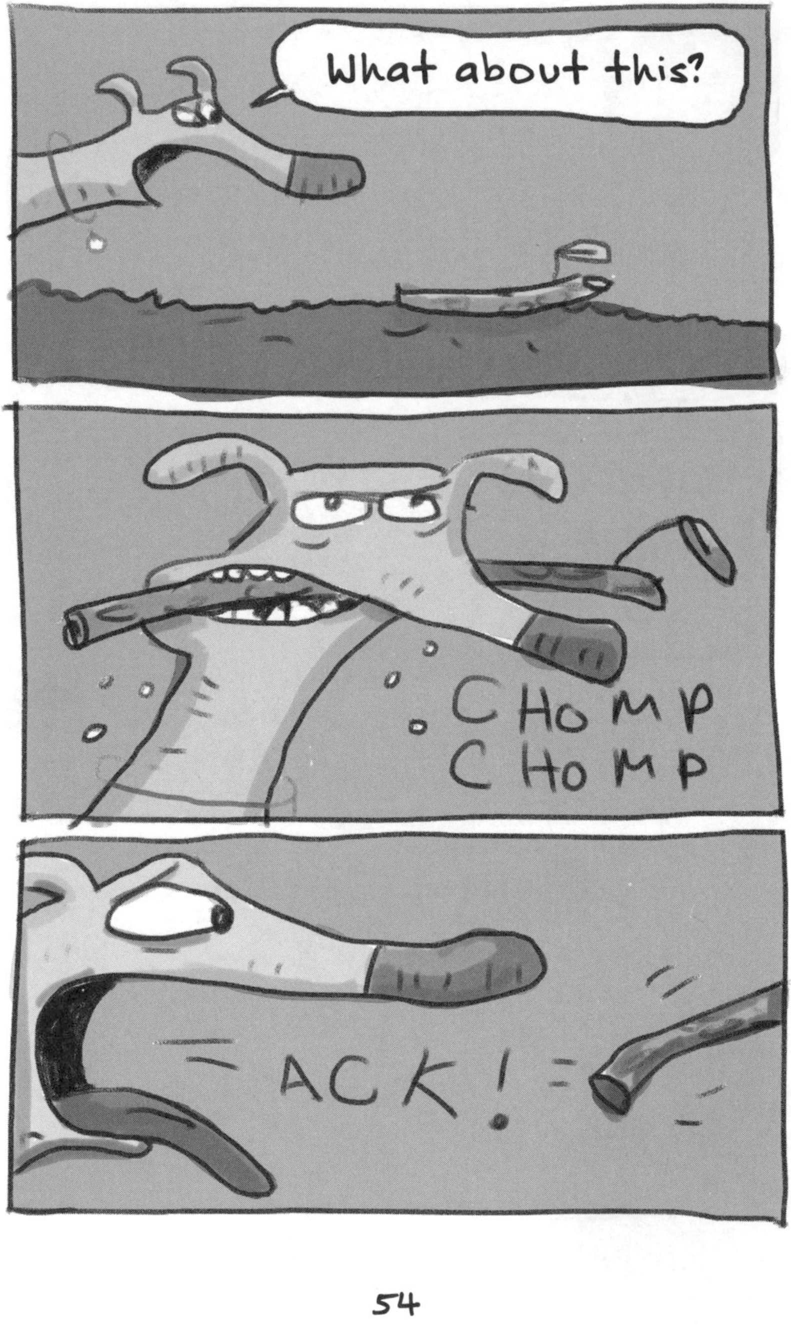
What about this?
CHOMP
CHOMP
ACK!

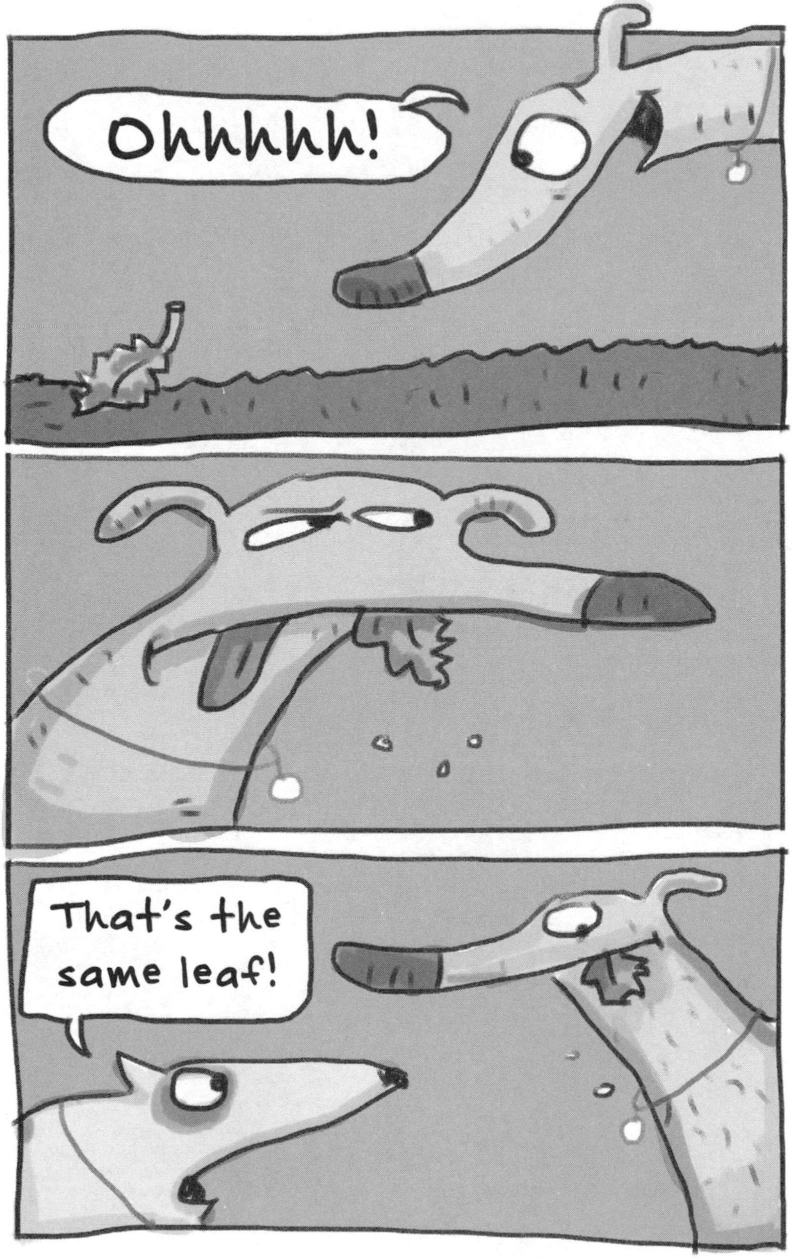
Ohhhhh!
That's the same leaf!

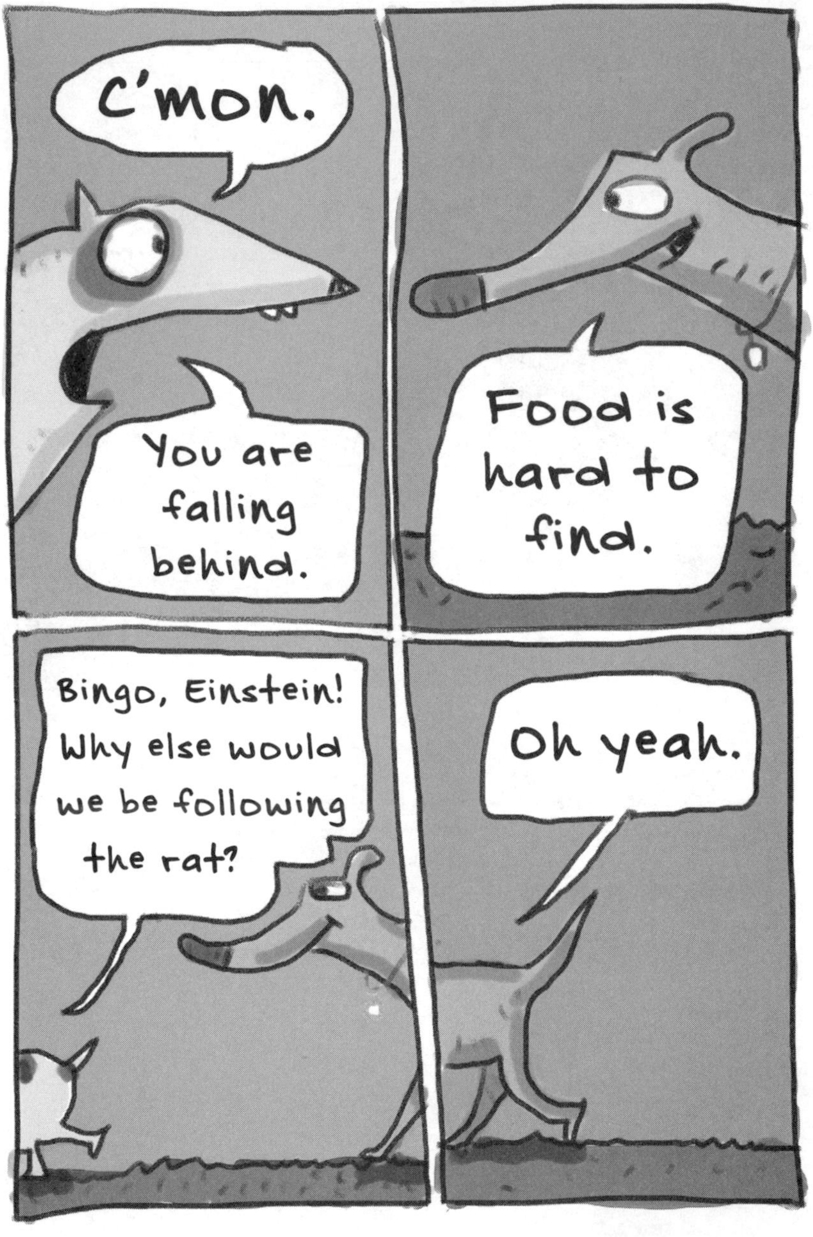
C'mon.
You are falling behind.
Food is hard to find.
Bingo, Einstein! Why else would we be following the rat?
Oh yeah.

Scene
Seven

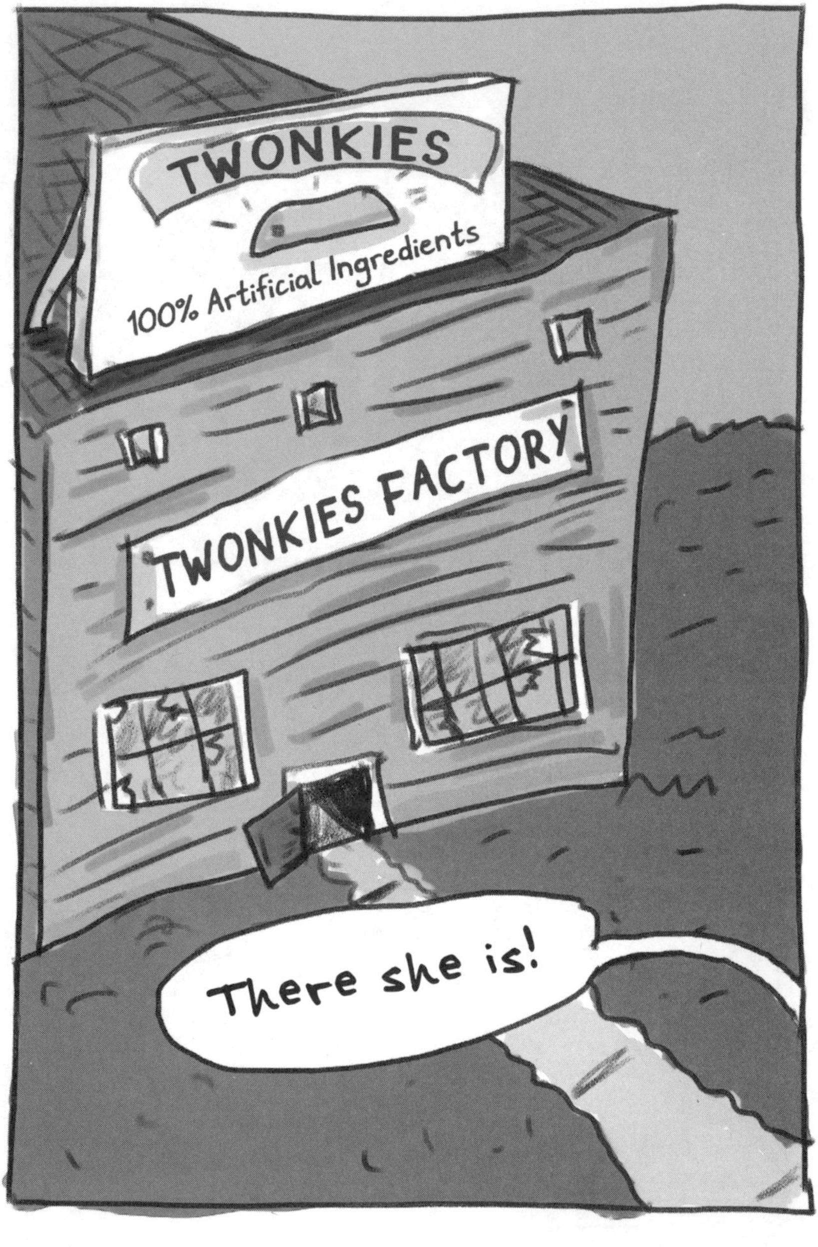
TWONKIES
100% Artificial Ingredients
TWONKIES FACTORY
There she is!

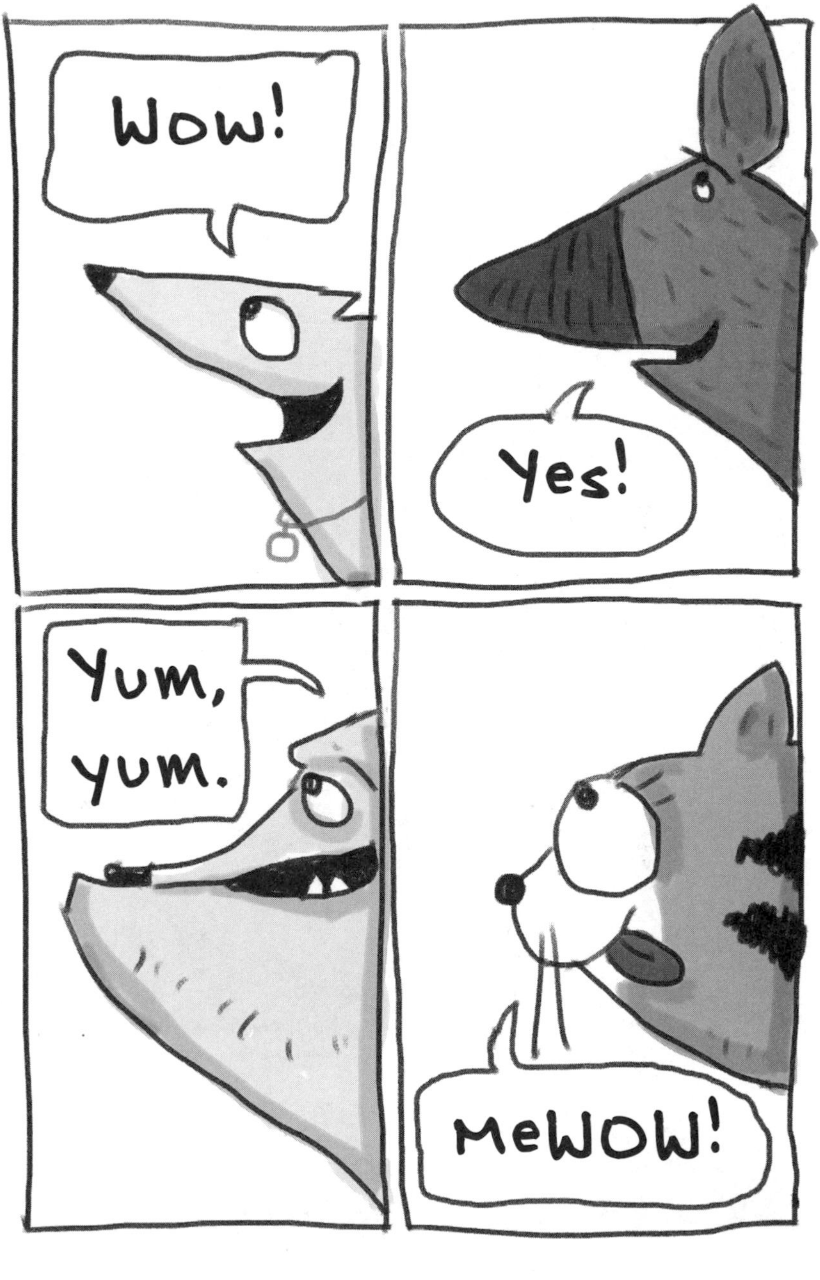
Wow!
Yes!
Yum, yum.
MeWOW!

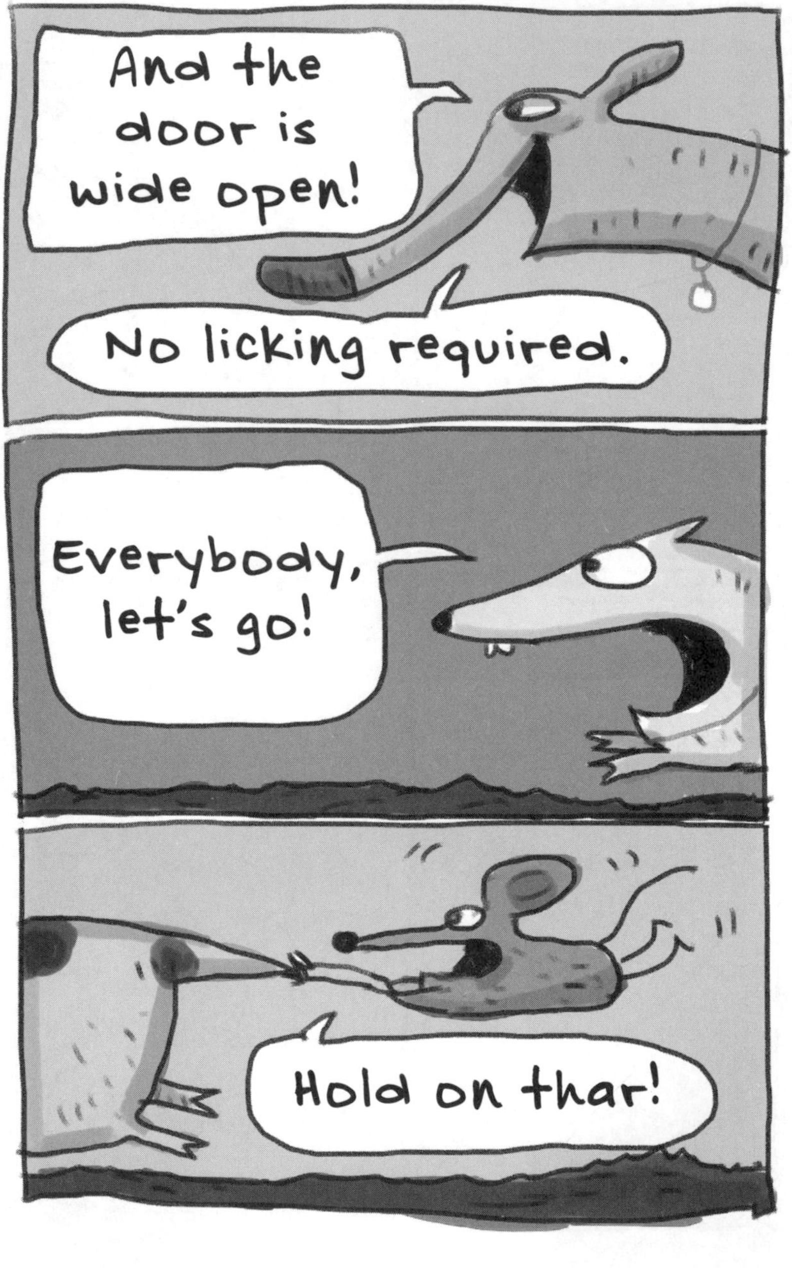
And the door is wide open!
No licking required.
Everybody, let's go!
Hold on thar!

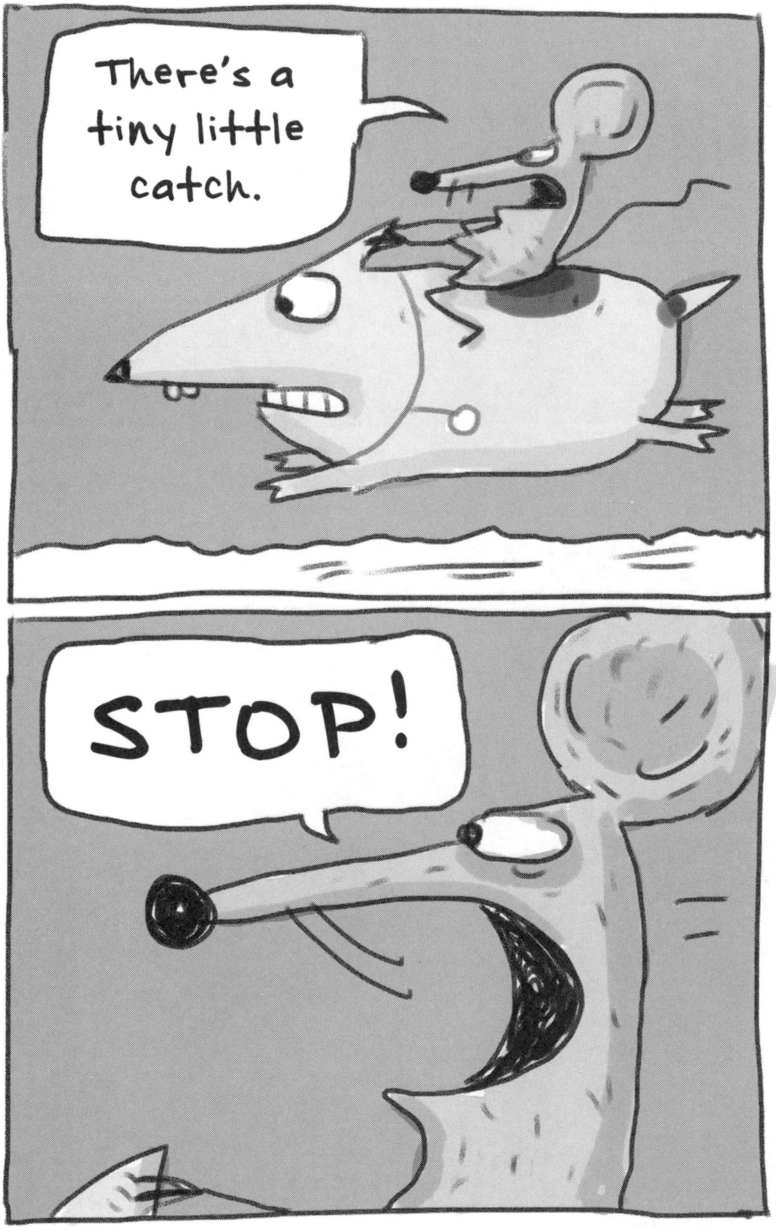
There's a tiny little catch.
STOP!

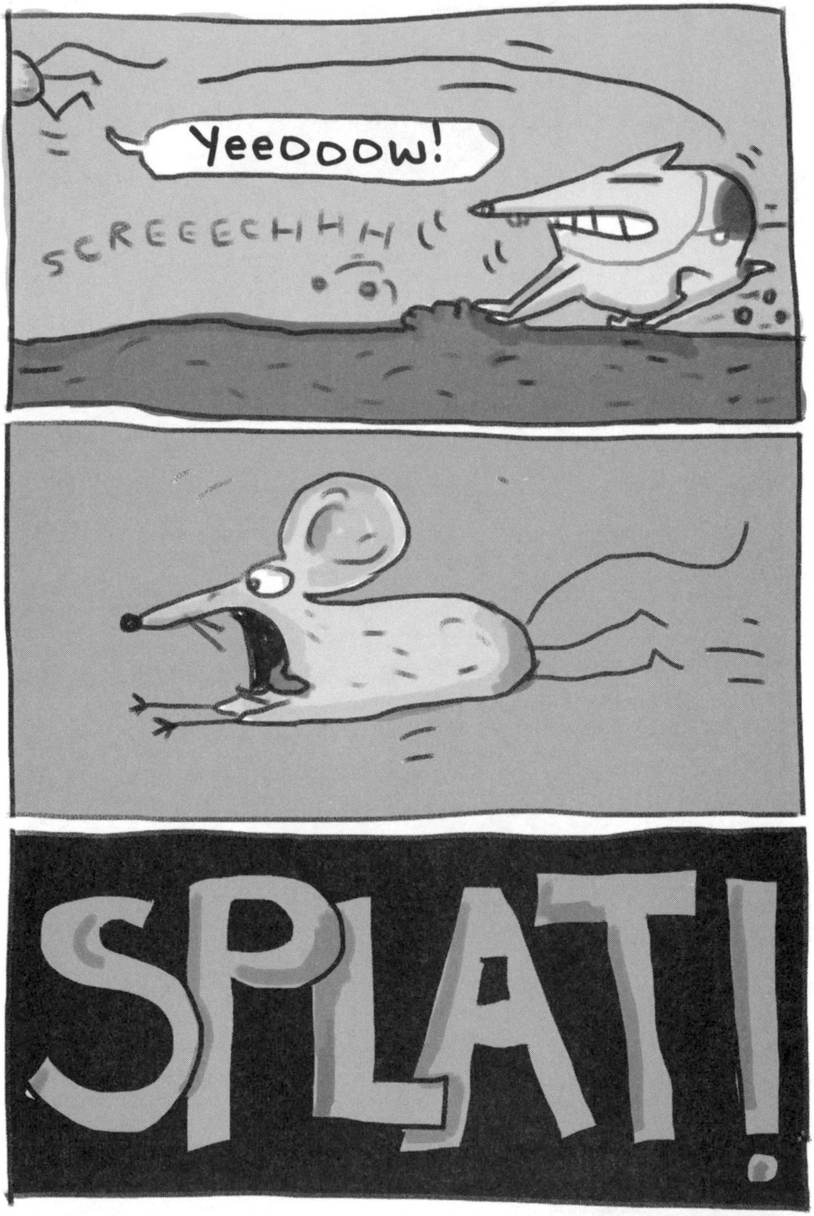
YEEOOOW!
SCREEEECHHHH
SPLAT!

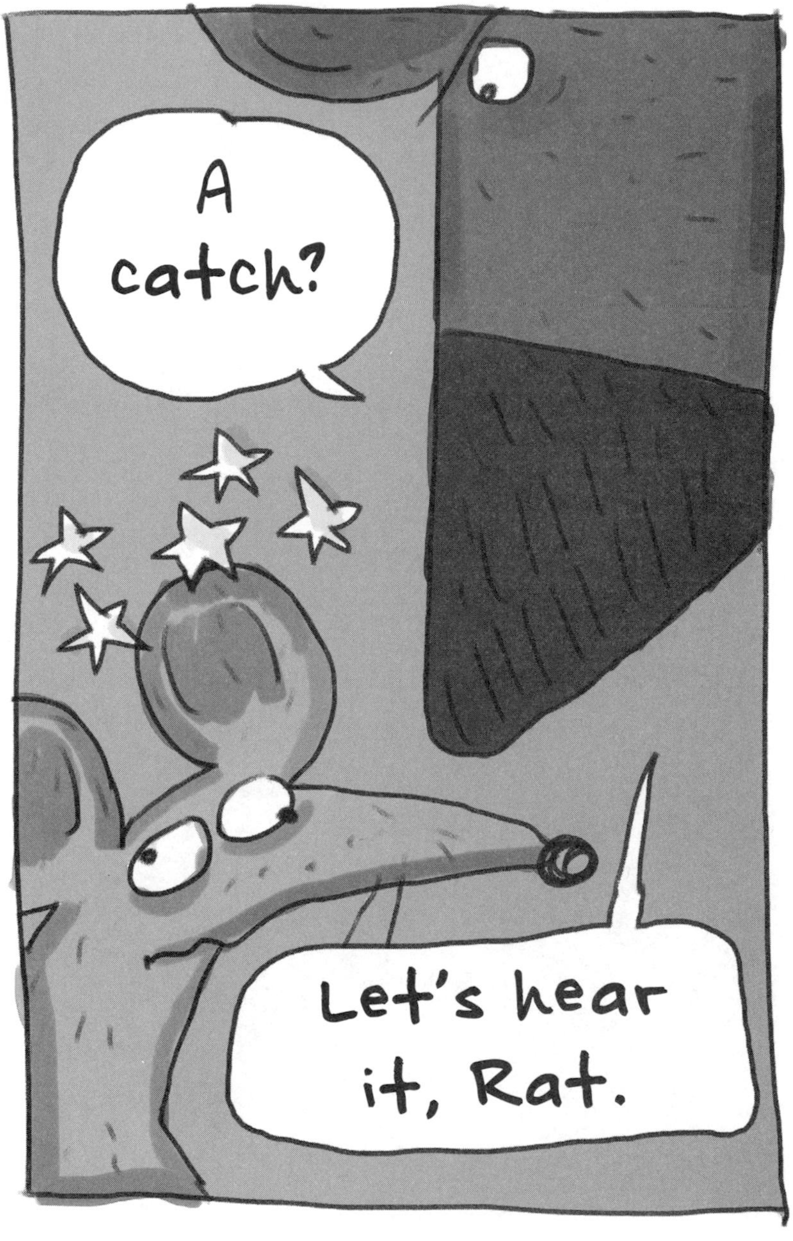
A catch?
Let's hear it, Rat.

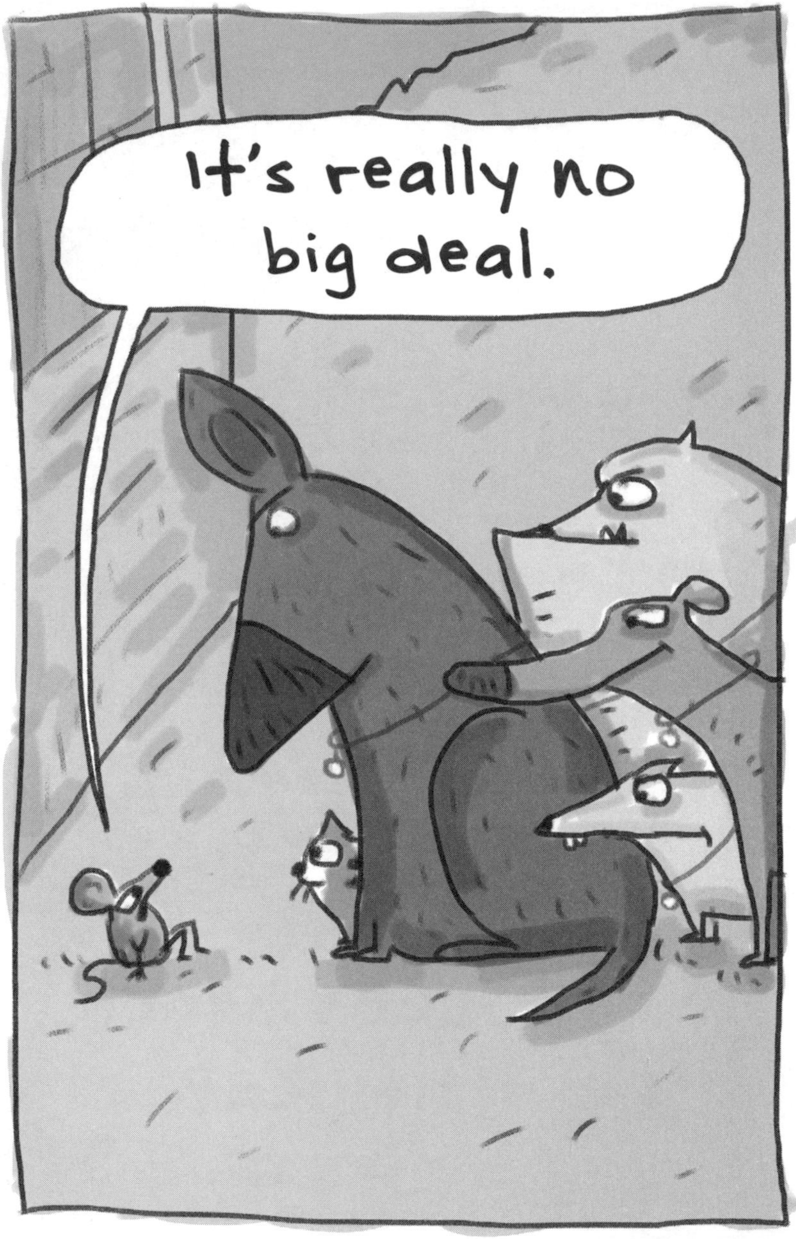
It's really no big deal.

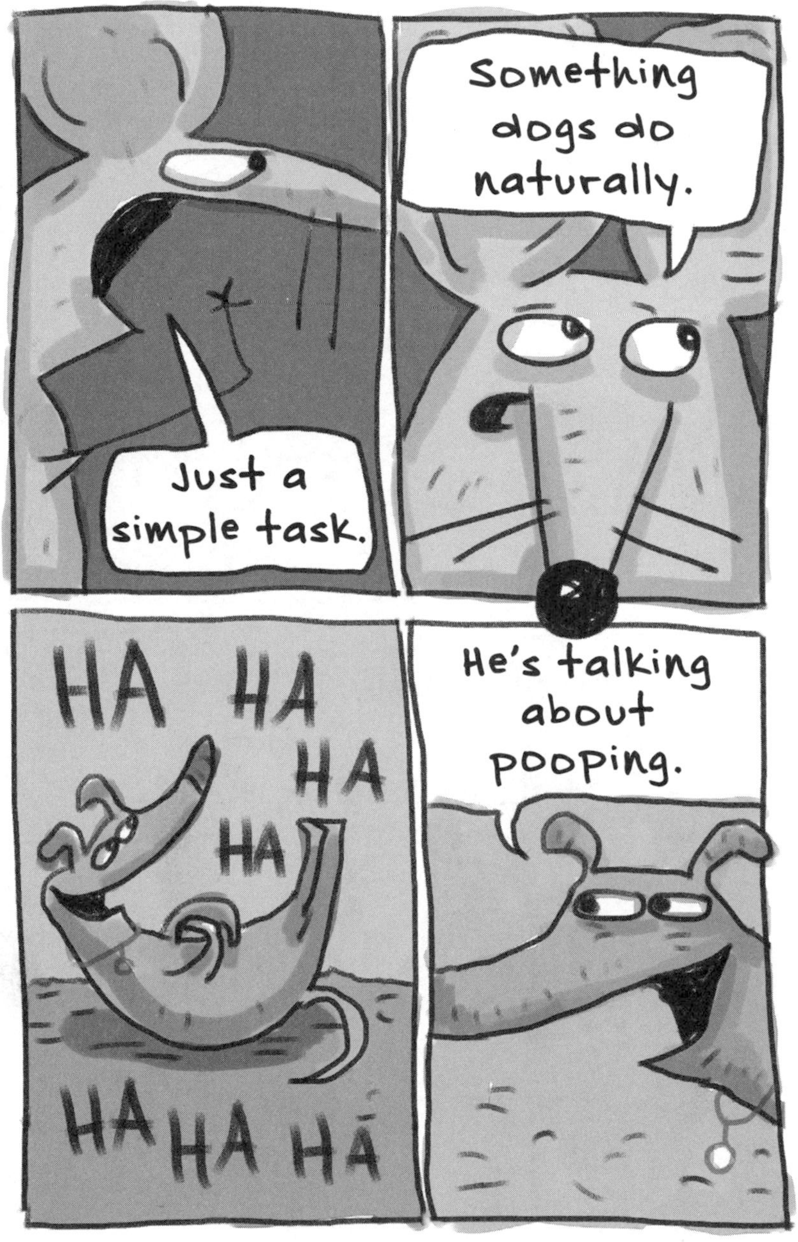
Just a simple task.
Something dogs do naturally.
HA HA HA HA
HA HA HA HA
He's talking about pooping.

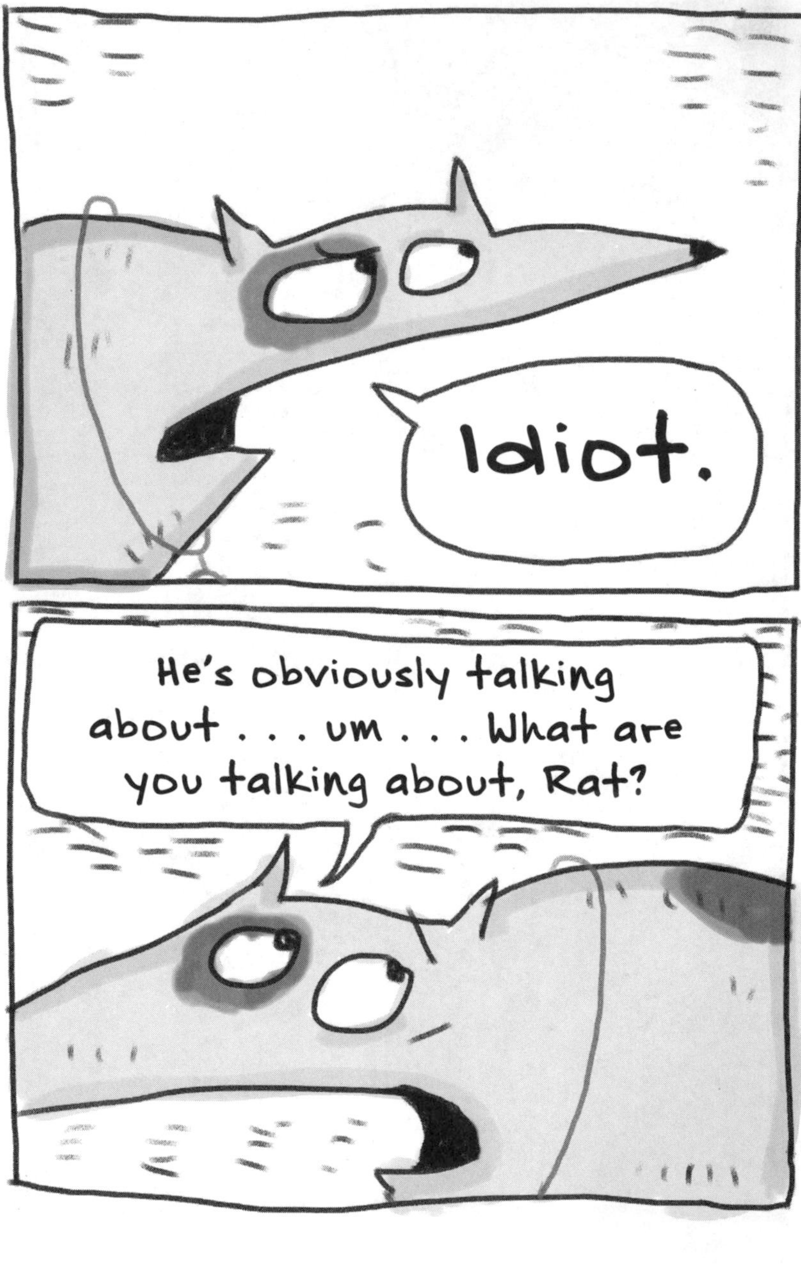
Idiot.
He's obviously talking about . . . um . . . What are you talking about, Rat?

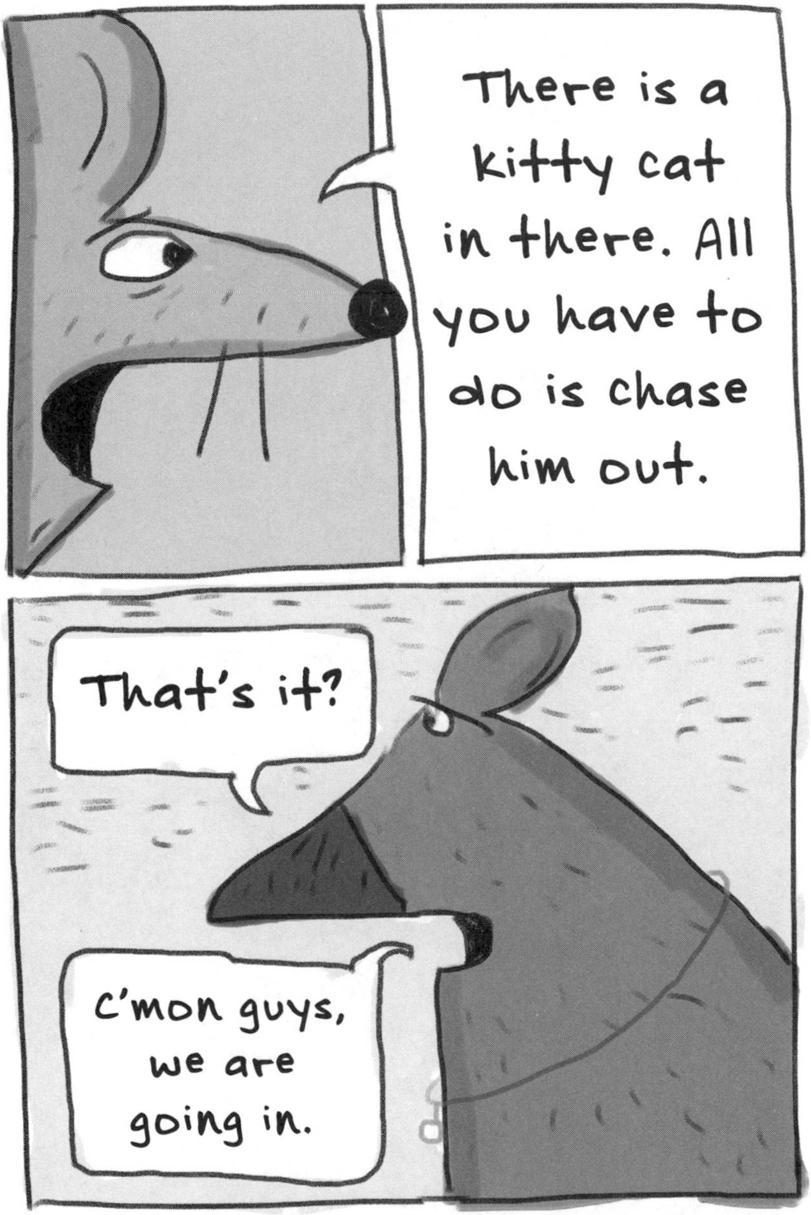
There is a kitty cat in there. All you have to do is chase him out.
That's it?
C'mon guys, we are going in.

Scene
Eight

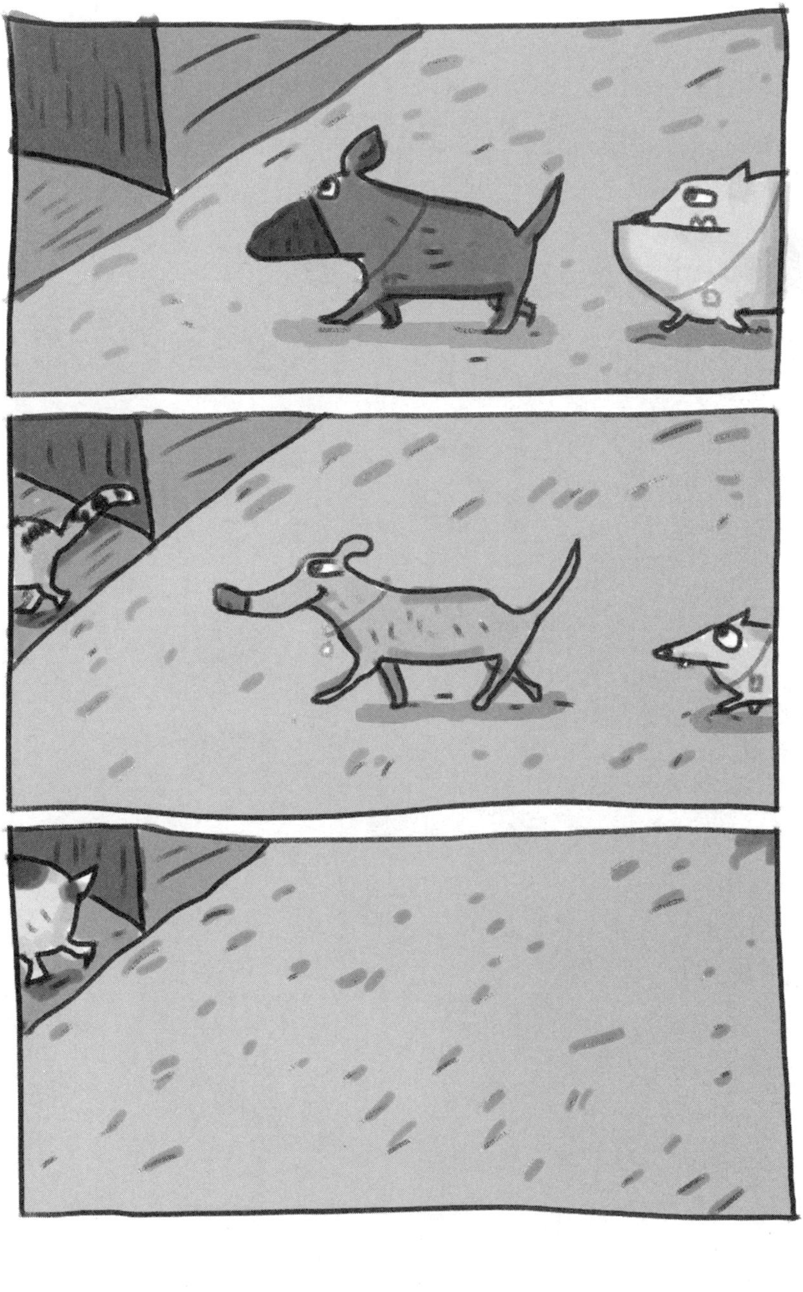

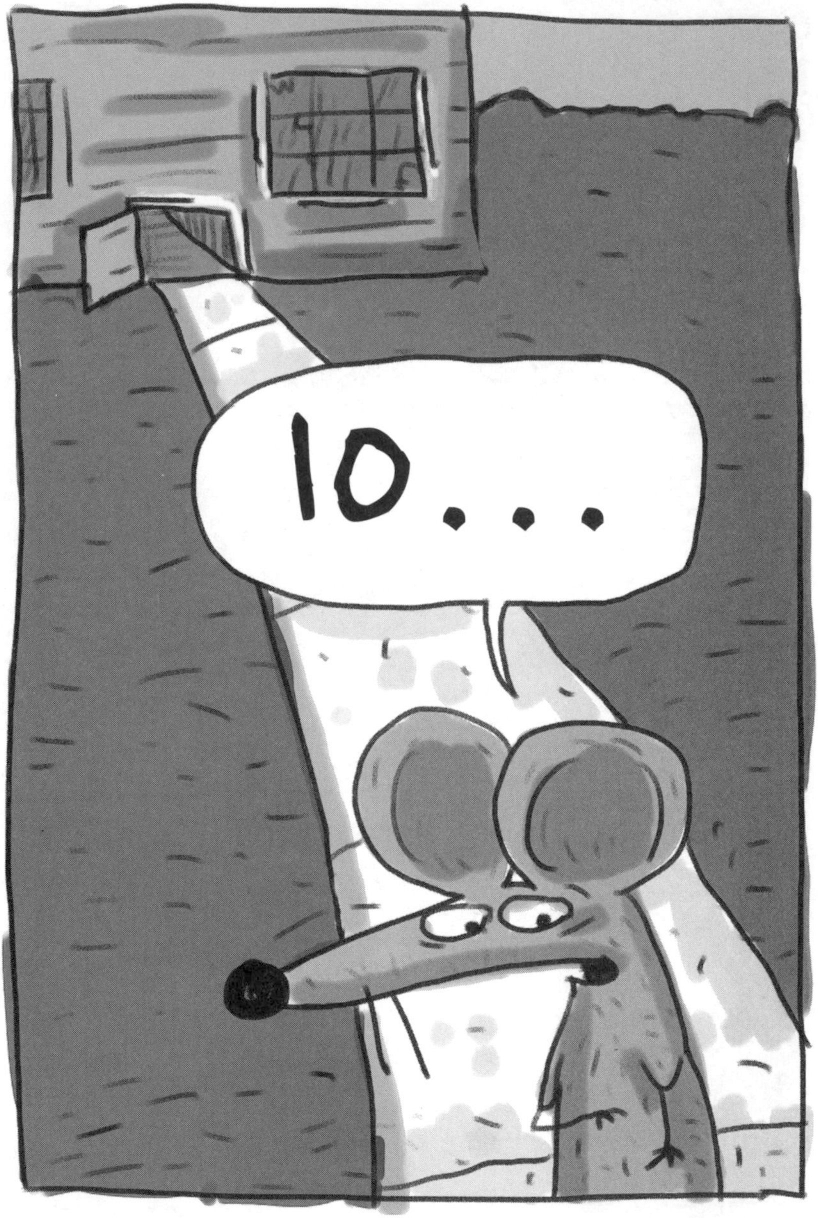
10...

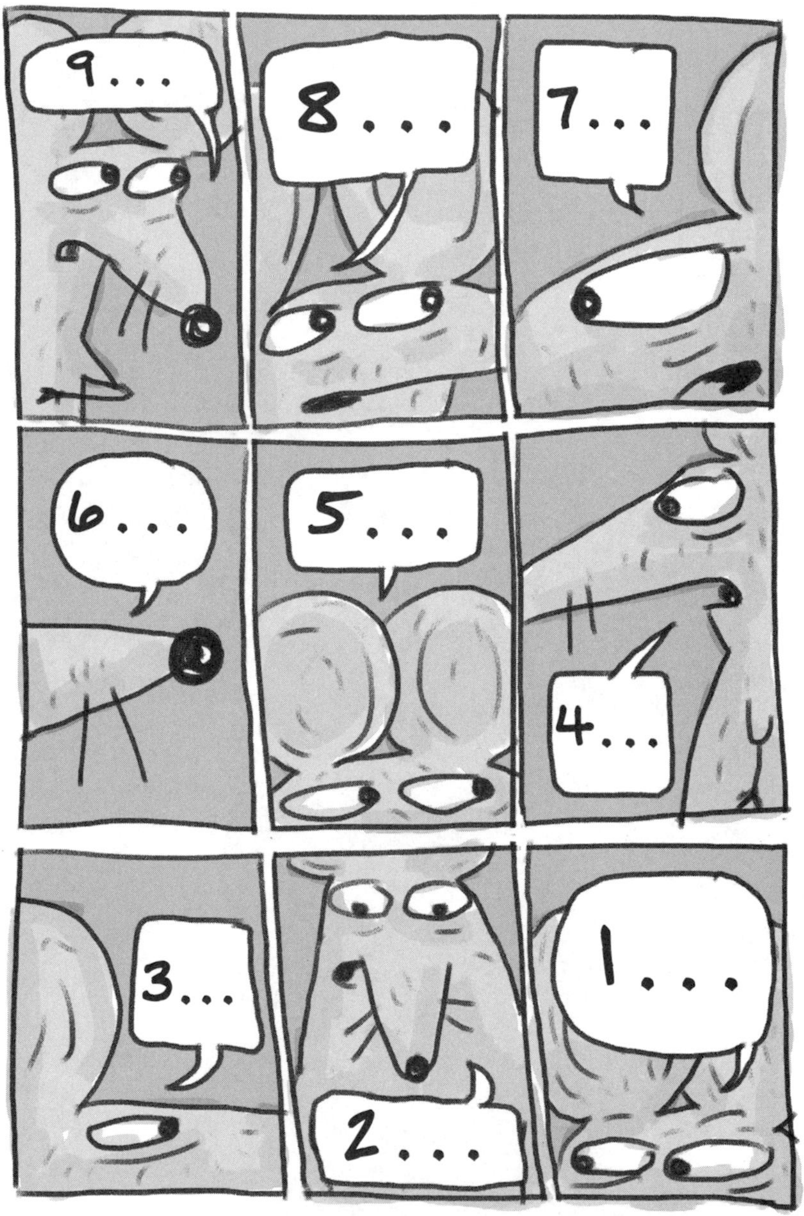
9...
8...
7...
6...
5...
4...
3...
2...
1...

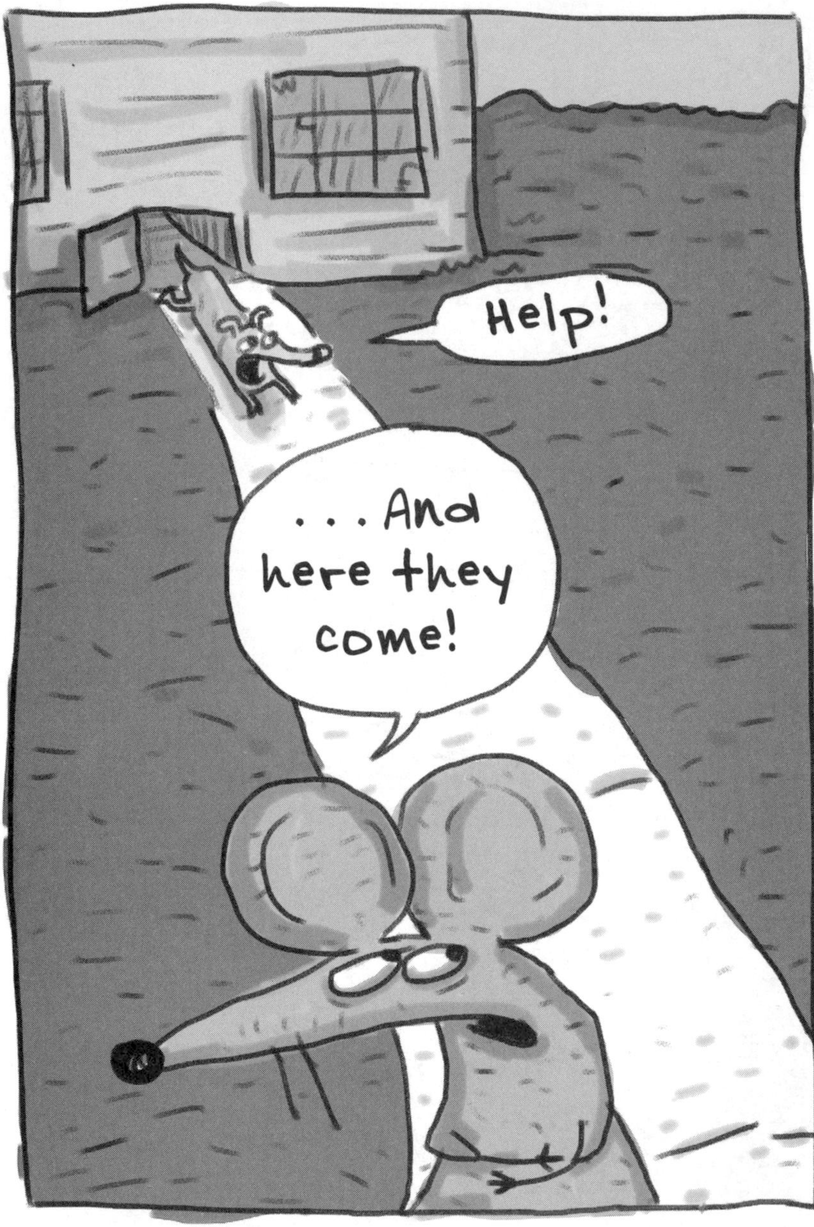
Help!
...And here they come!

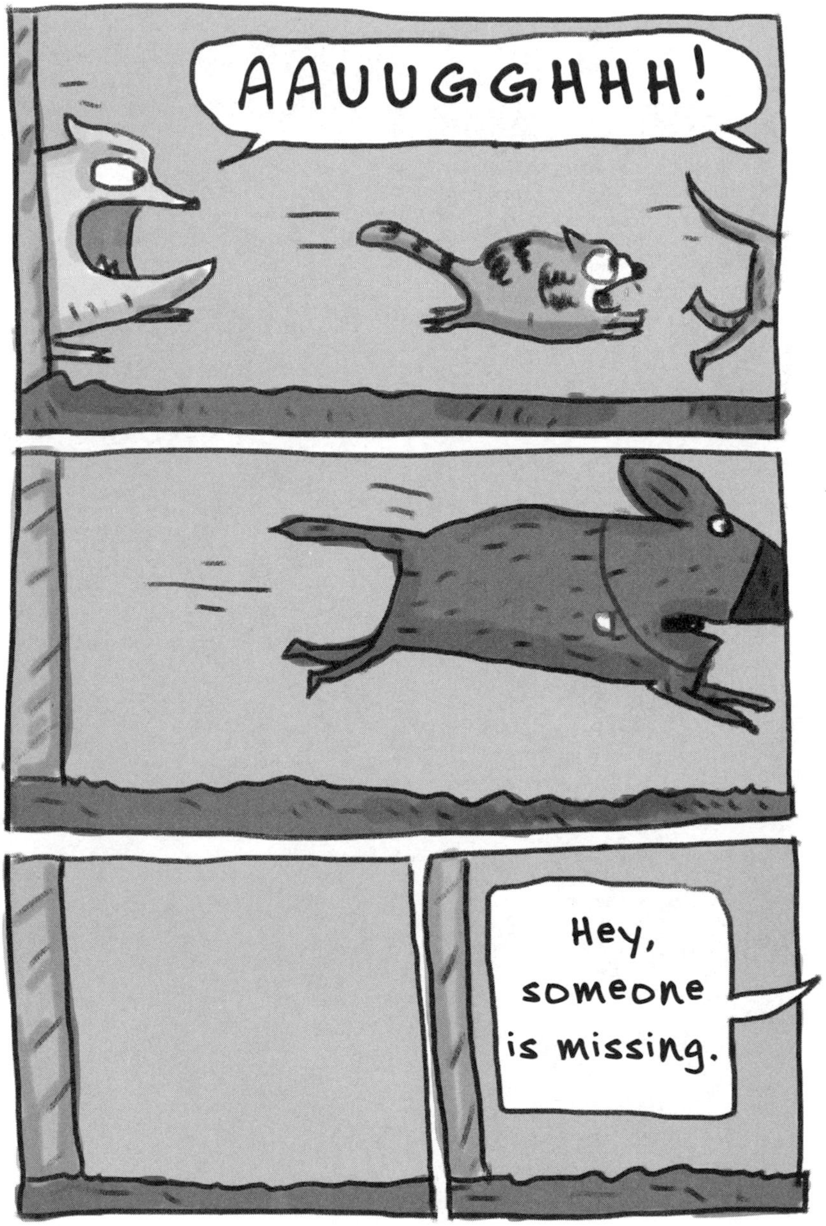
AAUUGGHHH!
Hey, someone is missing.

Scene
Nine

74

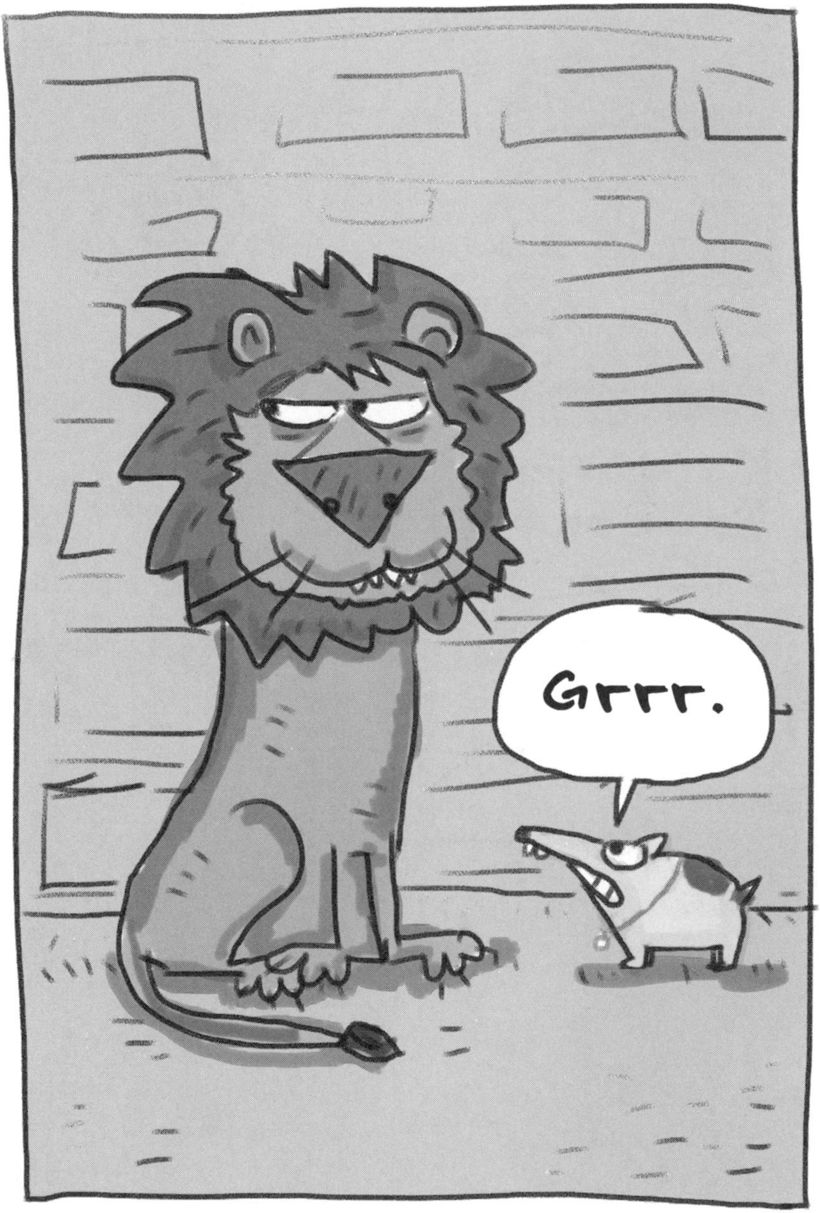
Grrr.

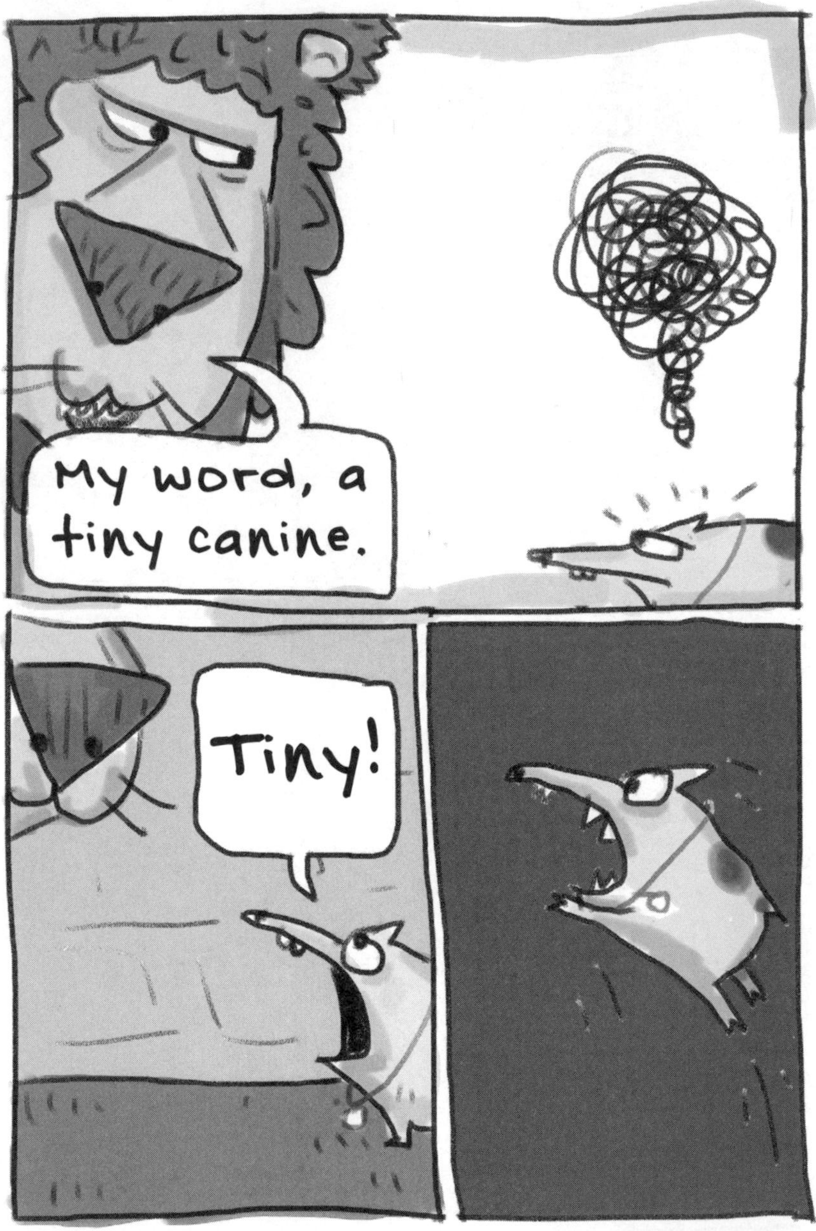
My word, a tiny canine.
Tiny!

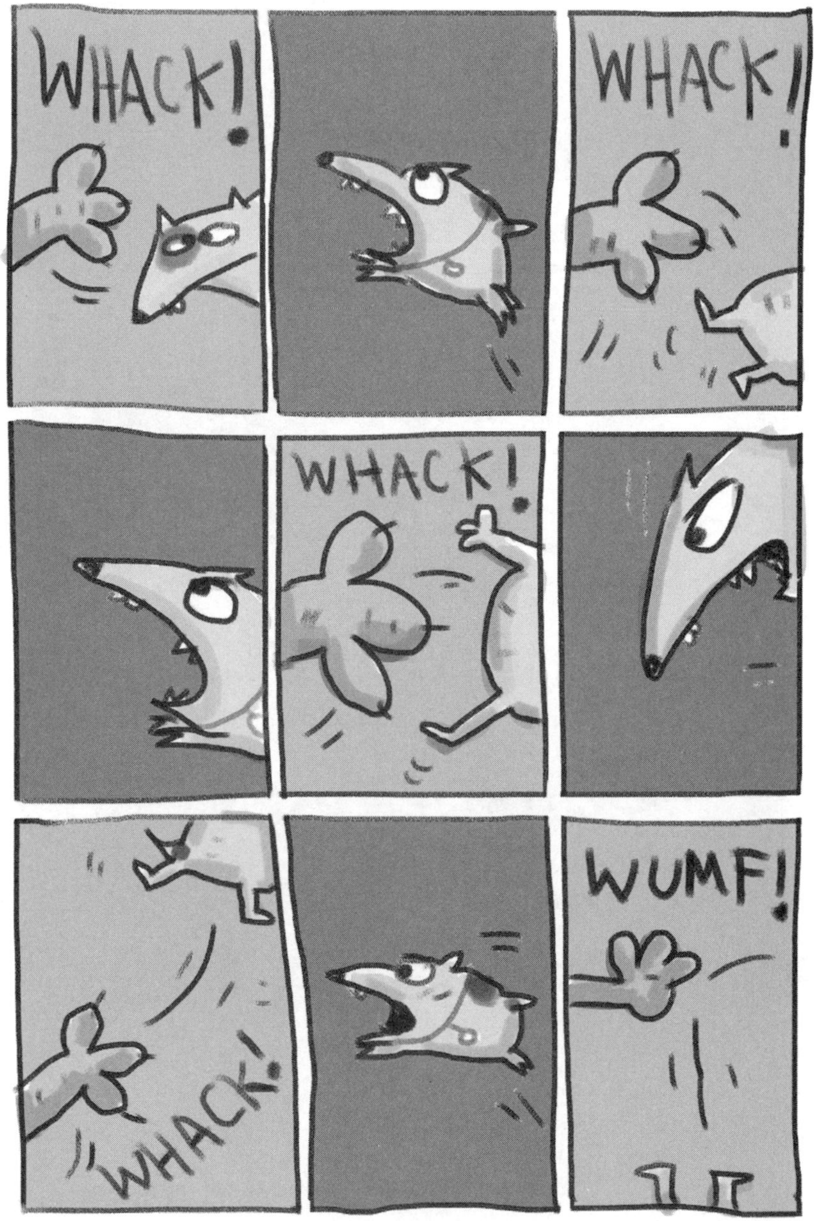
WHACK!
WHACK!
WHACK!
WHACK!
WUMF!

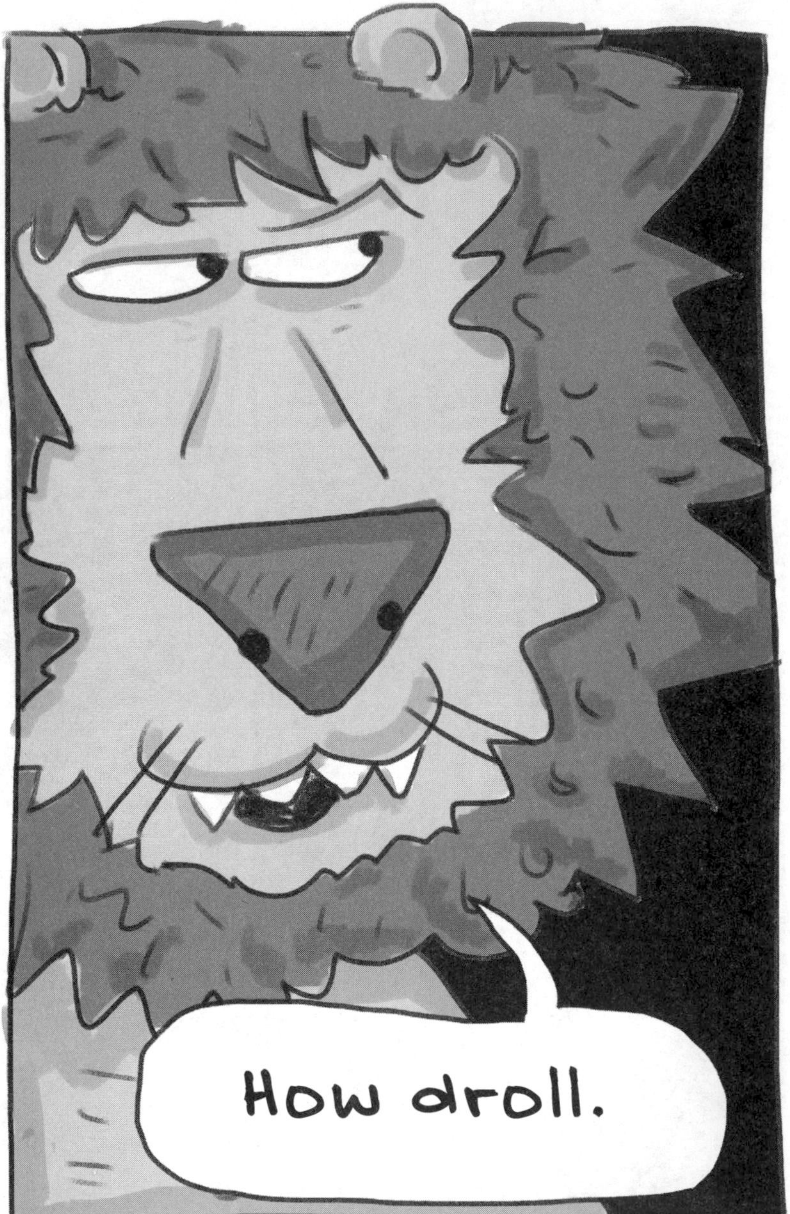
How droll.

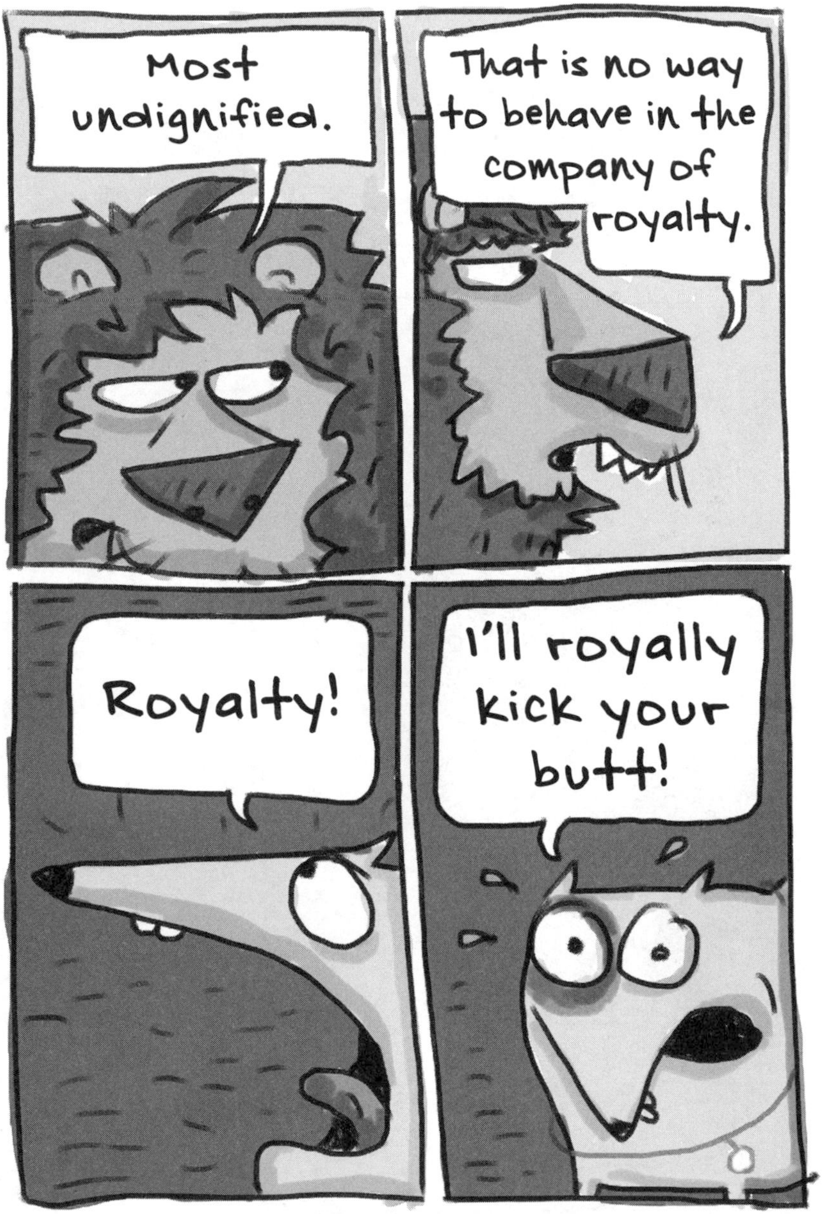
Most undignified.
That is no way to behave in the company of royalty.
Royalty!
I'll royally kick your butt!

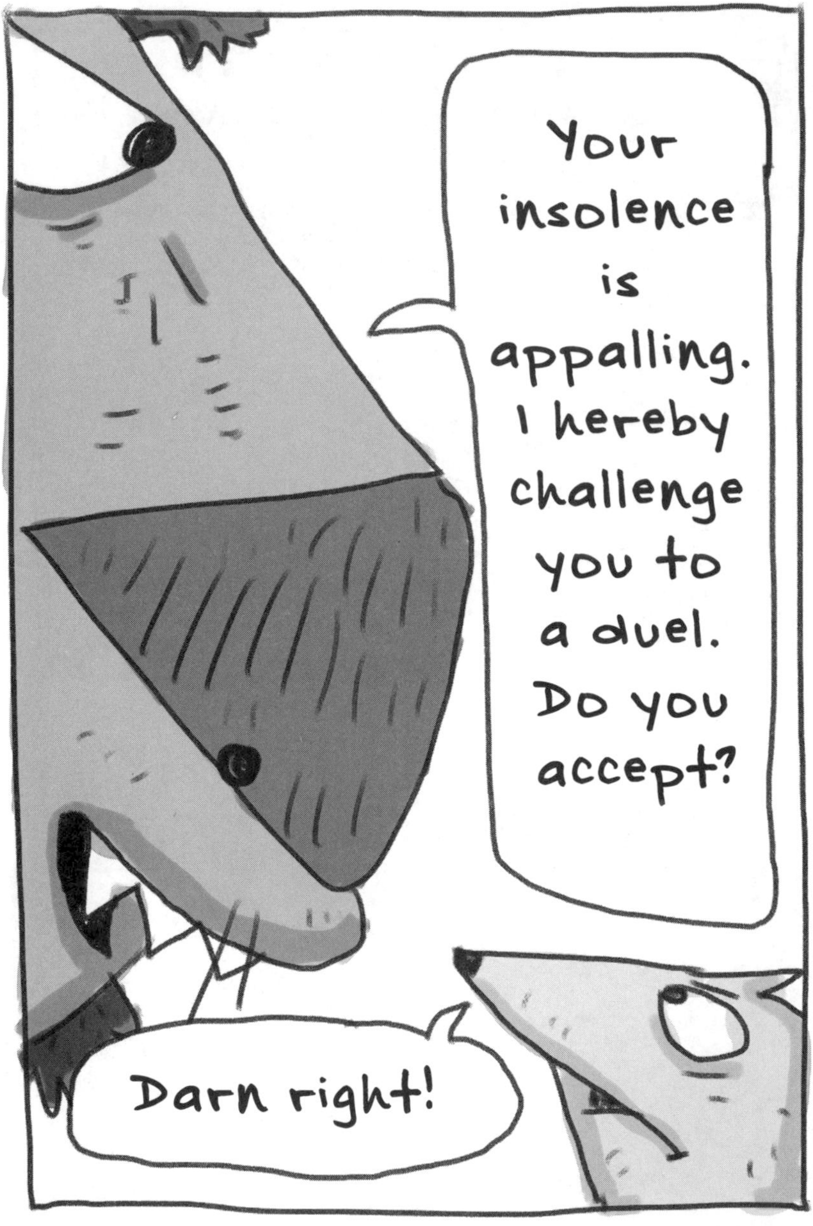
Your insolence is appalling. I hereby challenge you to a duel. Do you accept?
Darn right!

Scene
Ten

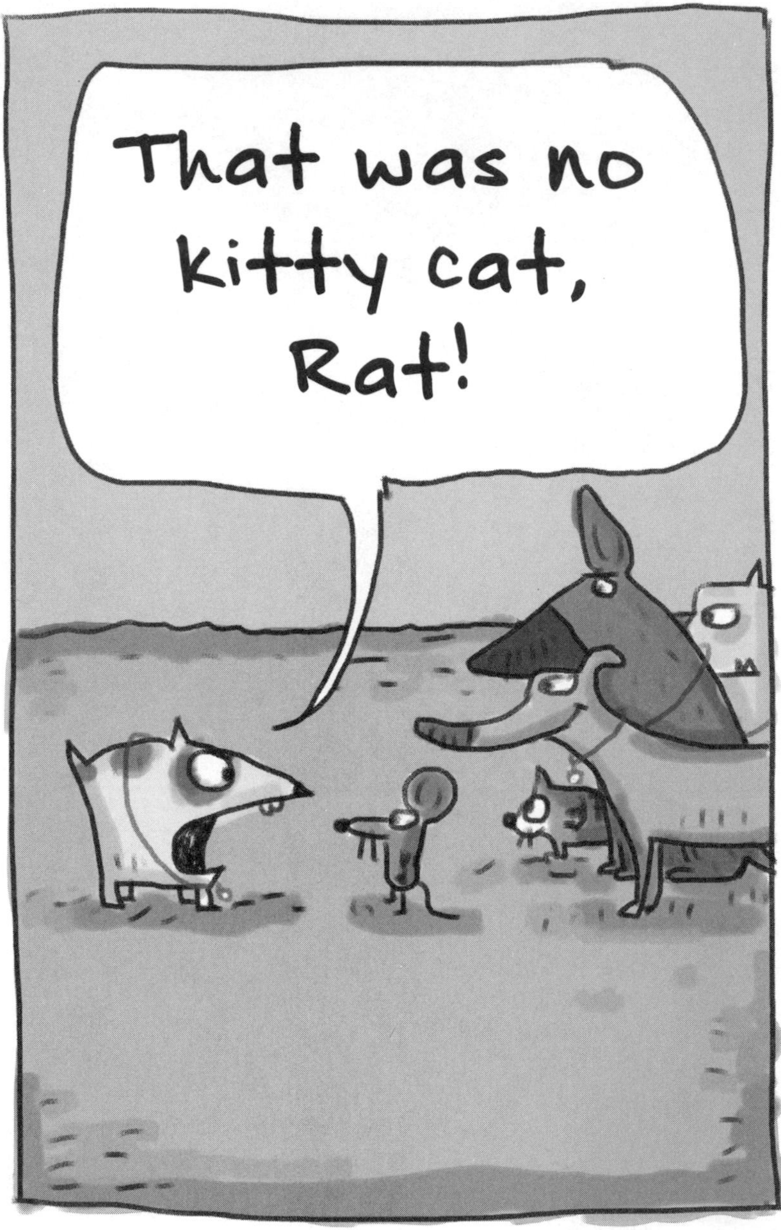
That was no kitty cat, Rat!

Scene
Eleven

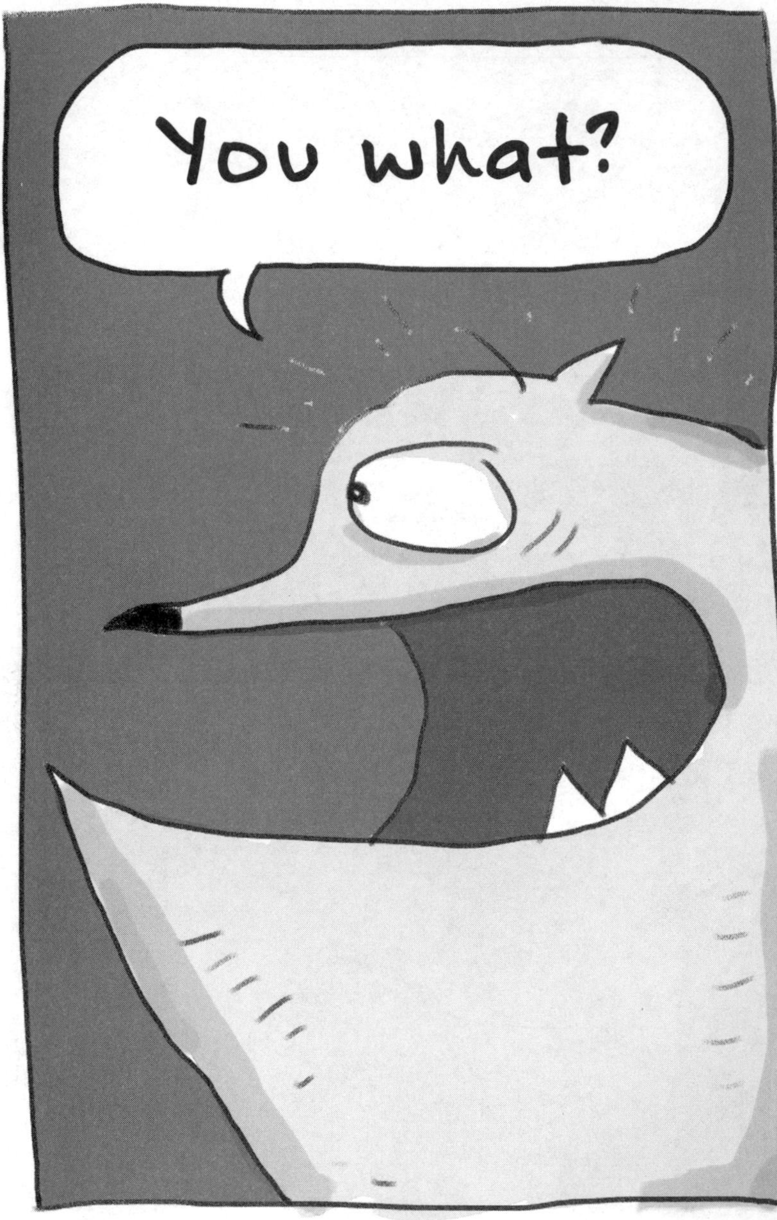
You what?

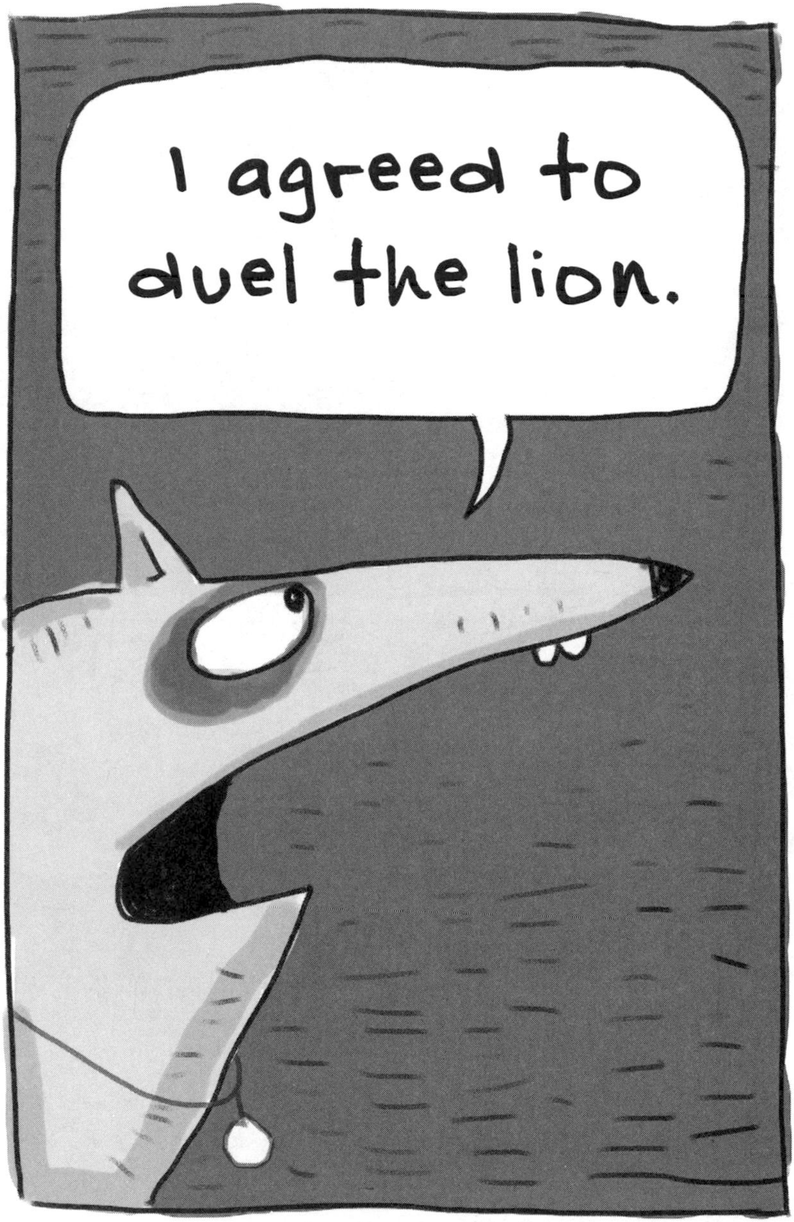
I agreed to duel the lion.

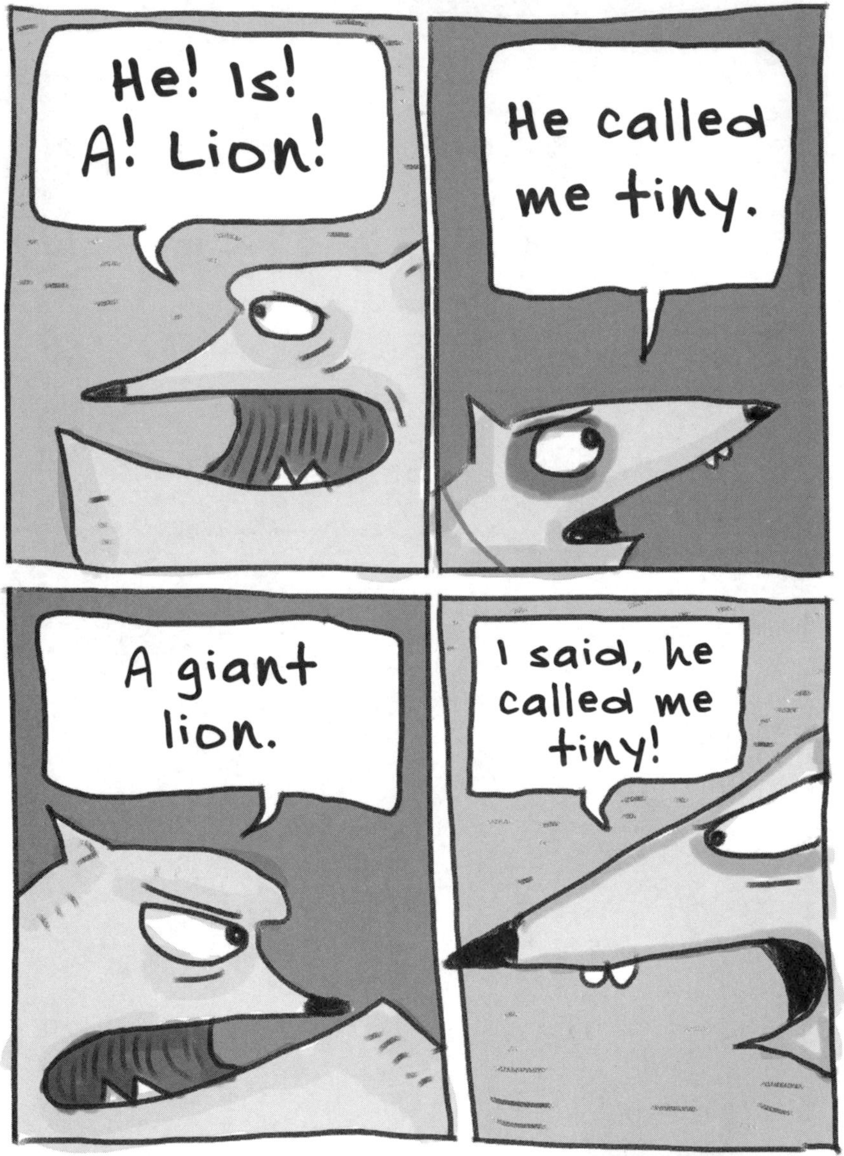
He! Is! A! Lion!
He called me tiny.
A giant lion.
I said, he called me tiny!

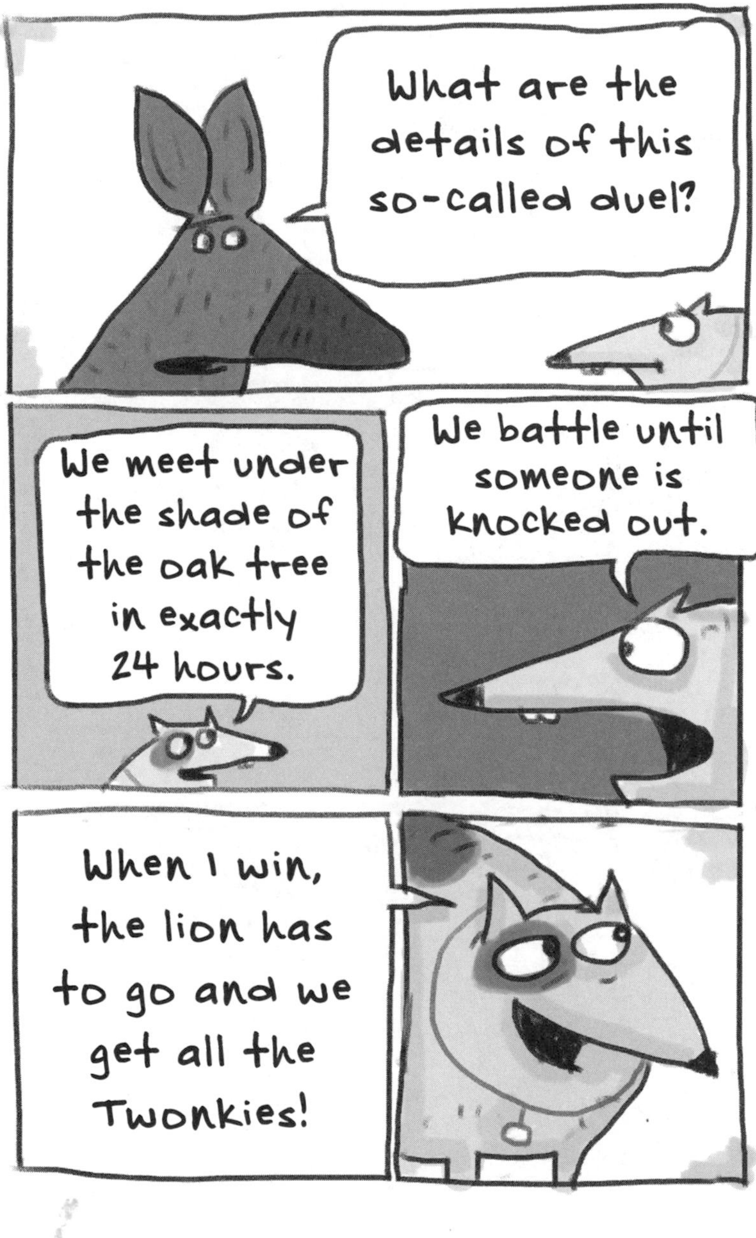
What are the details of this so-called duel?
We meet under the shade of the oak tree in exactly 24 hours.
We battle until someone is knocked out.
When I win, the lion has to go and we get all the Twonkies!

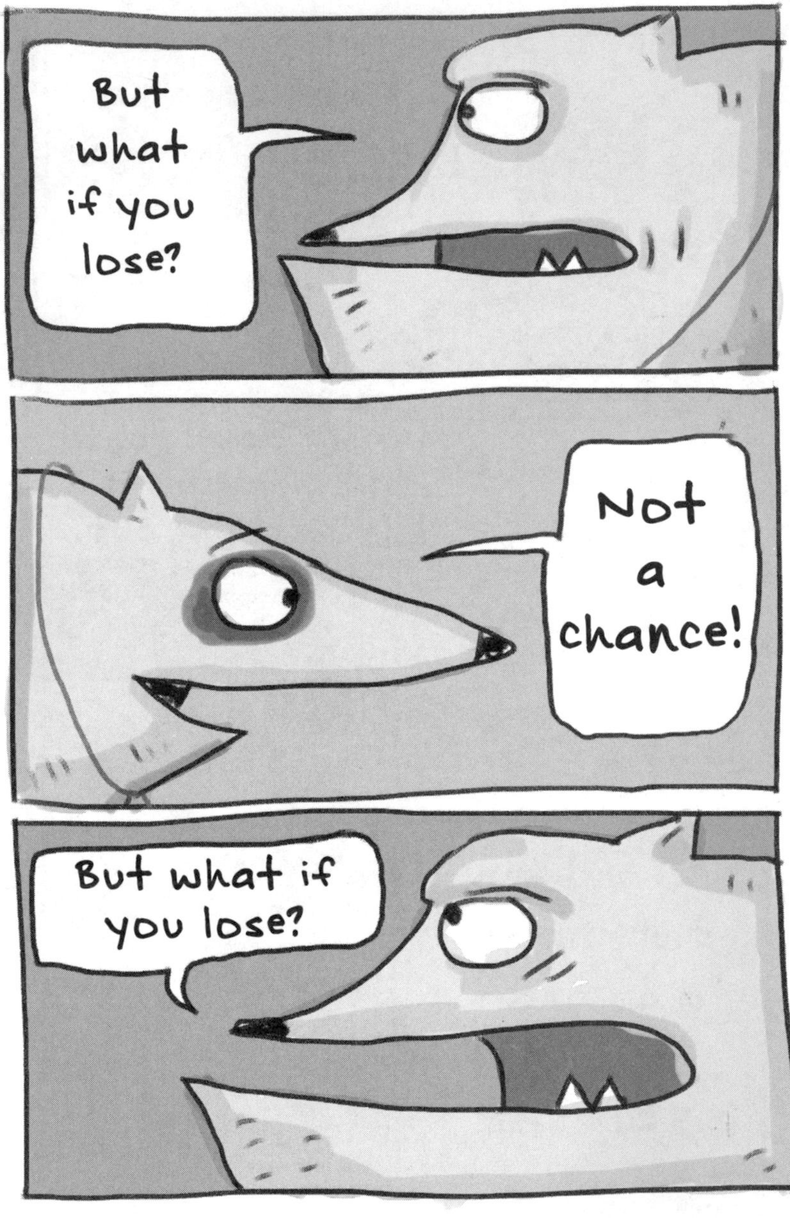
But what if you lose?
Not a chance!
But what if you lose?

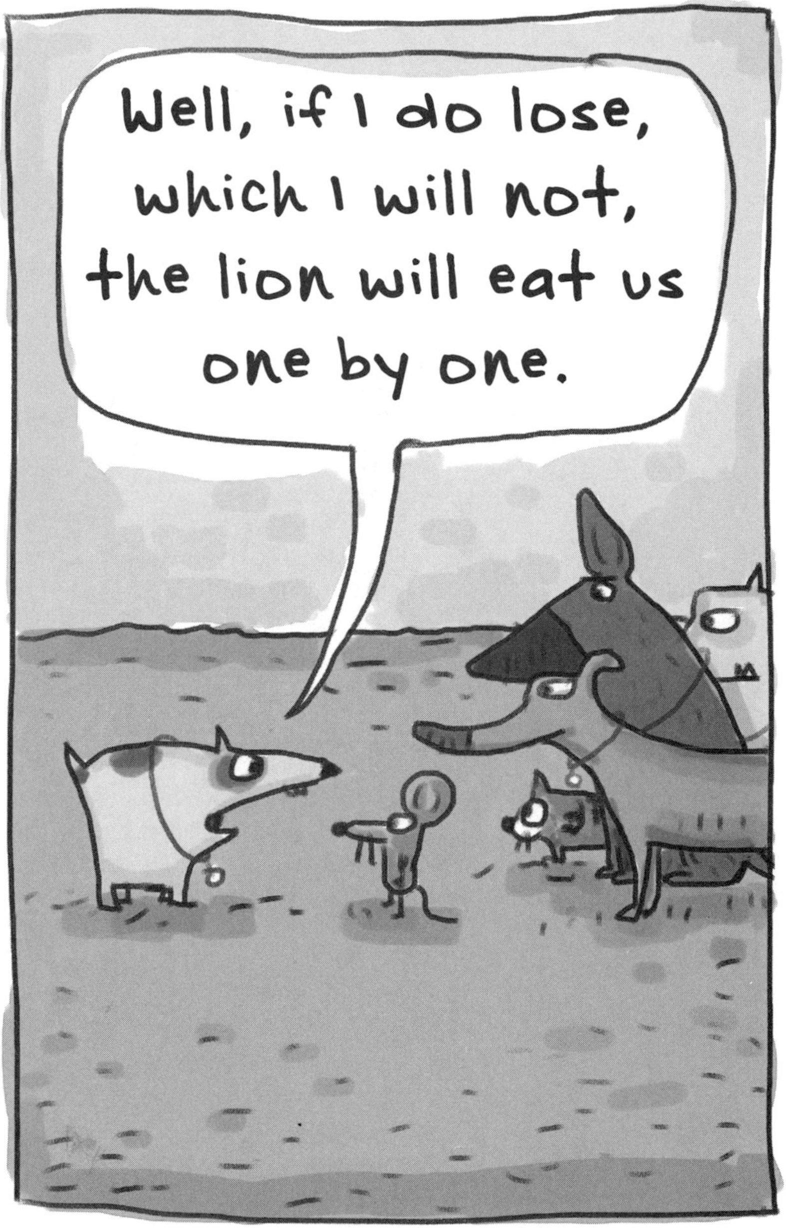
Well, if I do lose, which I will not, the lion will eat us one by one.

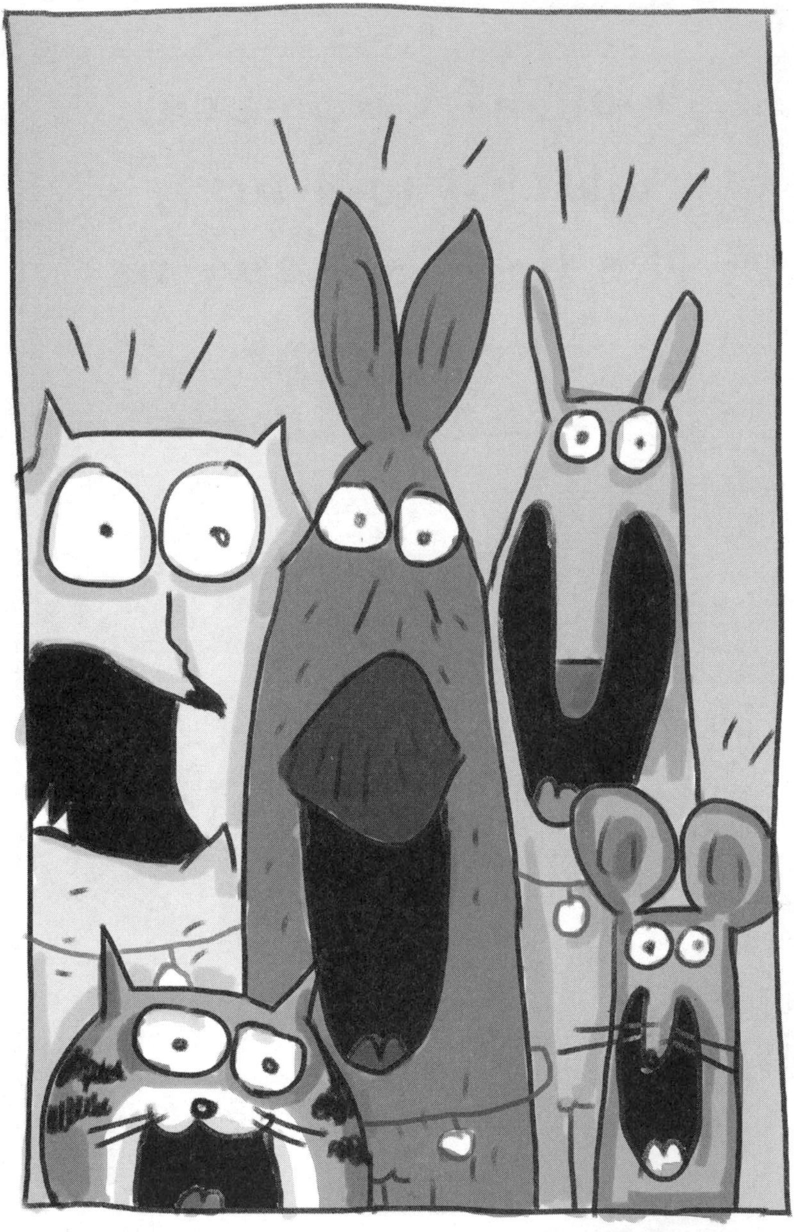

Scene
Twelve

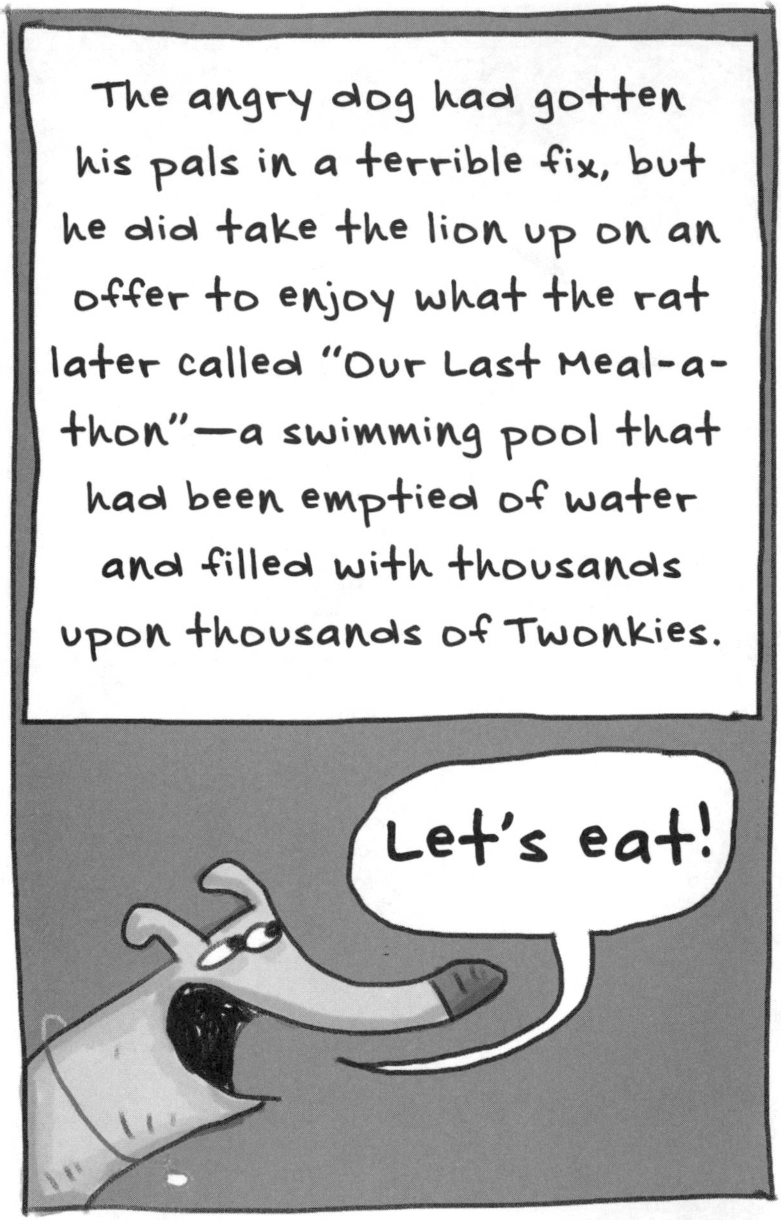
The angry dog had gotten his pals in a terrible fix, but he did take the lion up on an offer to enjoy what the rat later called "Our Last Meal-a-thon"—a swimming pool that had been emptied of water and filled with thousands upon thousands of Twonkies.
Let's eat!

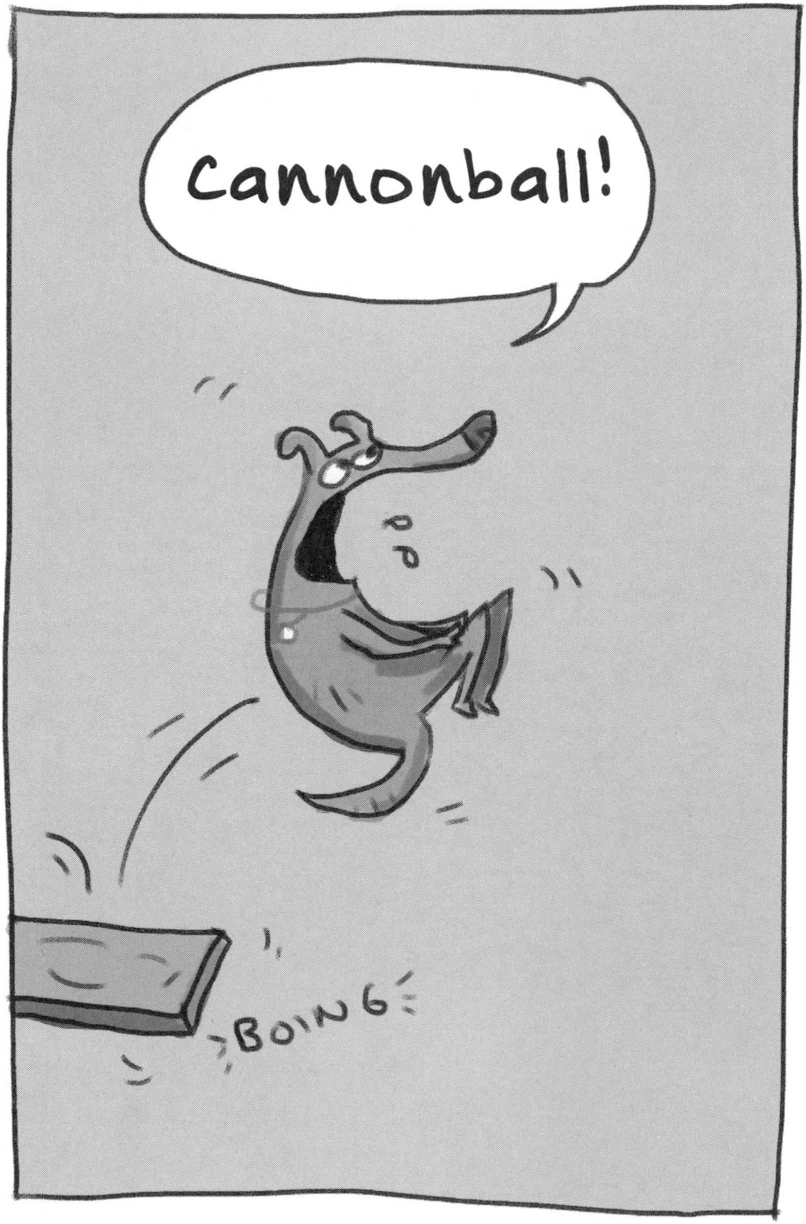
Cannonball!
BOING

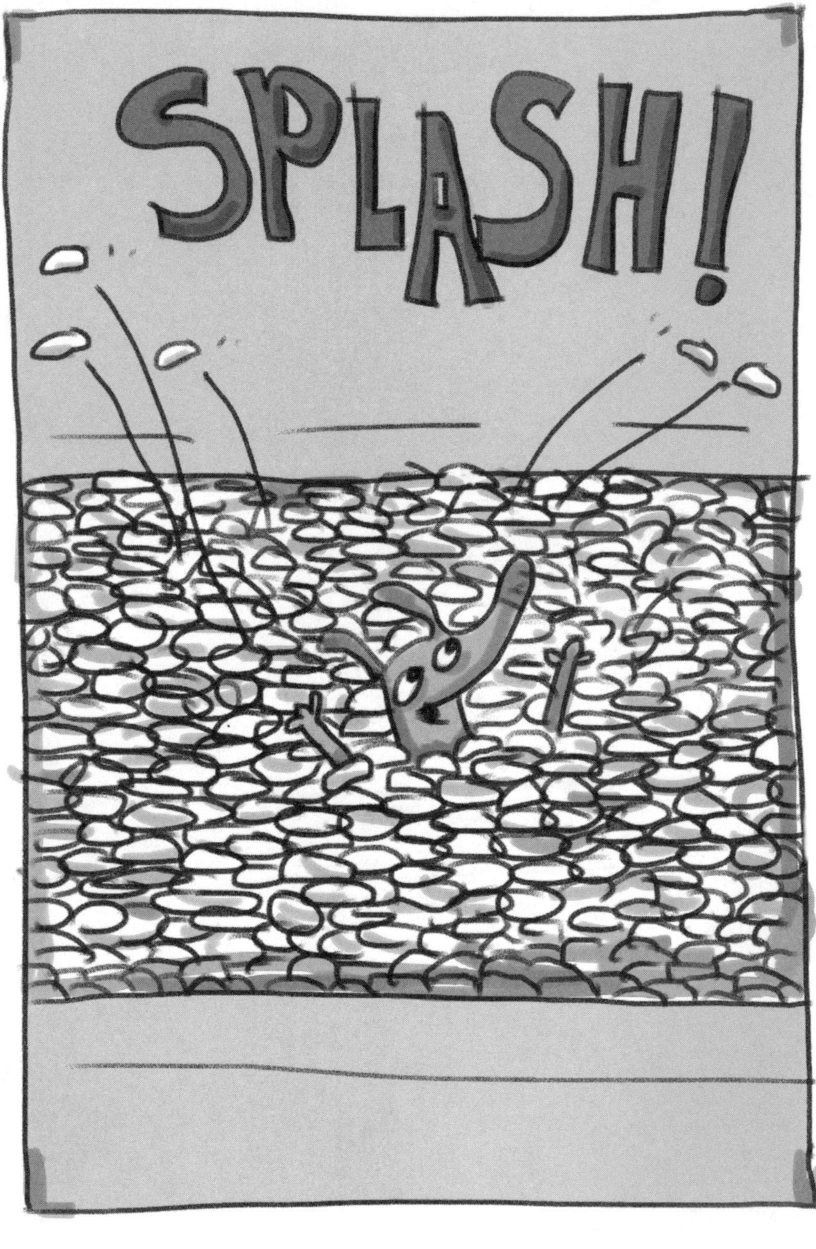
SPLASH!

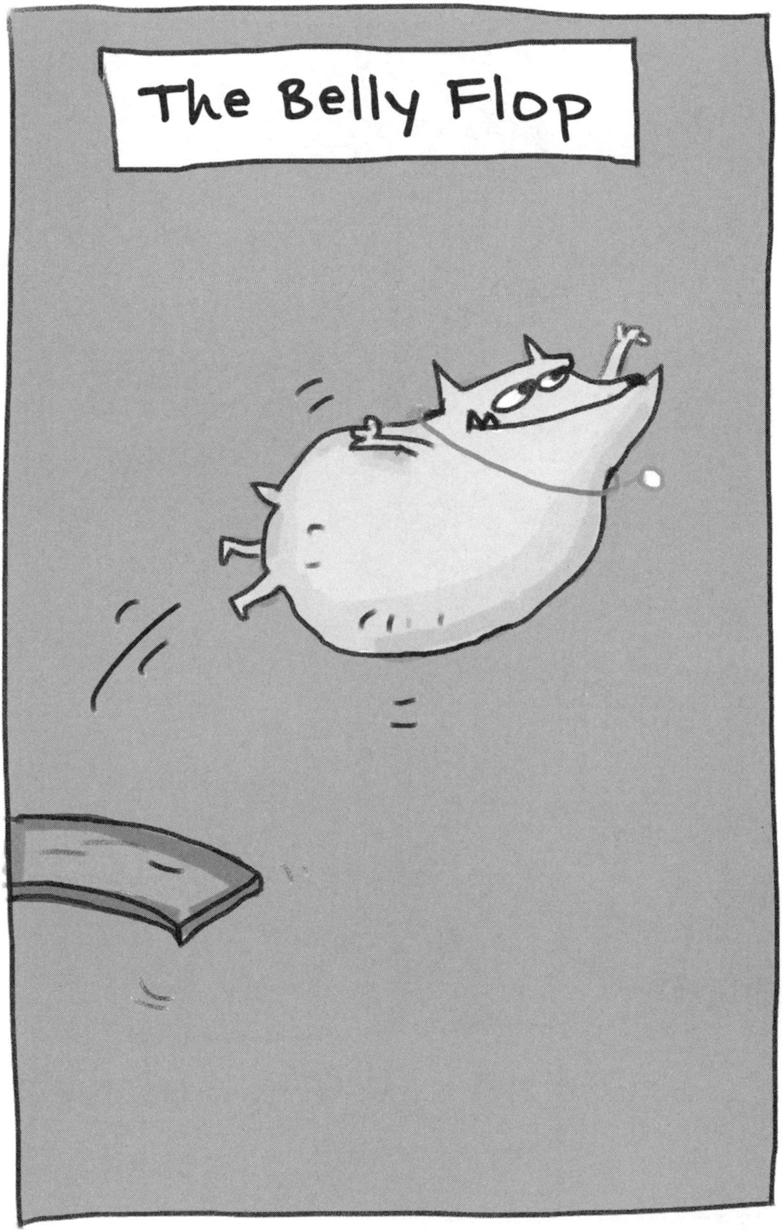
The Belly Flop

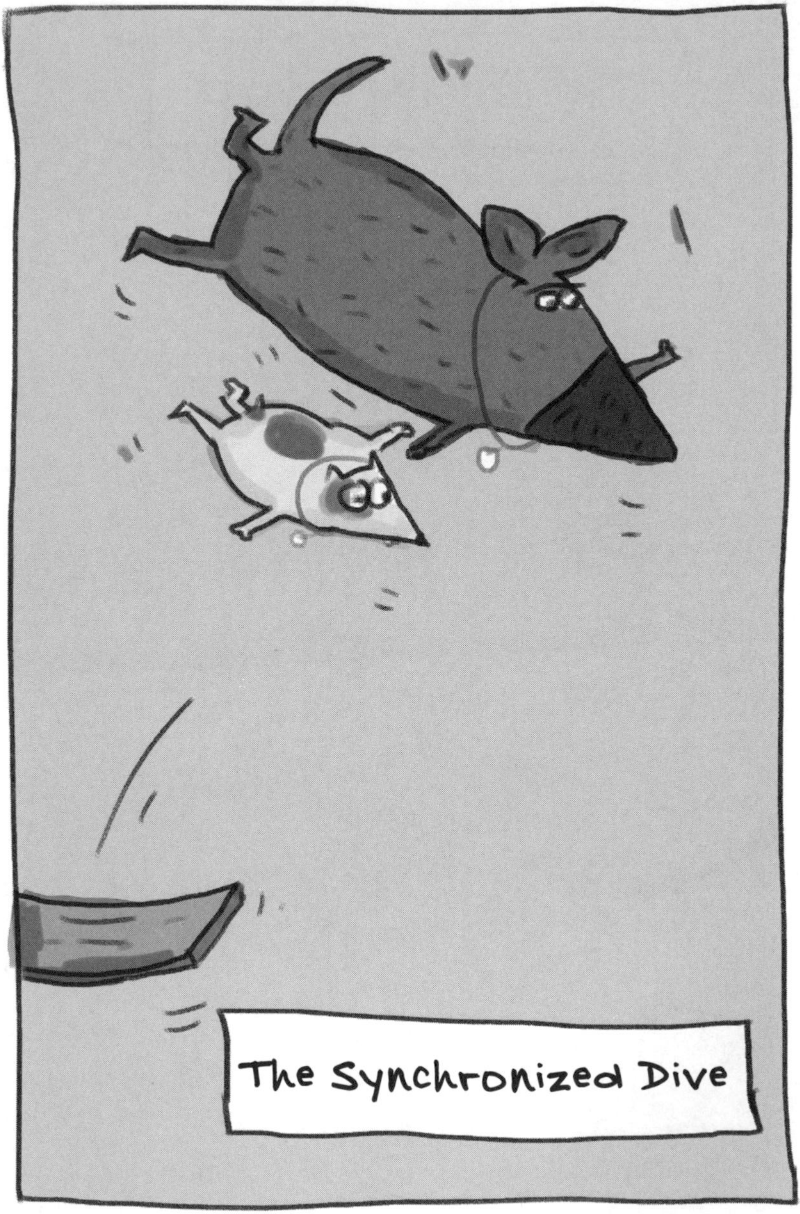
The Synchronized Dive

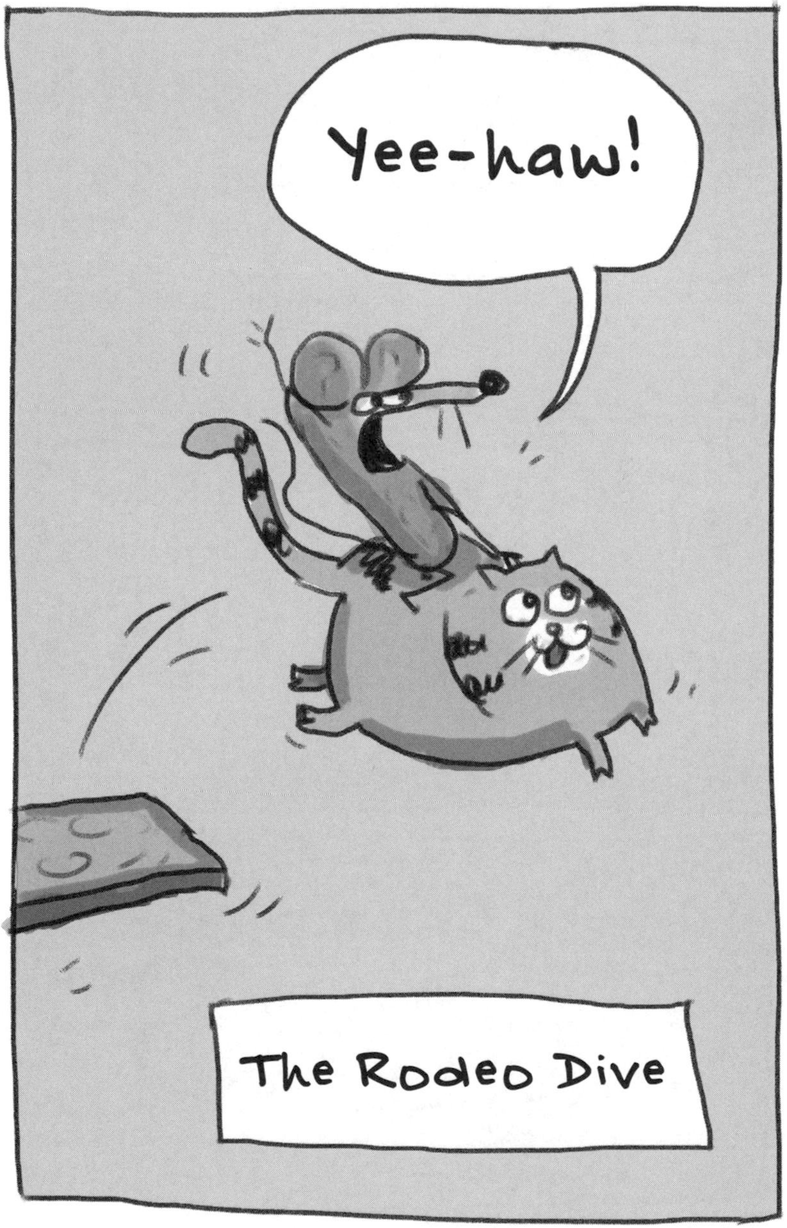
Yee-haw!
The Rodeo Dive

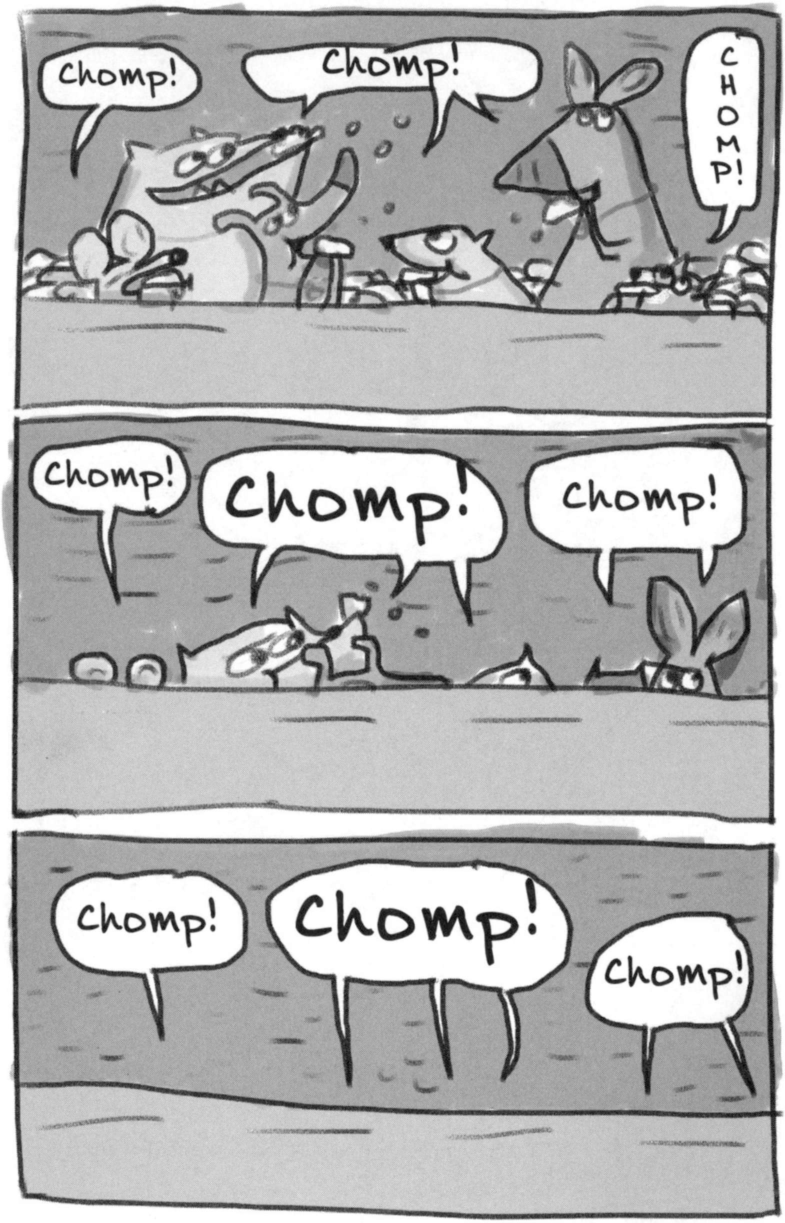
Chomp!
Chomp!
CHOMP!
Chomp!
Chomp!
Chomp!
Chomp!
Chomp!
Chomp!

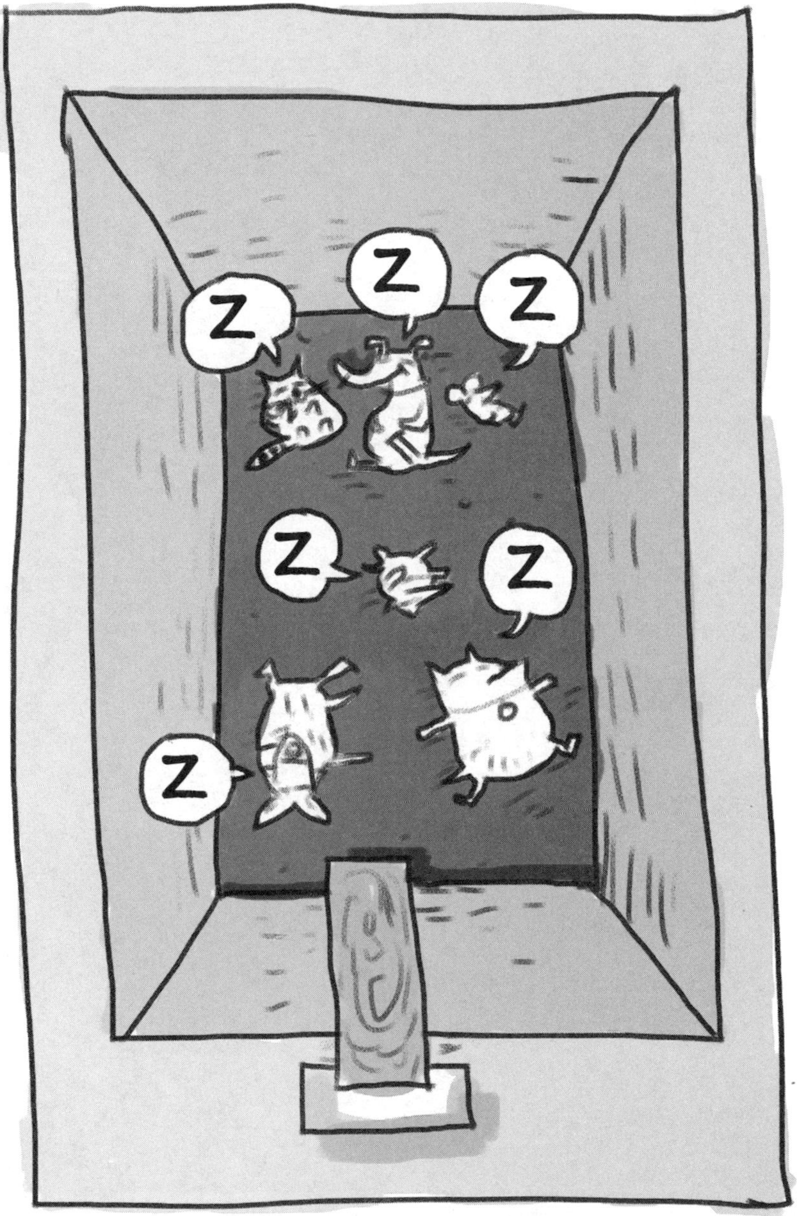
Z
Z
Z
Z
Z
Z

Scene
Thirteen

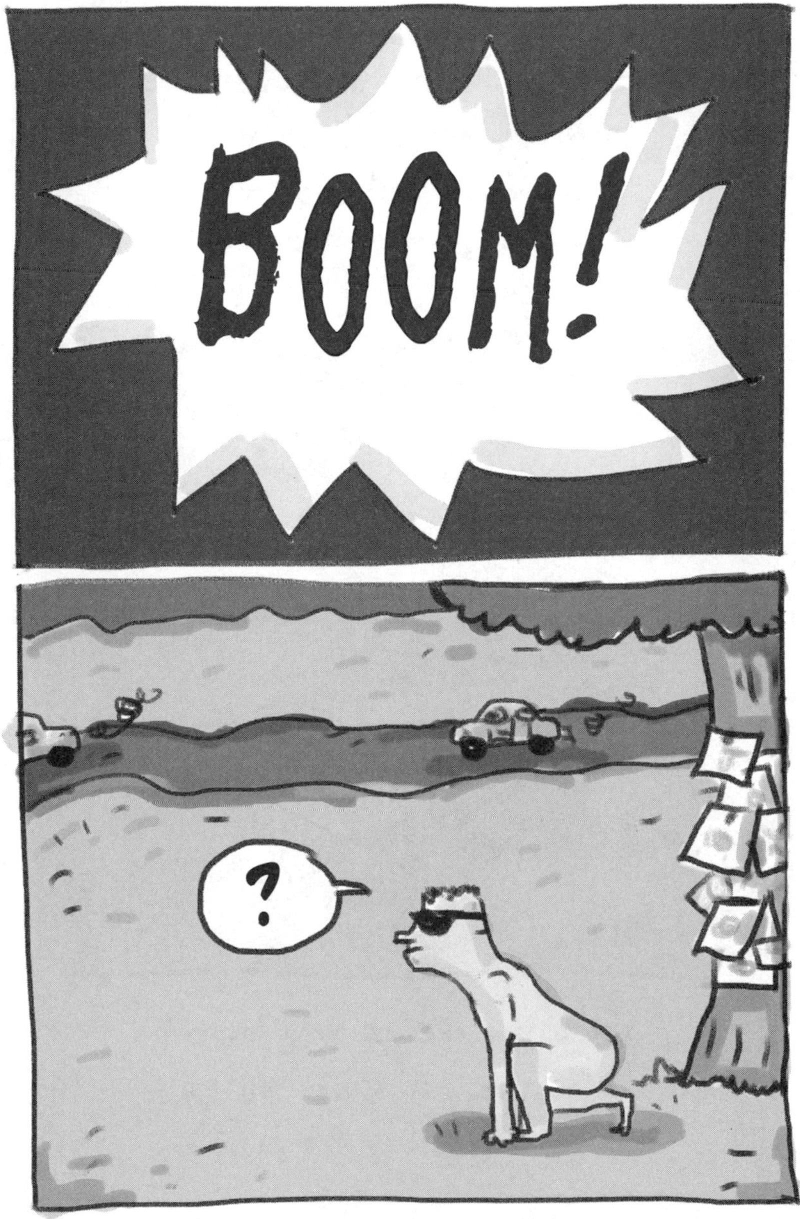
BOOM!
?

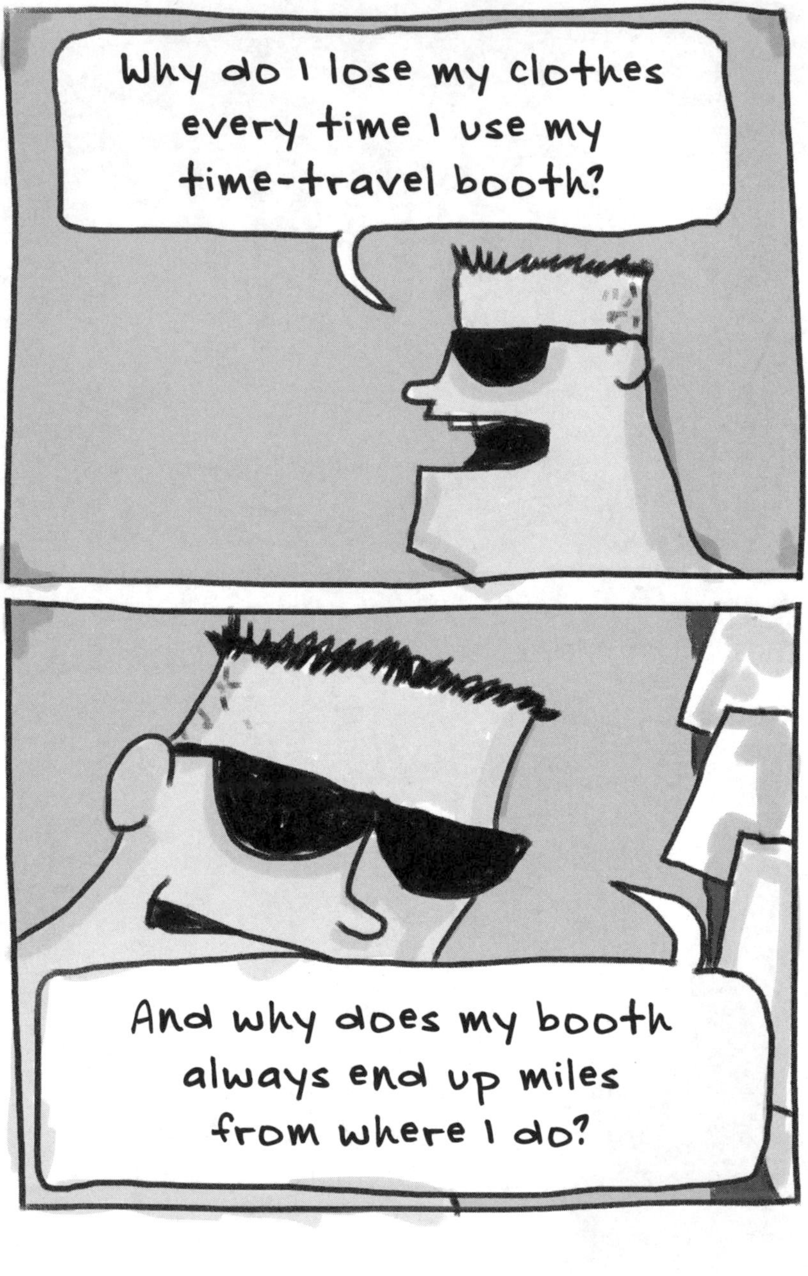
Why do I lose my clothes every time I use my time-travel booth?
And why does my booth always end up miles from where I do?

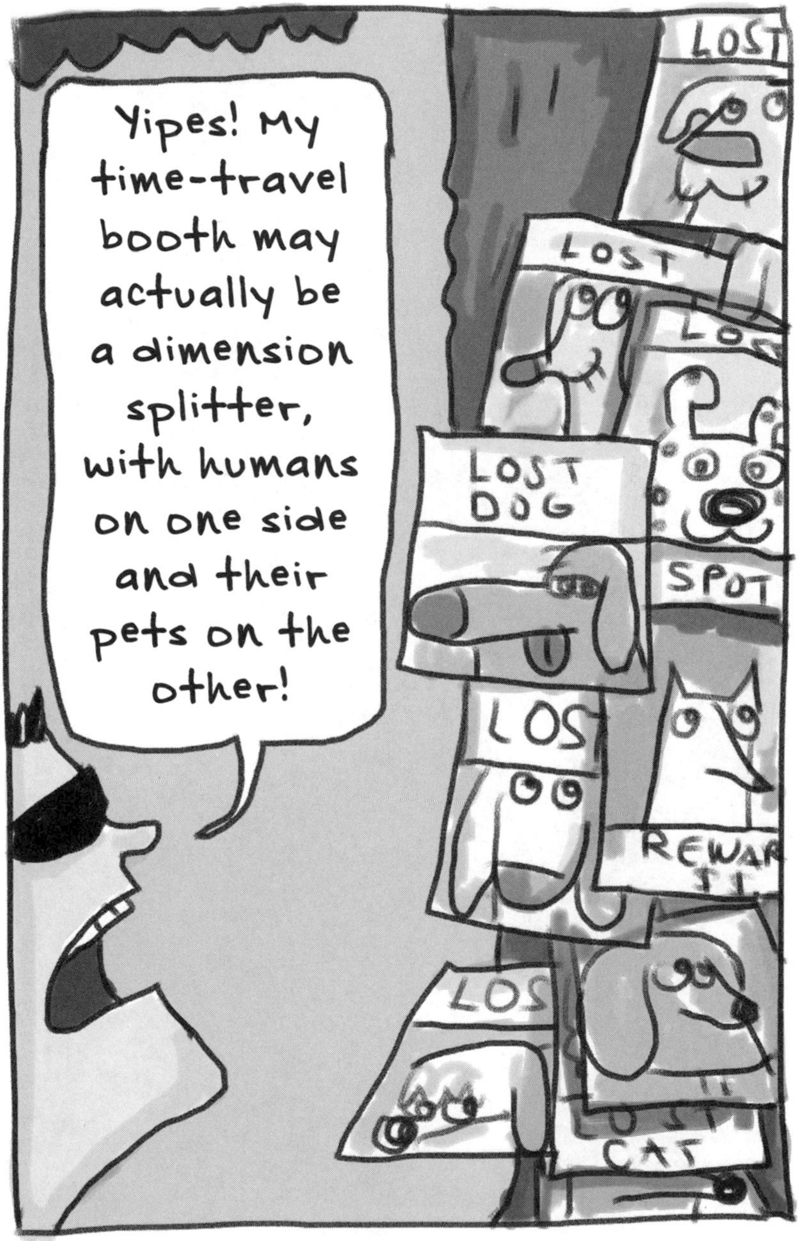
Yipes! My time-travel booth may actually be a dimension splitter, with humans on one side and their pets on the other!
LOST
LOST
LOST DOG
SPOT
CAT

Scene
Fourteen

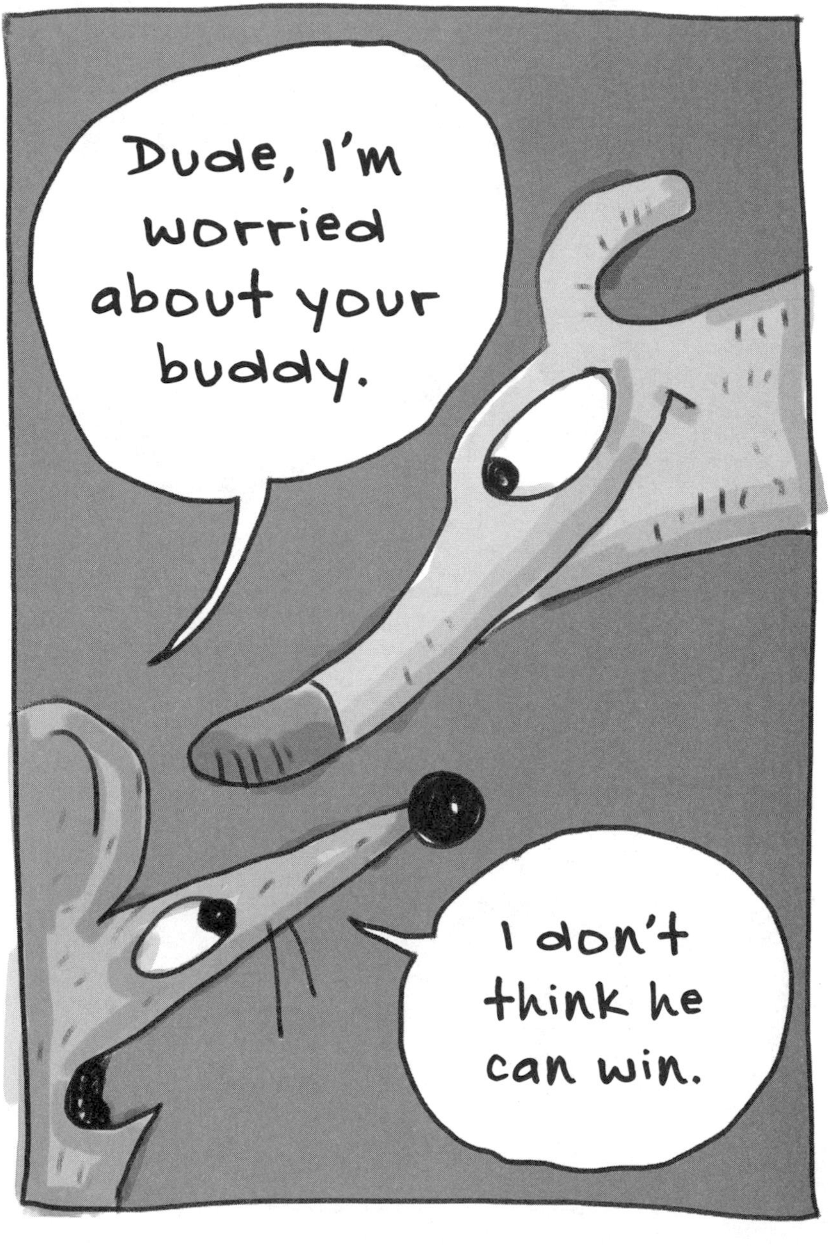
Dude, I'm worried about your buddy.
I don't think he can win.

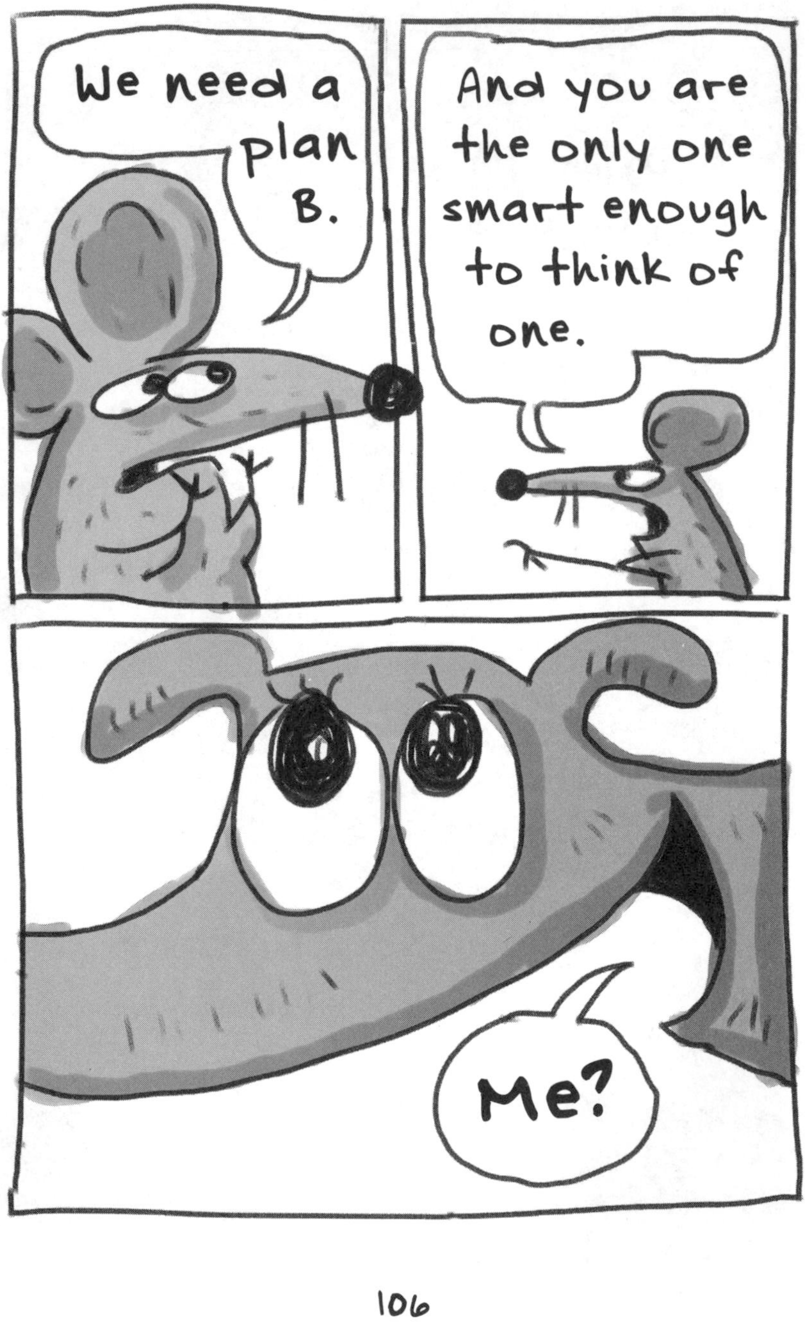
We need a plan B.
And you are the only one smart enough to think of one.
Me?

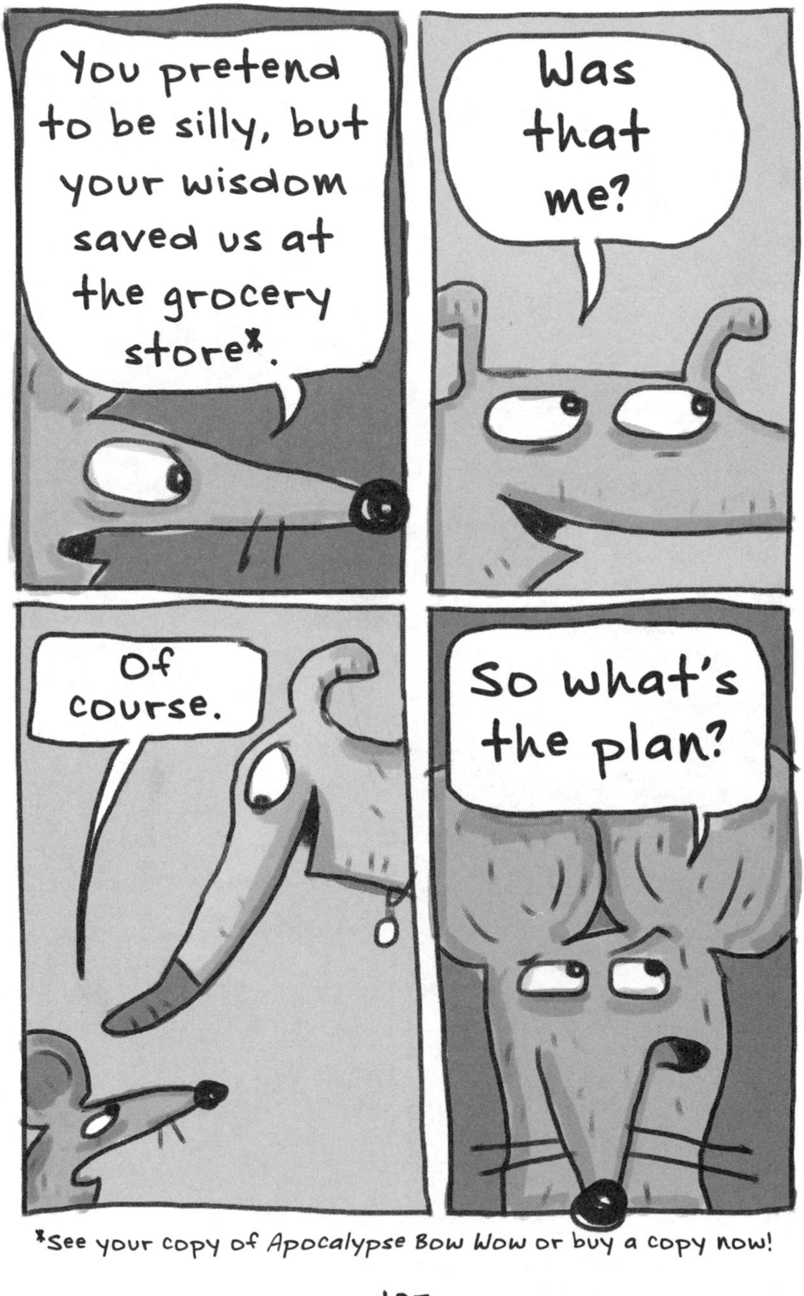
You pretend to be silly, but your wisdom saved us at the grocery store*.
Was that me?
Of course.
So what's the plan?

*See your copy of *Apocalypse Bow Wow* or buy a copy now!

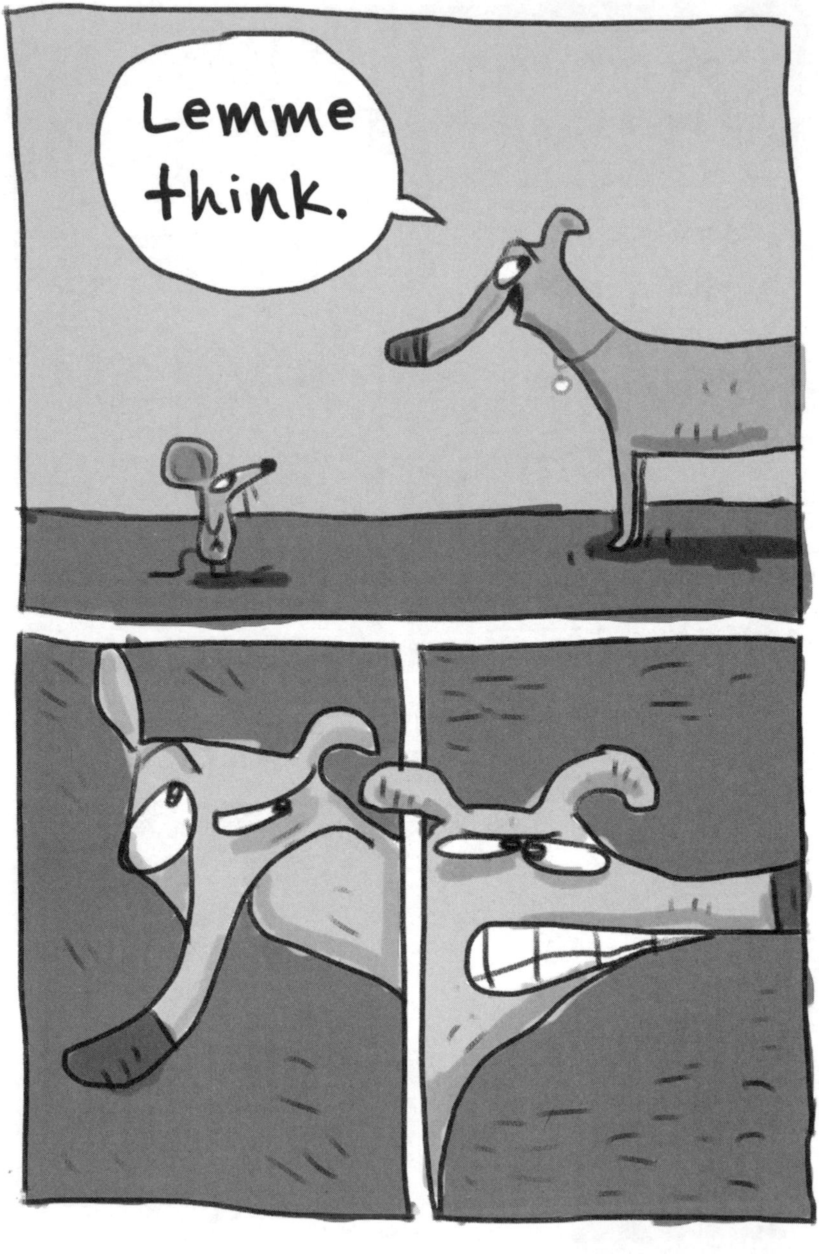
Lemme think.

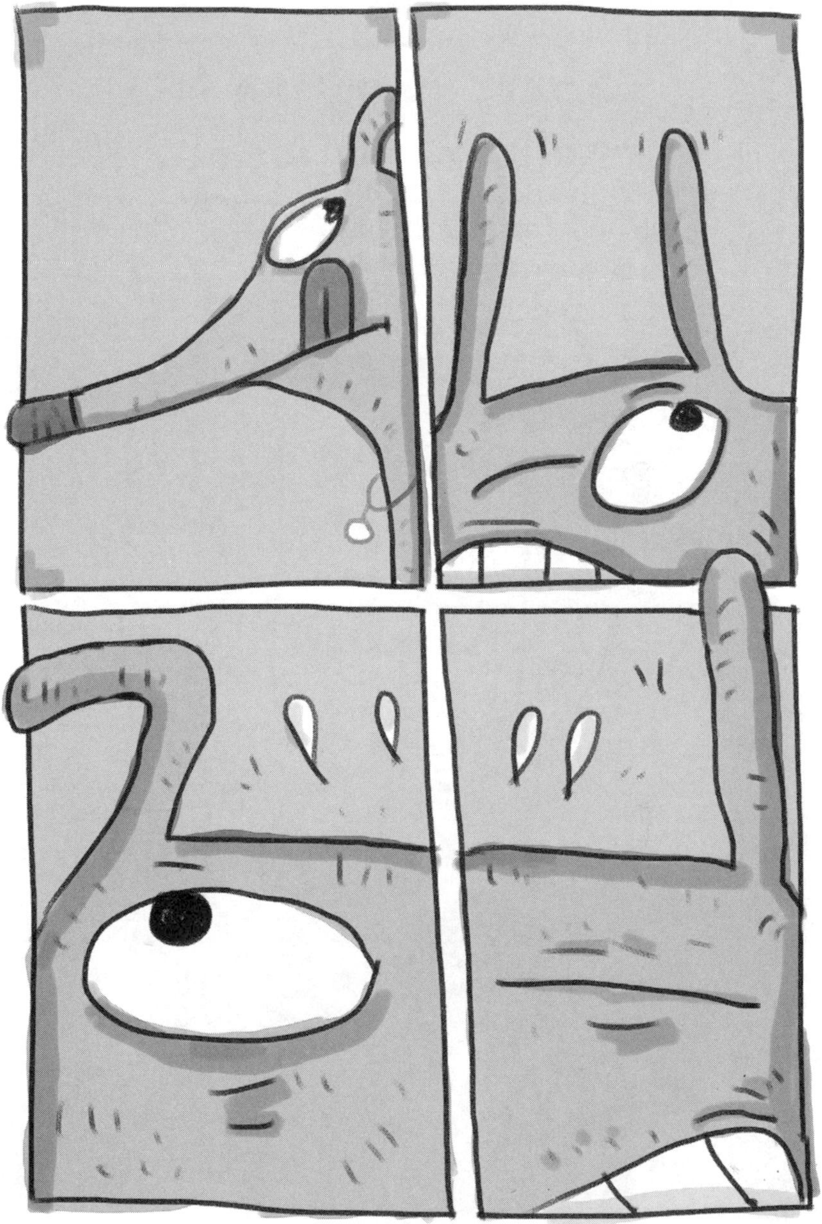

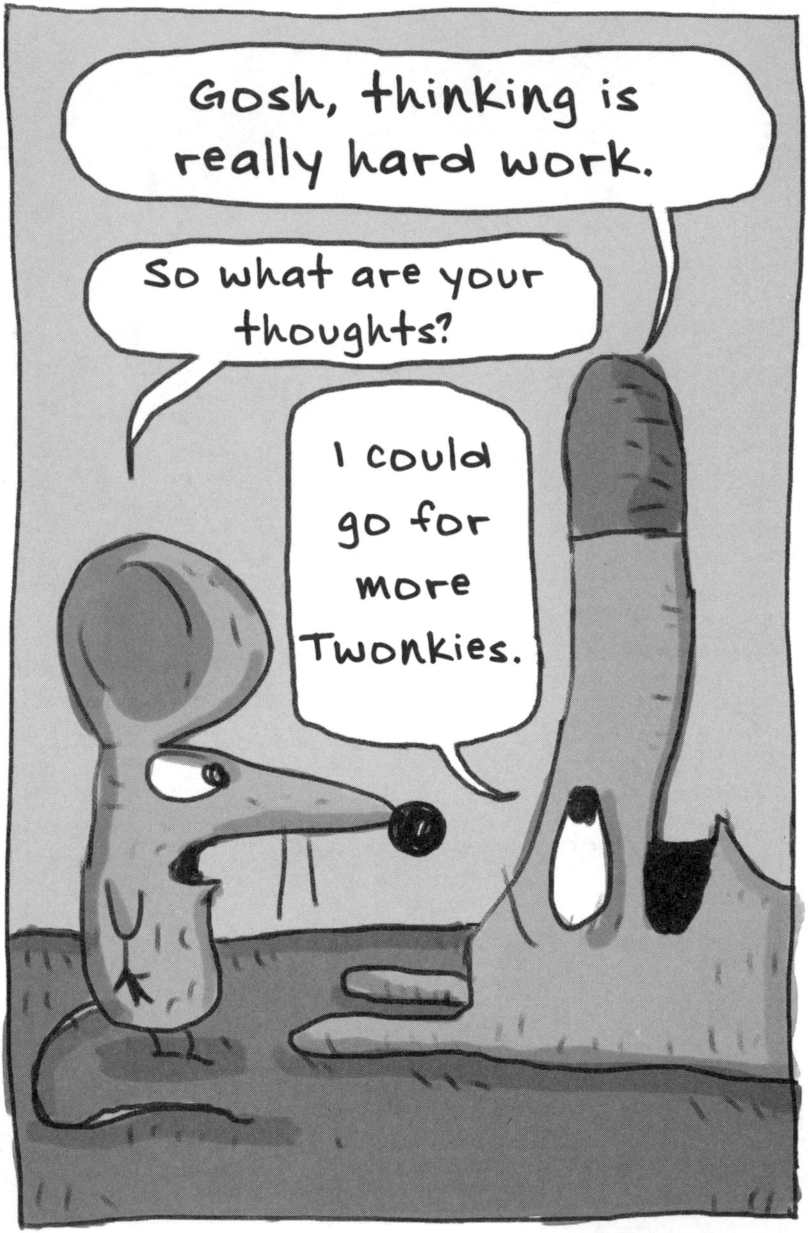
Gosh, thinking is really hard work.
So what are your thoughts?
I could go for more Twonkies.

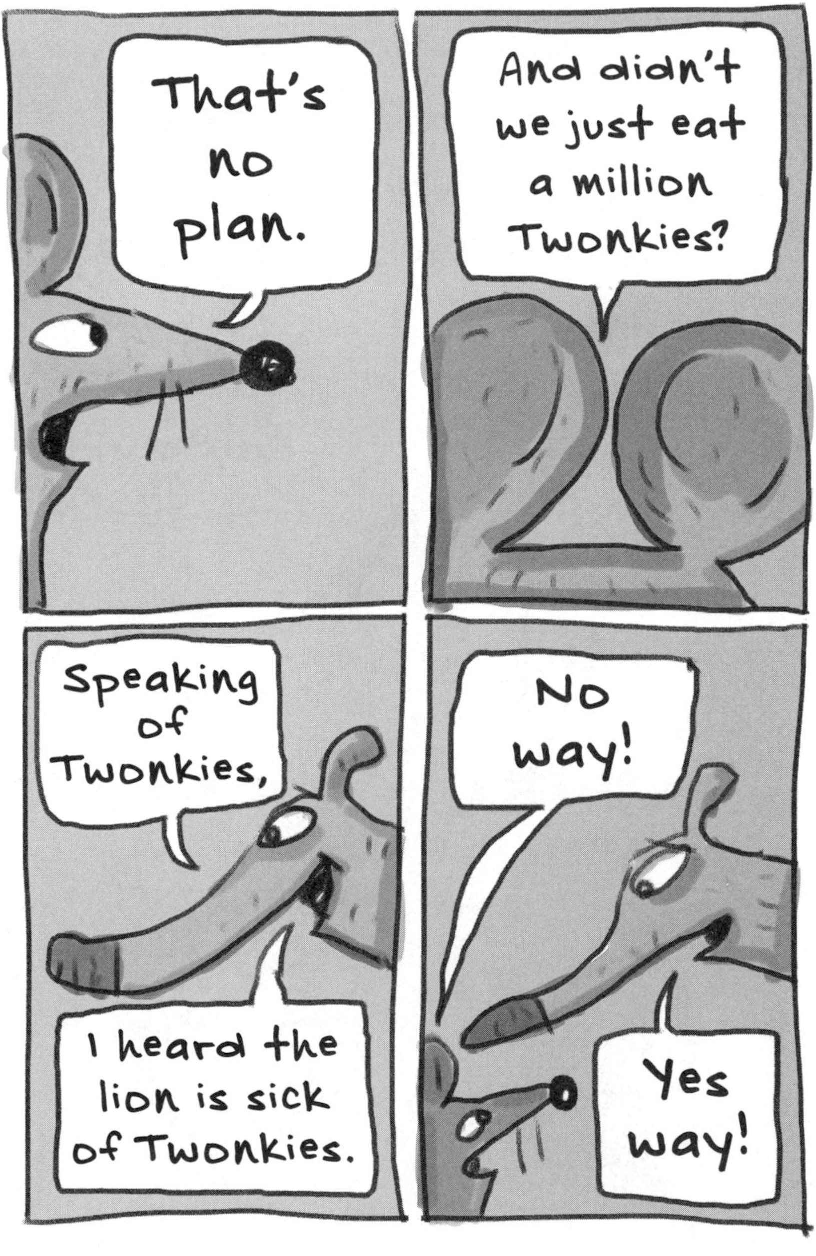
That's no plan.
And didn't we just eat a million Twonkies?
Speaking of Twonkies,
I heard the lion is sick of Twonkies.
No way!
Yes way!

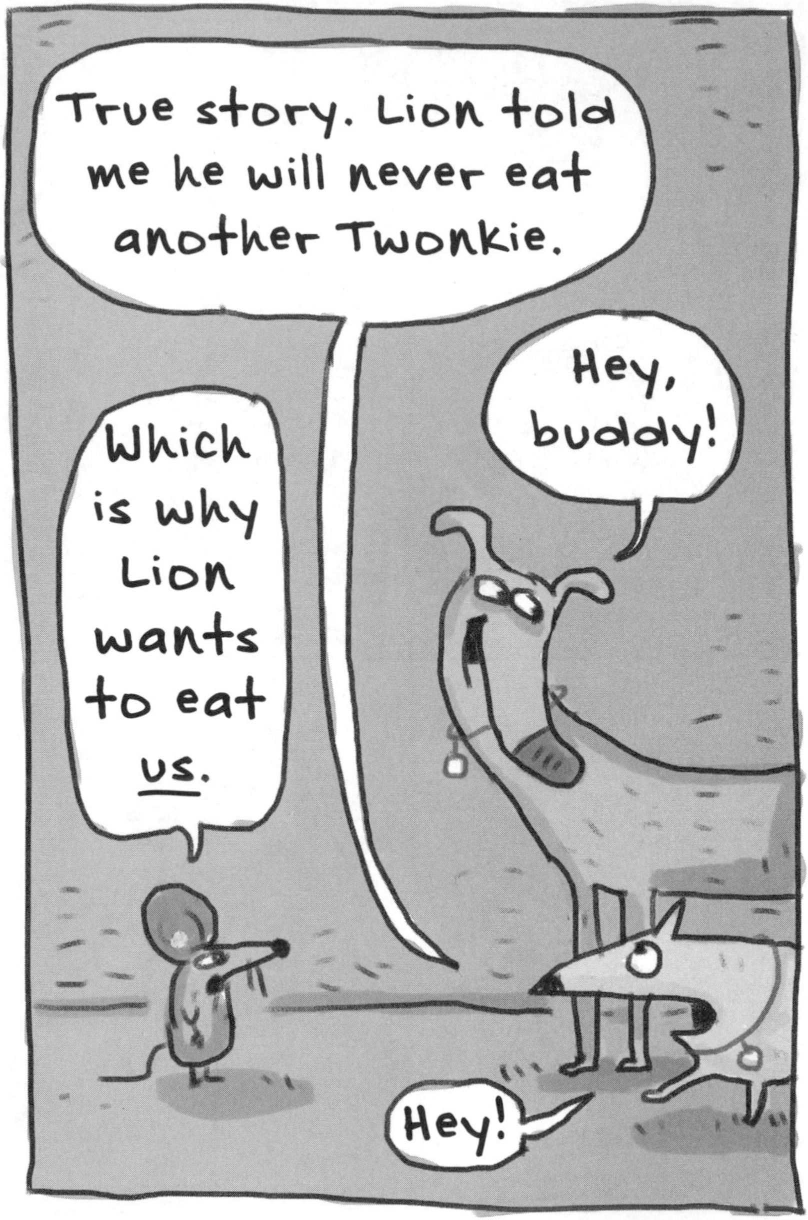
True story. Lion told me he will never eat another Twonkie.
Which is why Lion wants to eat us.
Hey, buddy!
Hey!

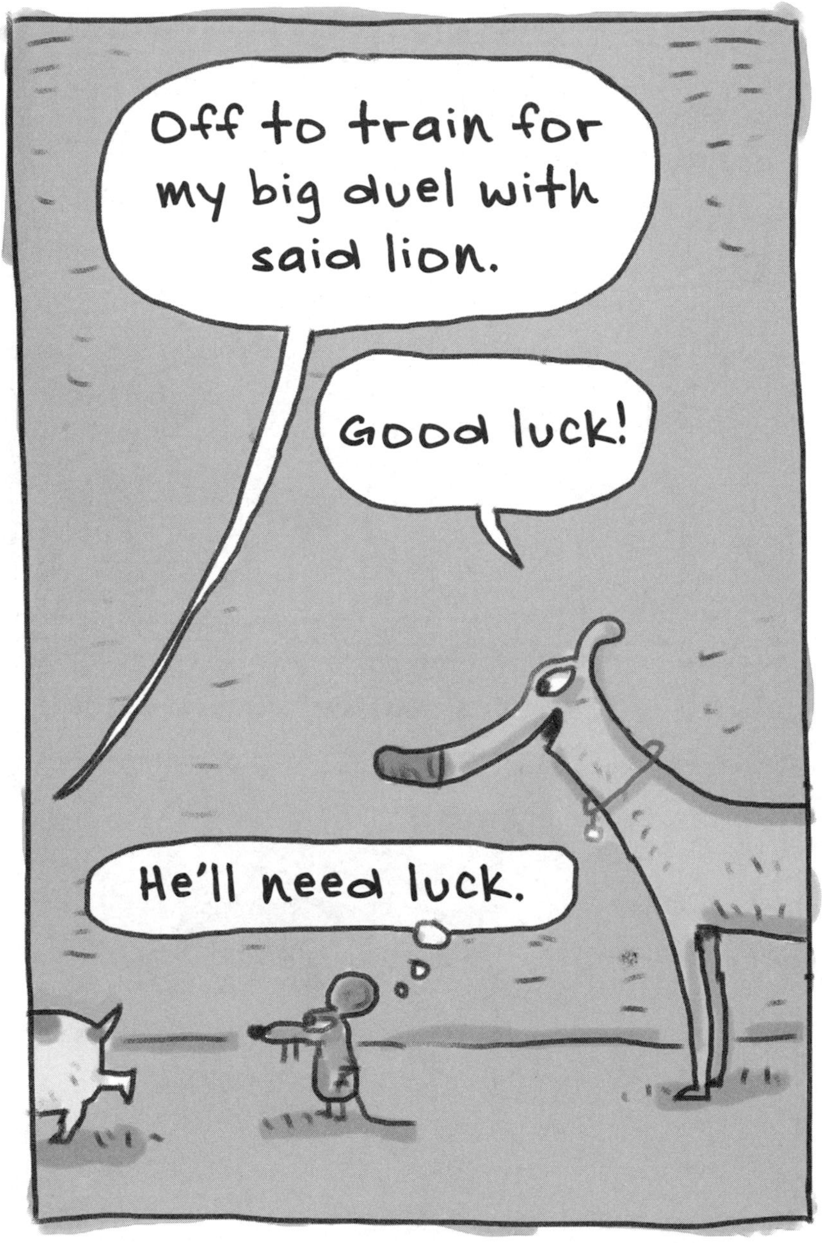
Off to train for my big duel with said lion.
Good luck!
He'll need luck.

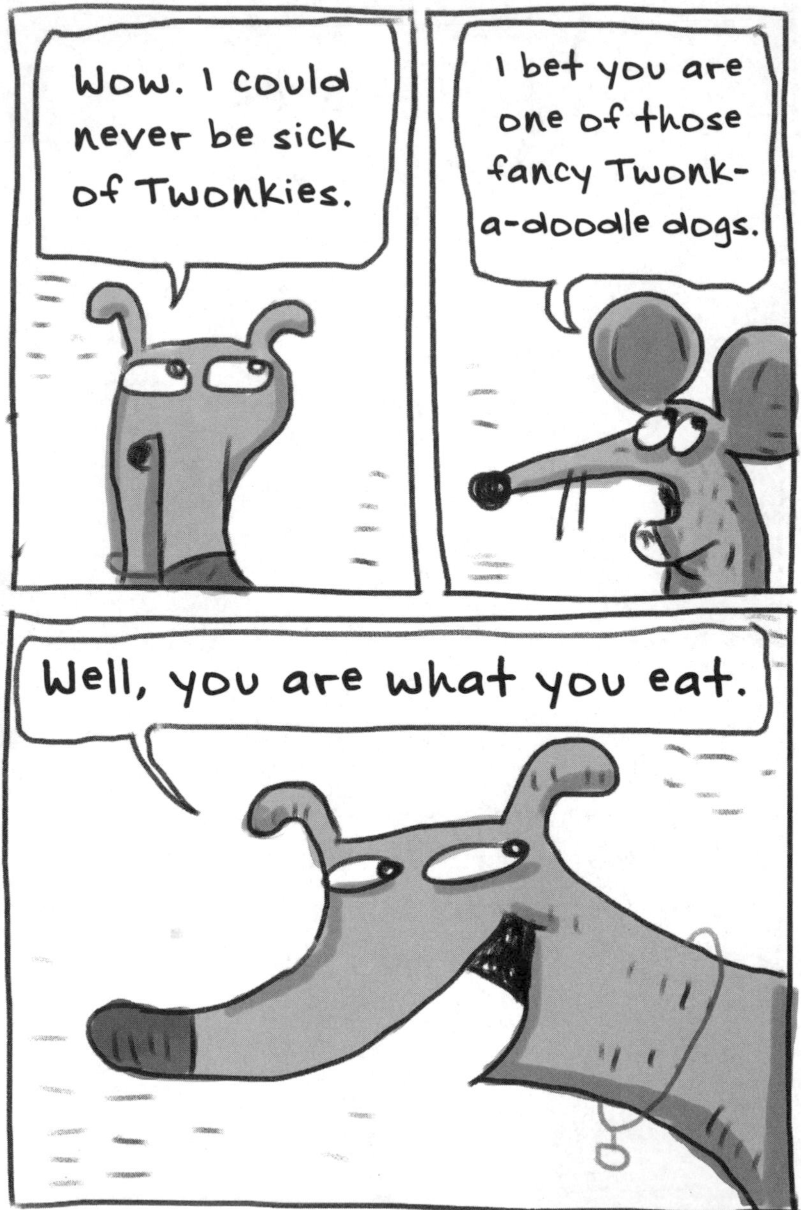
Wow. I could never be sick of Twonkies.
I bet you are one of those fancy Twonk-a-doodle dogs.
Well, you are what you eat.

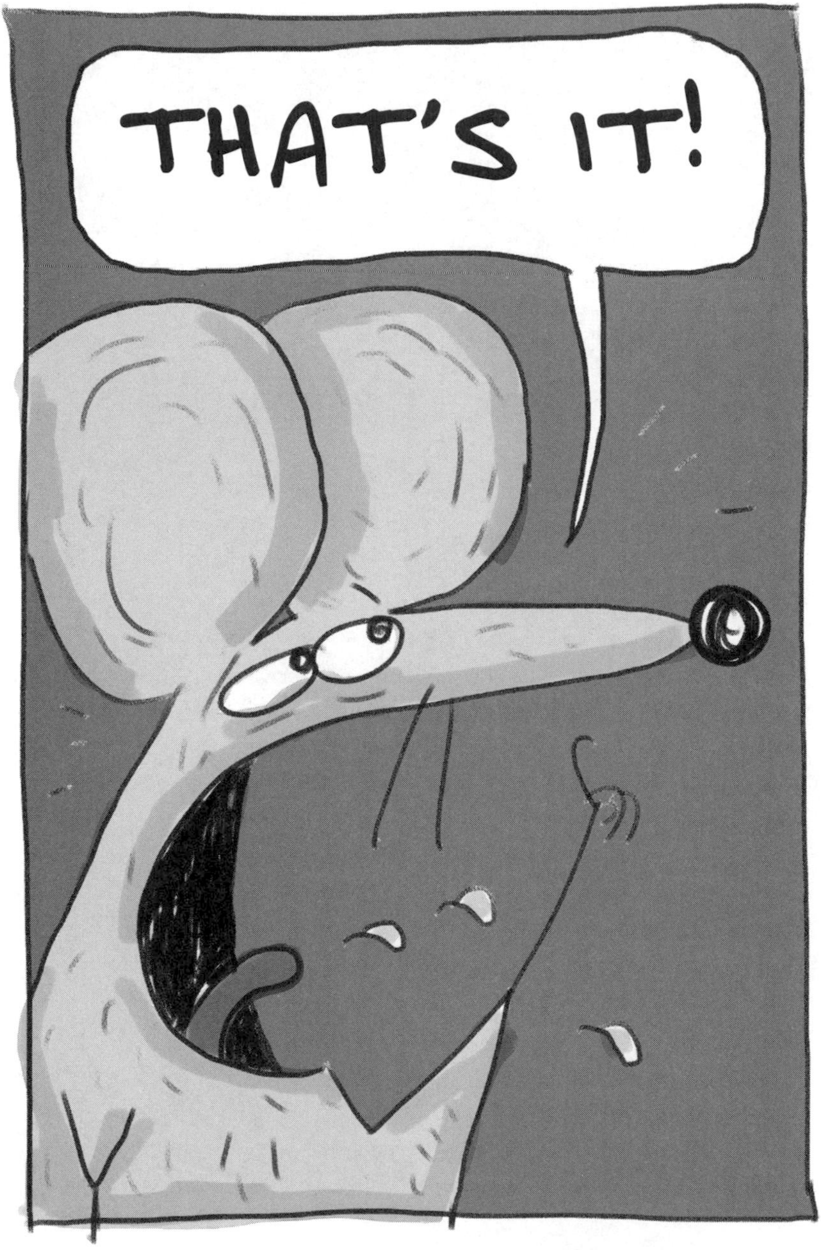
THAT'S IT!

Scene Fifteen

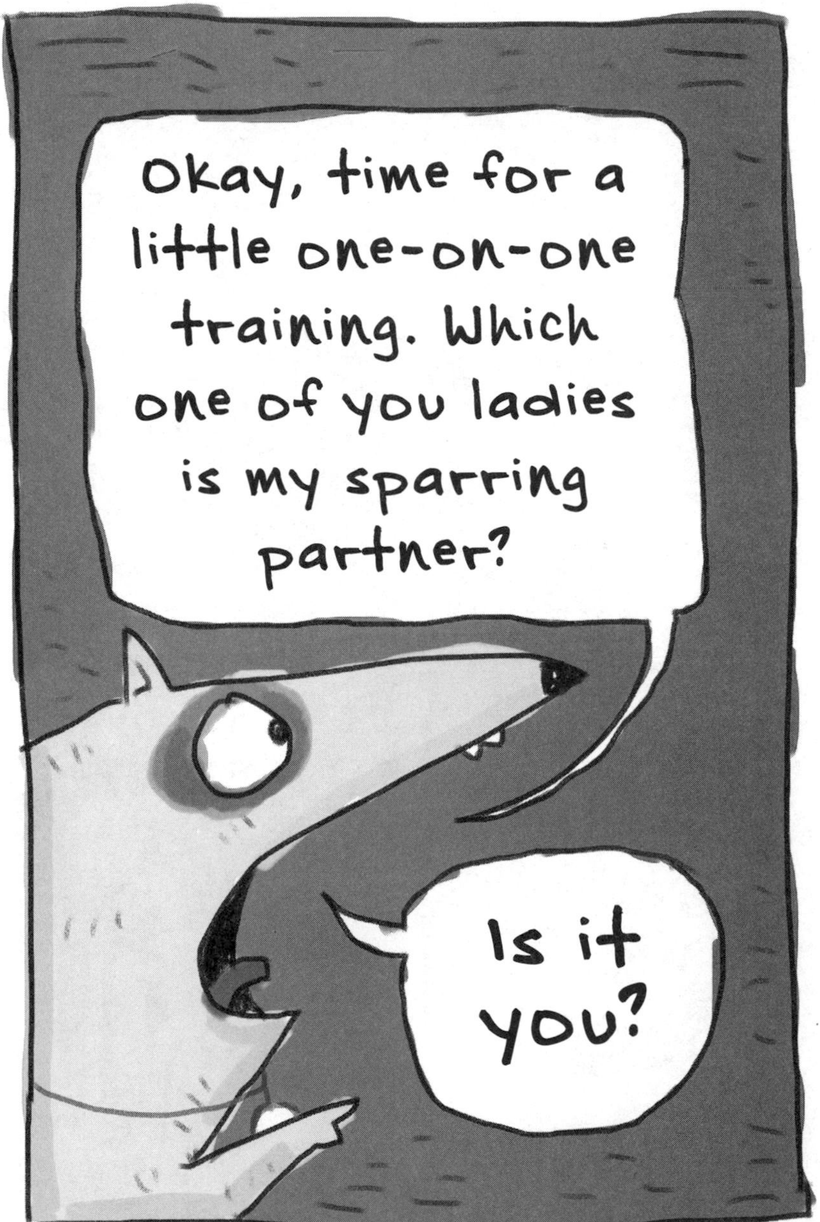
Okay, time for a little one-on-one training. Which one of you ladies is my sparring partner?
Is it you?

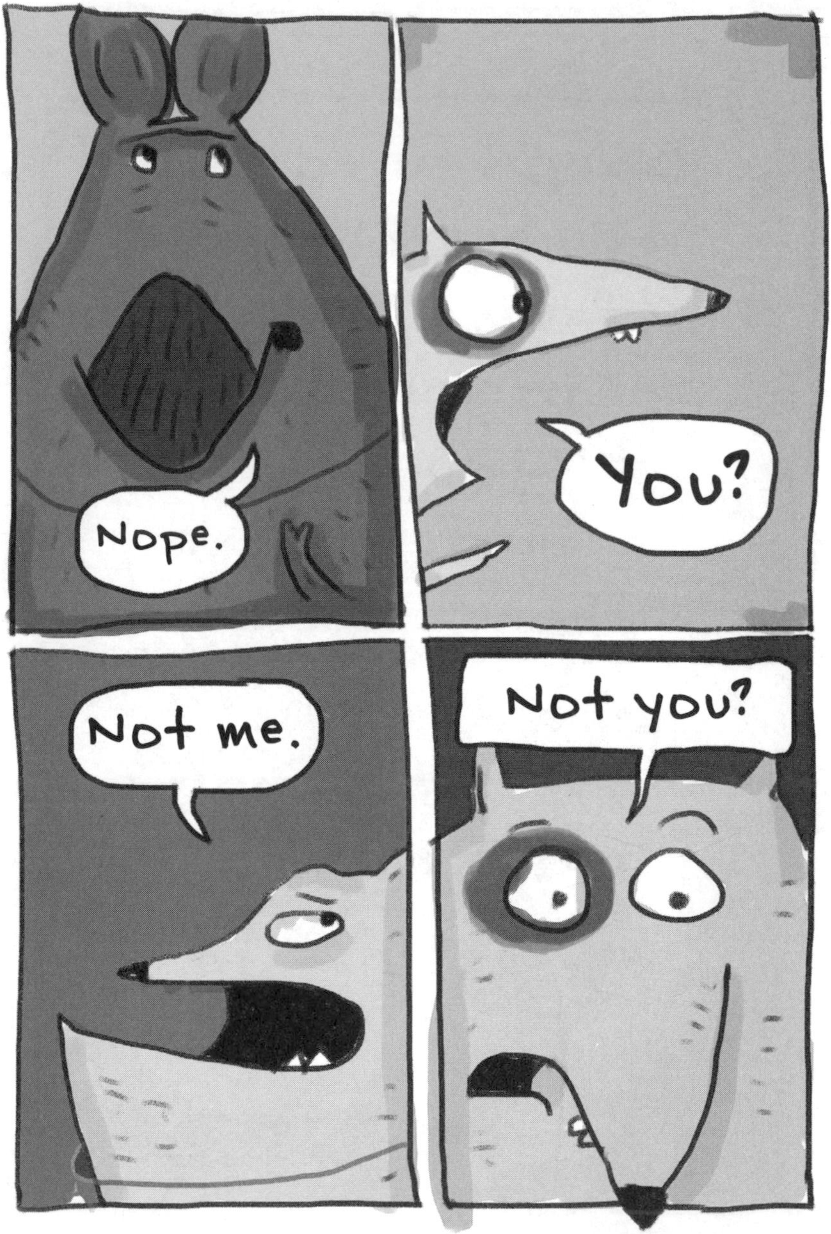
Nope.
You?
Not me.
Not you?

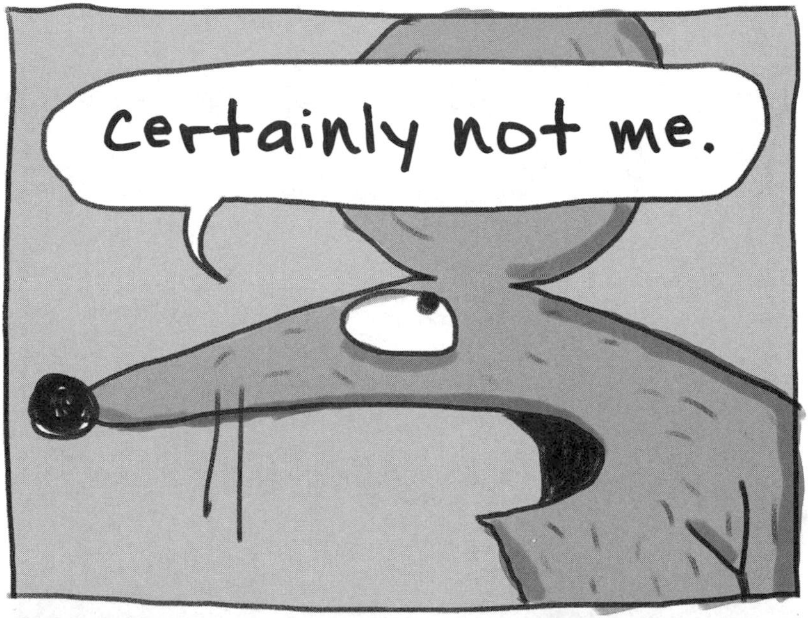
Certainly not me.

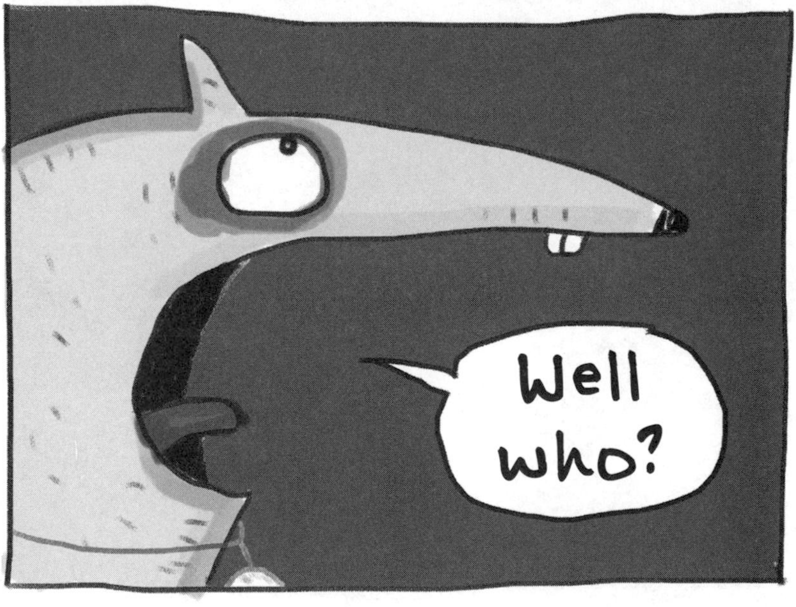
Well who?

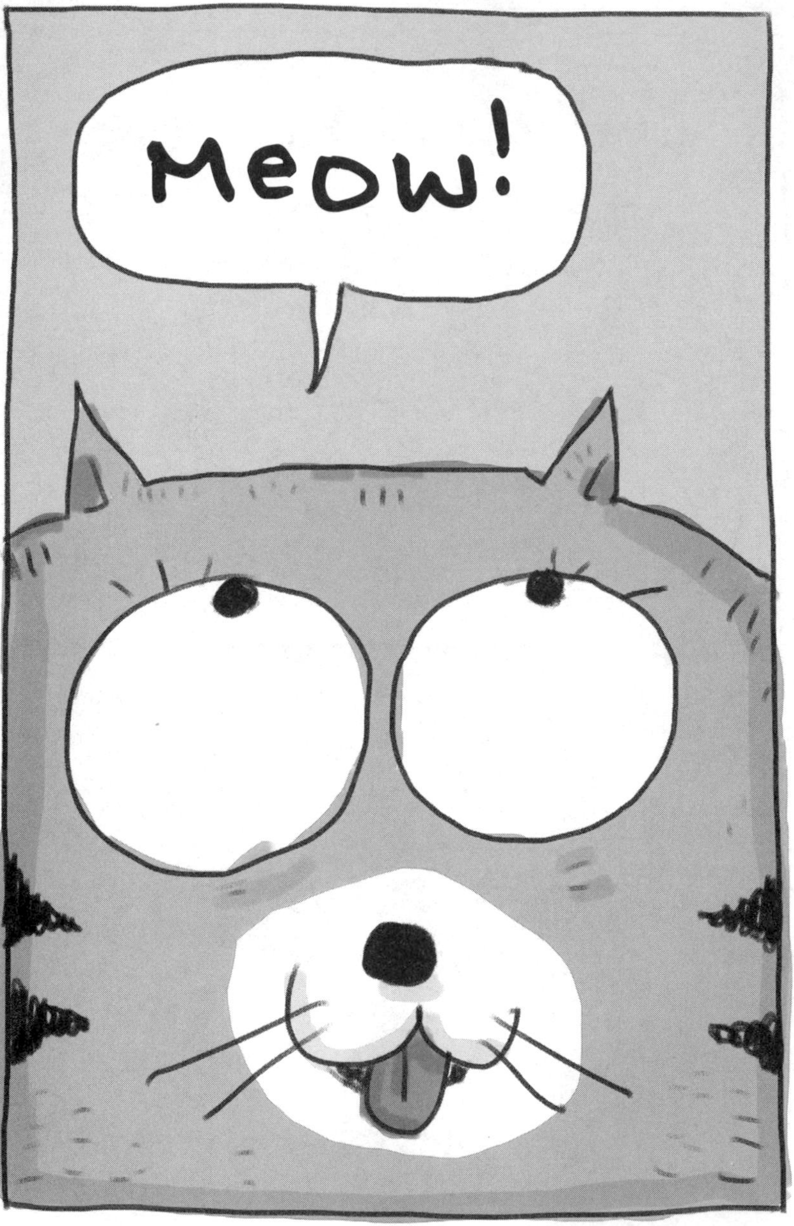
Meow!

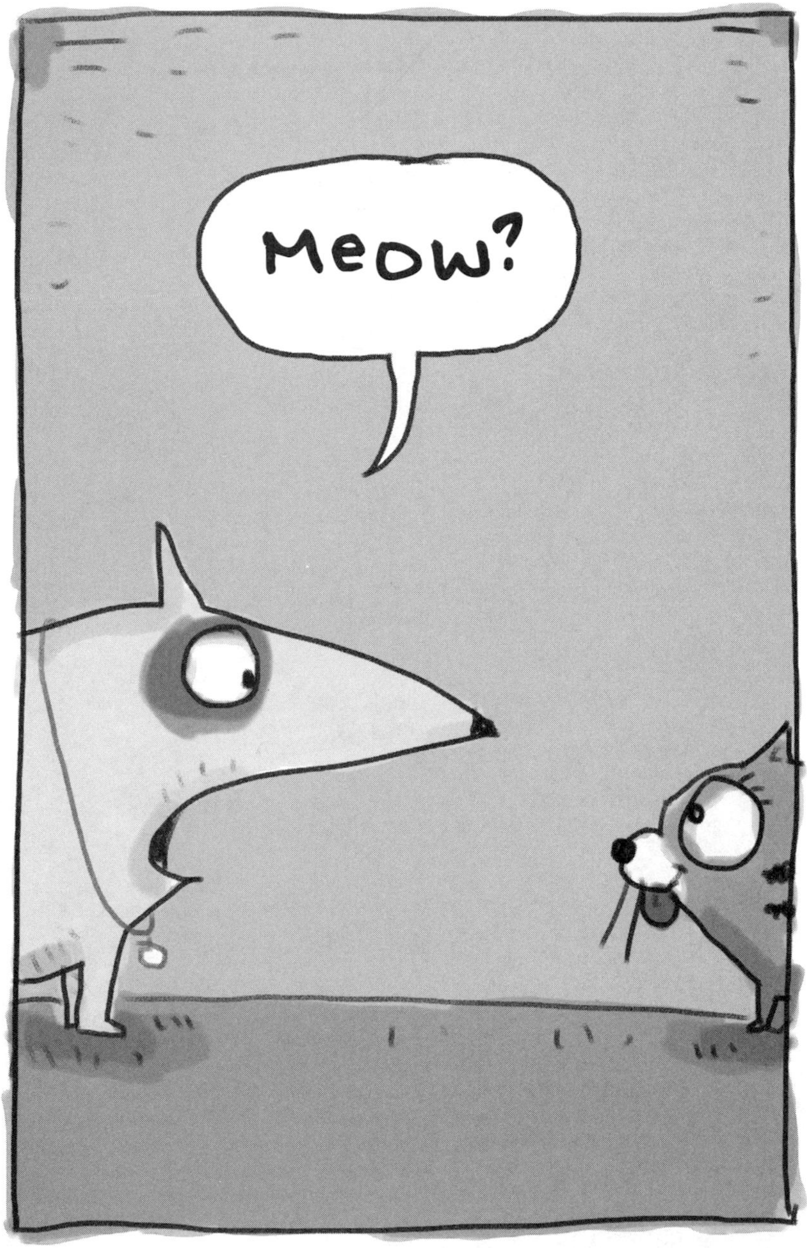
Meow?

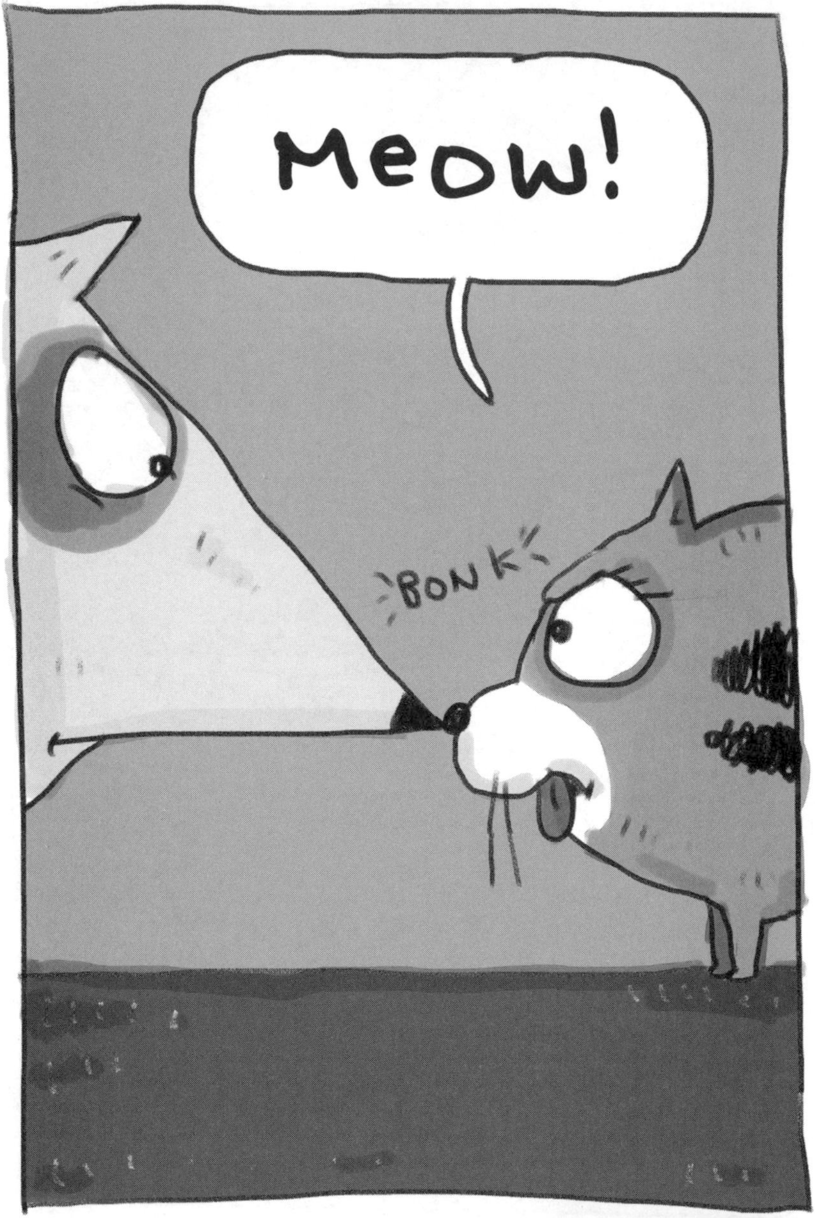
MEOW!
BONK

Scene
Sixteen

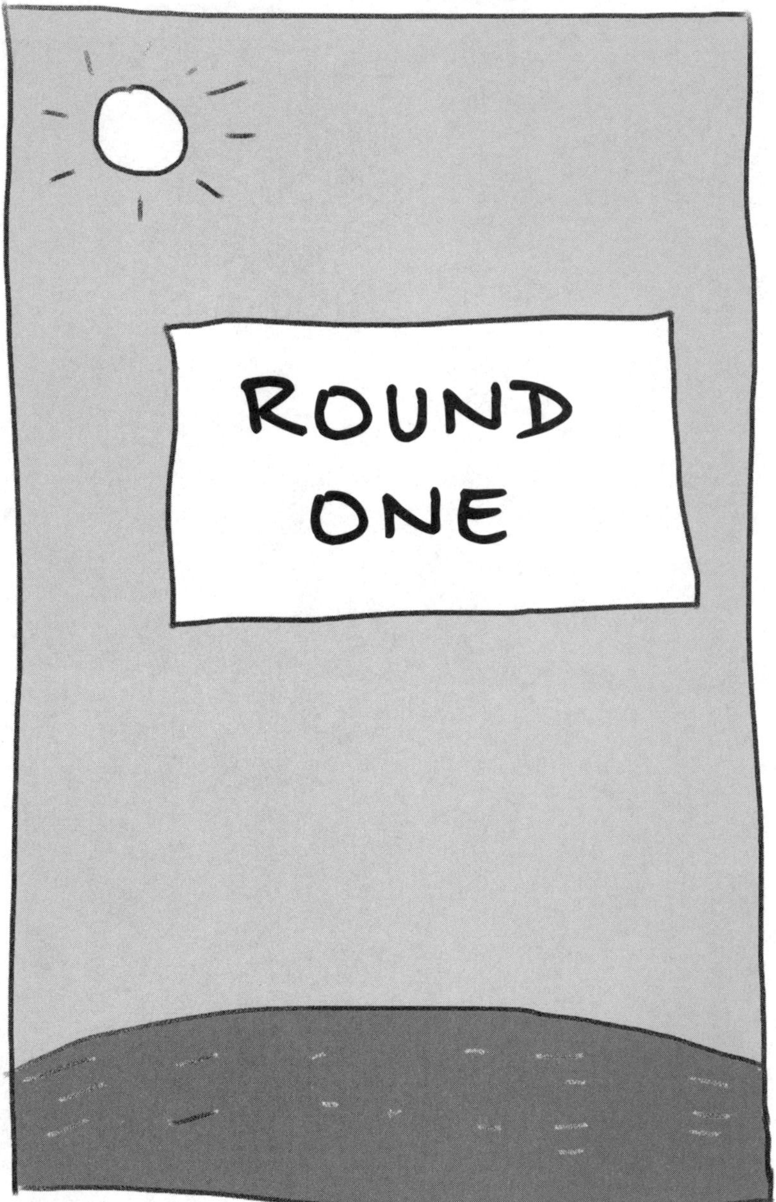
ROUND ONE

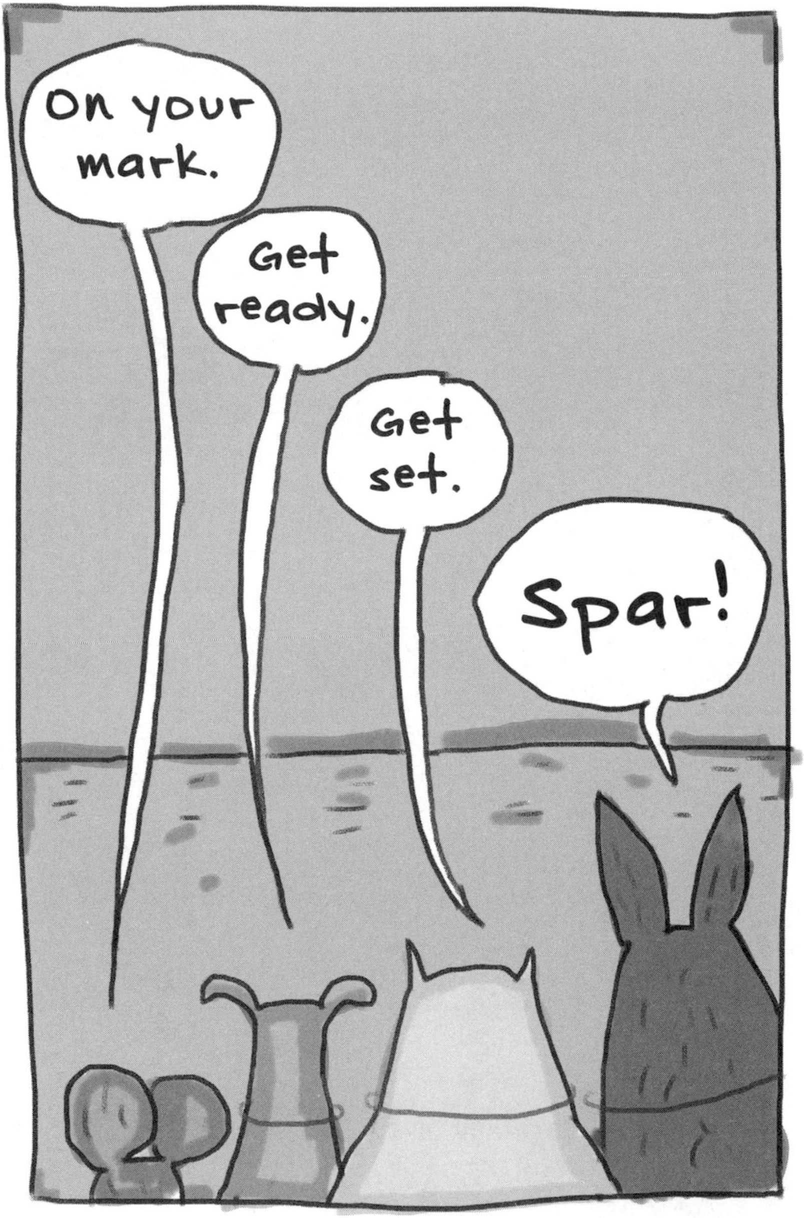
On your mark.
Get ready.
Get set.
Spar!

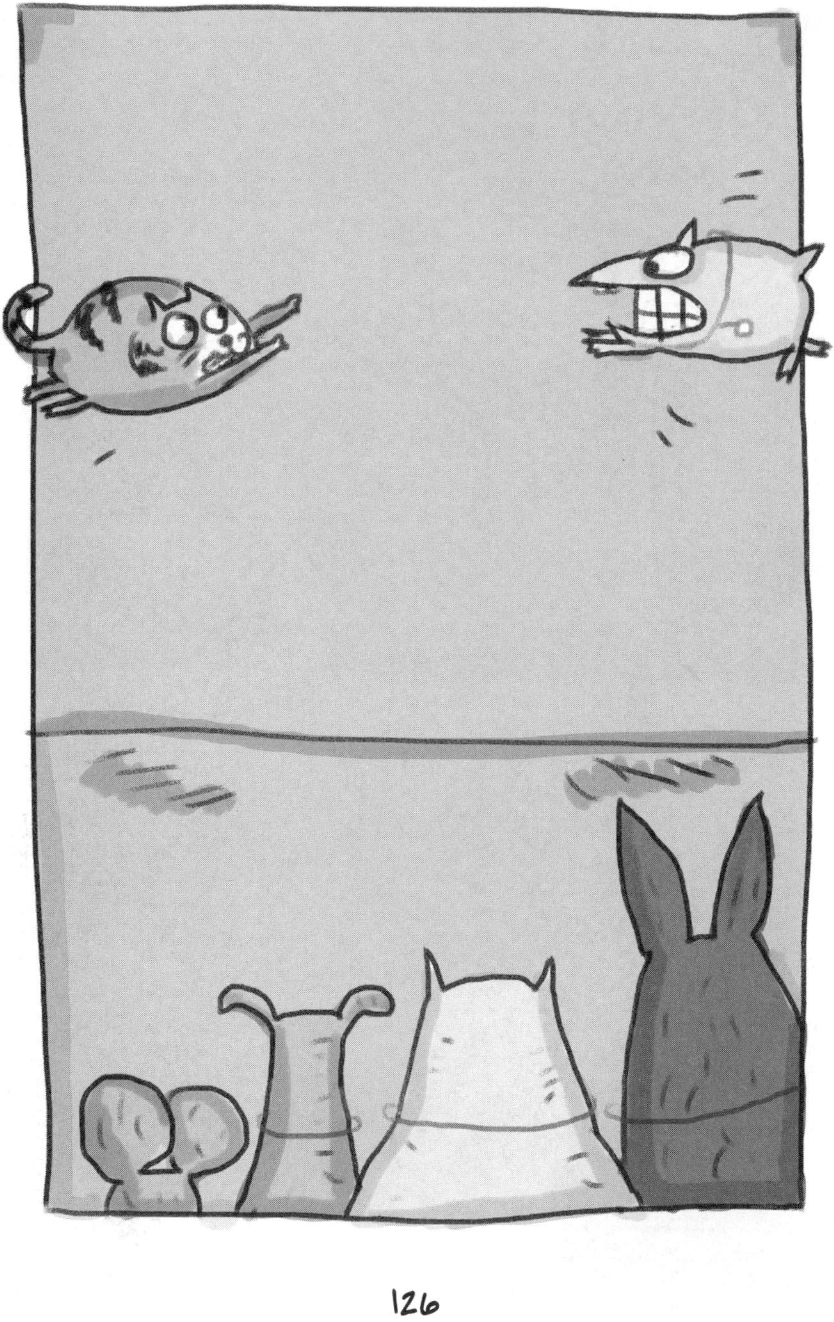

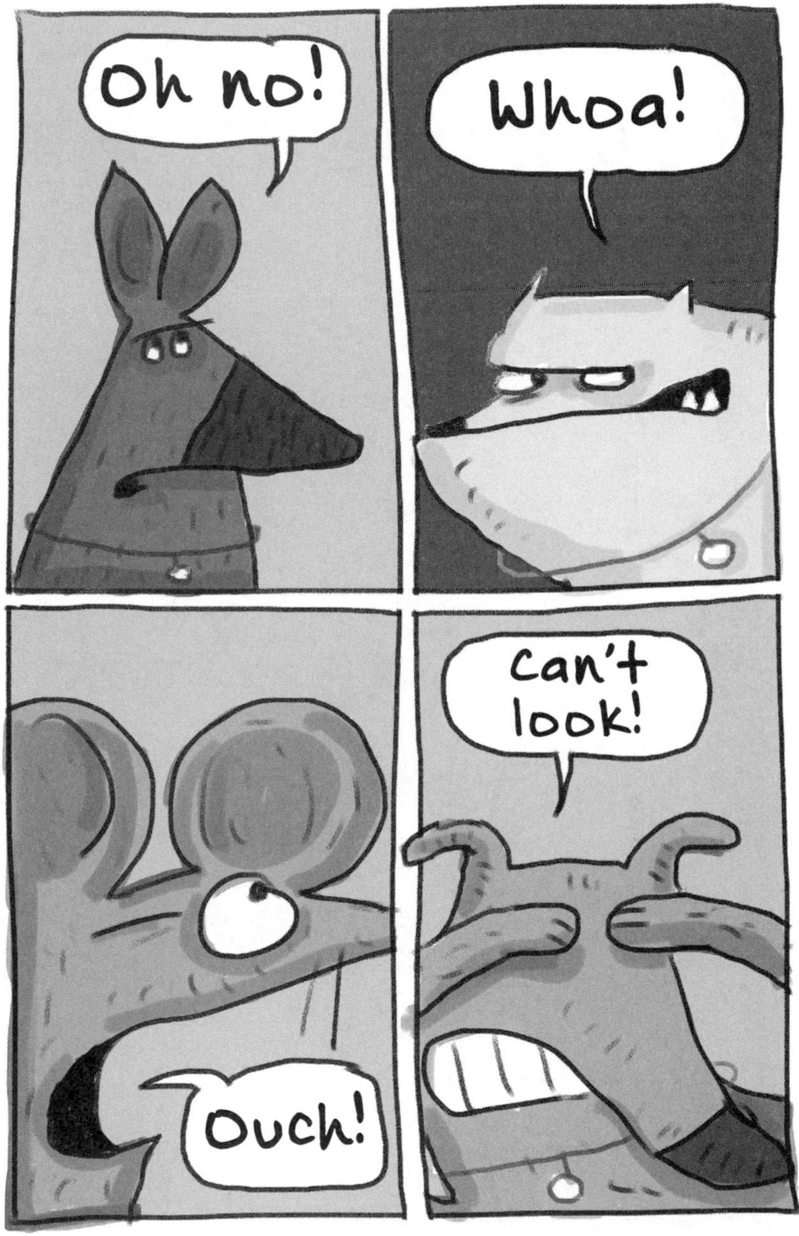
Oh no!
Whoa!
Ouch!
Can't look!

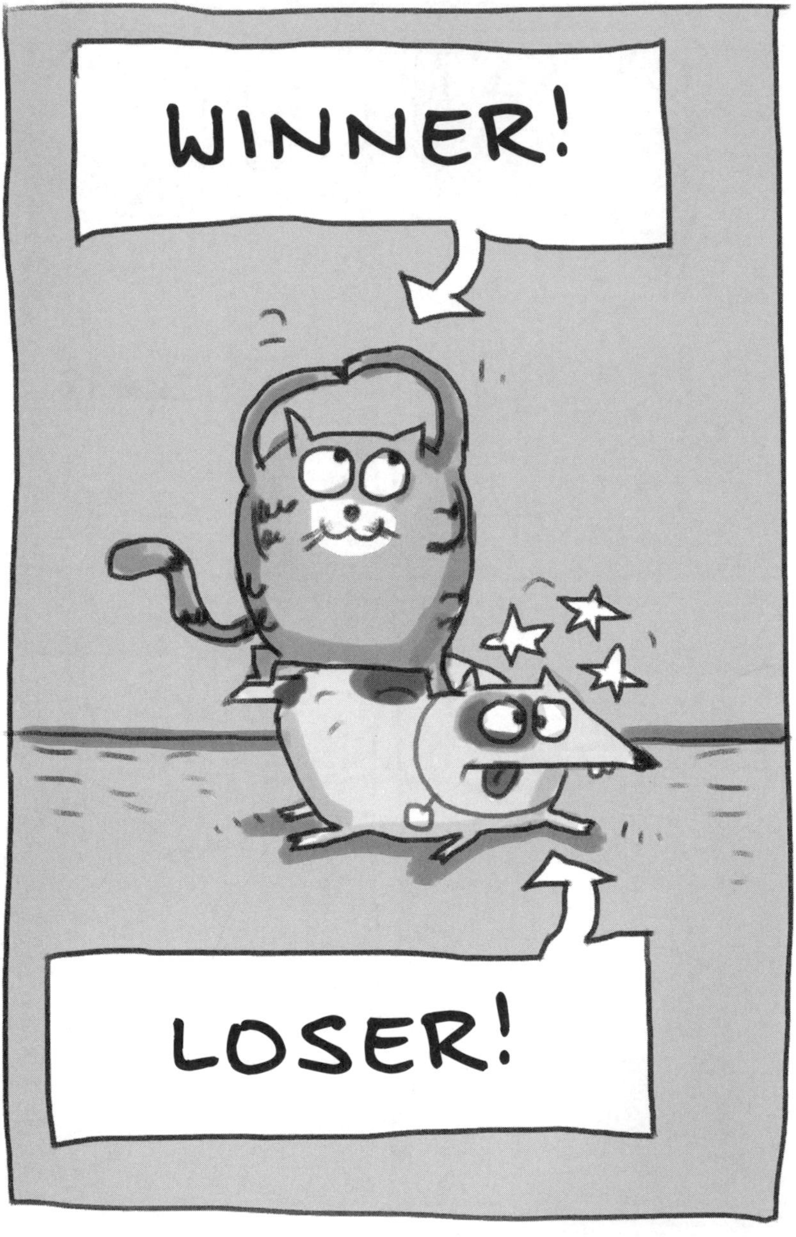
WINNER!
LOSER!

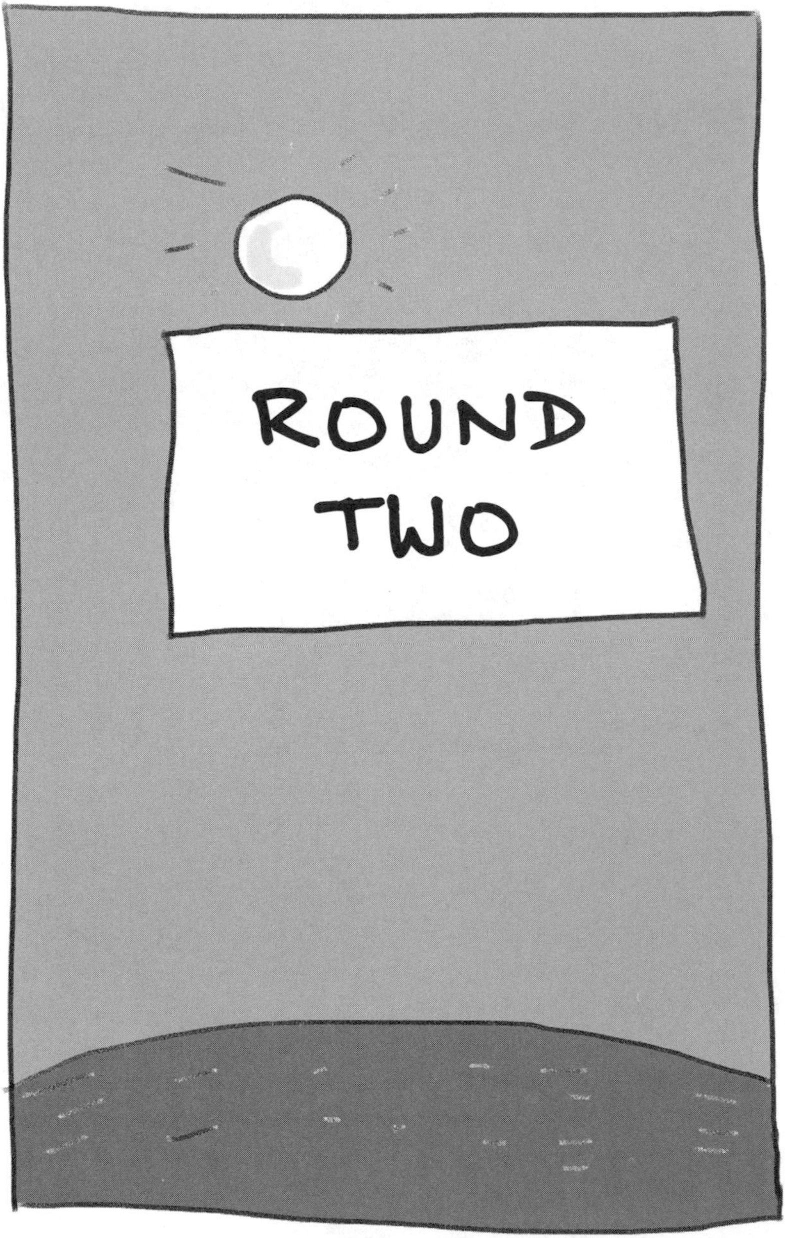
ROUND TWO

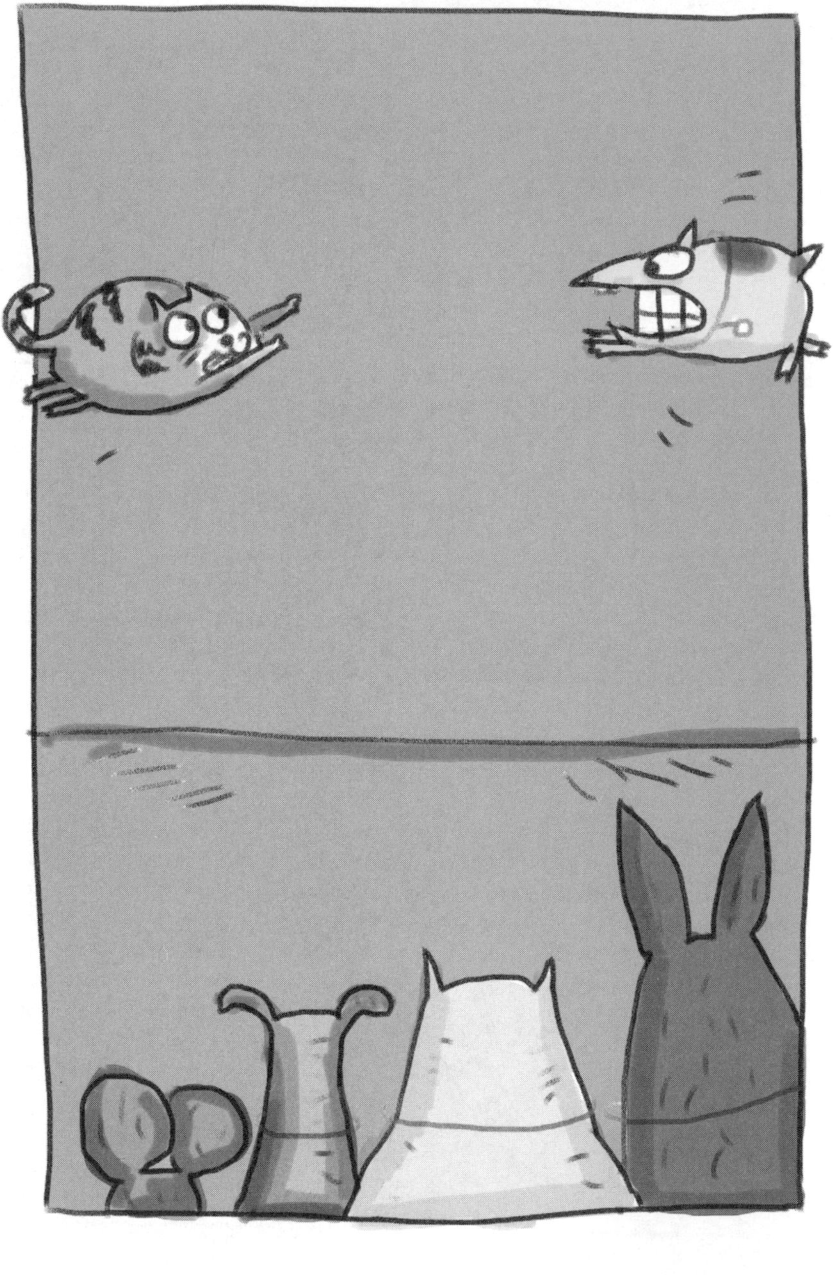

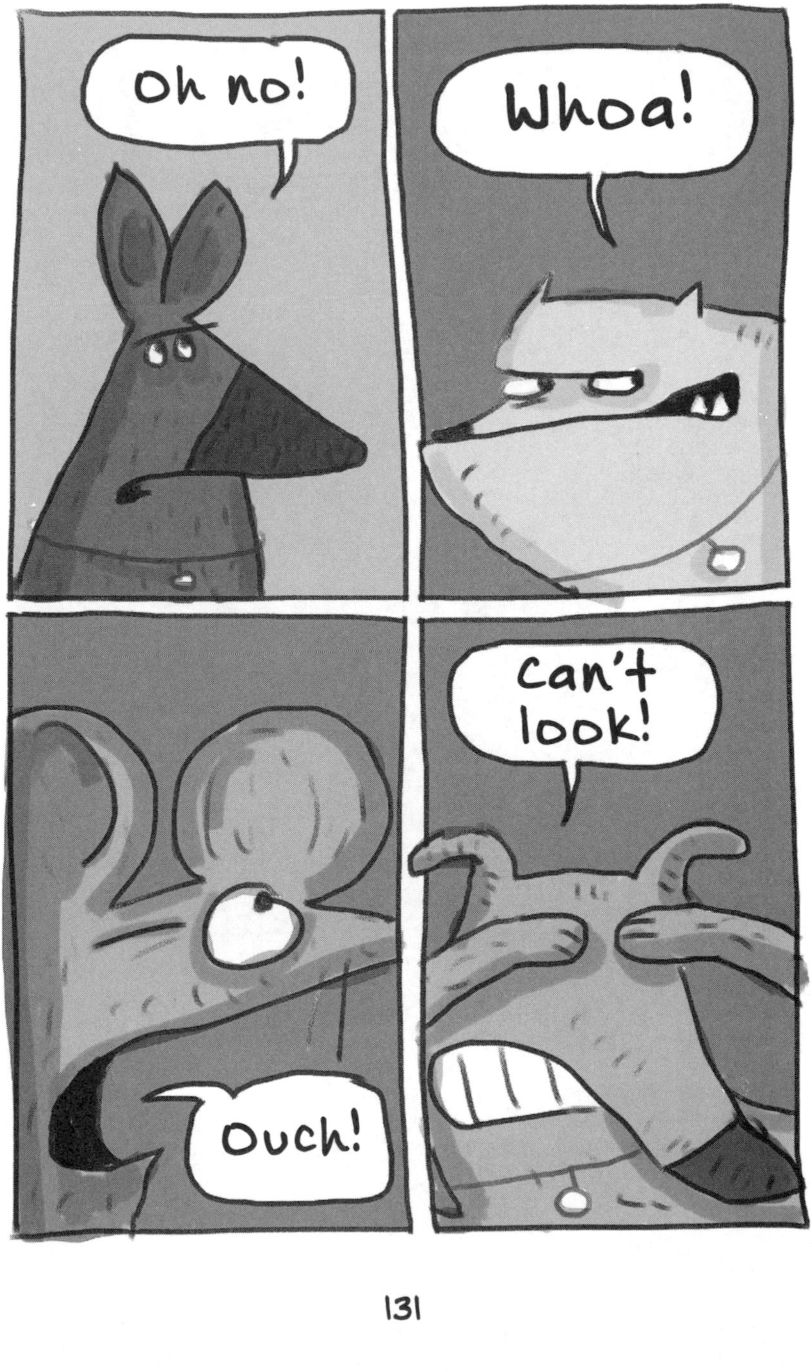
Oh no!
Whoa!
Ouch!
Can't look!

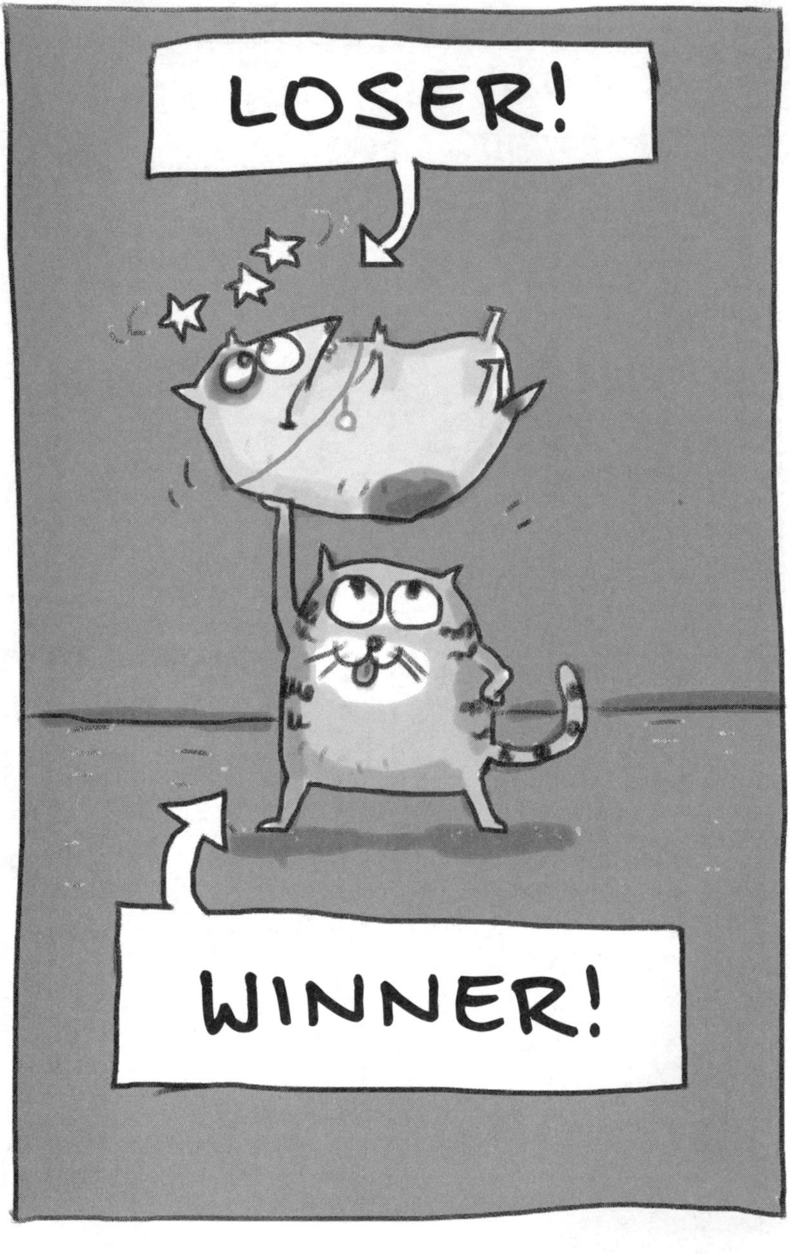
LOSER!
WINNER!

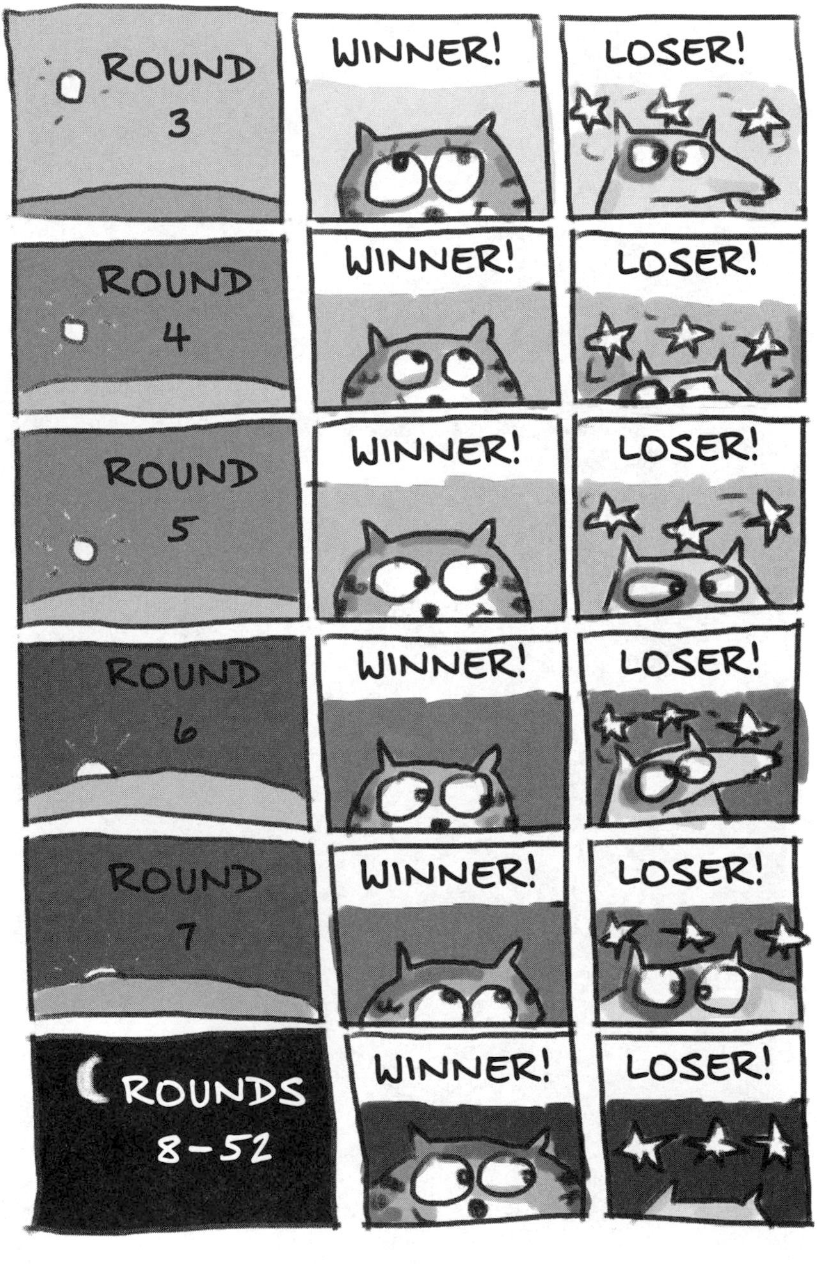
ROUND 3
WINNER!
LOSER!
ROUND 4
WINNER!
LOSER!
ROUND 5
WINNER!
LOSER!
ROUND 6
WINNER!
LOSER!
ROUND 7
WINNER!
LOSER!
ROUNDS 8–52
WINNER!
LOSER!

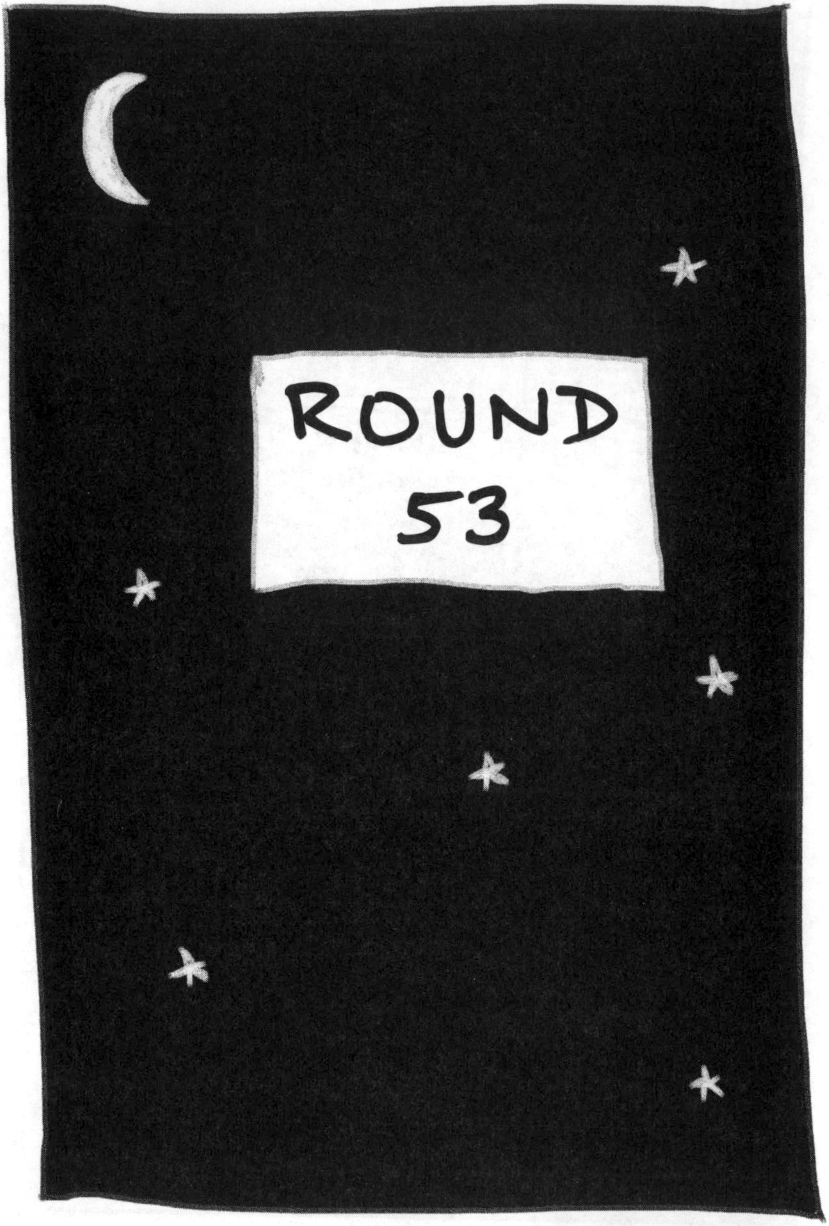
ROUND
53

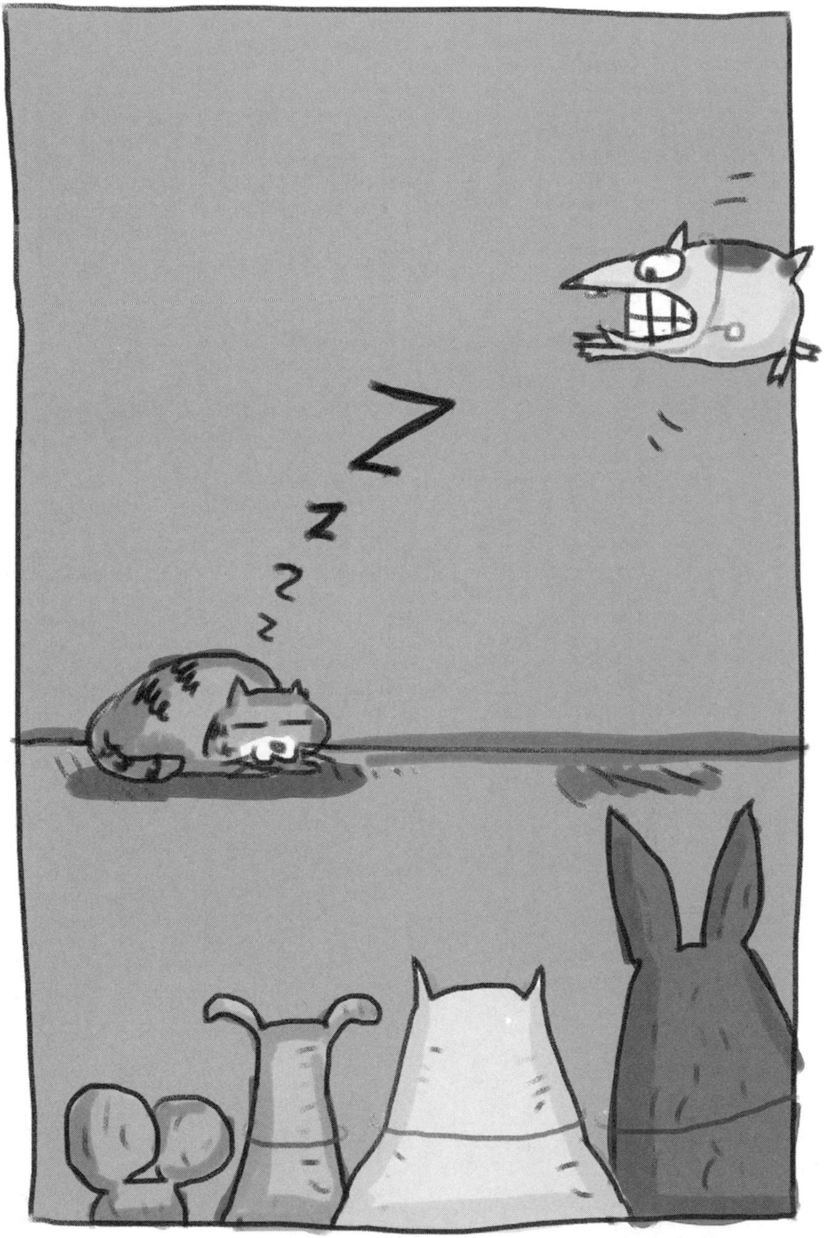
Z Z Z Z

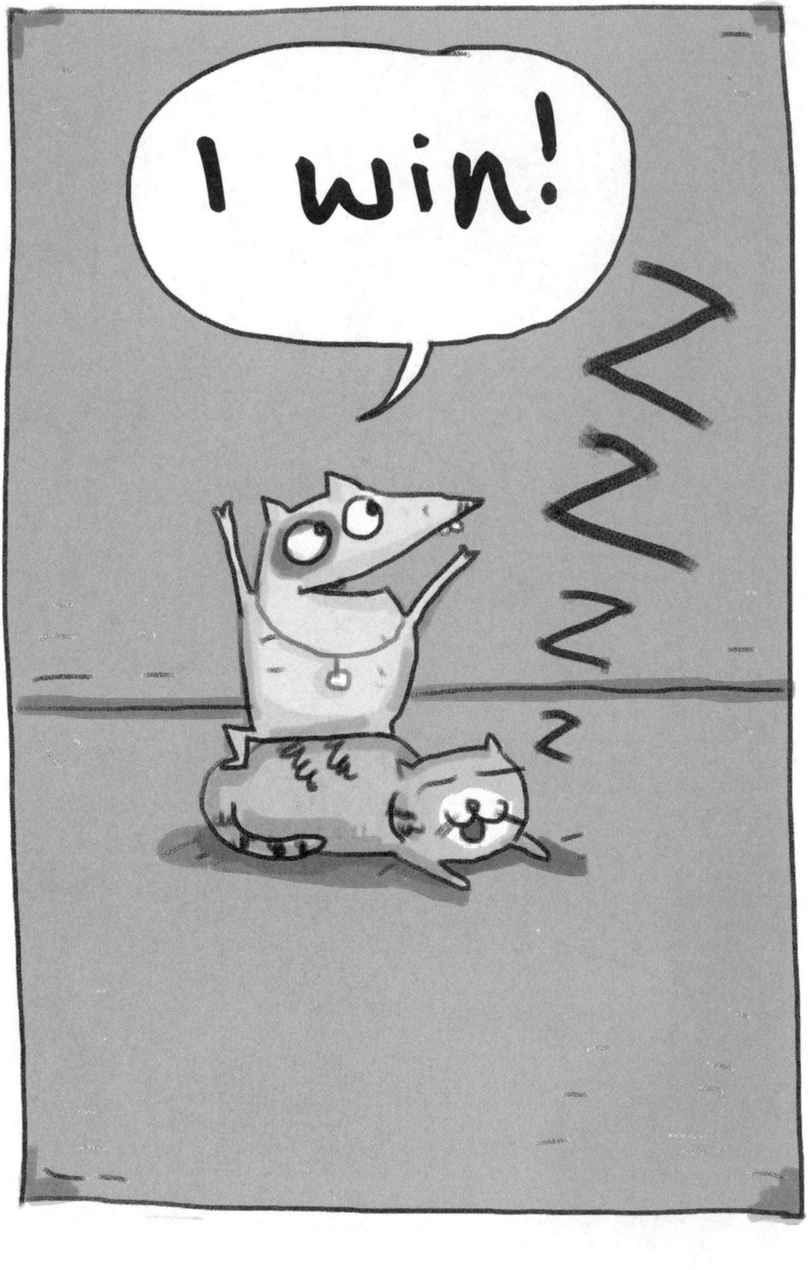
I win!
ZZZZ

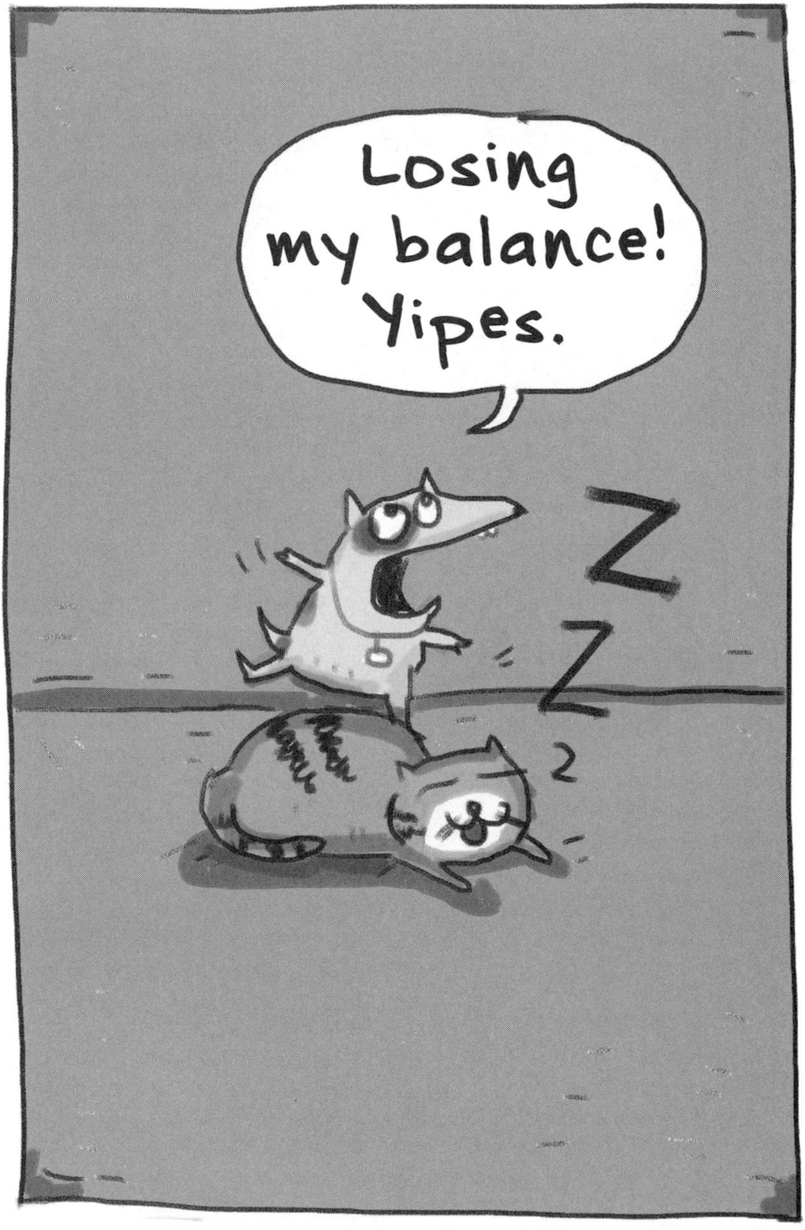
Losing my balance! Yipes.
Z
Z
z

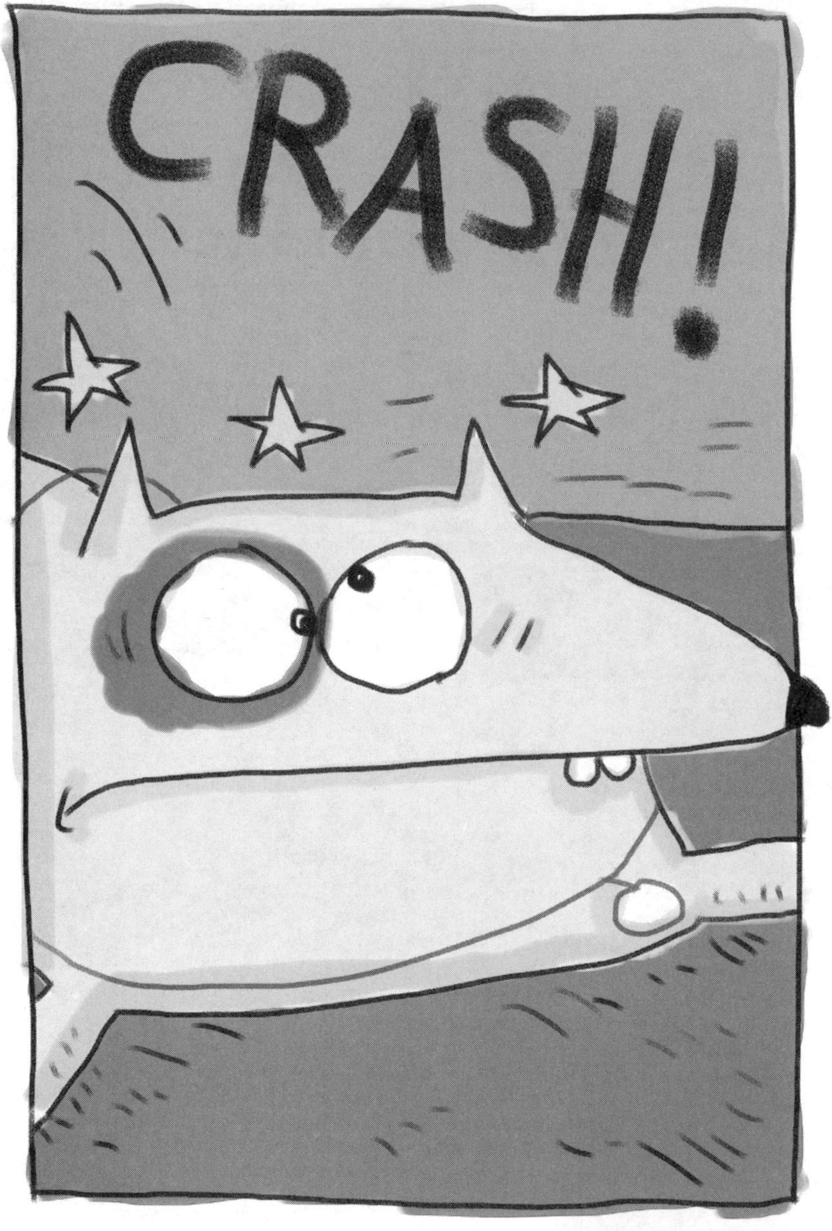
CRASH!

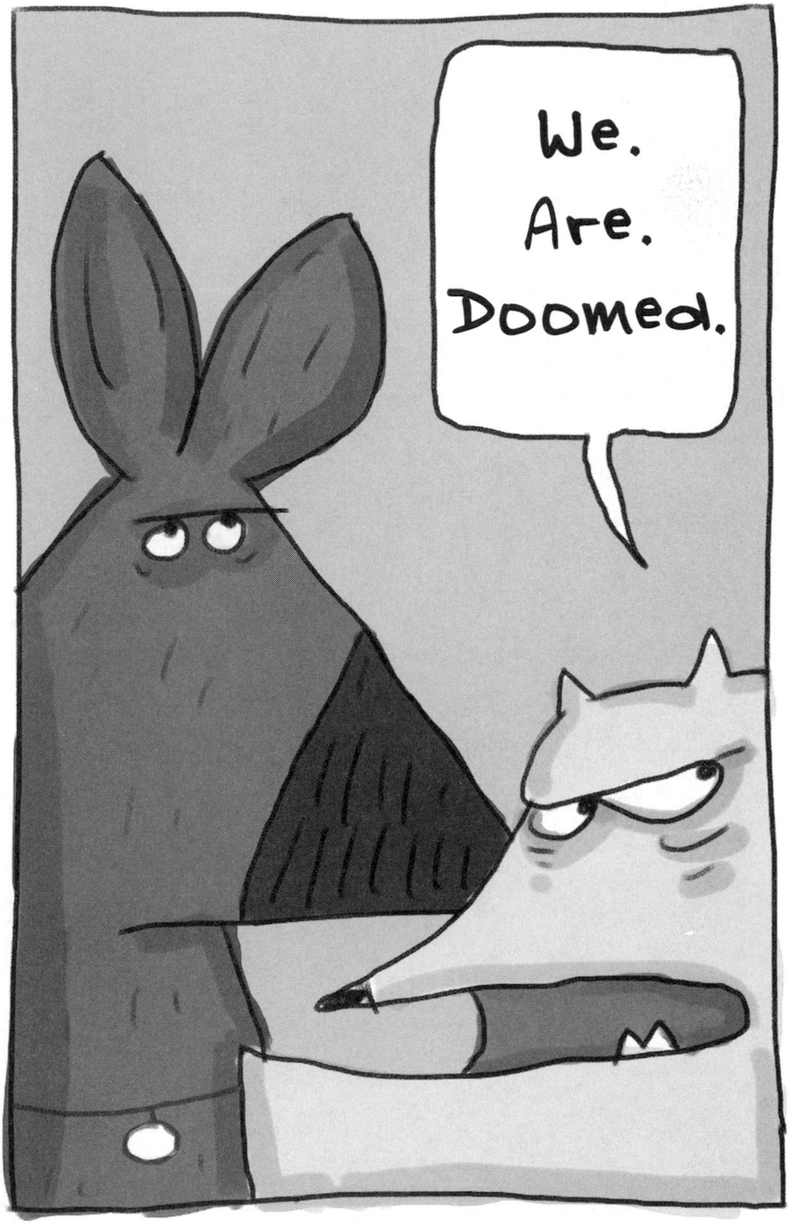
We. Are. Doomed.

Scene
Seventeen

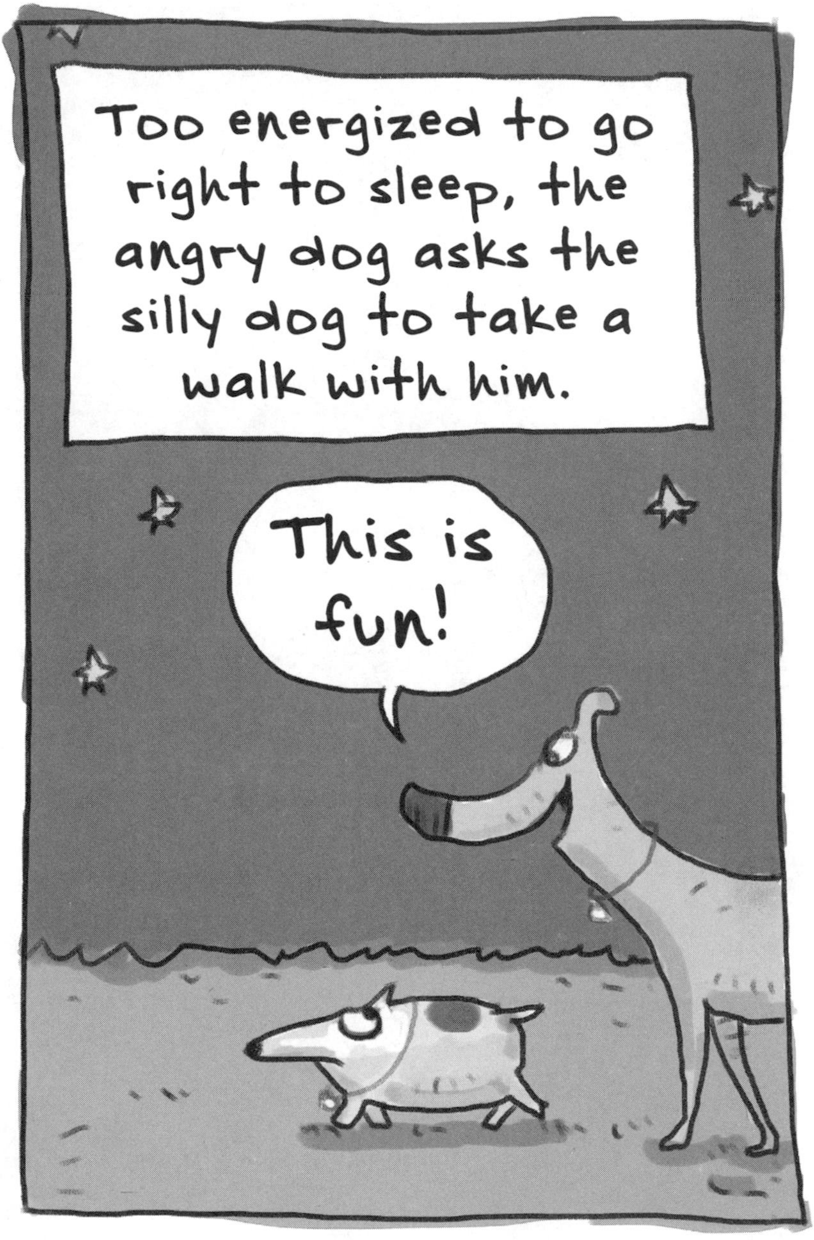
Too energized to go right to sleep, the angry dog asks the silly dog to take a walk with him.
This is fun!

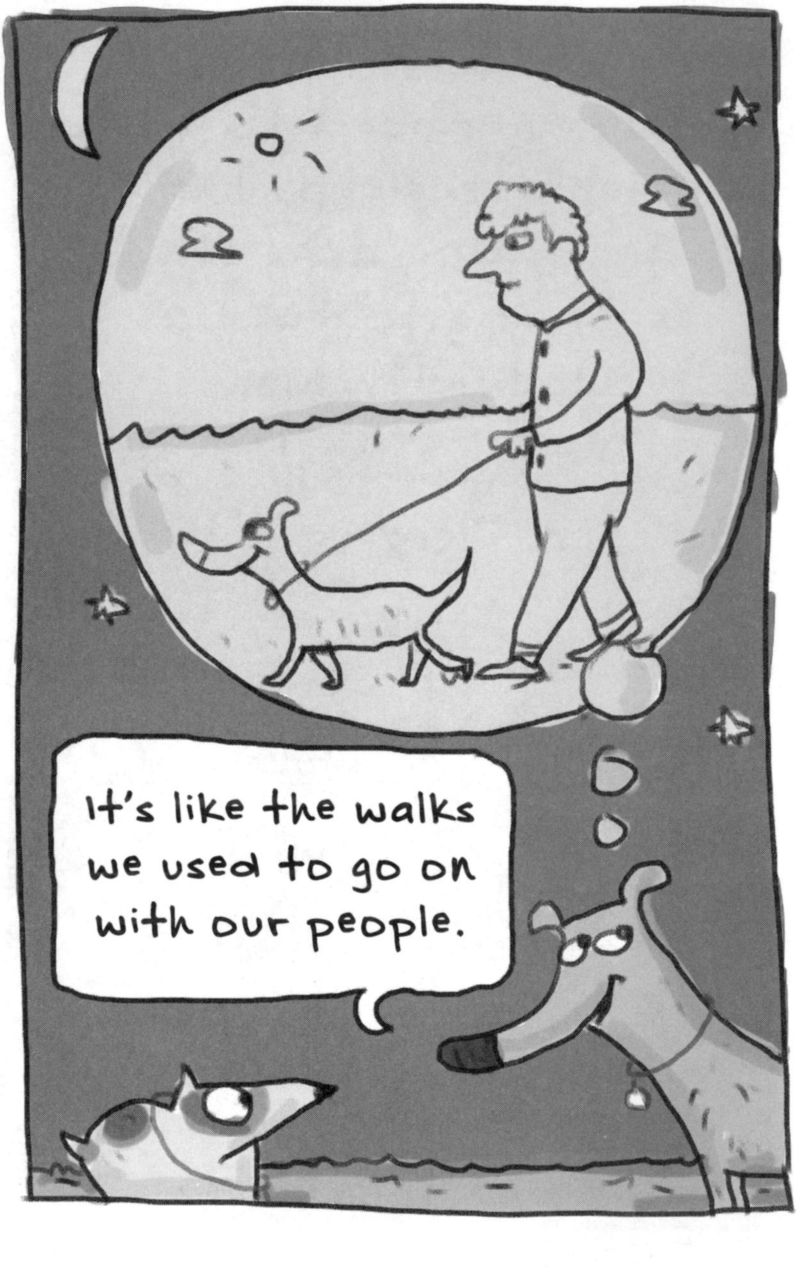
It's like the walks we used to go on with our people.

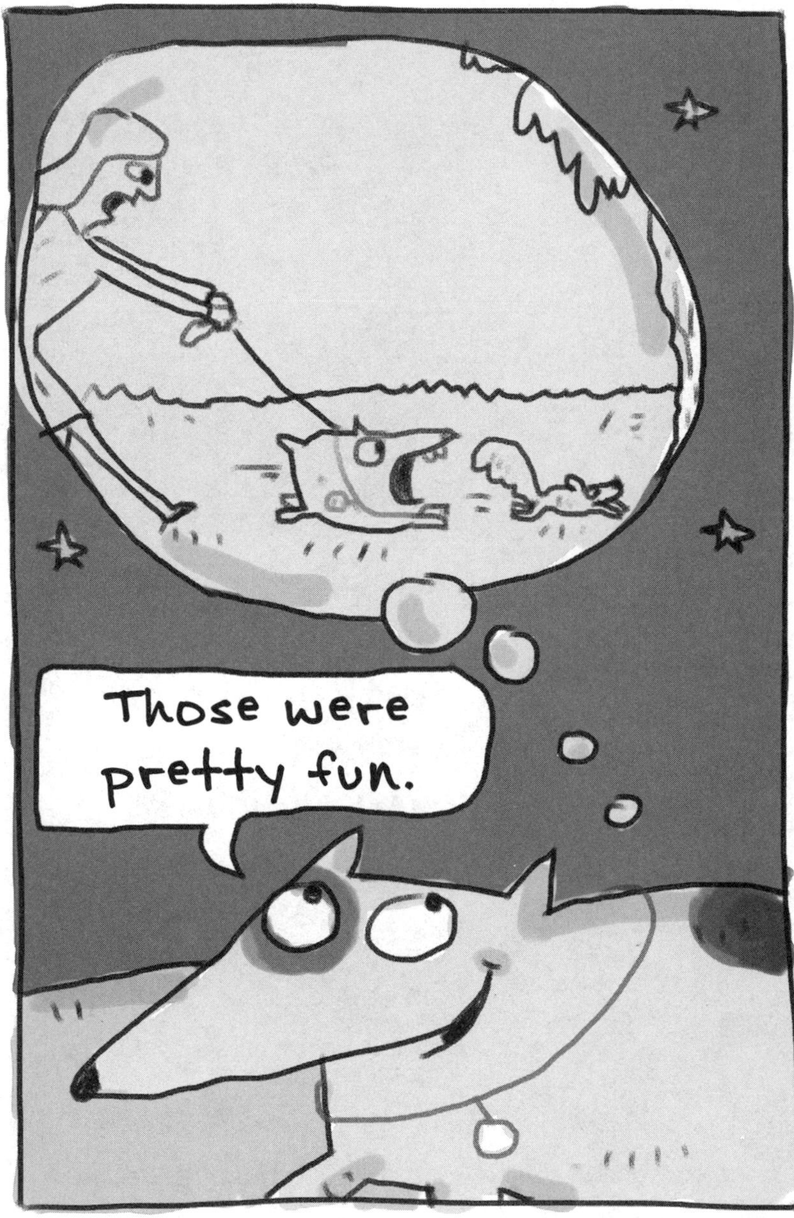
Those were pretty fun.

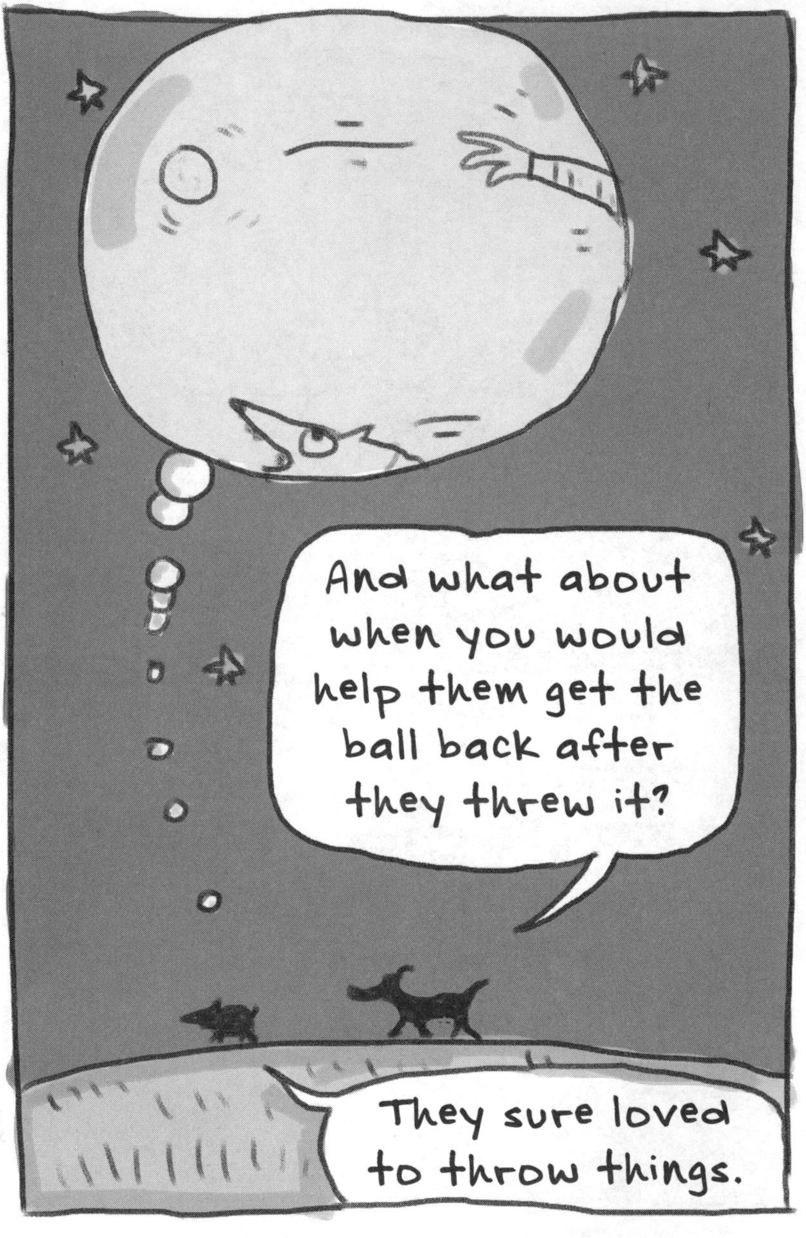
And what about when you would help them get the ball back after they threw it?
They sure loved to throw things.

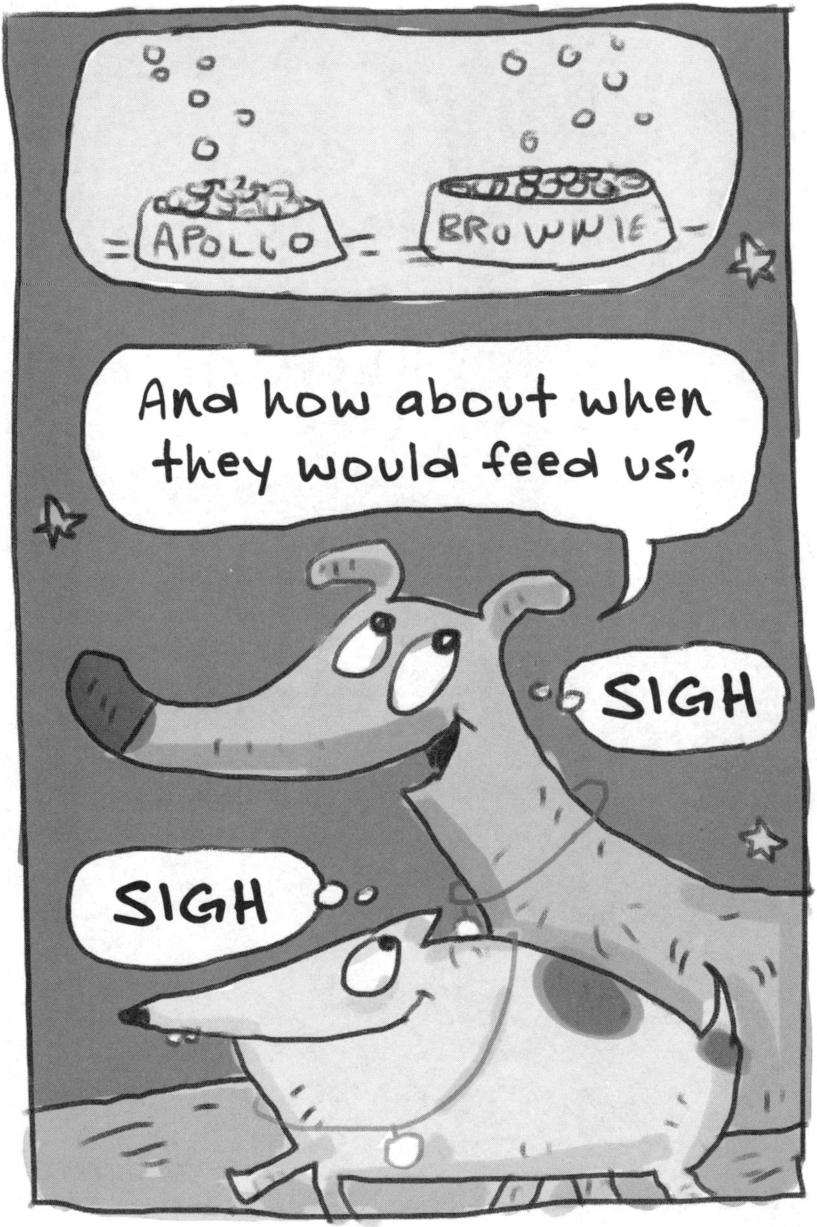
APOLLO
BROWNIE
And how about when they would feed us?
SIGH
SIGH

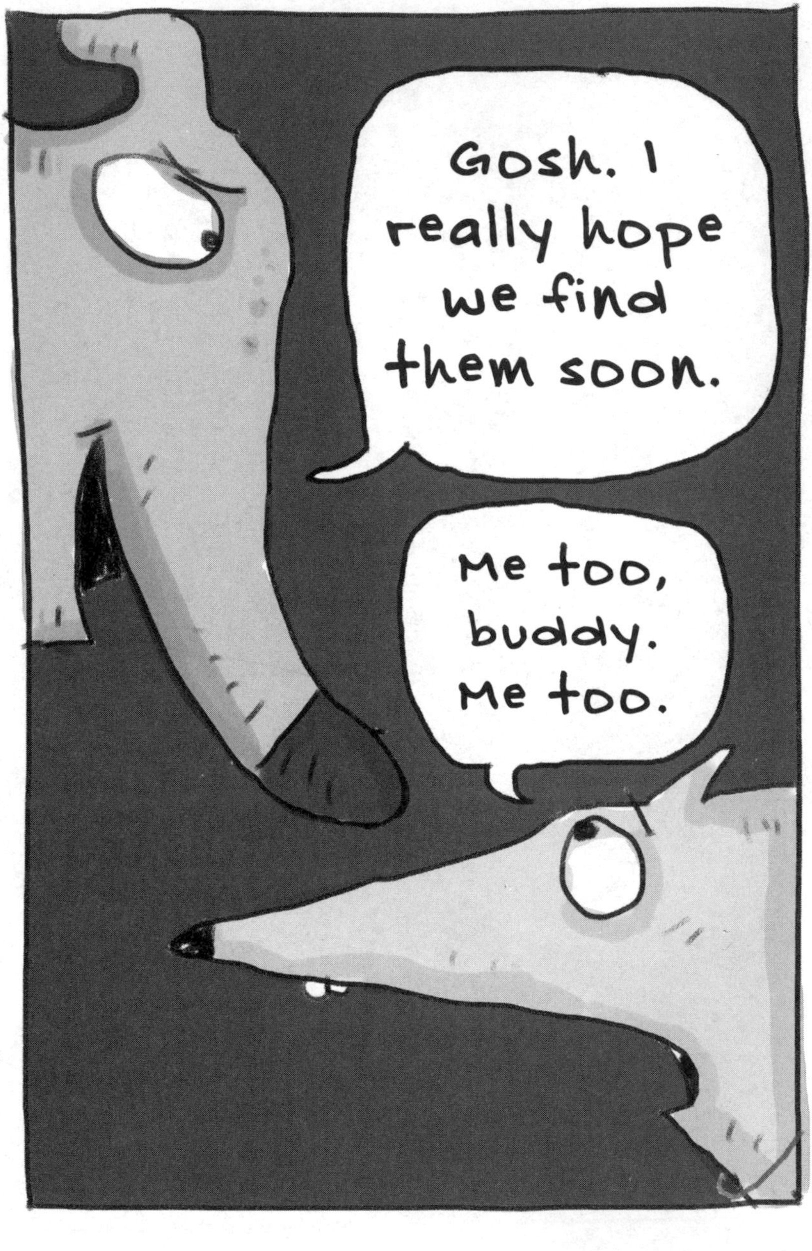
Gosh. I really hope we find them soon.
Me too, buddy. Me too.

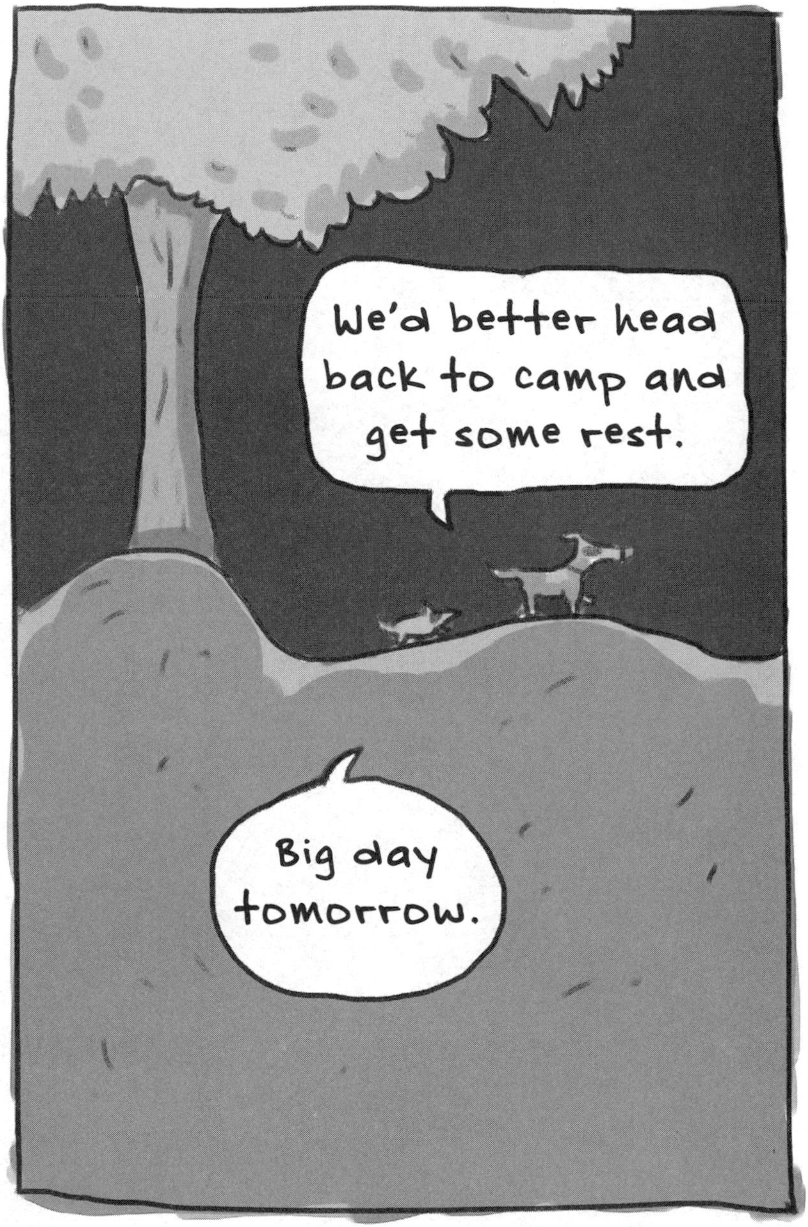
We'd better head back to camp and get some rest.
Big day tomorrow.

Scene
Eighteen

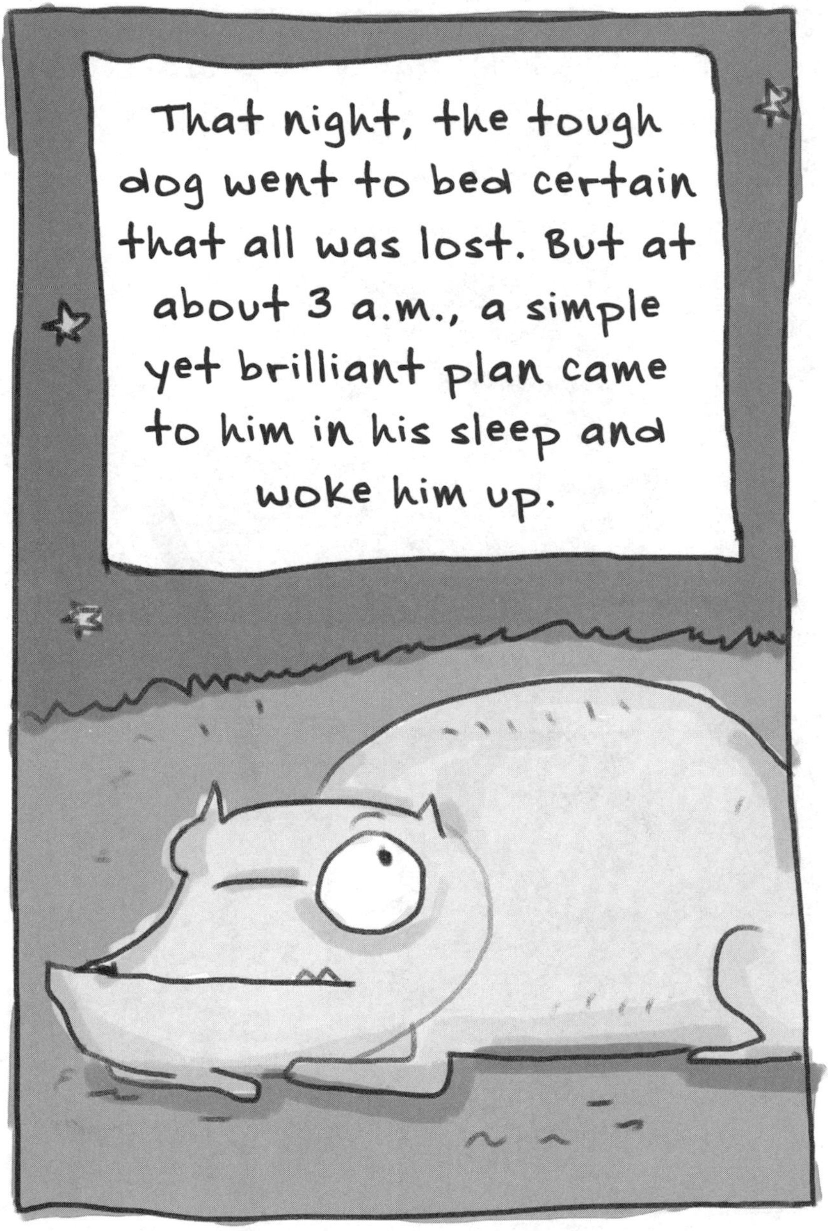
That night, the tough dog went to bed certain that all was lost. But at about 3 a.m., a simple yet brilliant plan came to him in his sleep and woke him up.

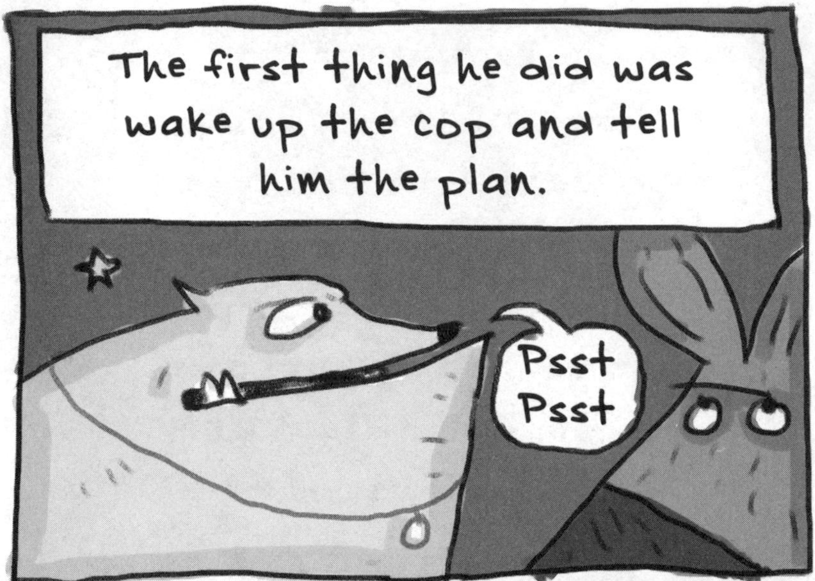
The first thing he did was wake up the cop and tell him the plan.
Psst Psst

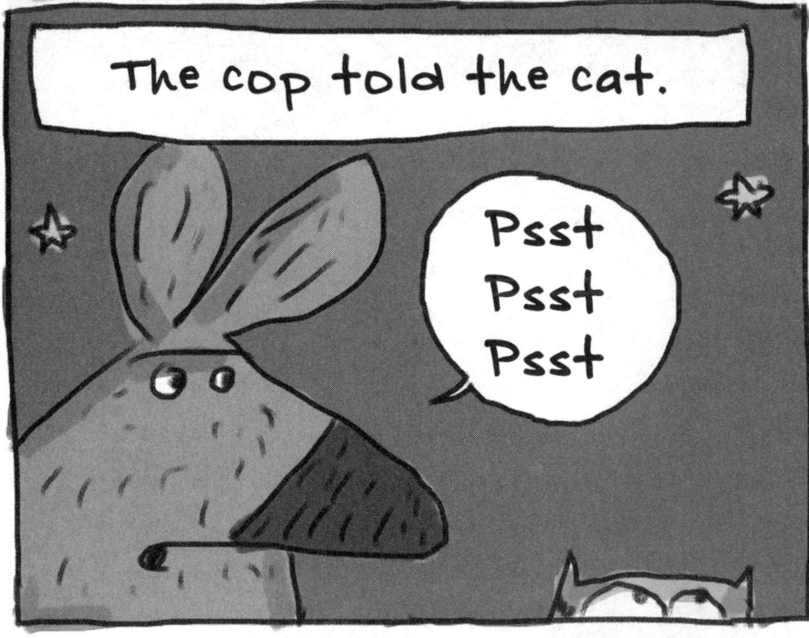
The cop told the cat.
Psst Psst Psst

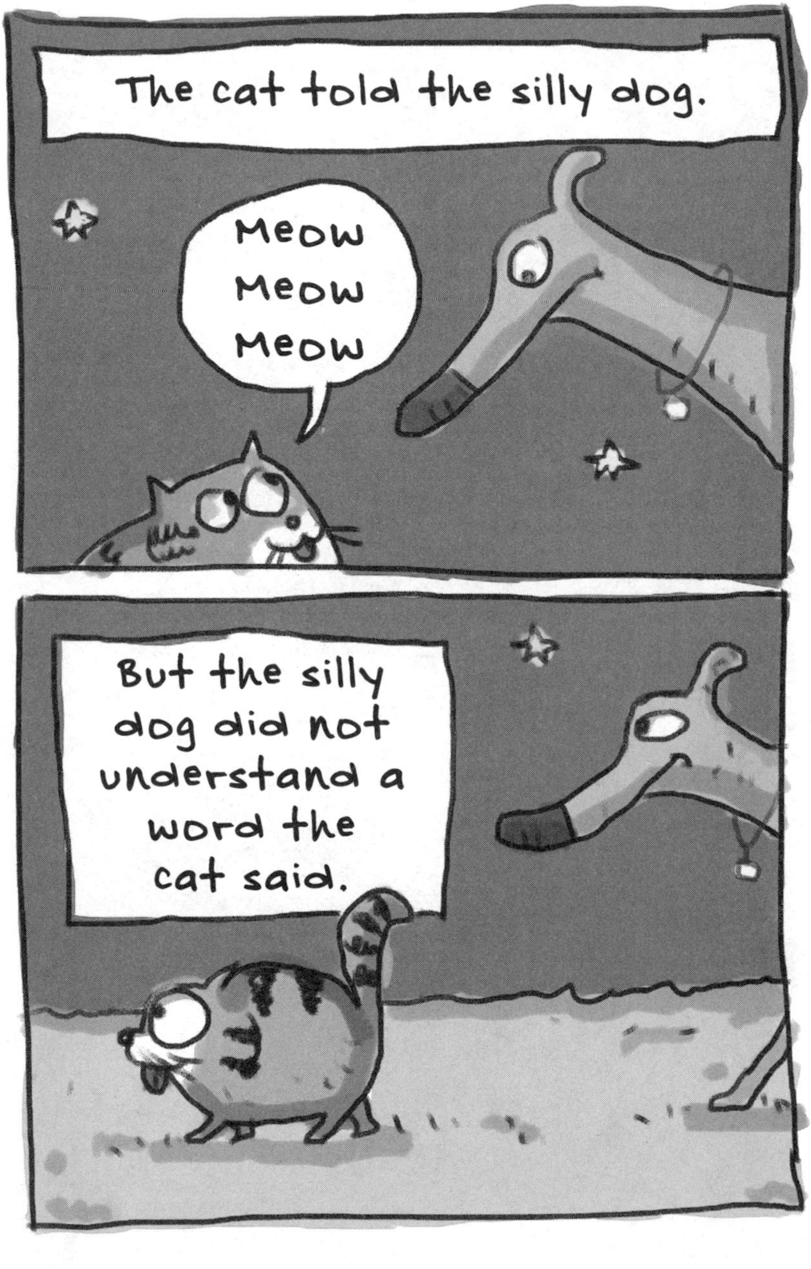
The cat told the silly dog.
Meow Meow Meow
But the silly dog did not understand a word the cat said.

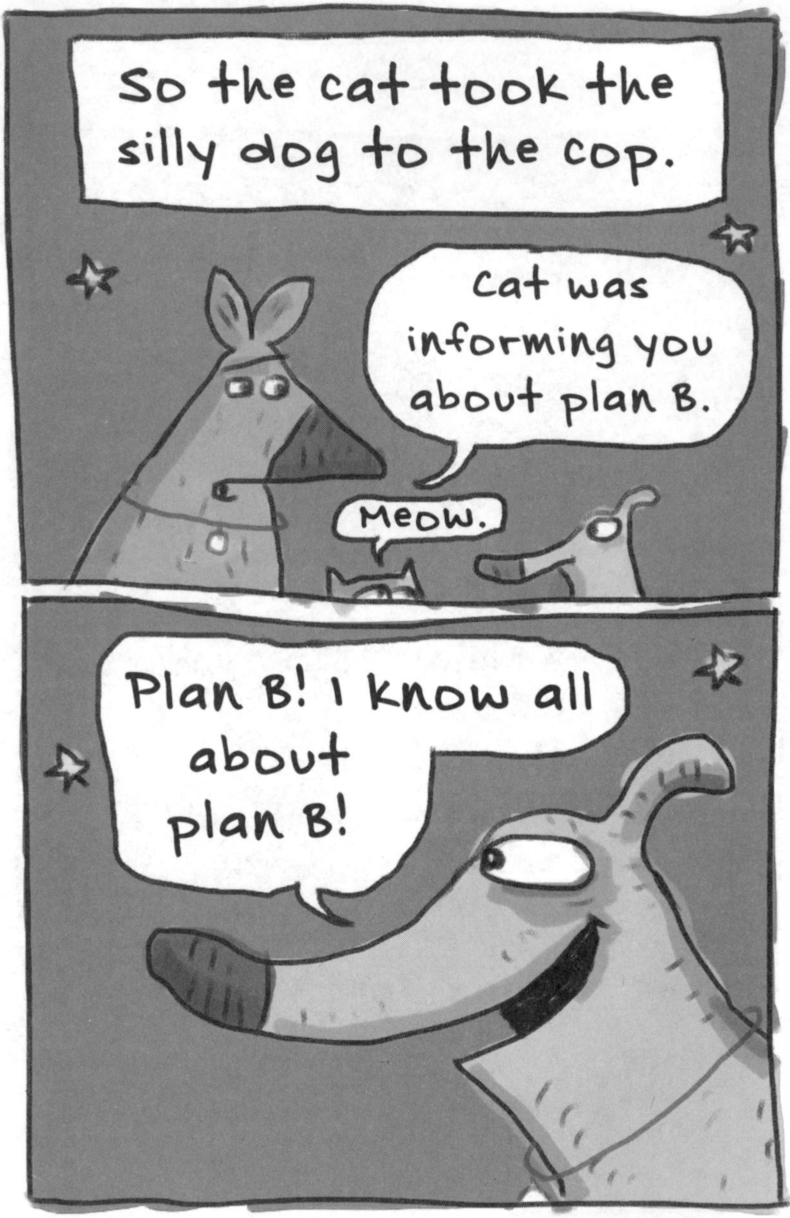
So the cat took the silly dog to the cop.
Cat was informing you about plan B.
MEOW.
Plan B! I know all about plan B!

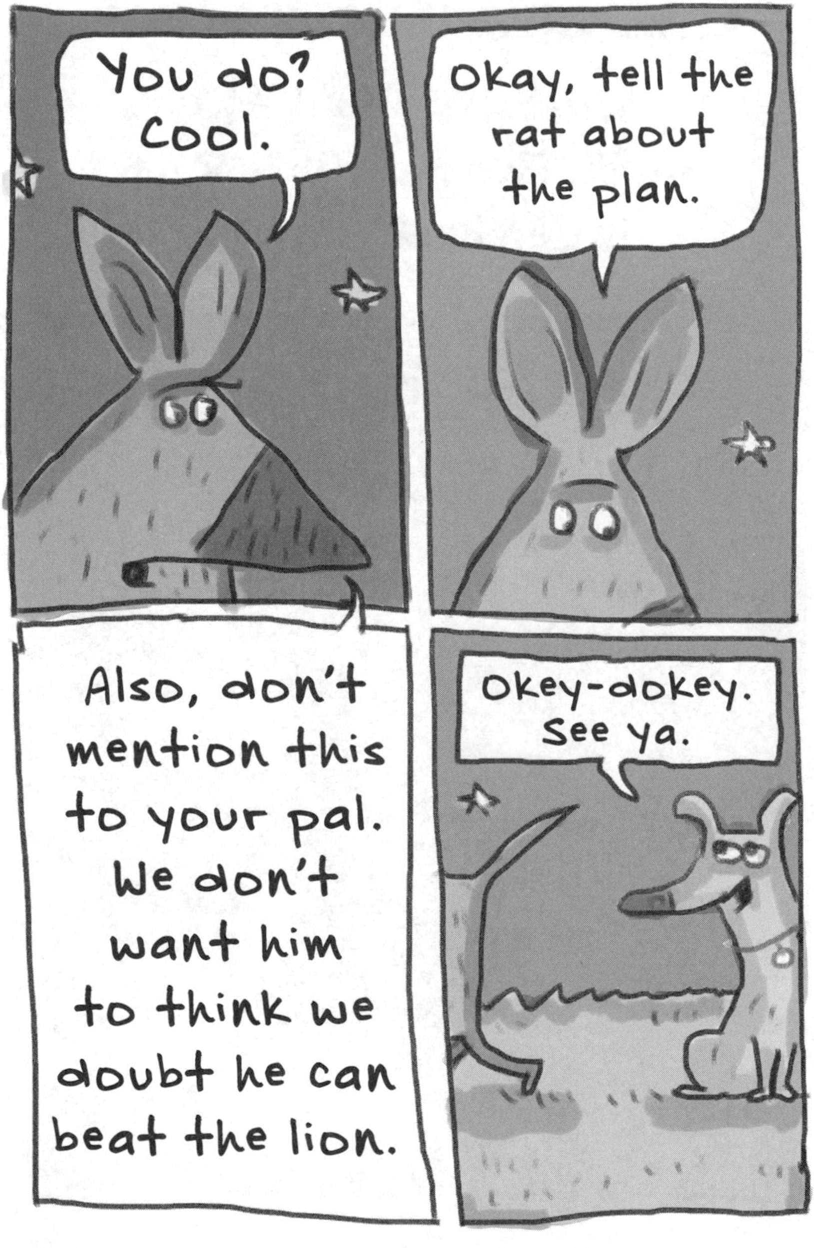
You do? Cool.
Okay, tell the rat about the plan.
Also, don't mention this to your pal. We don't want him to think we doubt he can beat the lion.
Okey-dokey. See ya.

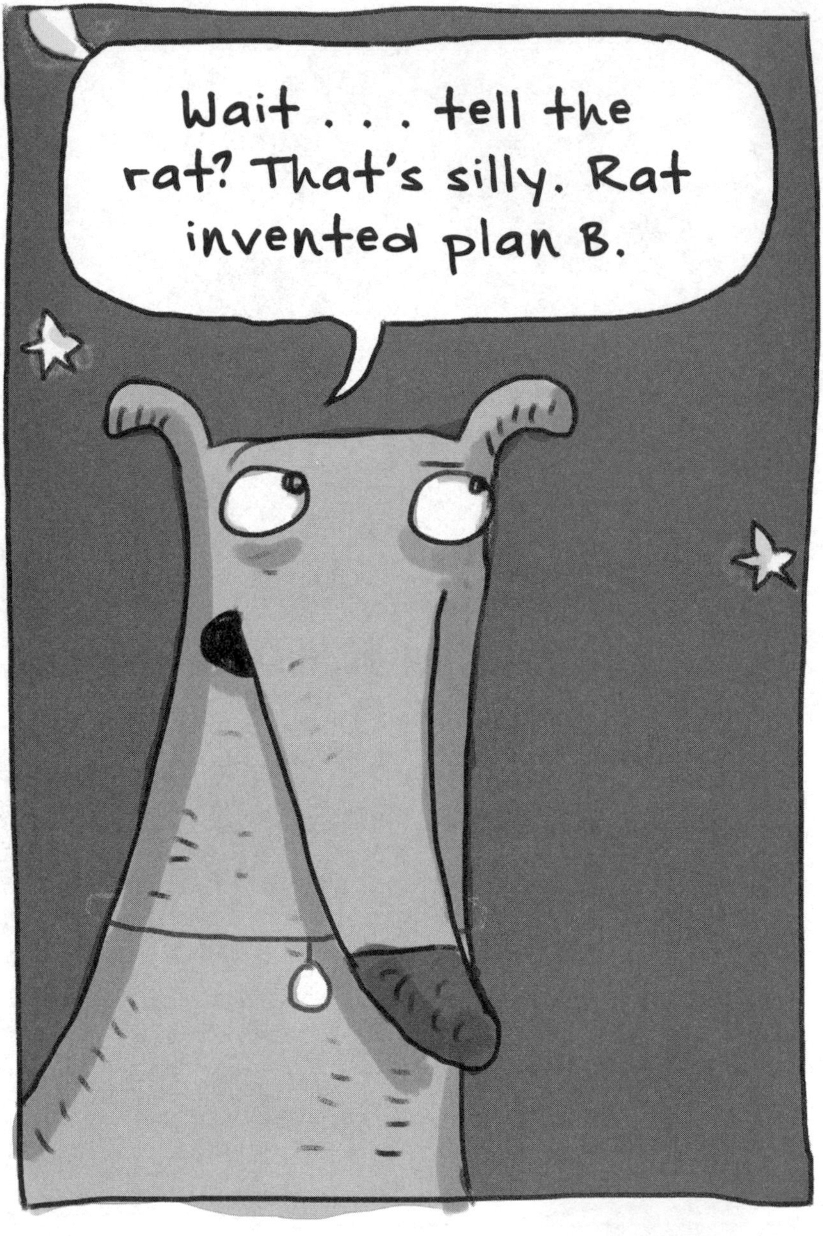
Wait . . . tell the rat? That's silly. Rat invented plan B.

Scene
Nineteen

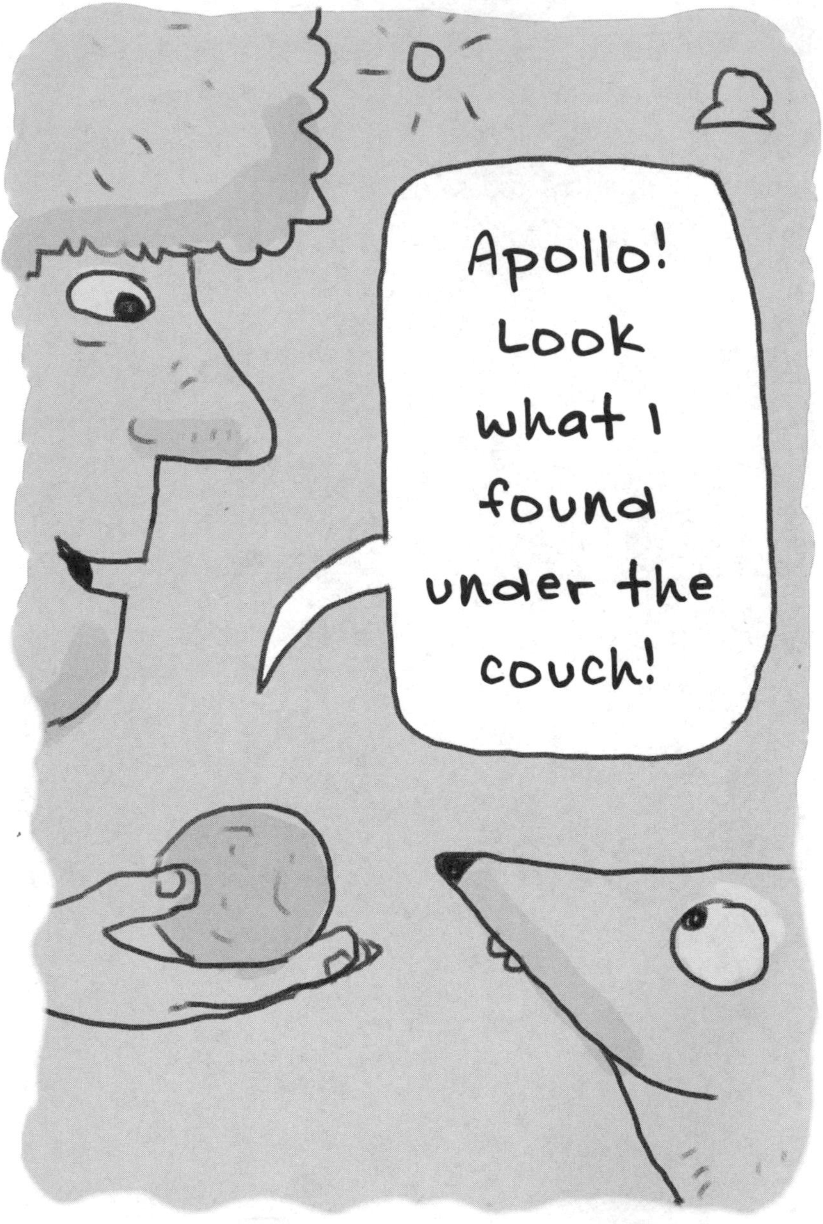
Apollo! Look what I found under the couch!

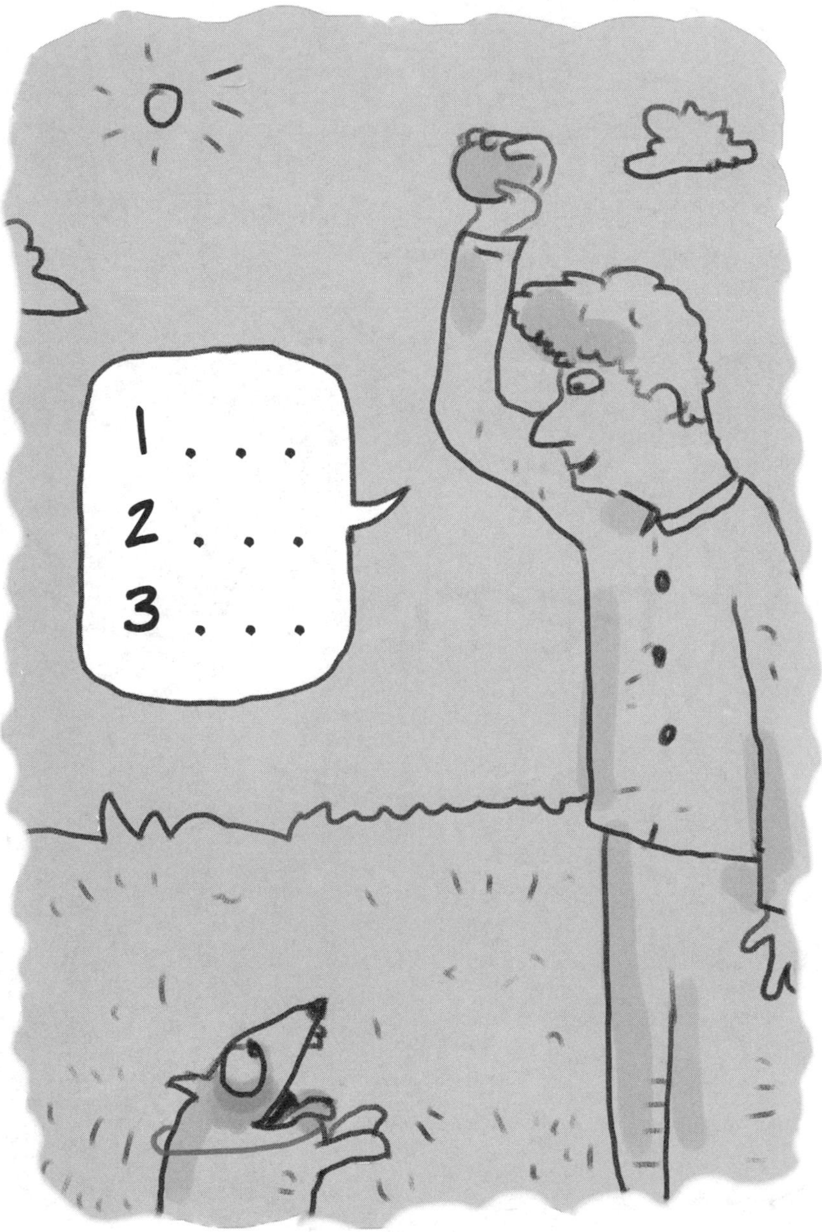
1....
2....
3....

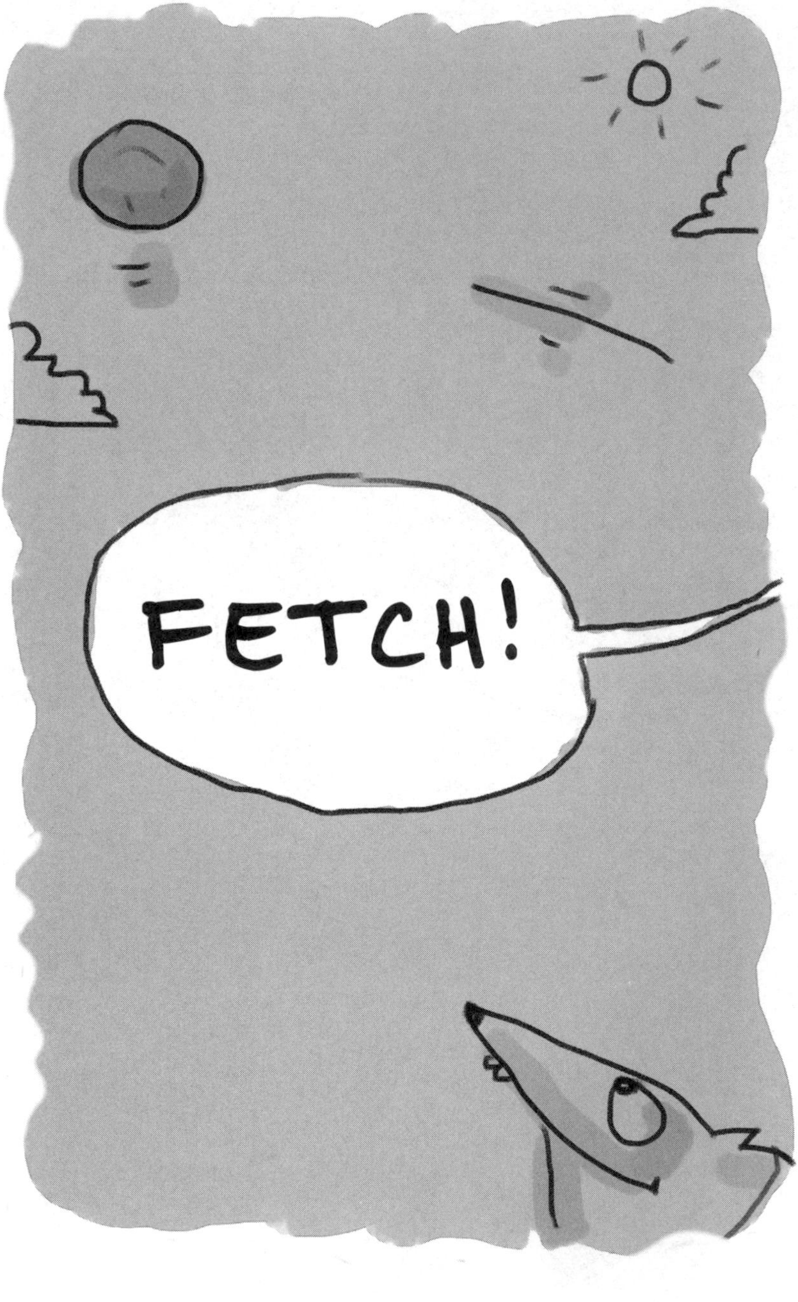
FETCH!

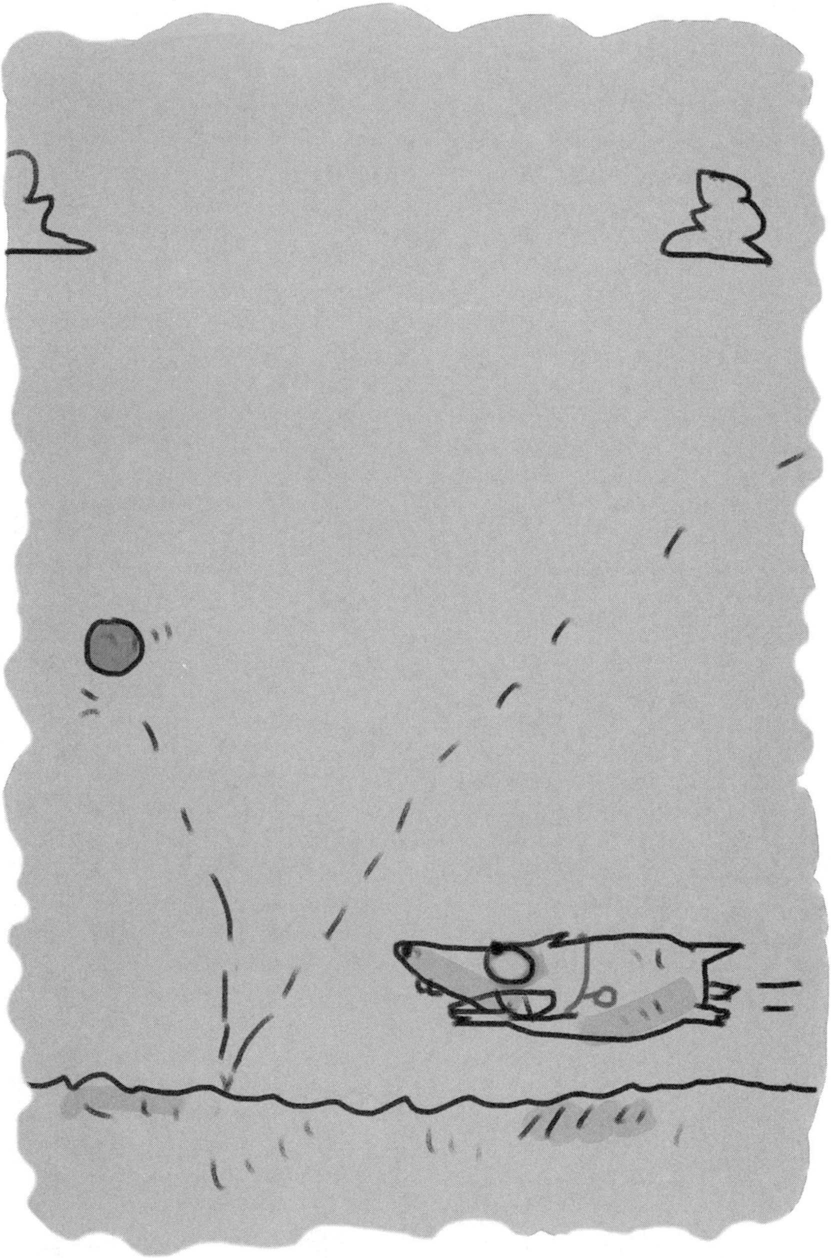

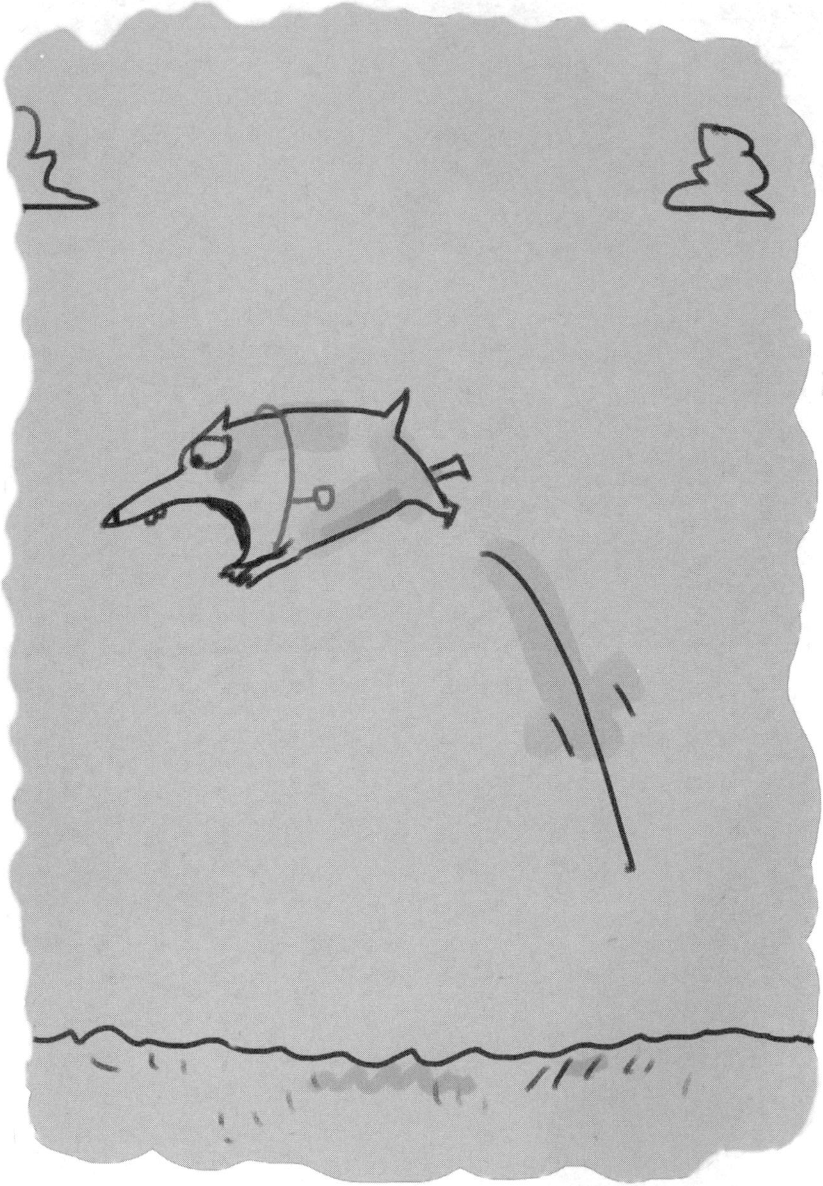

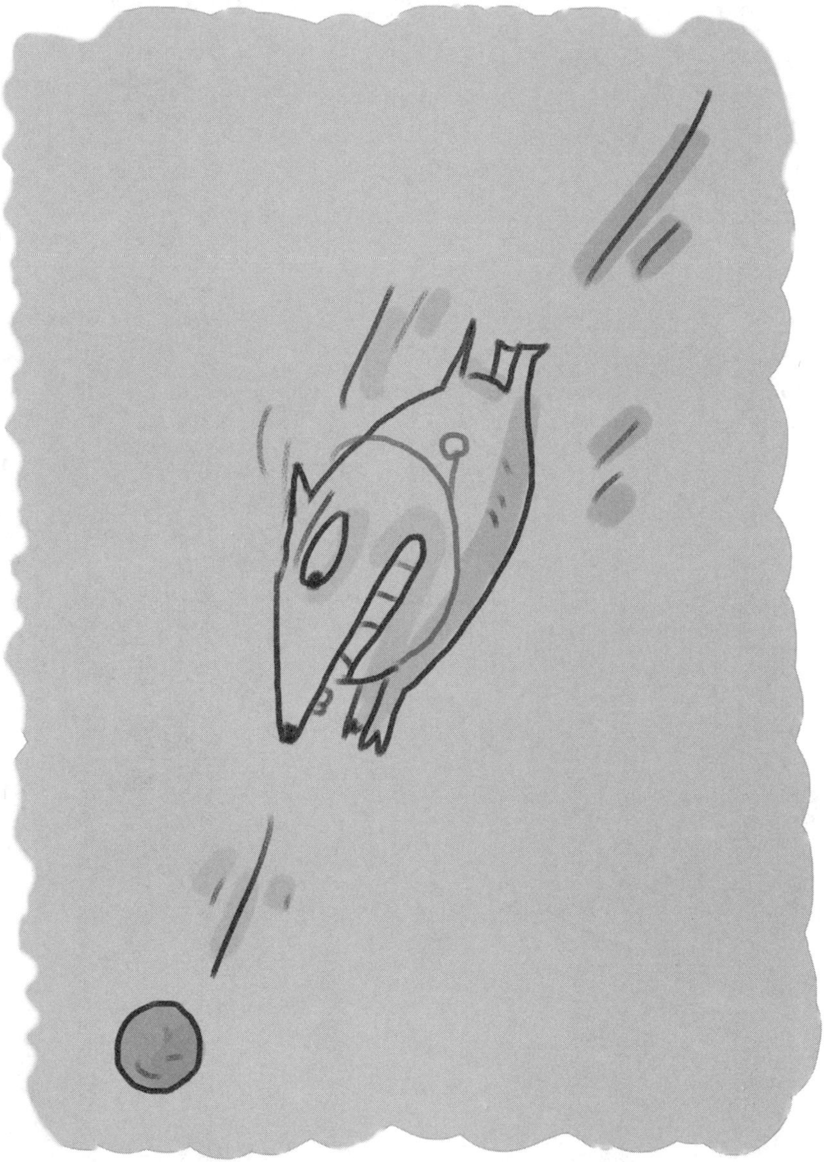

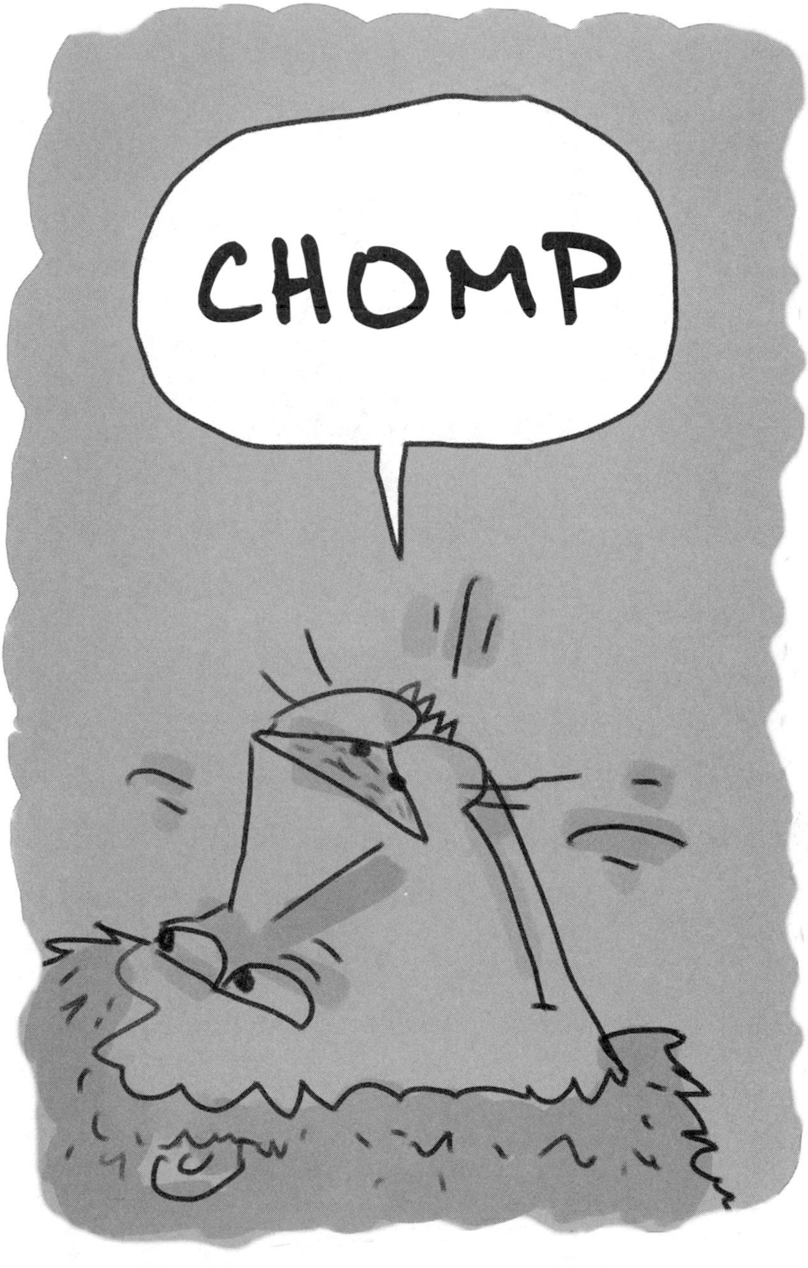
CHOMP

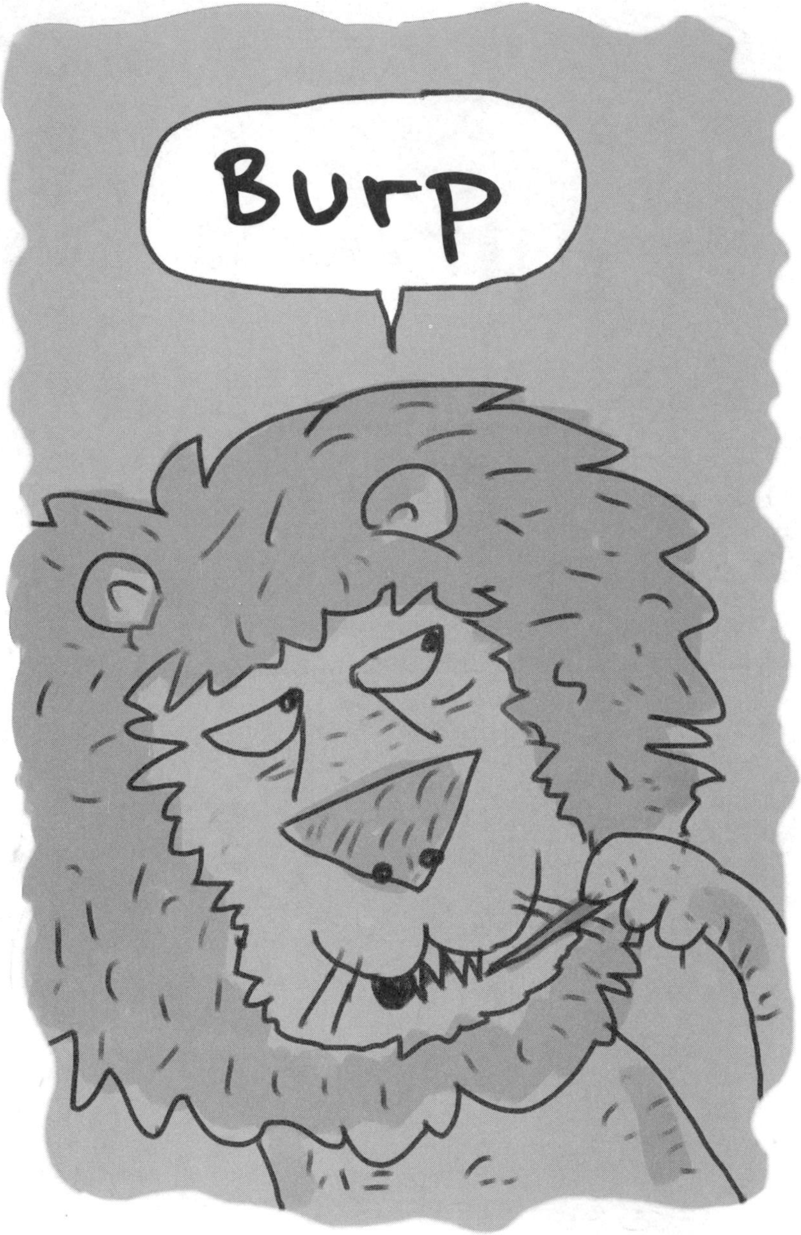
Burp

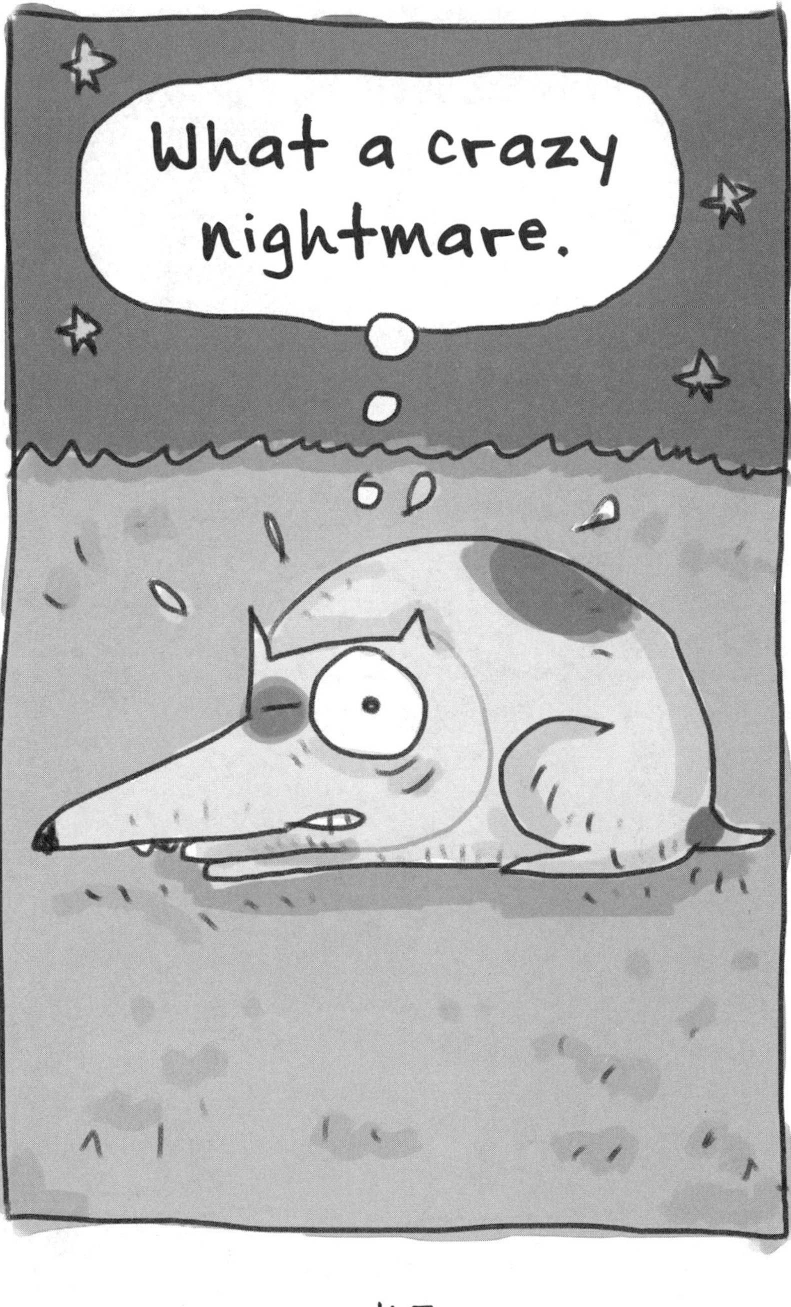
What a crazy nightmare.

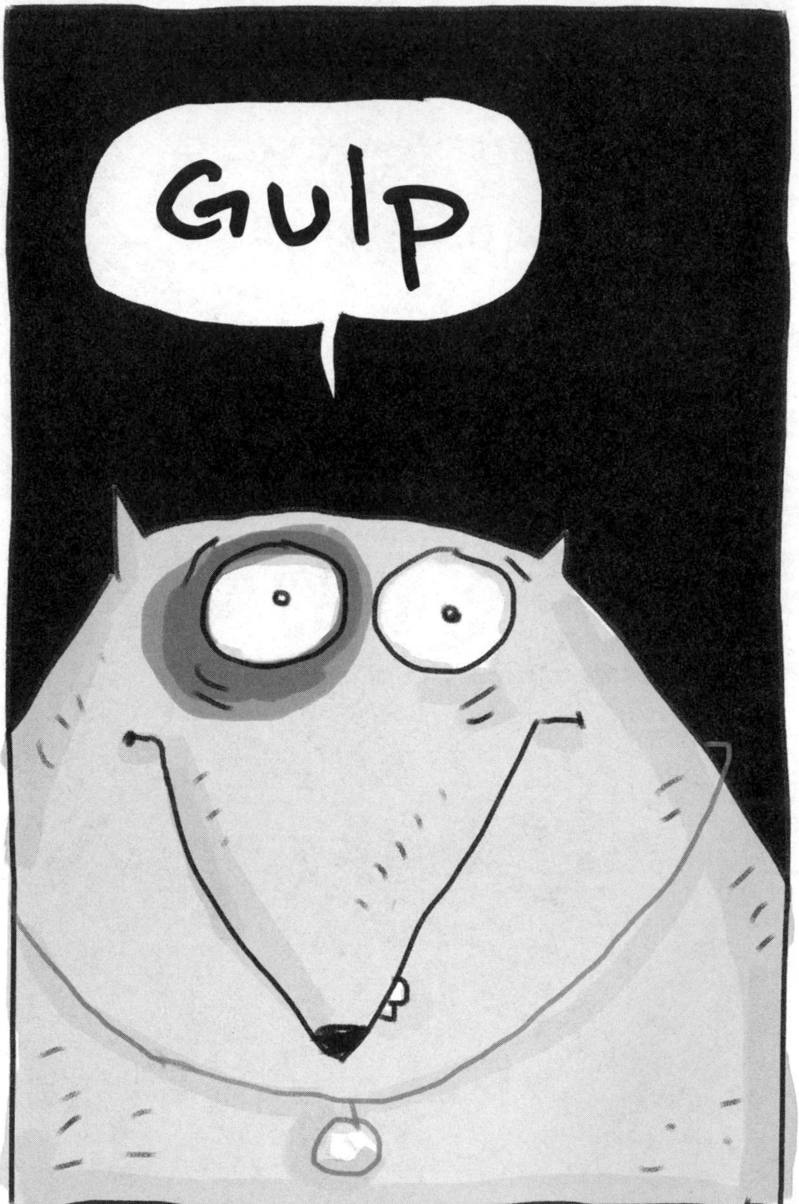
Gulp

Scene
Twenty

167

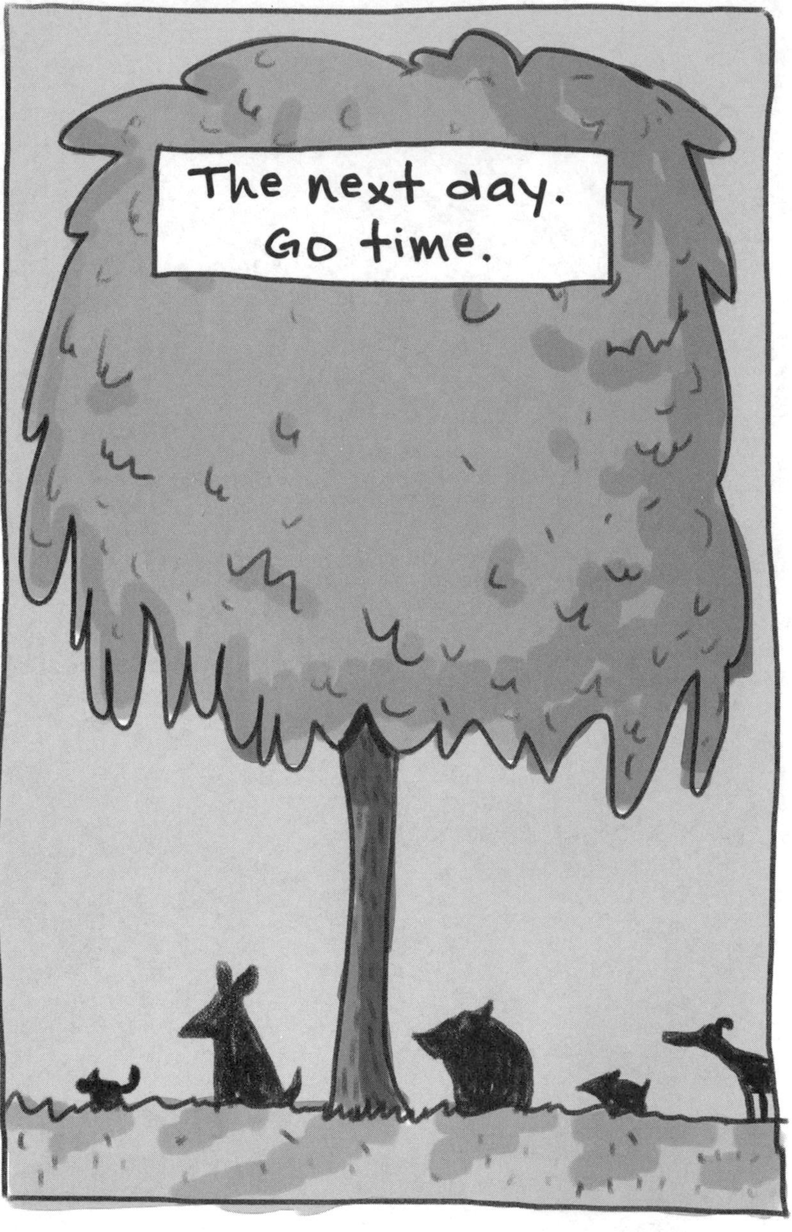
The next day.
Go time.

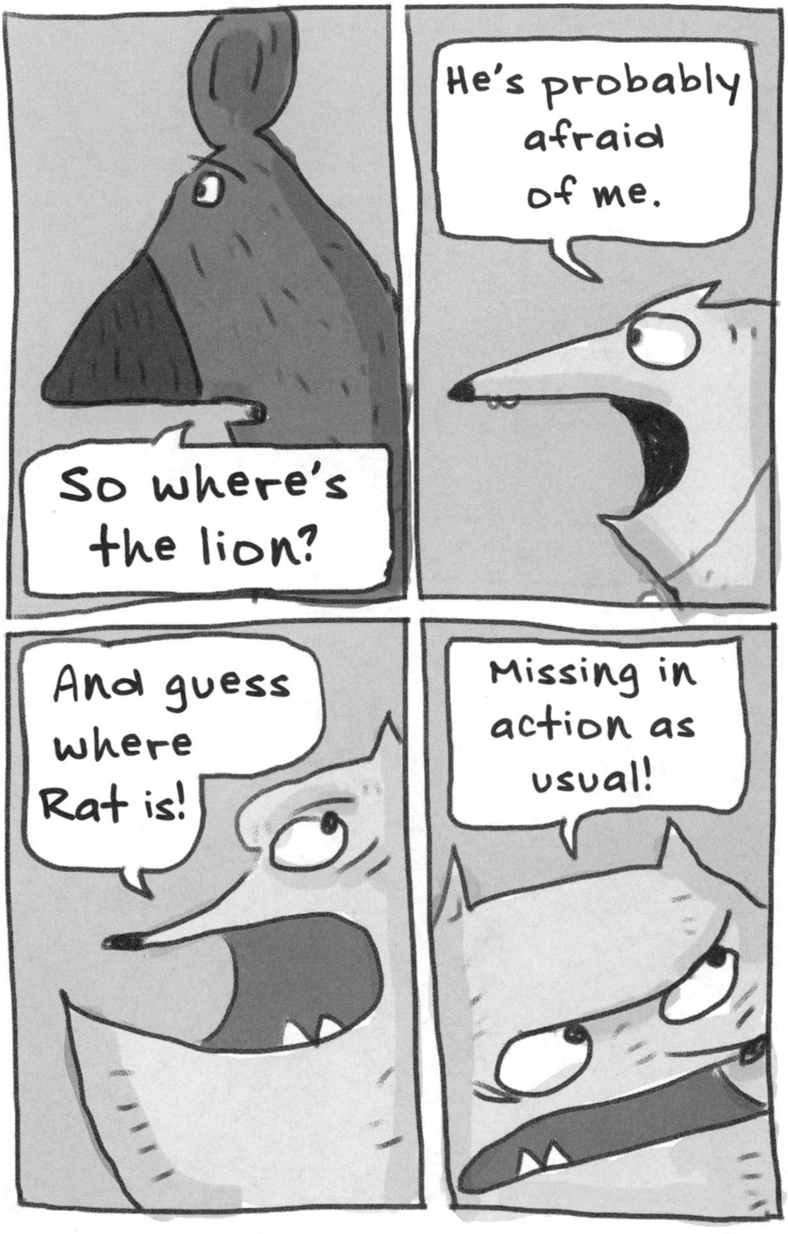
So where's the lion?
He's probably afraid of me.
And guess where Rat is!
Missing in action as usual!

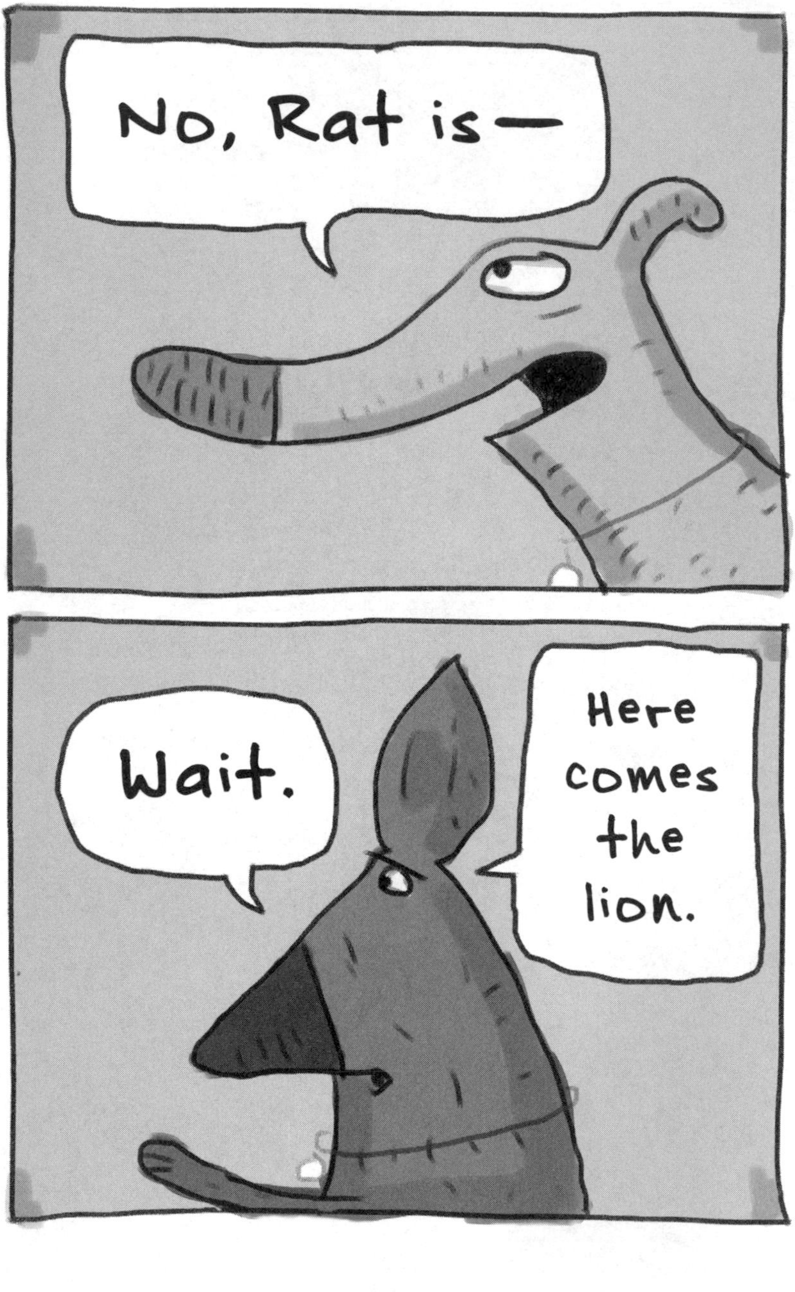
No, Rat is—
Wait.
Here comes the lion.

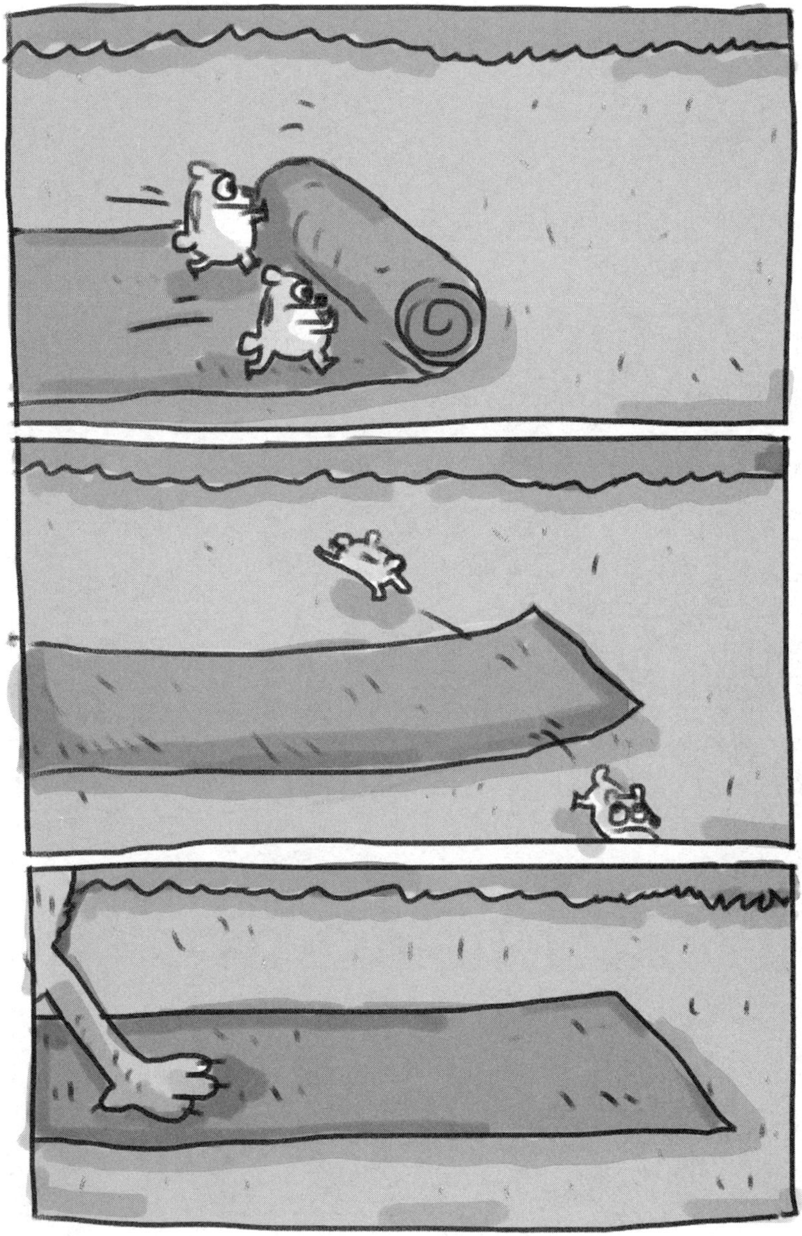

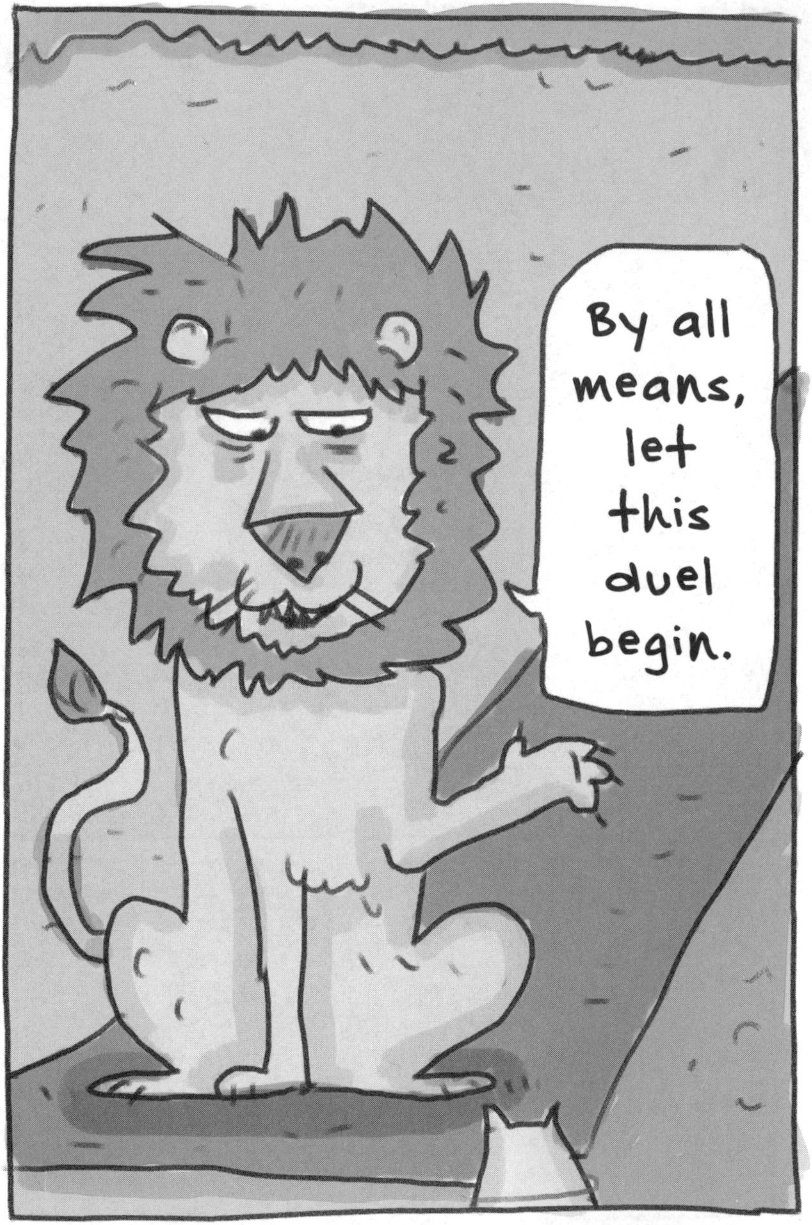
By all means, let this duel begin.

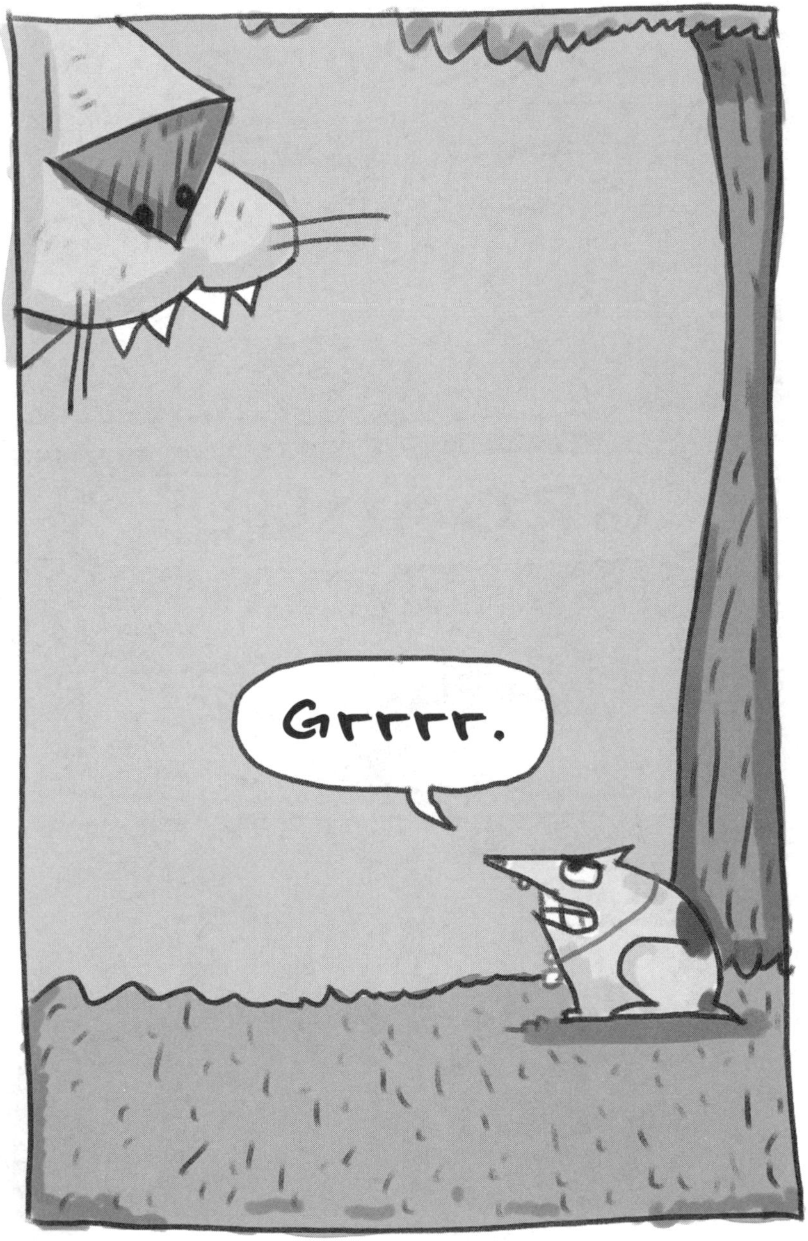
Grrrr.

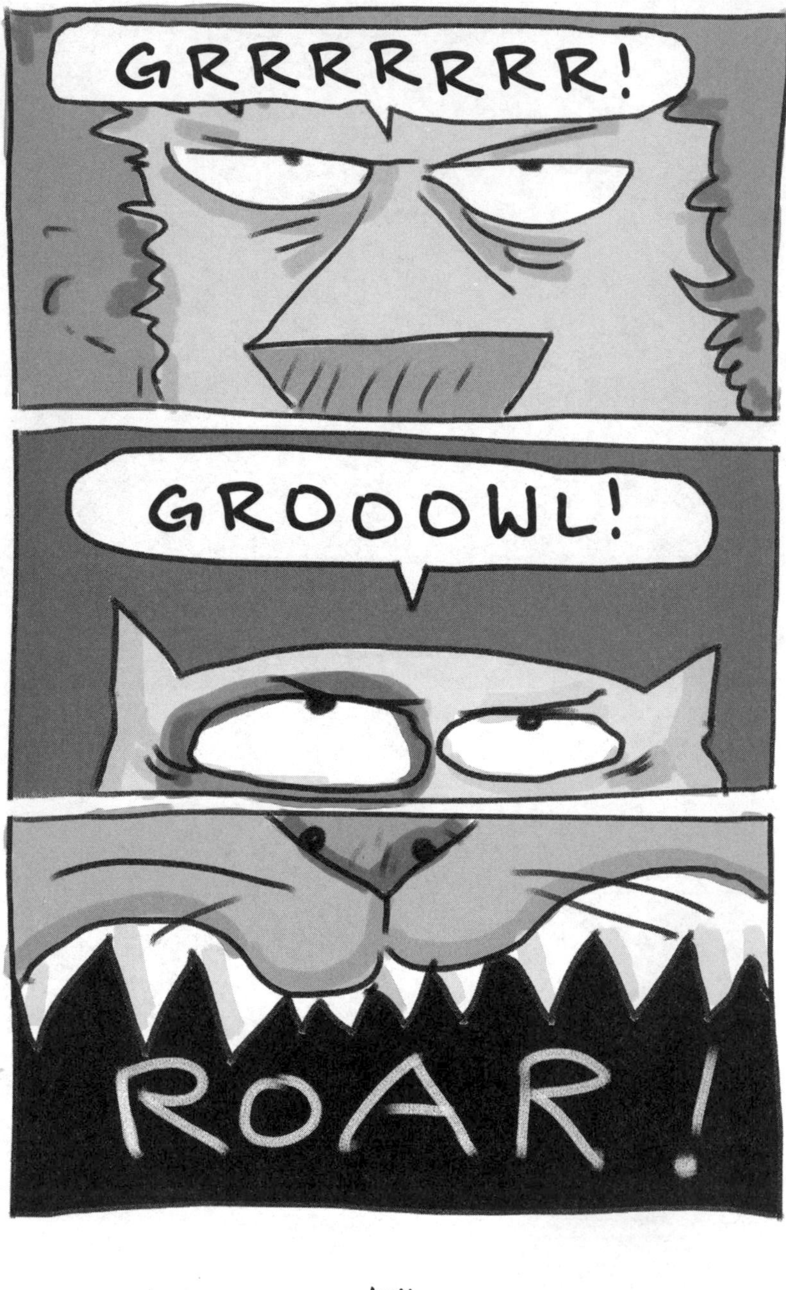
GRRRRRRR!
GROOOWL!
ROAR!

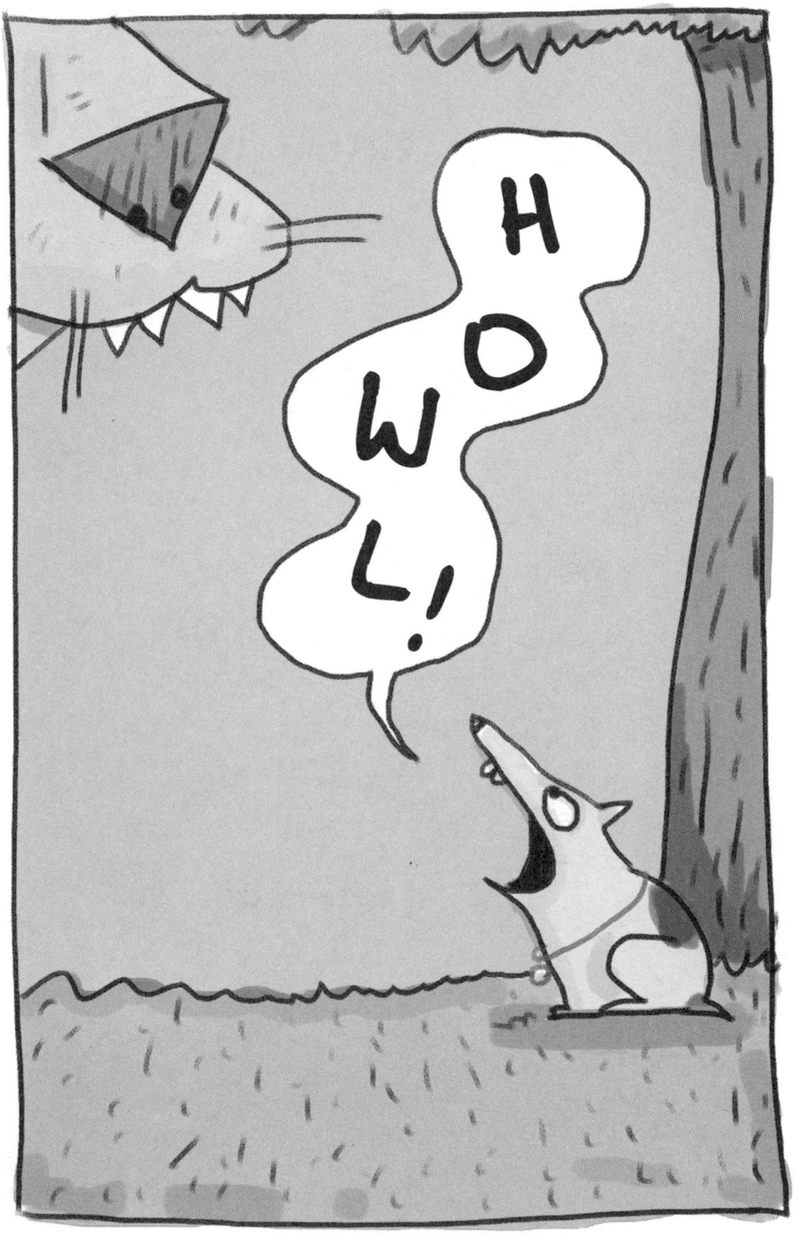
HOWL!

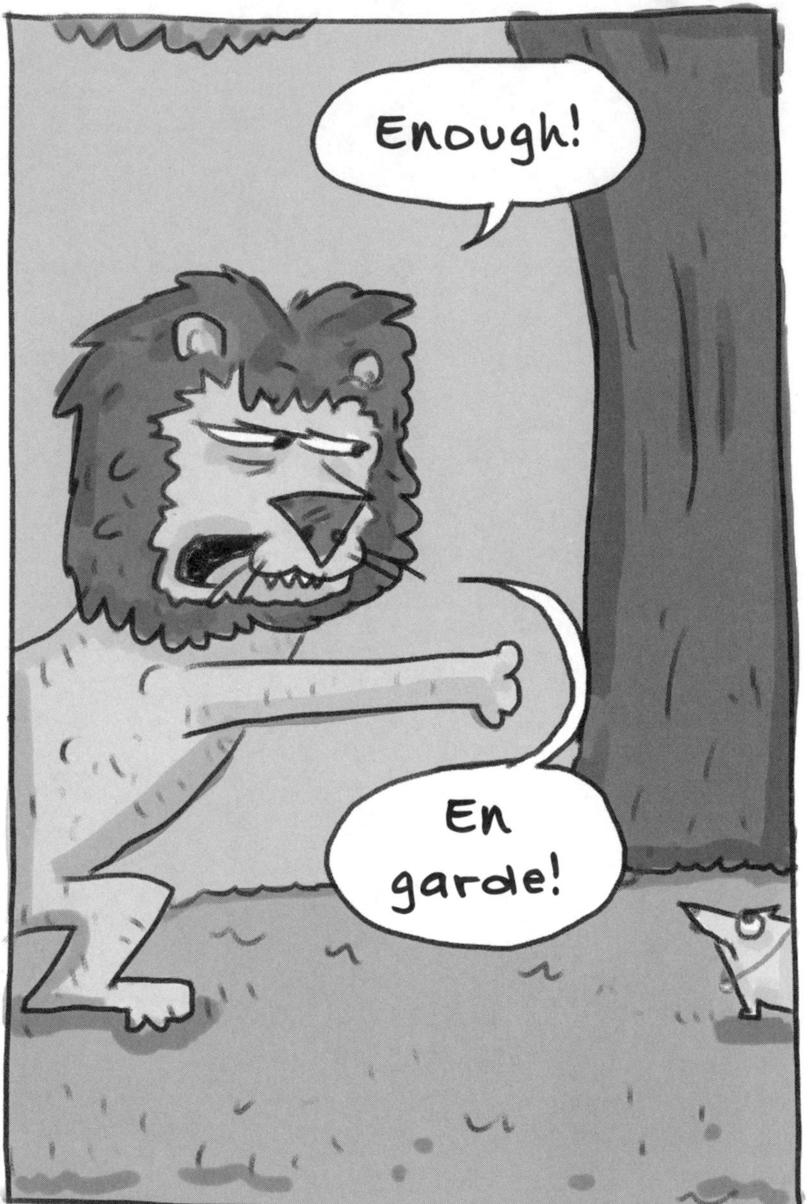
Enough!
En garde!

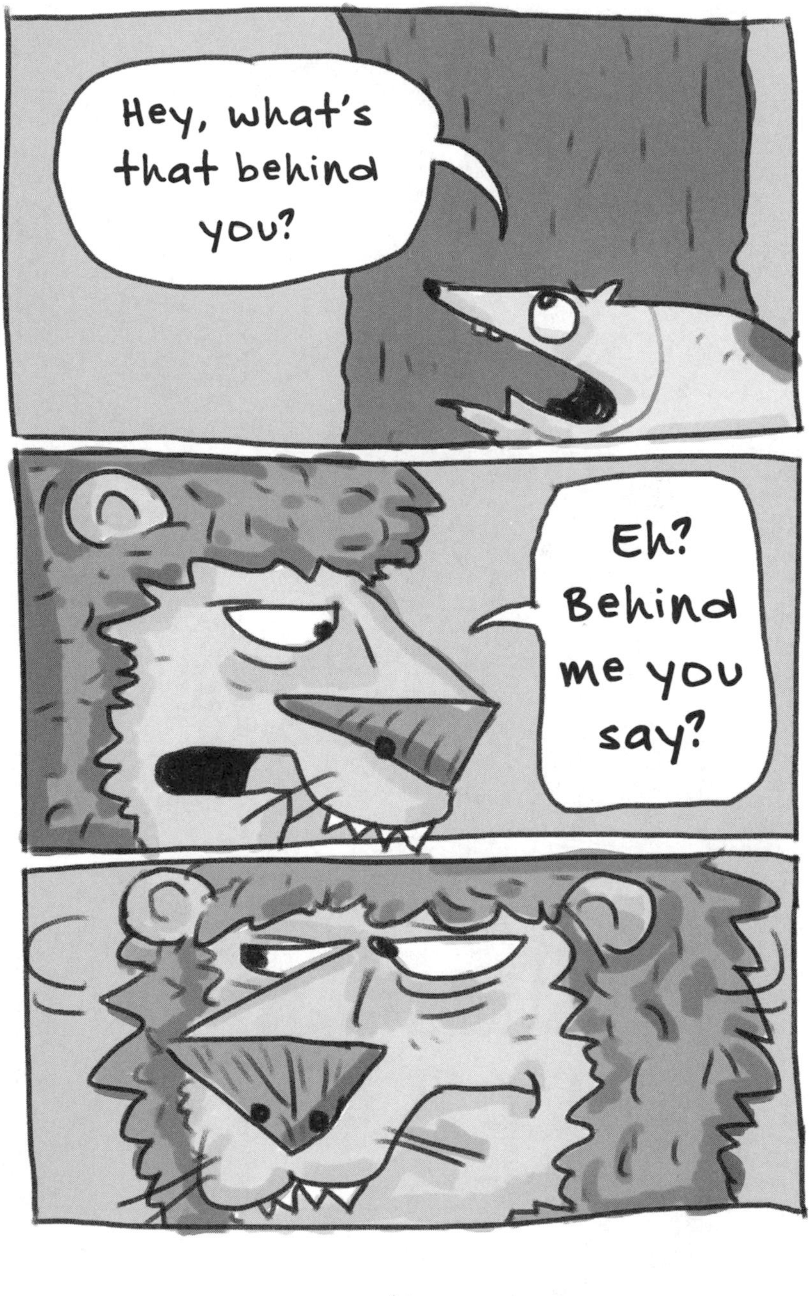
Hey, what's that behind you?
Eh? Behind me you say?

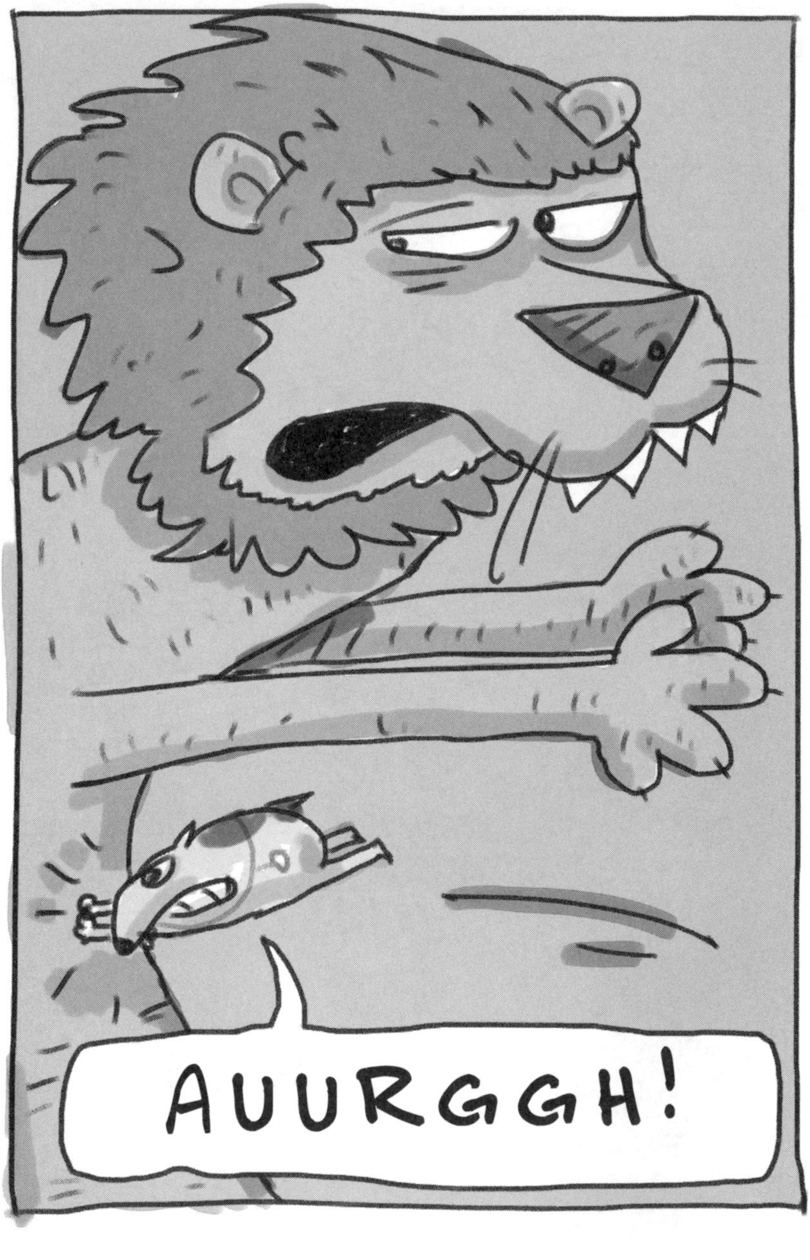
AUURGGH!

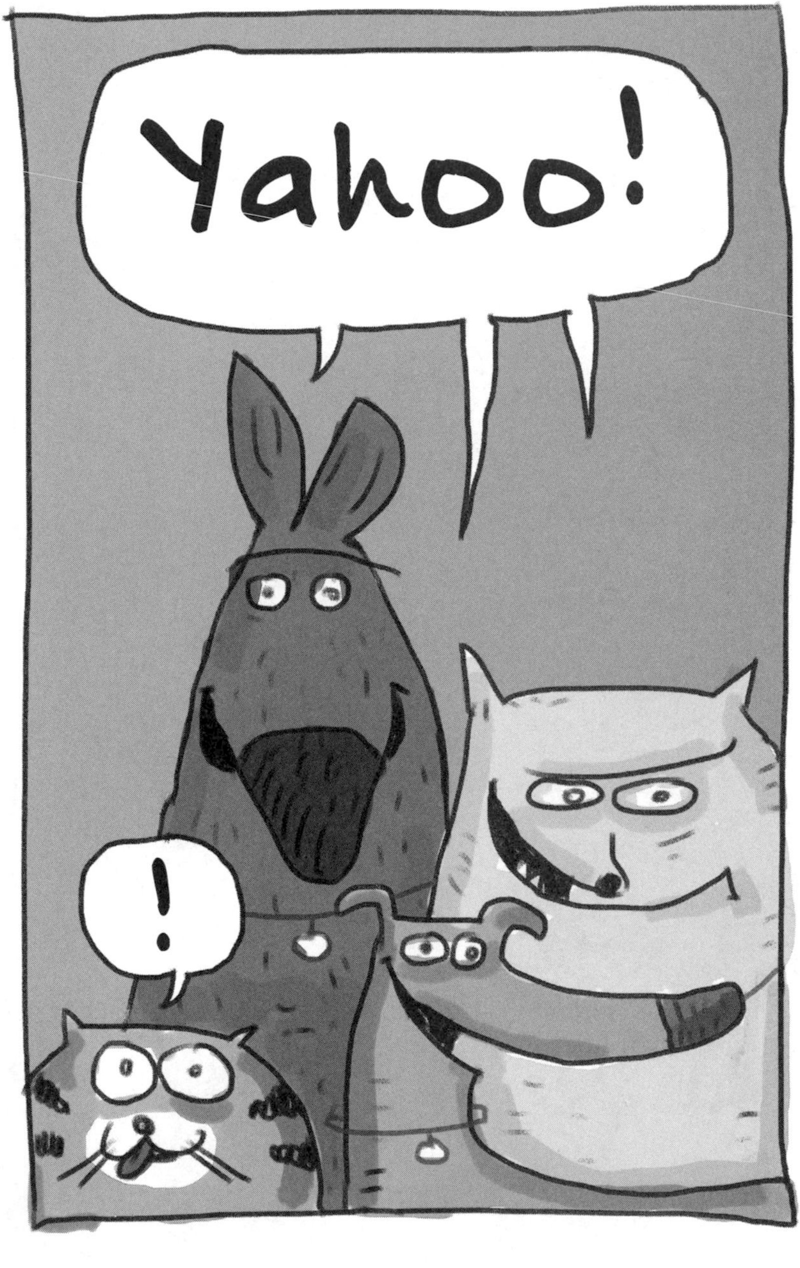
Yahoo!
!

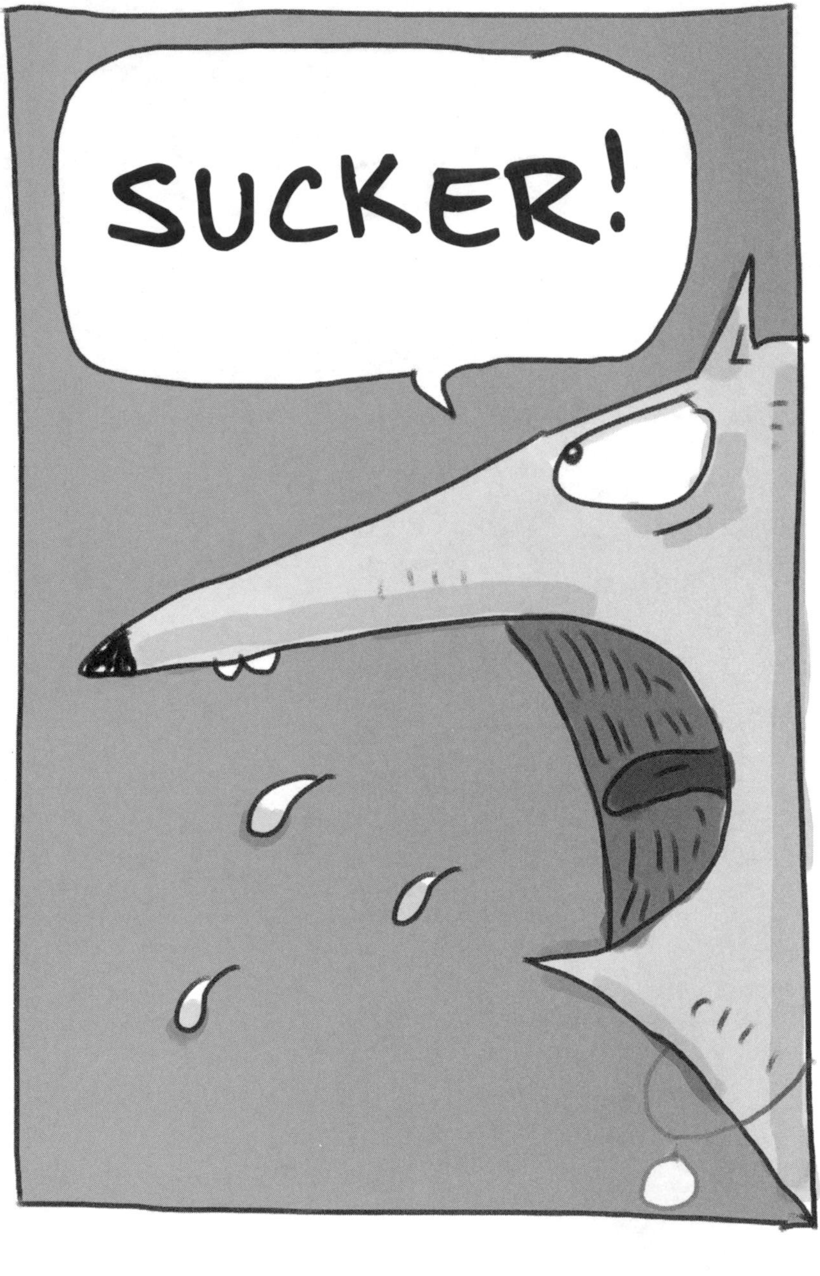
SUCKER!

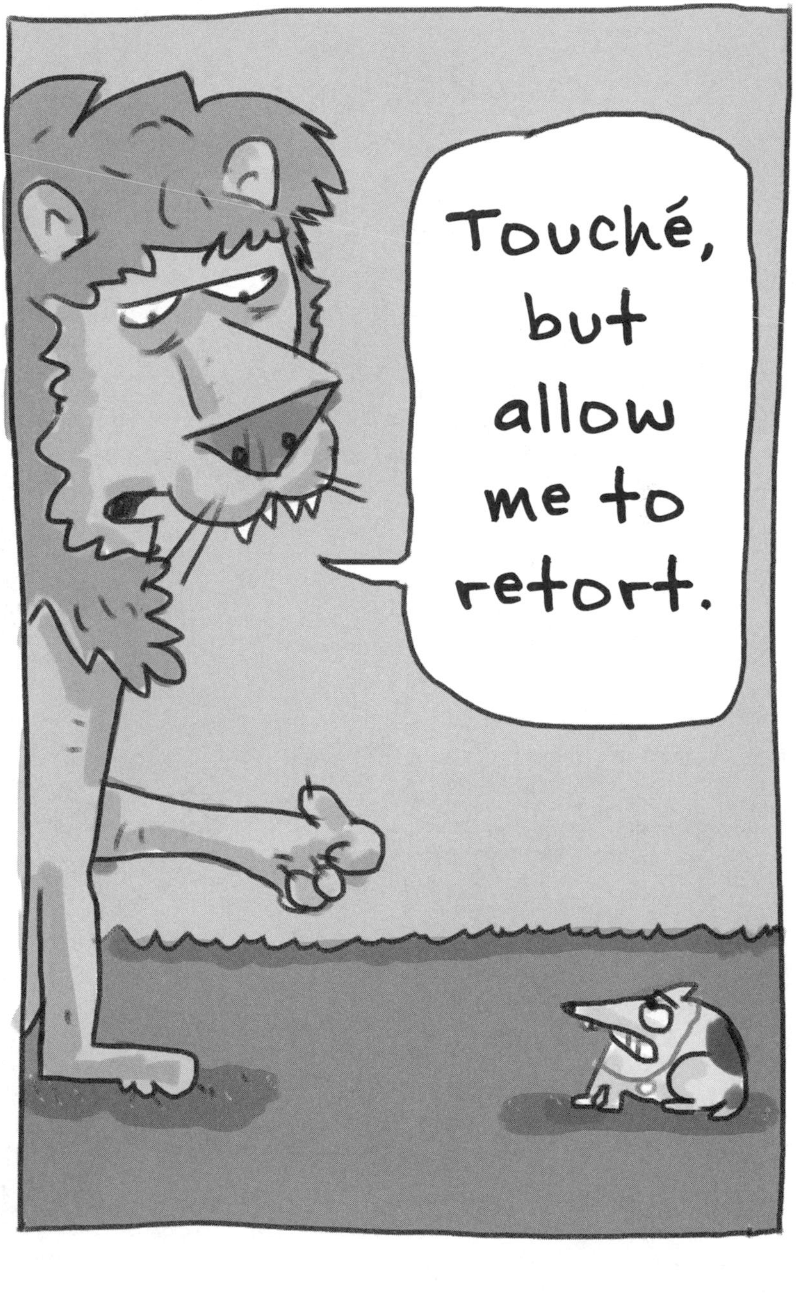
Touché, but allow me to retort.

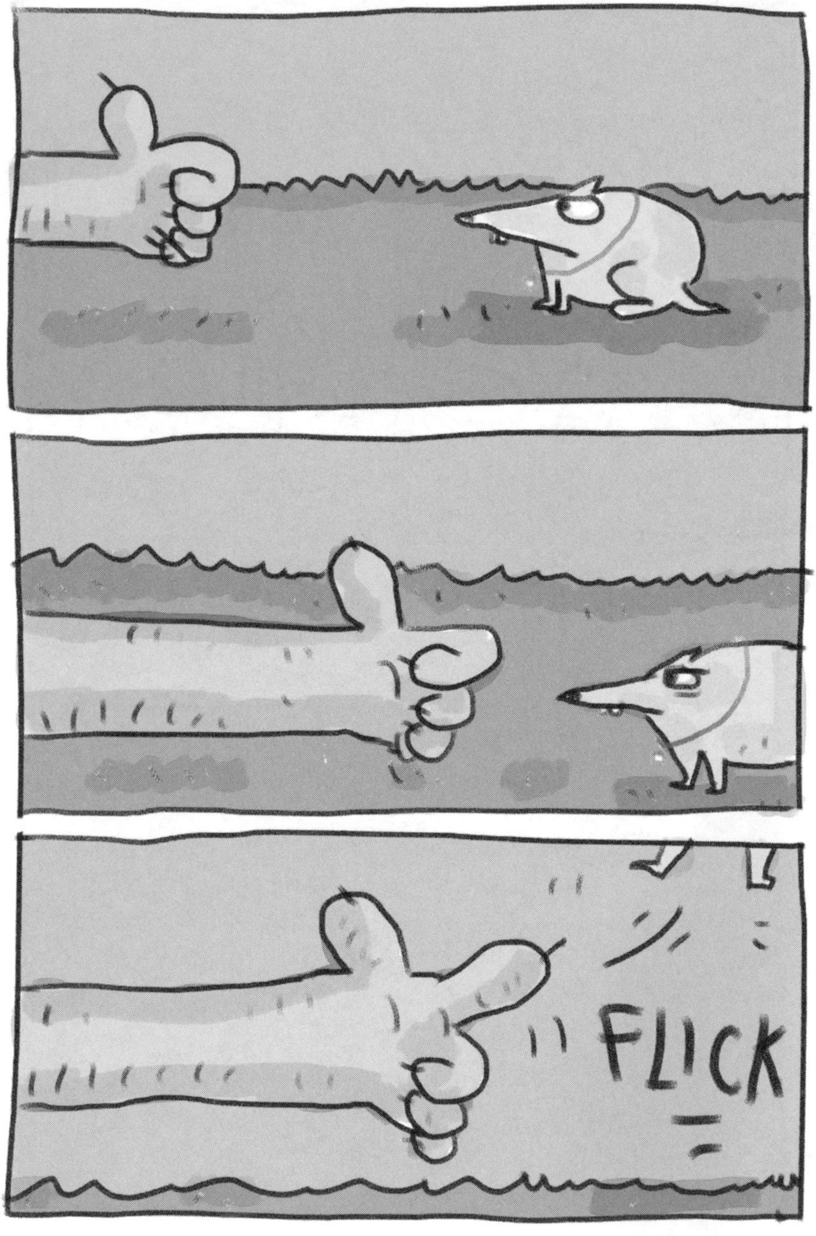
FLICK

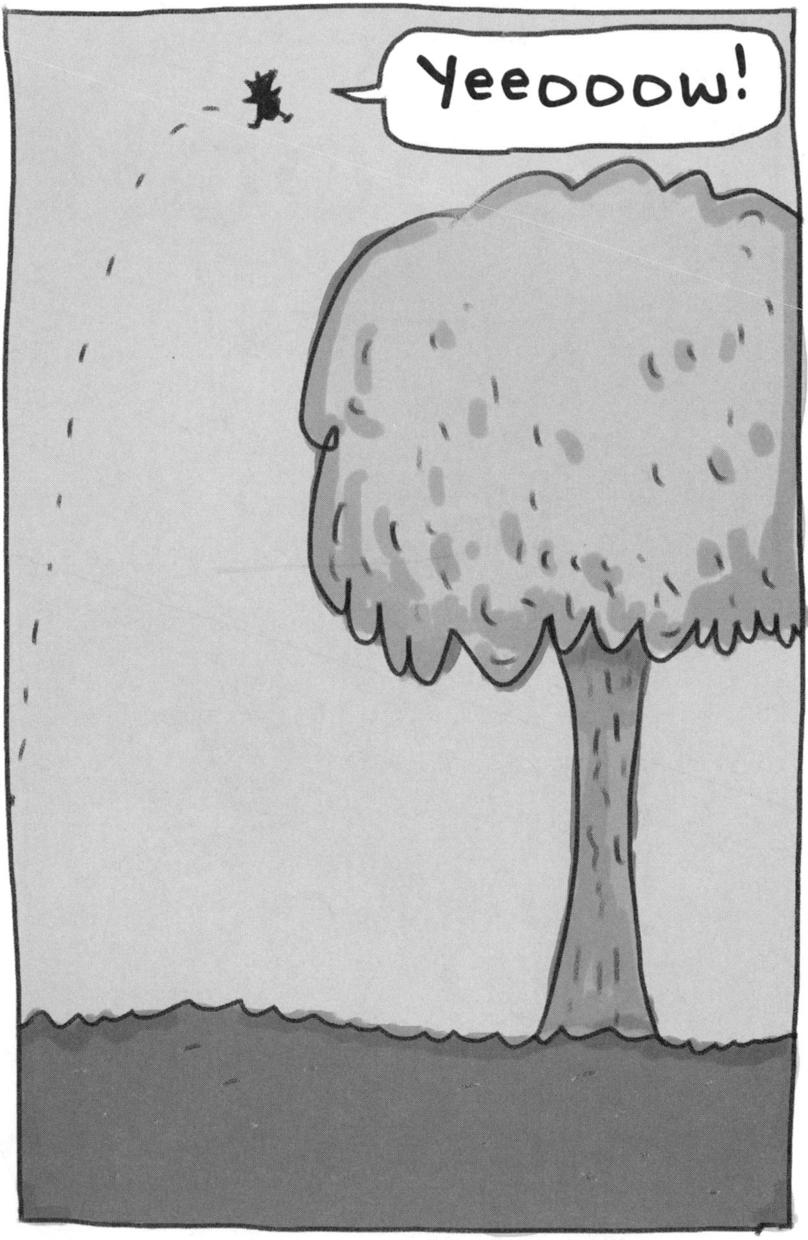
Yeeooow!

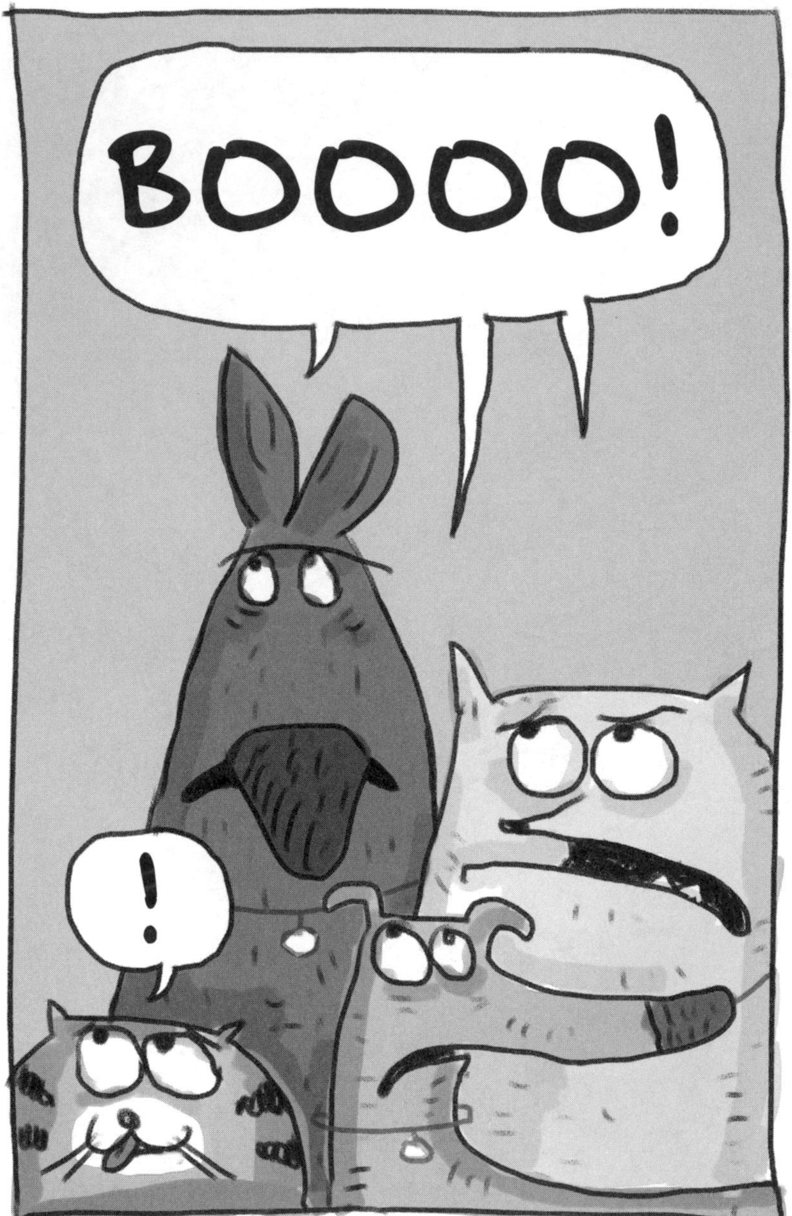
BOOOO!
!

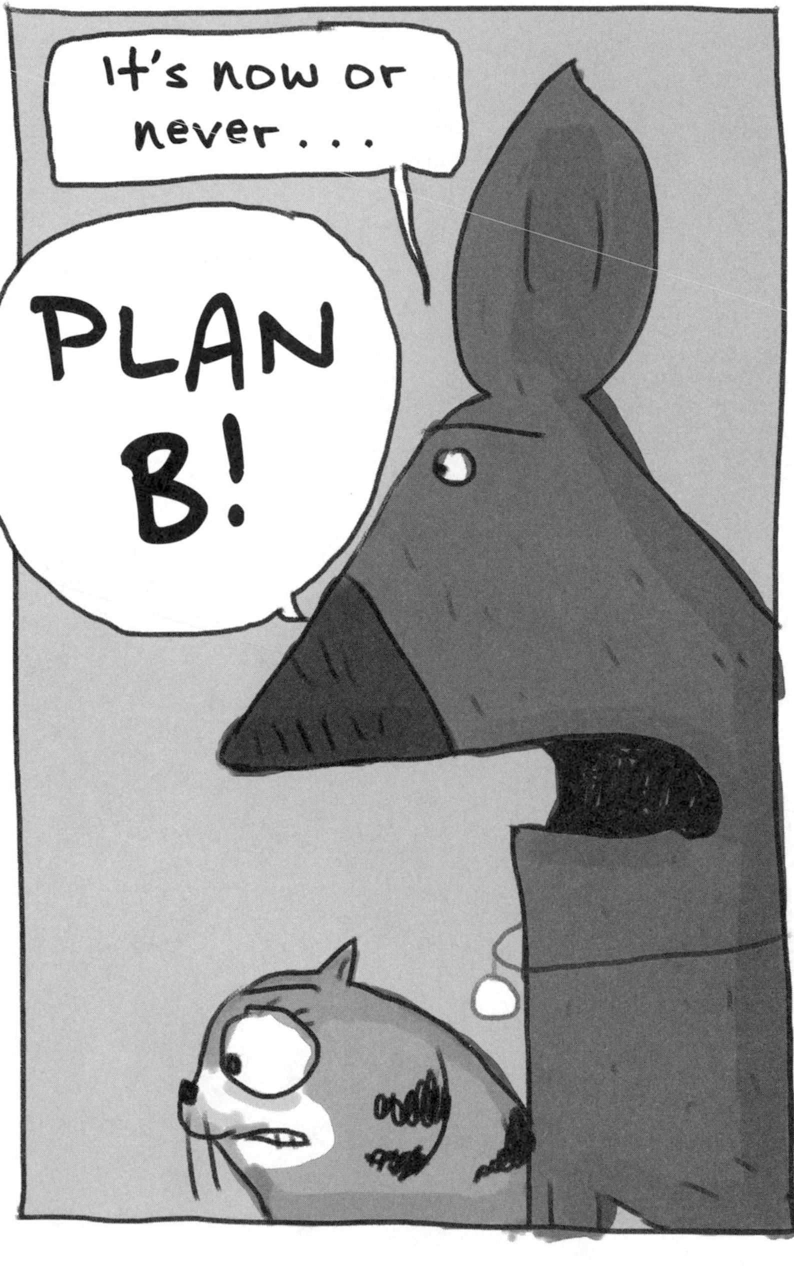
It's now or never . . .
PLAN B!

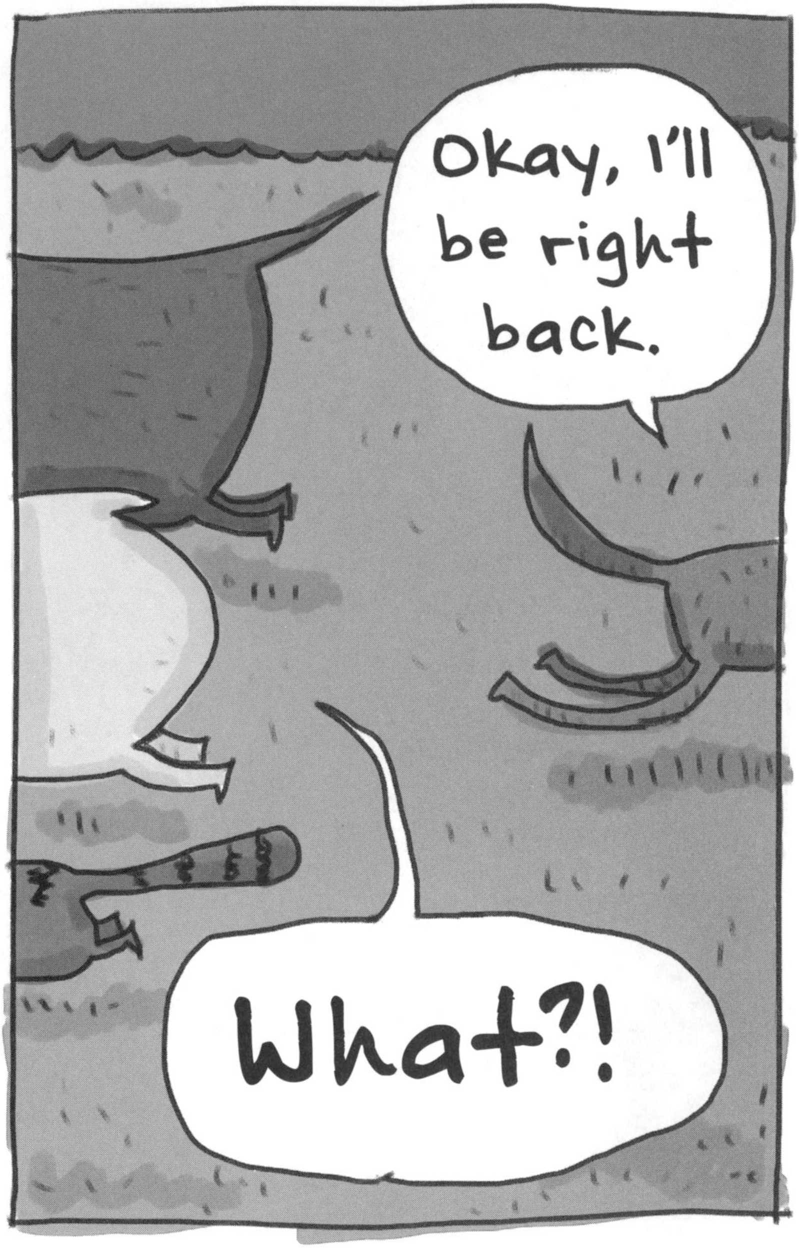
Okay, I'll be right back.
What?!

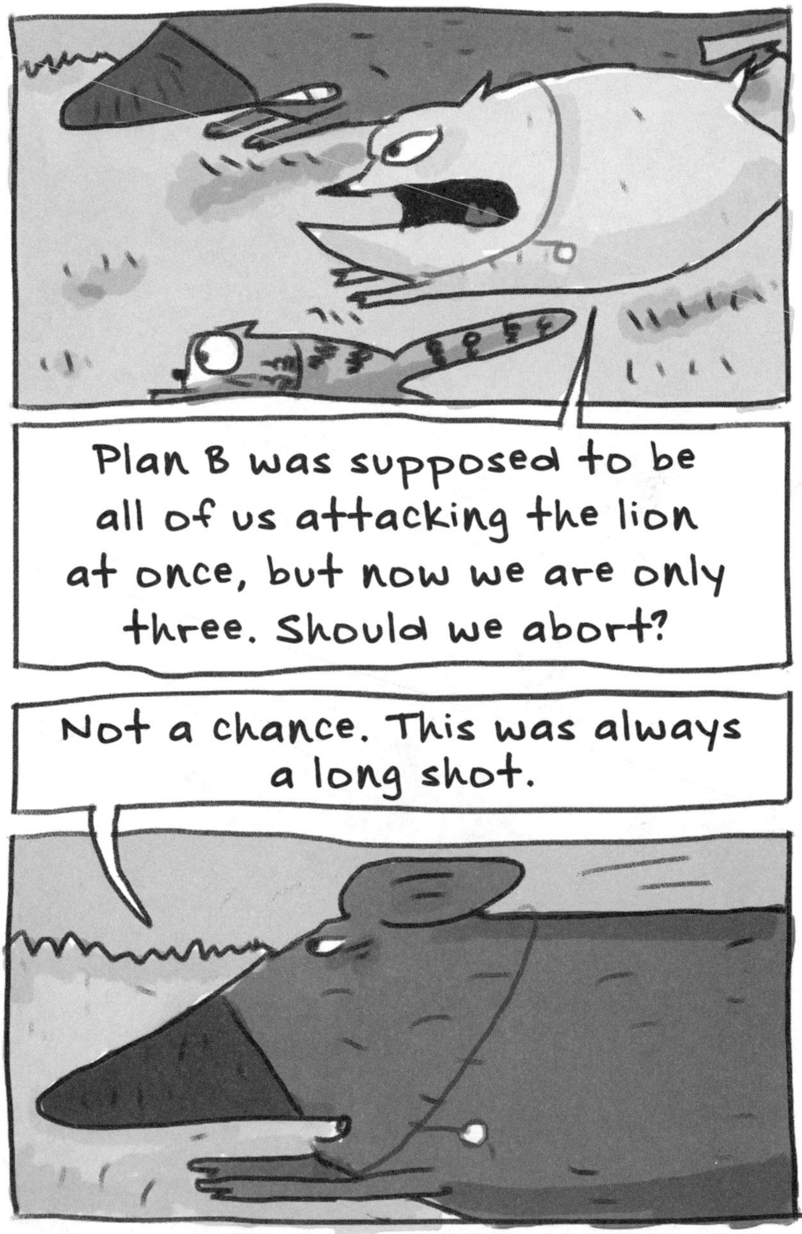
Plan B was supposed to be all of us attacking the lion at once, but now we are only three. Should we abort?
Not a chance. This was always a long shot.

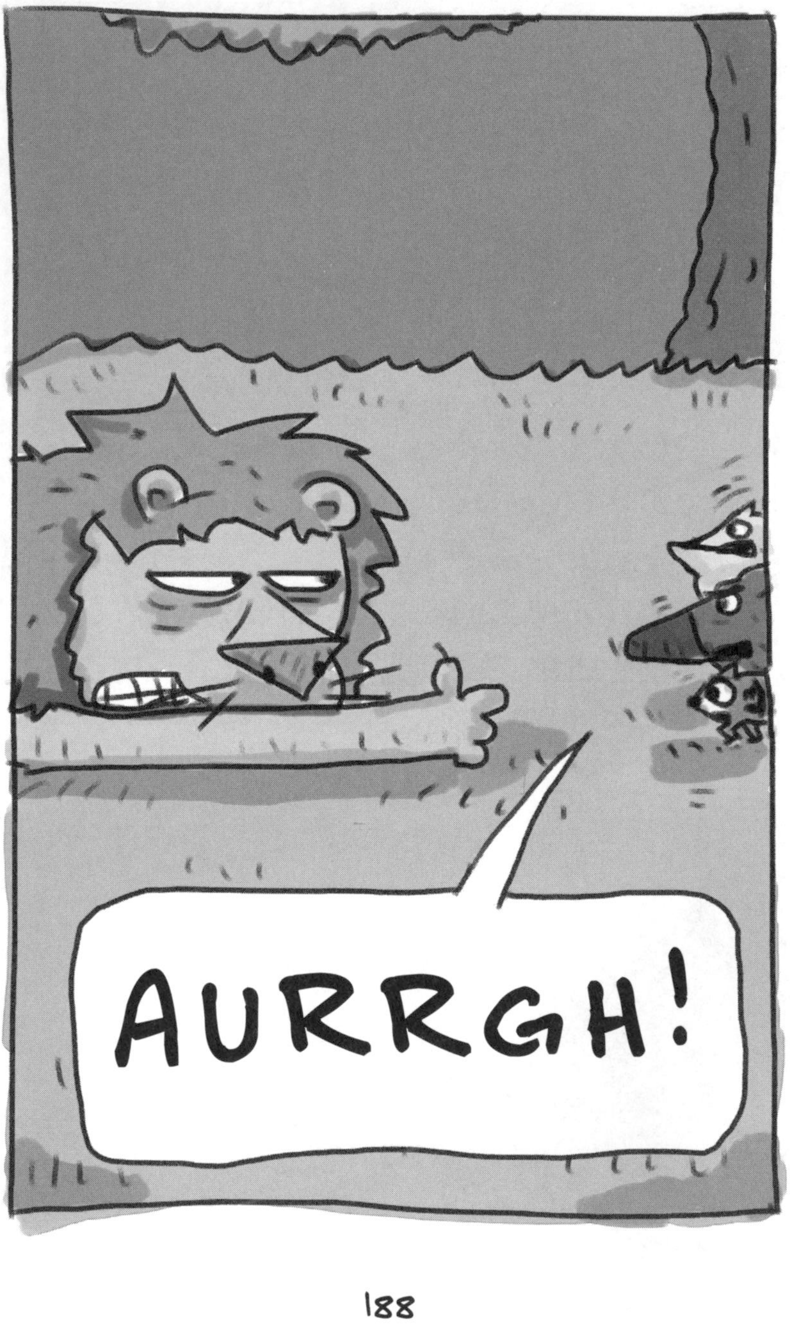
AURRGH!

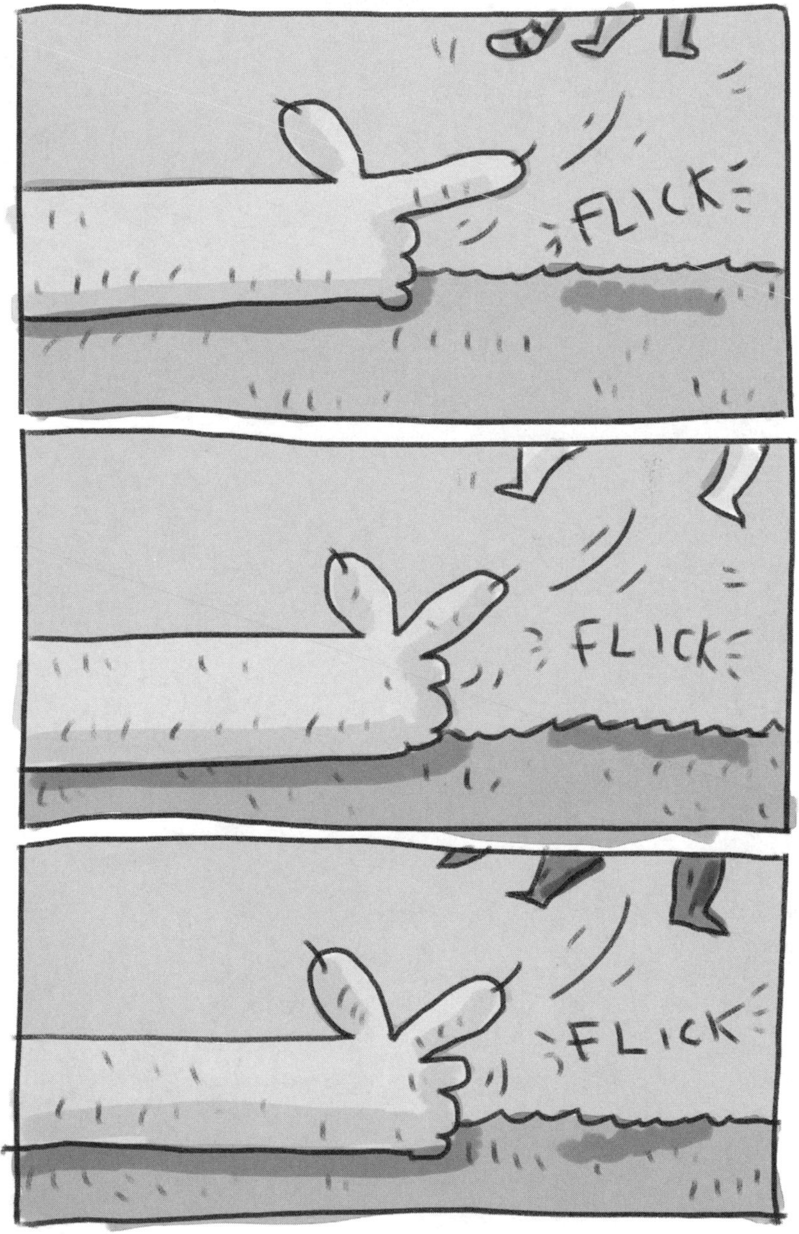
FLICK
FLICK
FLICK

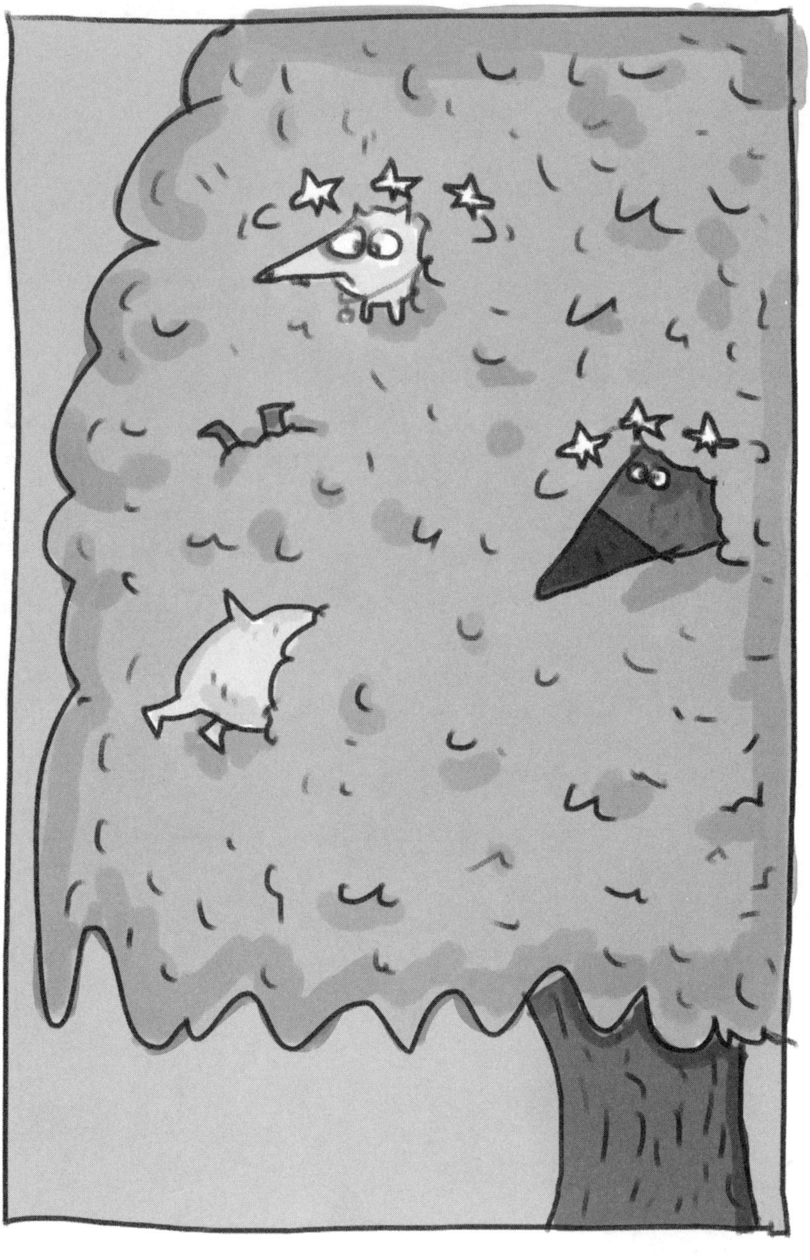

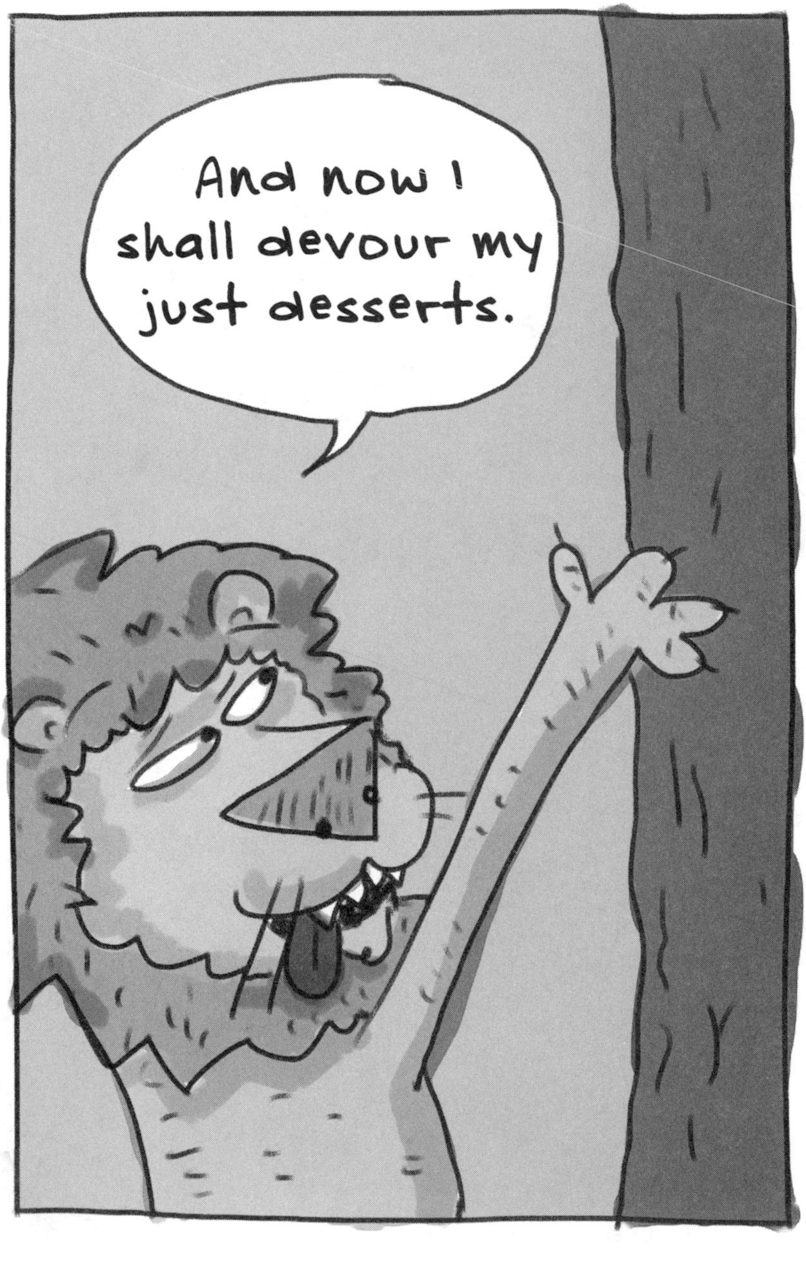
And now I shall devour my just desserts.

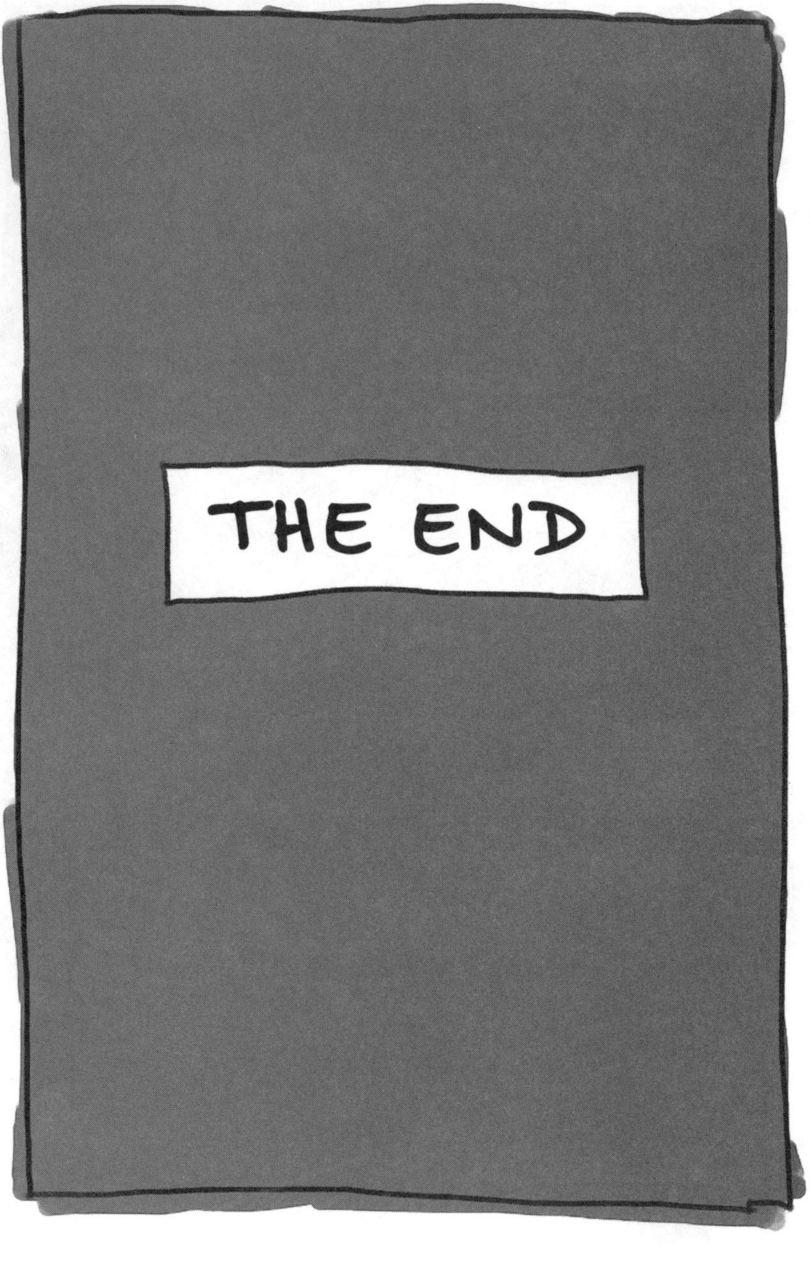
THE END

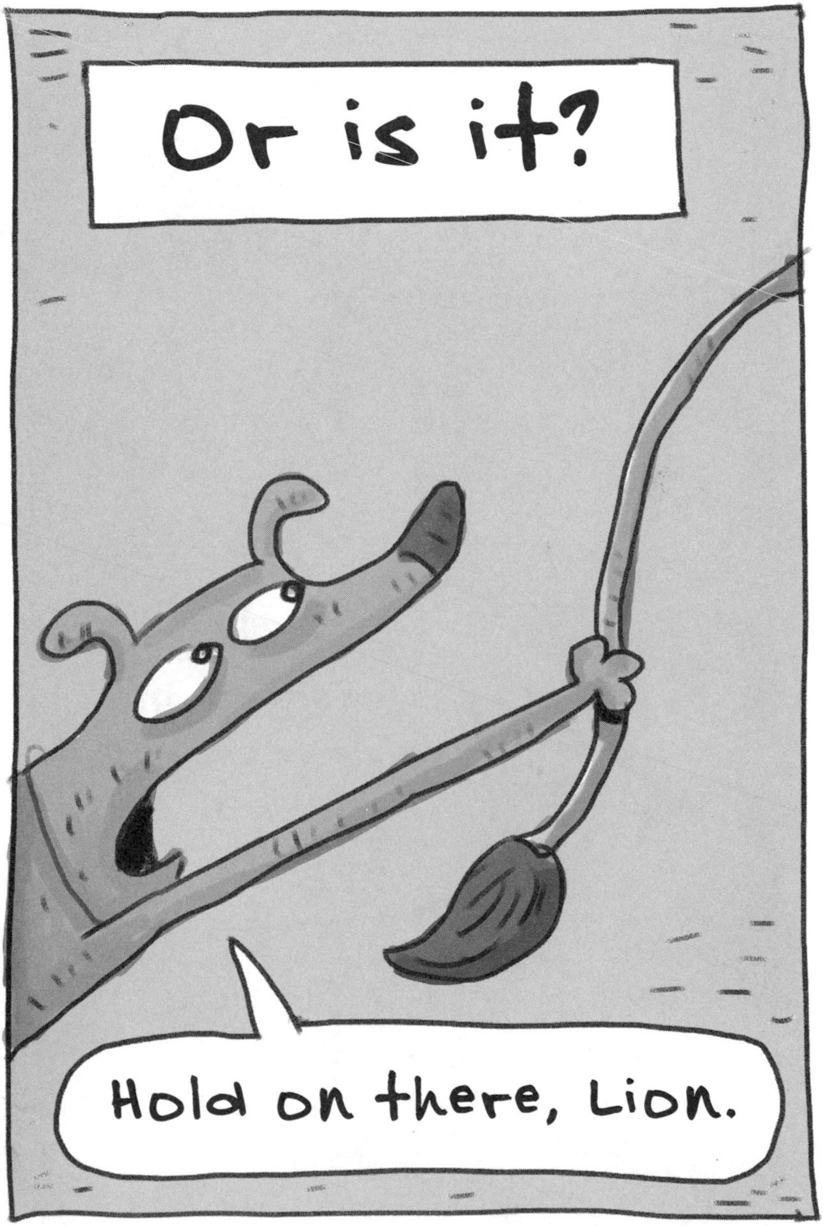
Or is it?
Hold on there, Lion.

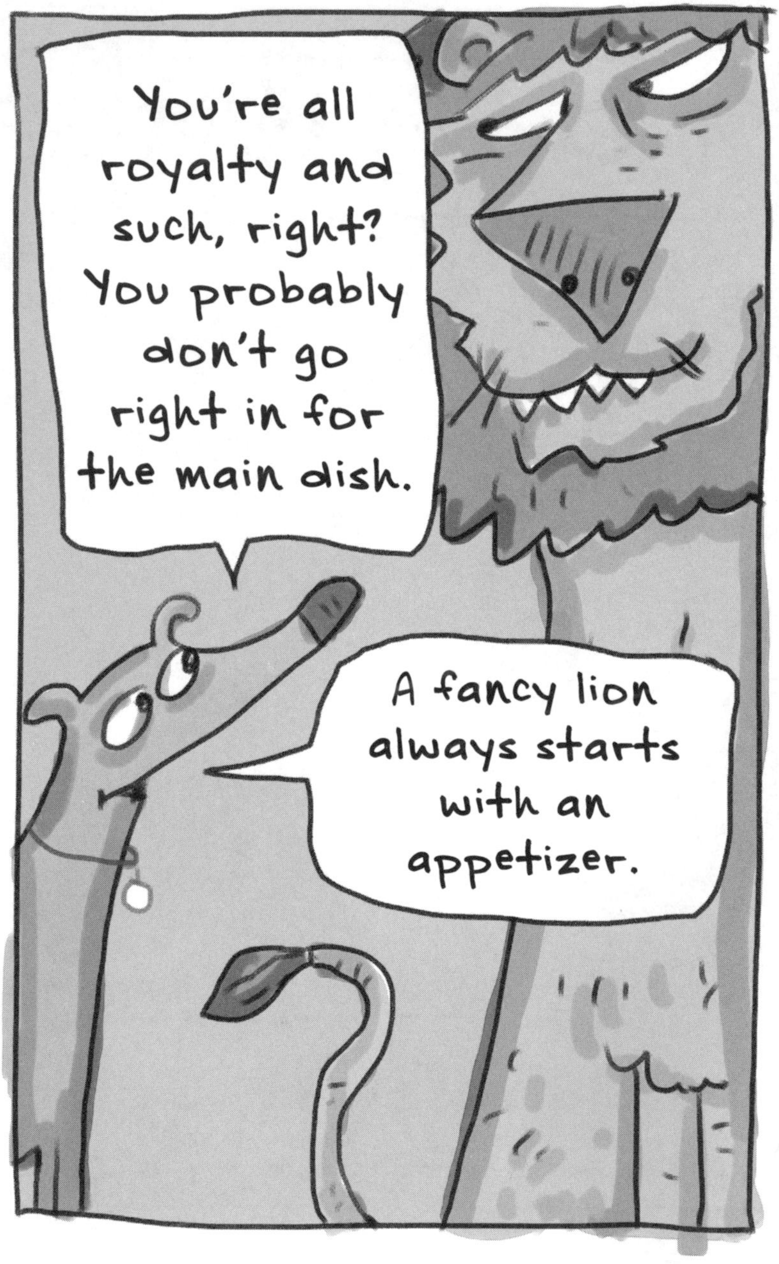
You're all royalty and such, right? You probably don't go right in for the main dish.
A fancy lion always starts with an appetizer.

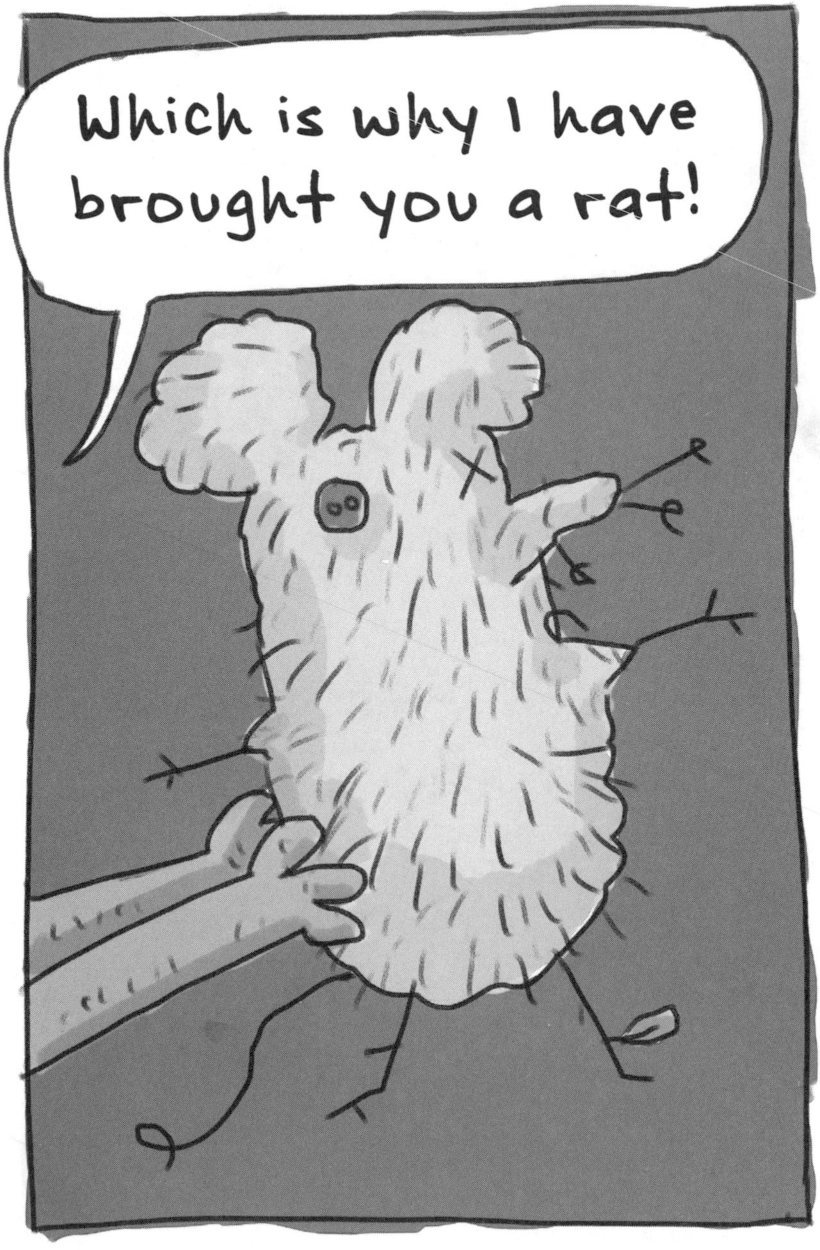
Which is why I have brought you a rat!

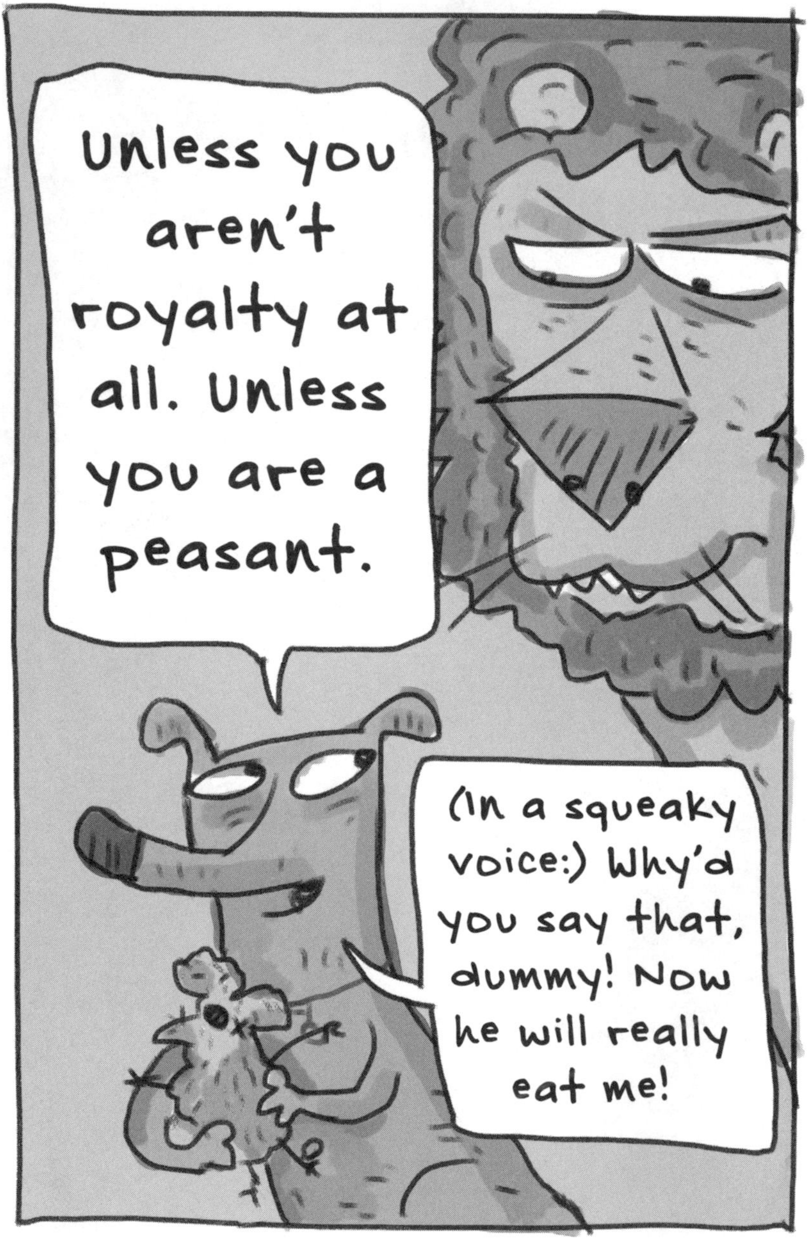
Unless you aren't royalty at all. Unless you are a peasant.
(In a squeaky voice:) Why'd you say that, dummy! Now he will really eat me!

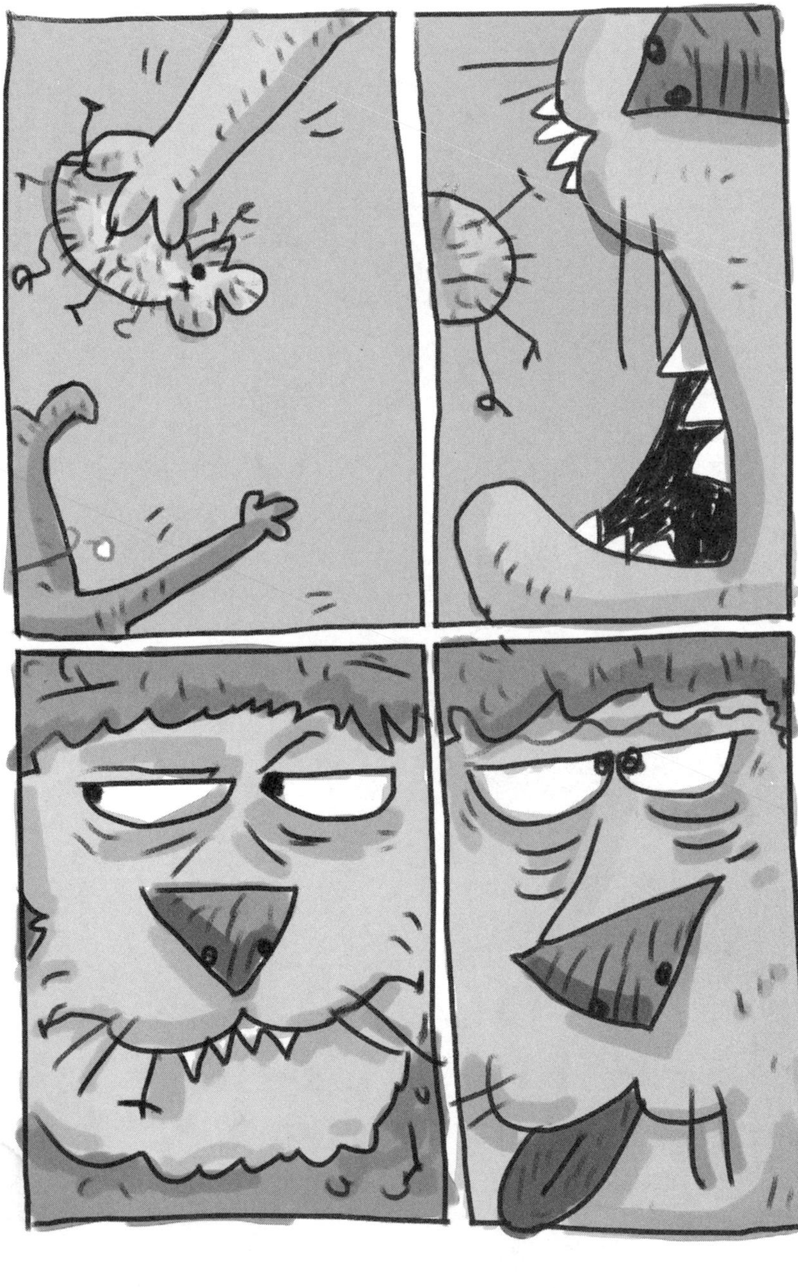

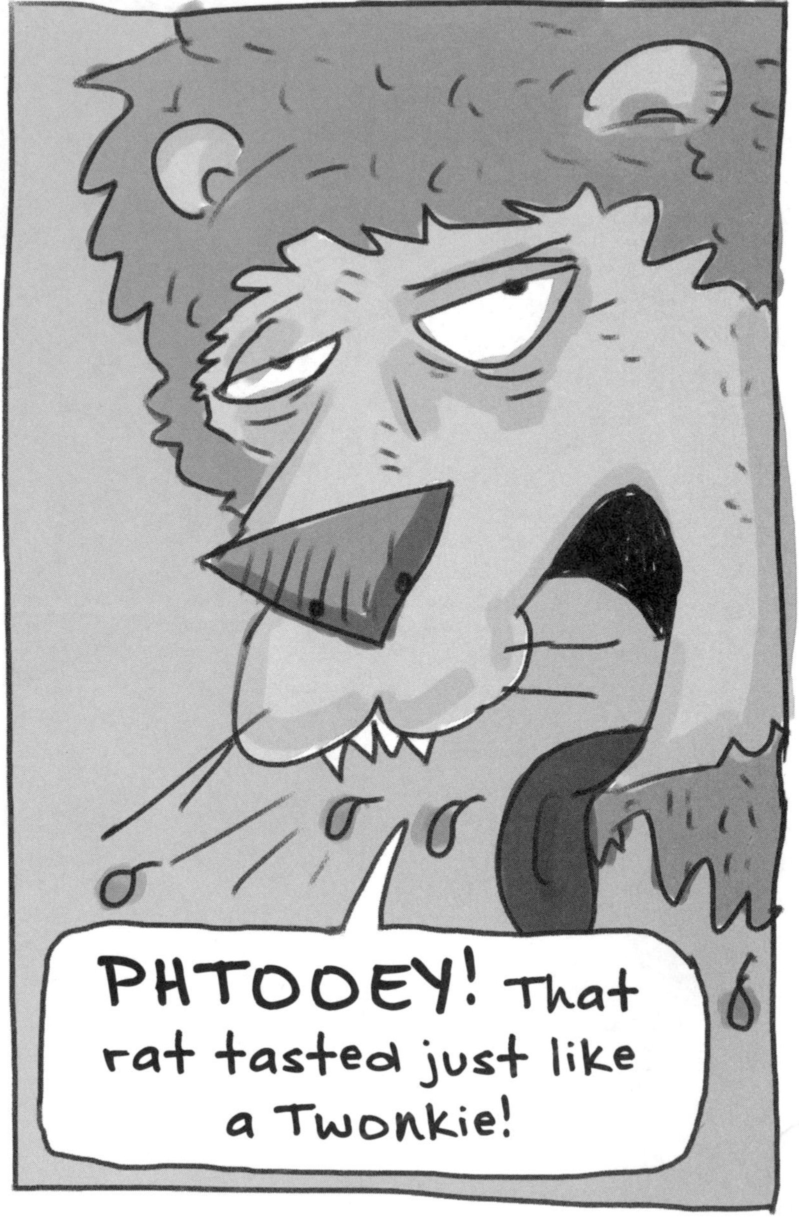
PHTOOEY! That rat tasted just like a Twonkie!

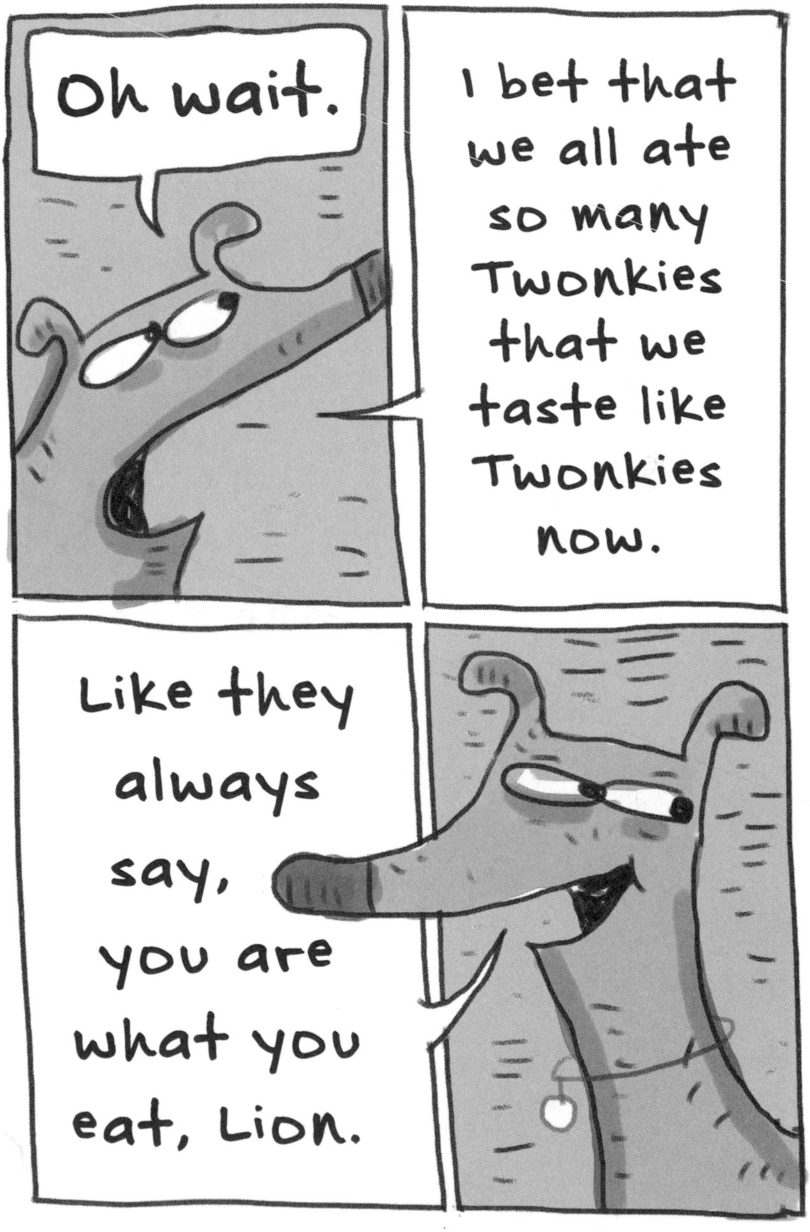
Oh wait.
I bet that we all ate so many Twonkies that we taste like Twonkies now.
Like they always say, you are what you eat, Lion.

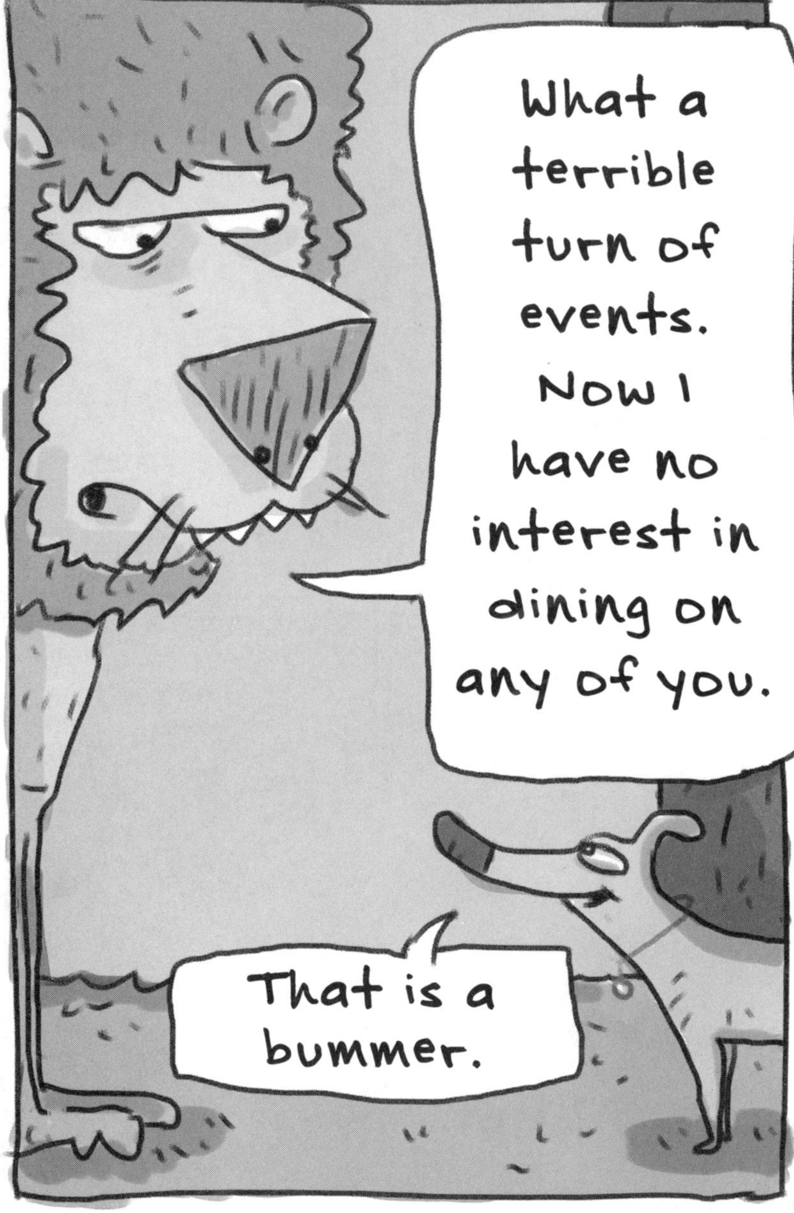
What a terrible turn of events. Now I have no interest in dining on any of you.
That is a bummer.

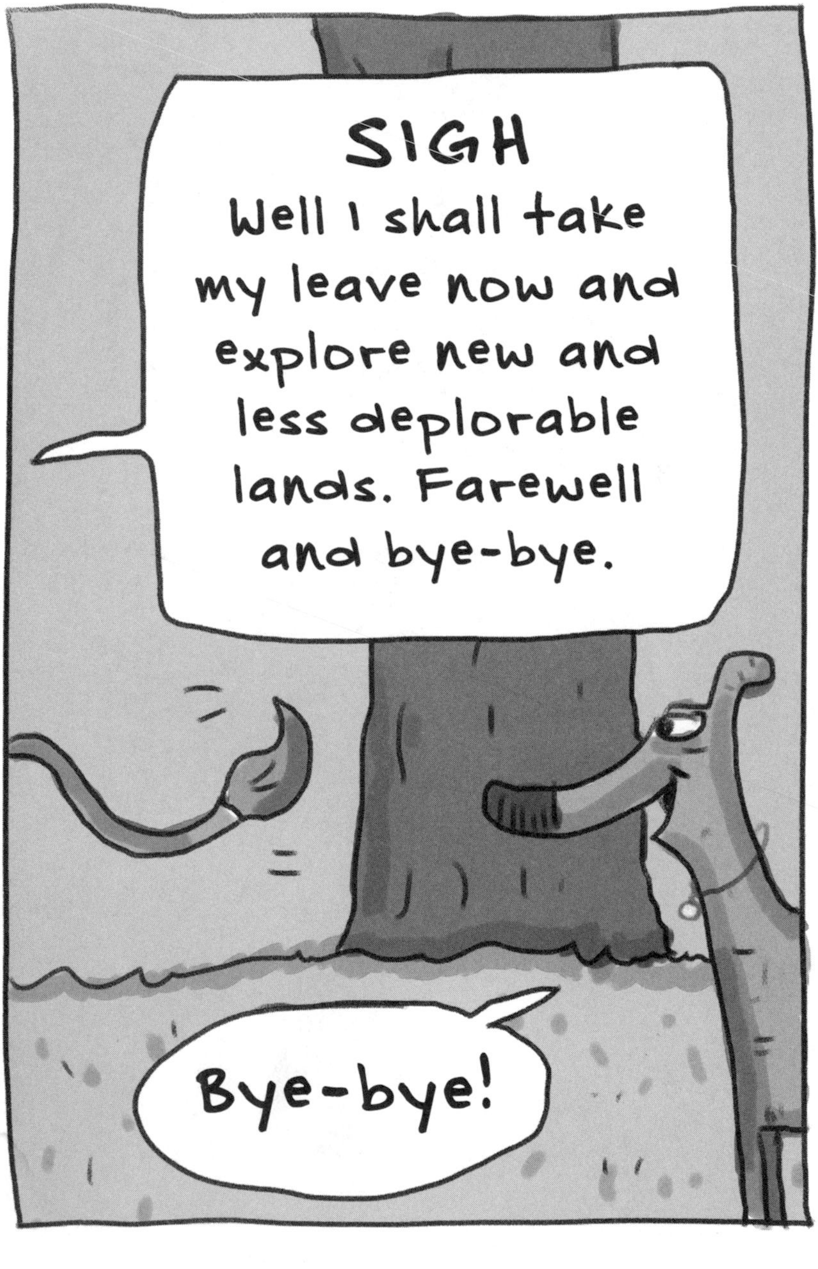
SIGH
Well I shall take my leave now and explore new and less deplorable lands. Farewell and bye-bye.
Bye-bye!

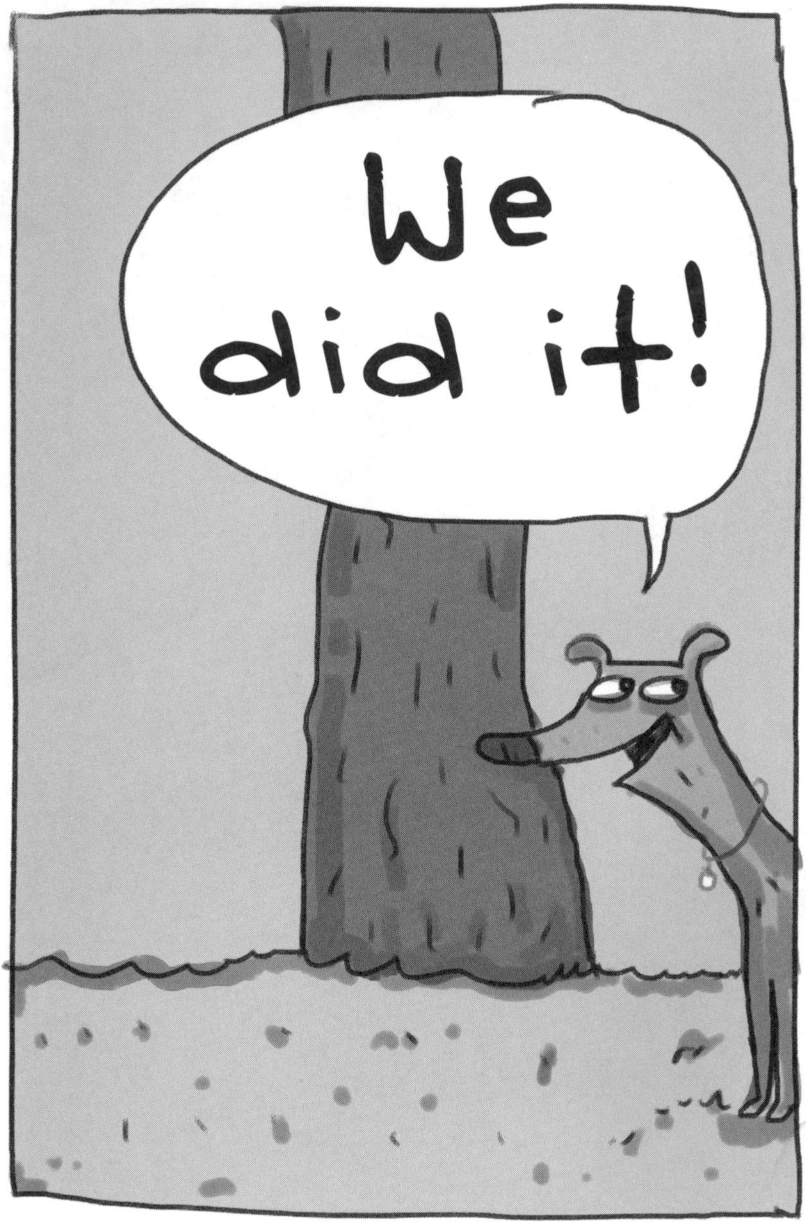
We did it!

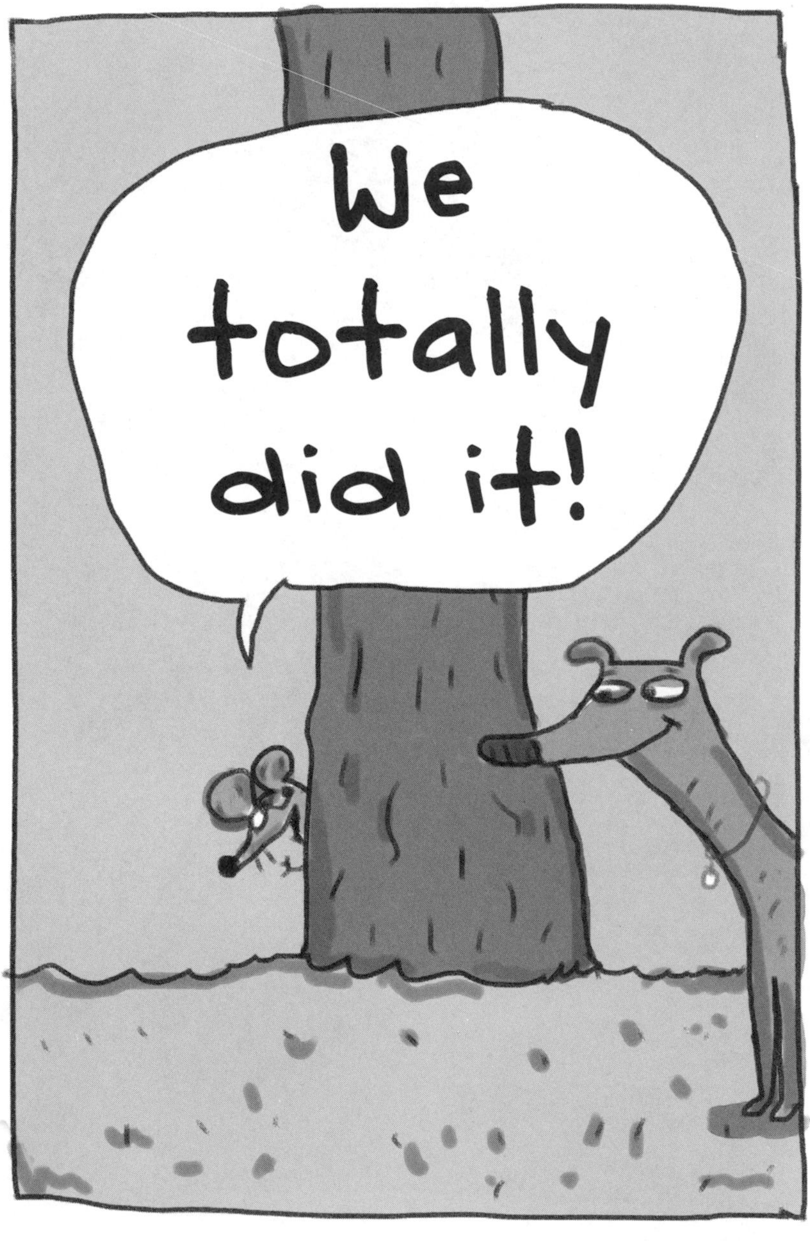
We totally did it!

Scene
Twenty-Two

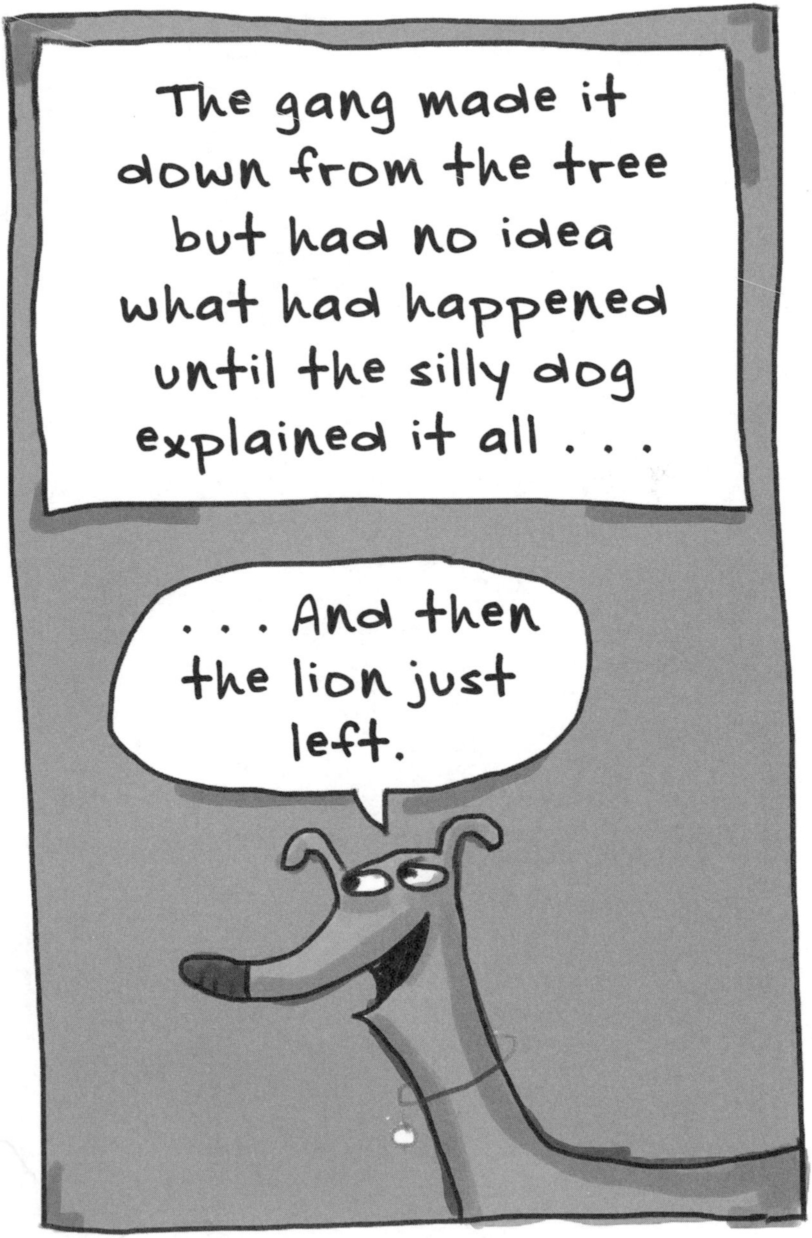
The gang made it down from the tree but had no idea what had happened until the silly dog explained it all . . .
. . . And then the lion just left.

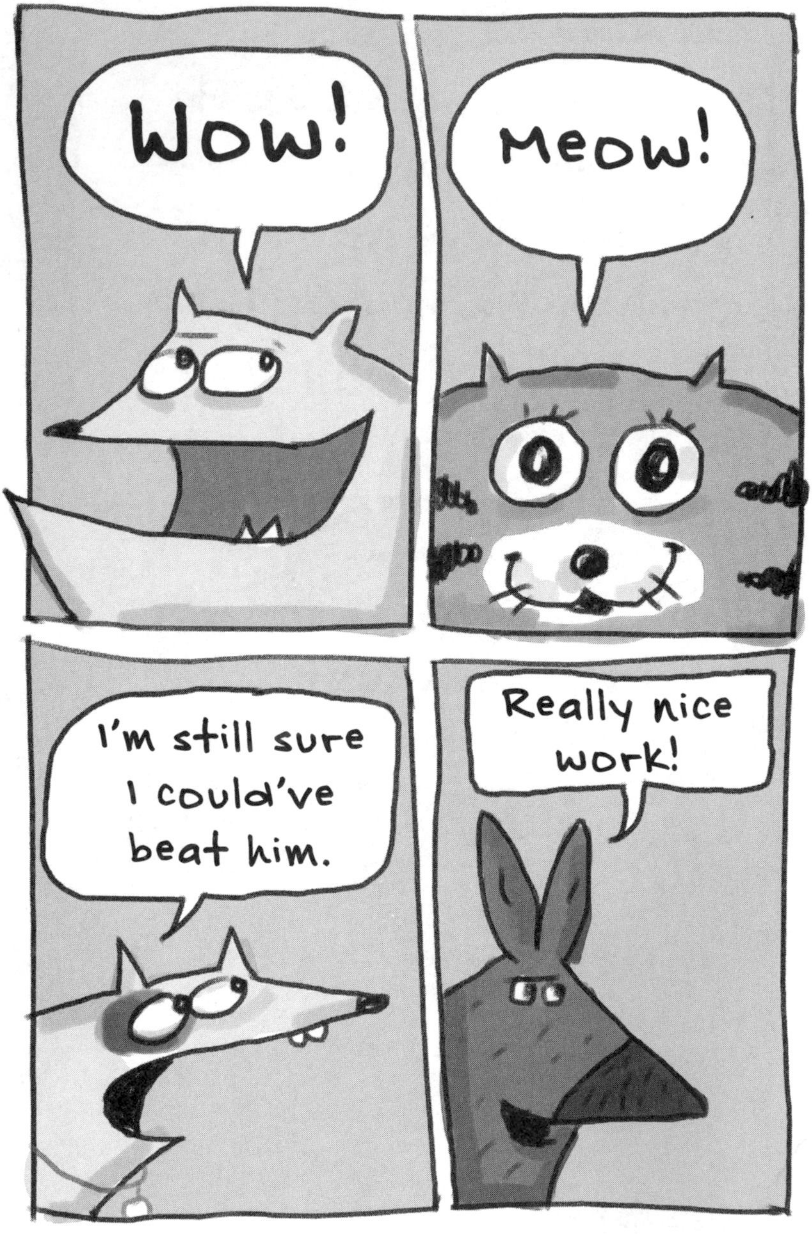
Wow!
Meow!
I'm still sure I could've beat him.
Really nice work!

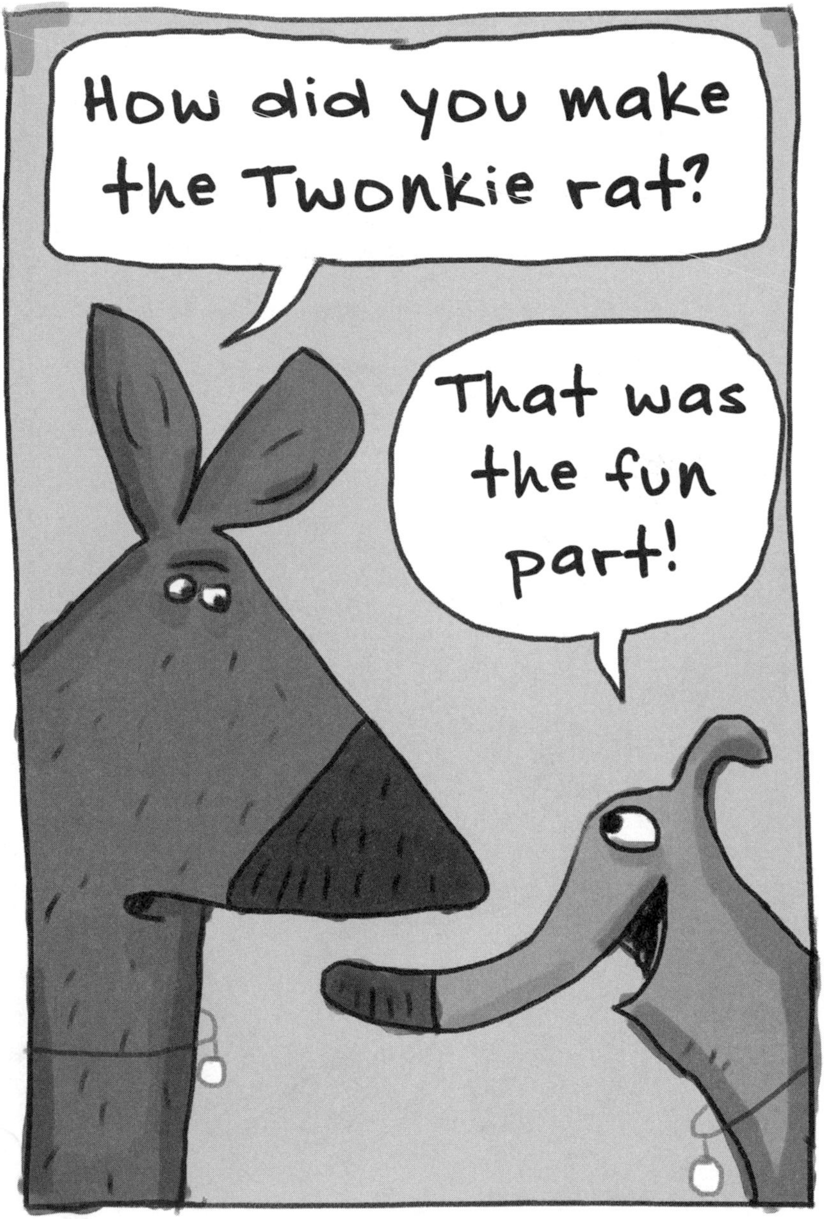
How did you make the Twonkie rat?
That was the fun part!

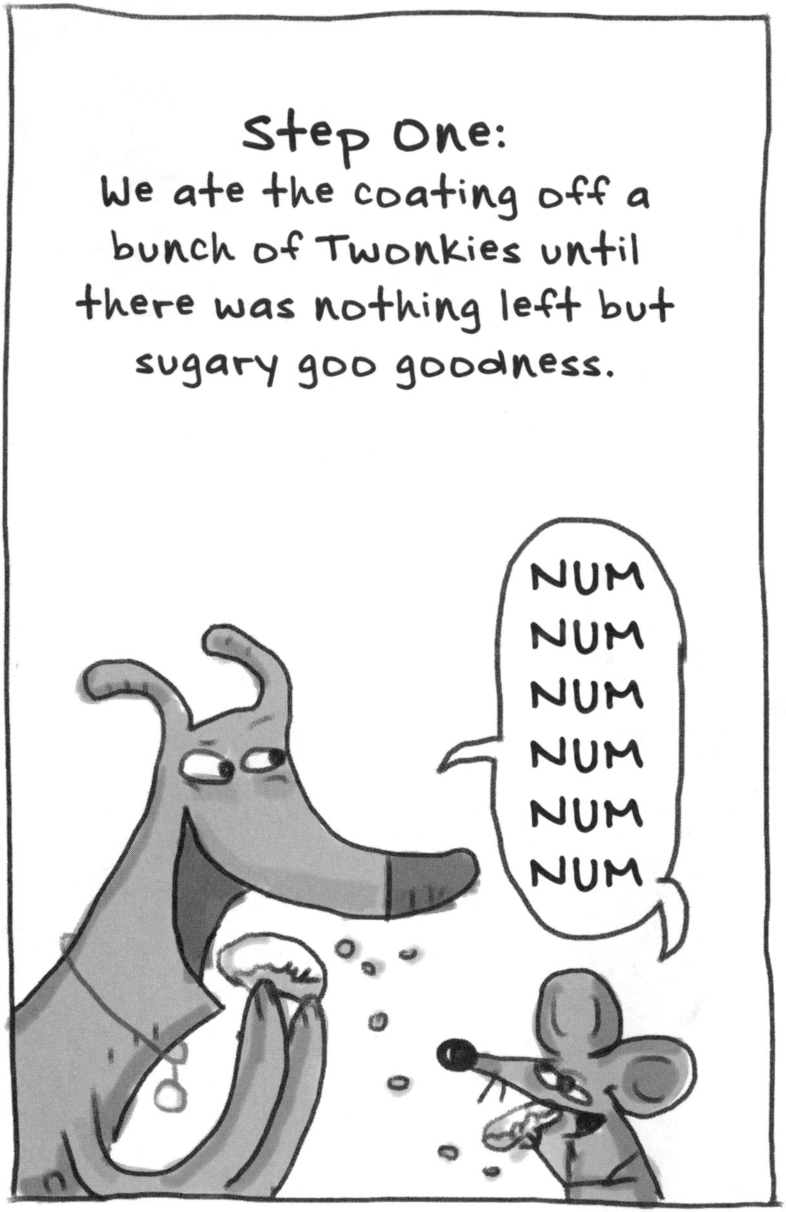
Step One:
We ate the coating off a bunch of Twonkies until there was nothing left but sugary goo goodness.
NUM NUM NUM NUM NUM NUM

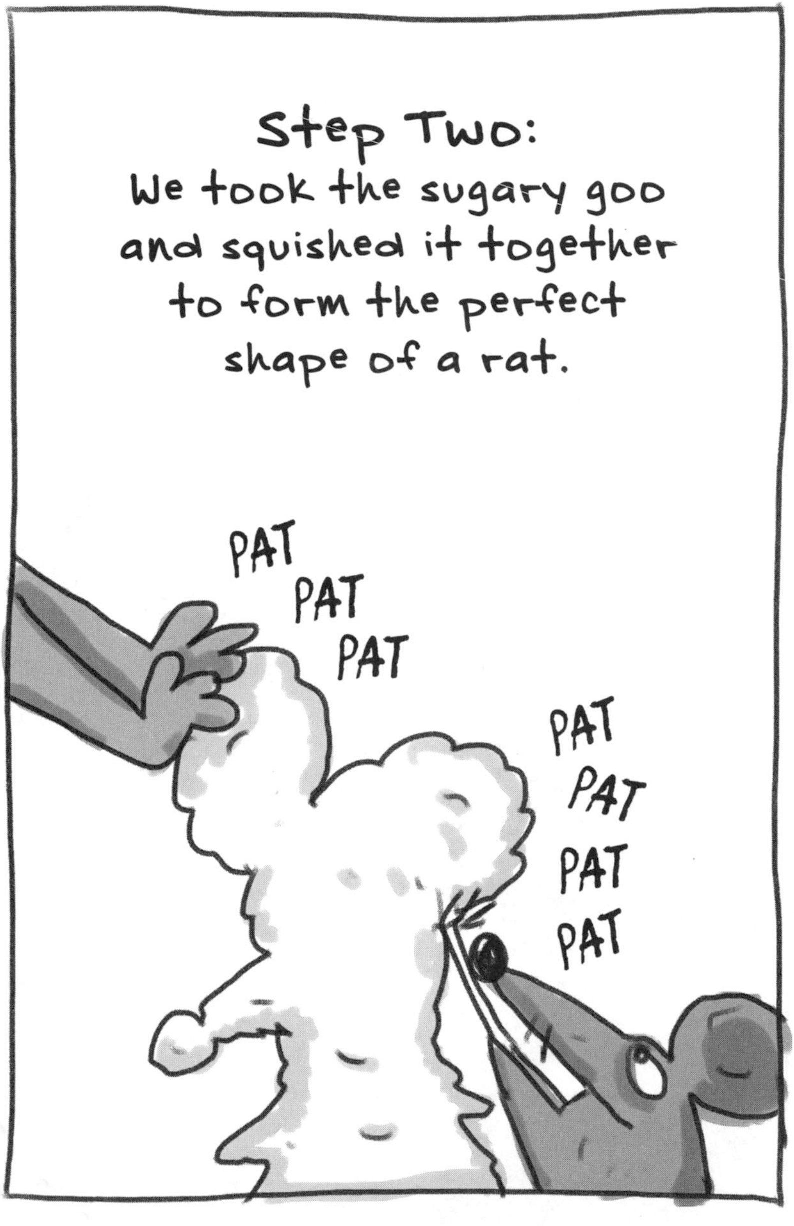
Step Two:
We took the sugary goo and squished it together to form the perfect shape of a rat.
PAT PAT PAT
PAT PAT PAT PAT

Step Three:
We added eyes.

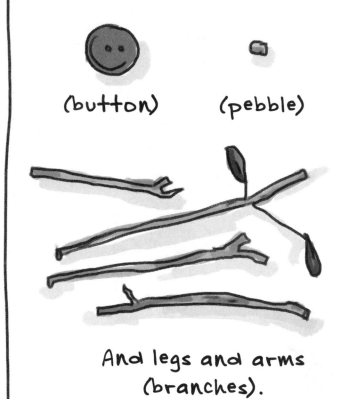

(button)   (pebble)

And legs and arms
(branches).

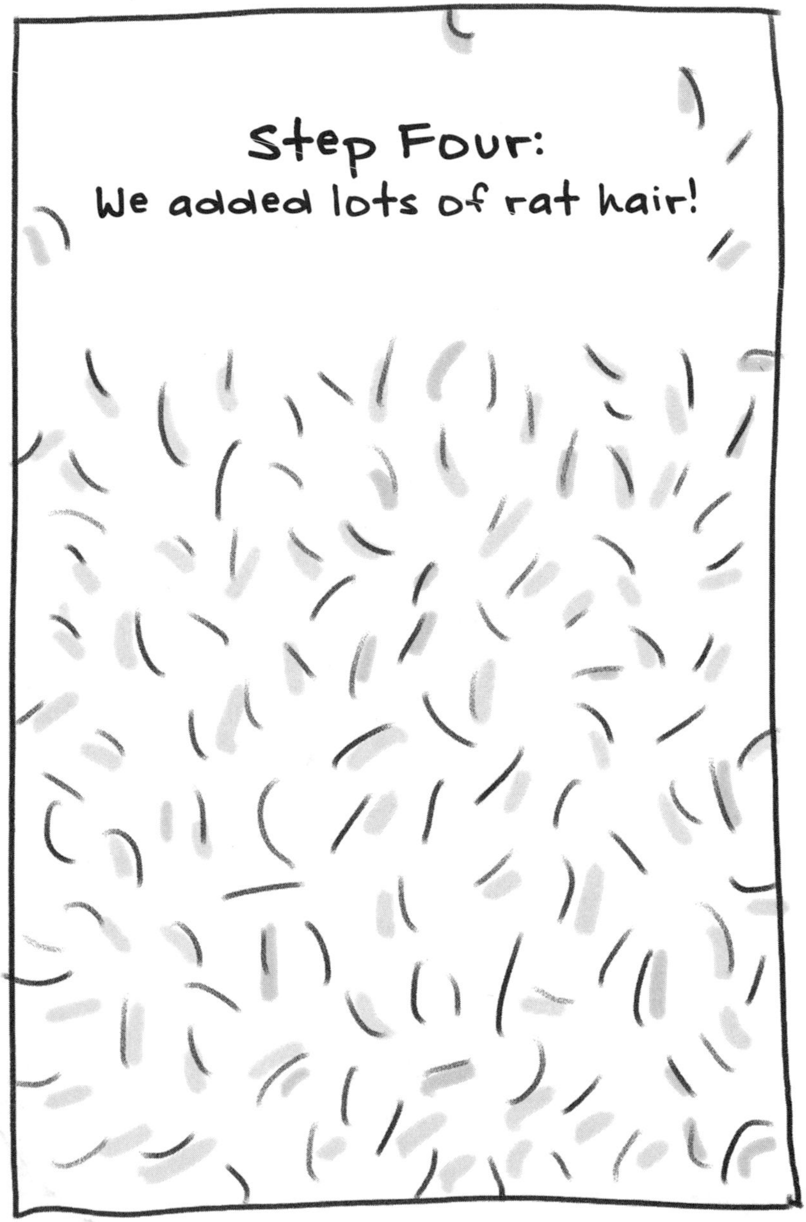
Step Four:
We added lots of rat hair!

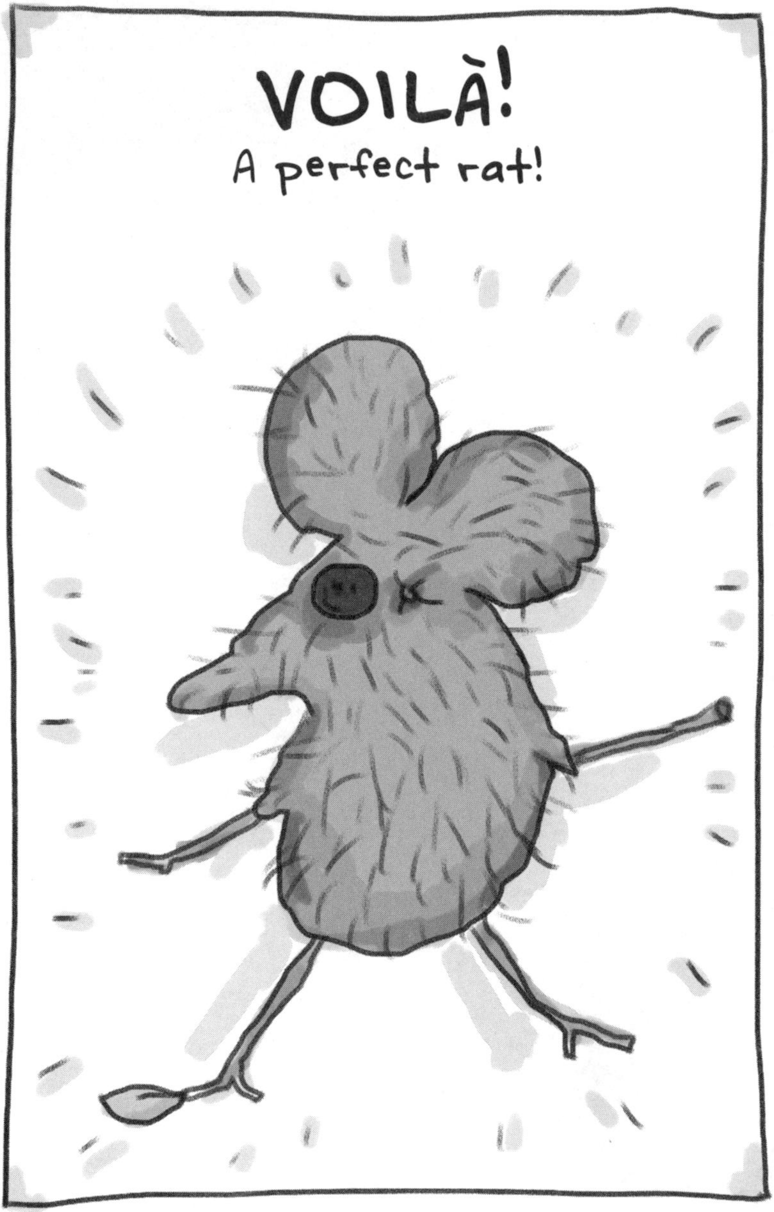
VOILÀ!
A perfect rat!

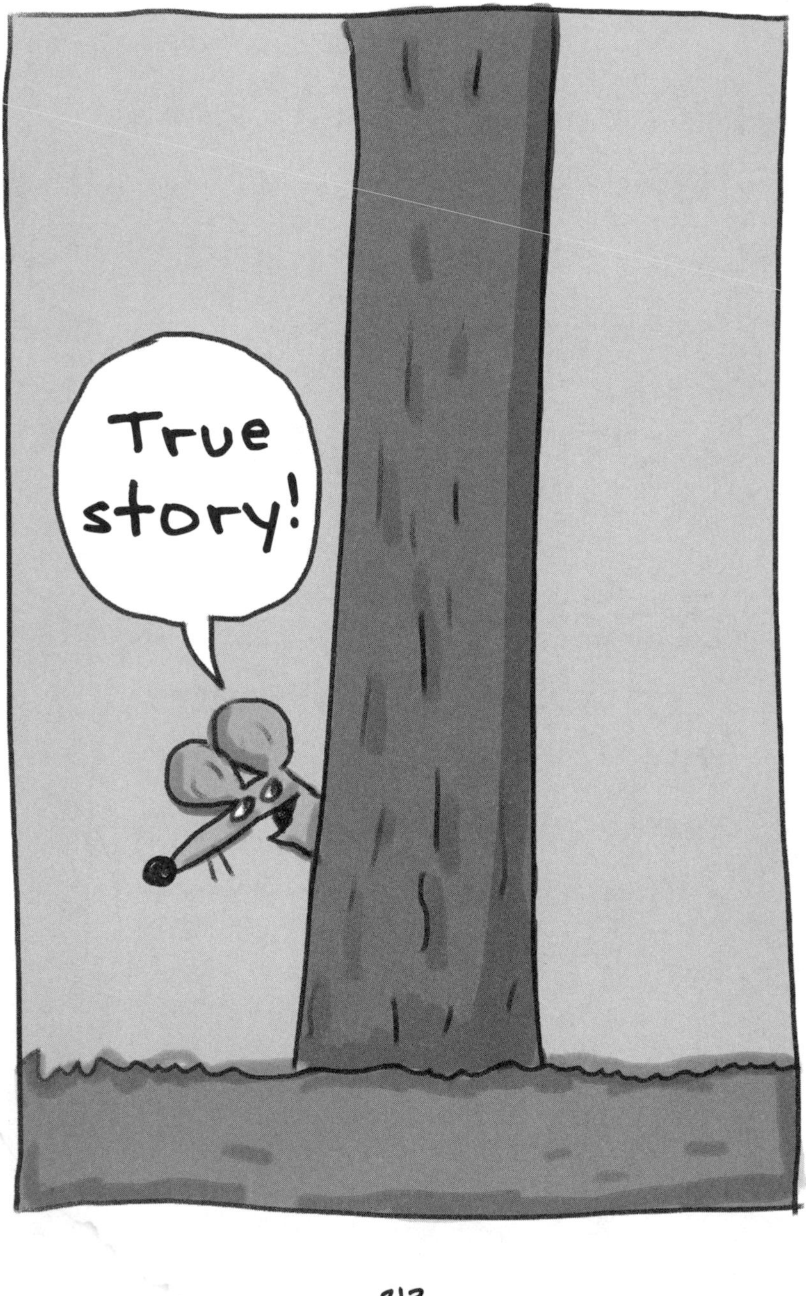
True story!

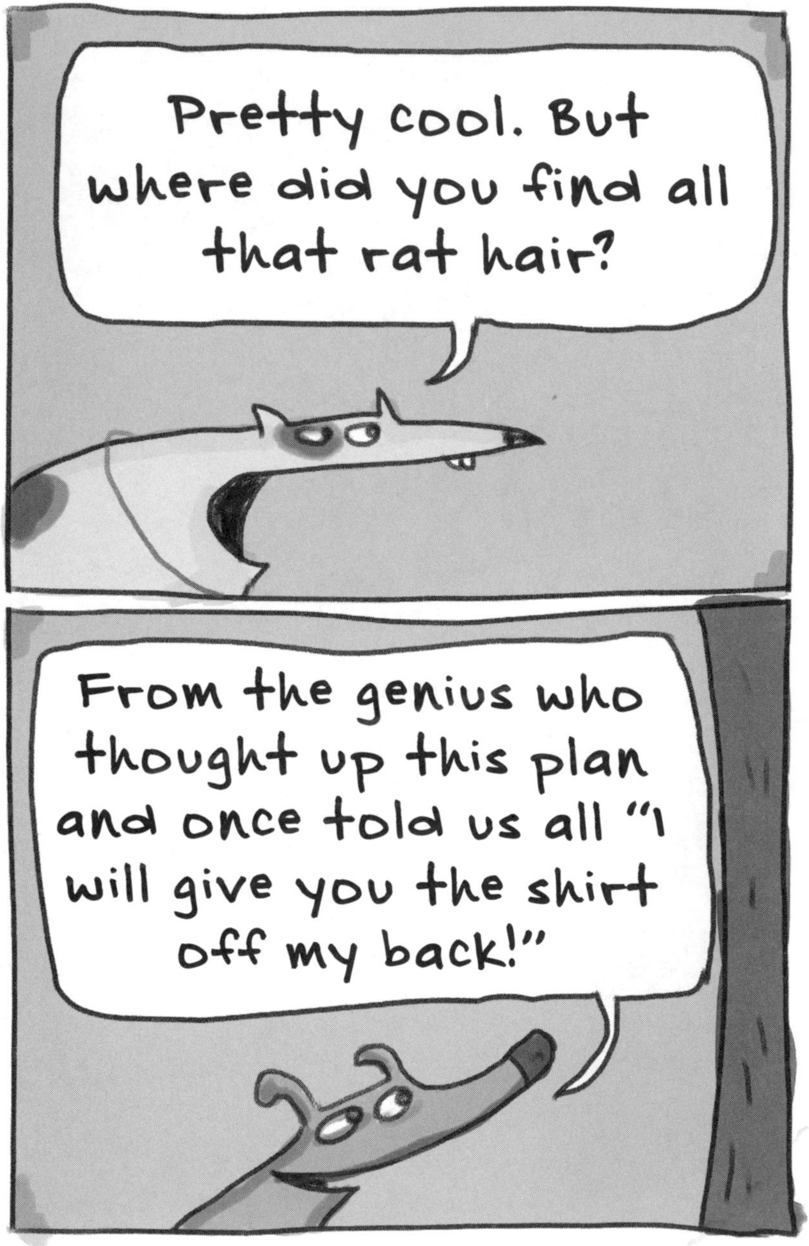
Pretty cool. But where did you find all that rat hair?
From the genius who thought up this plan and once told us all "I will give you the shirt off my back!"

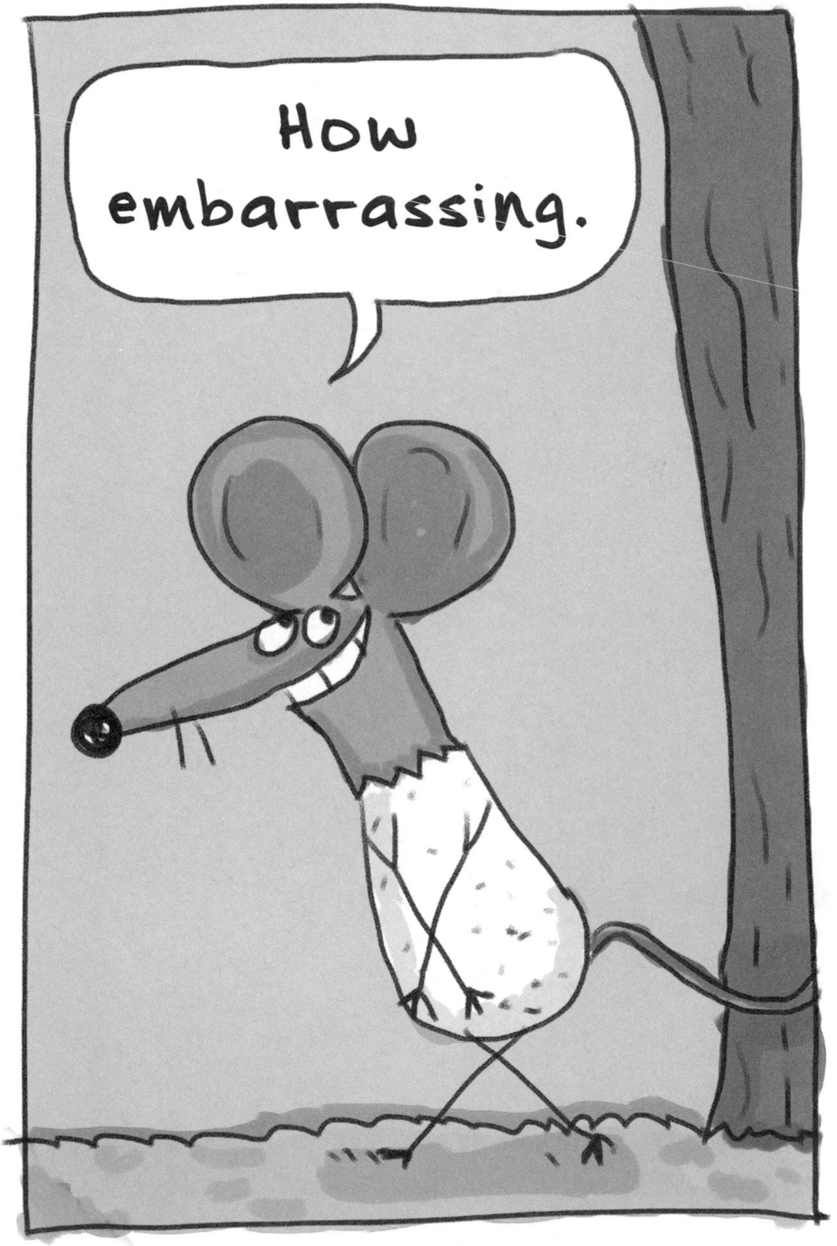
How embarrassing.

Scene
Twenty-Three

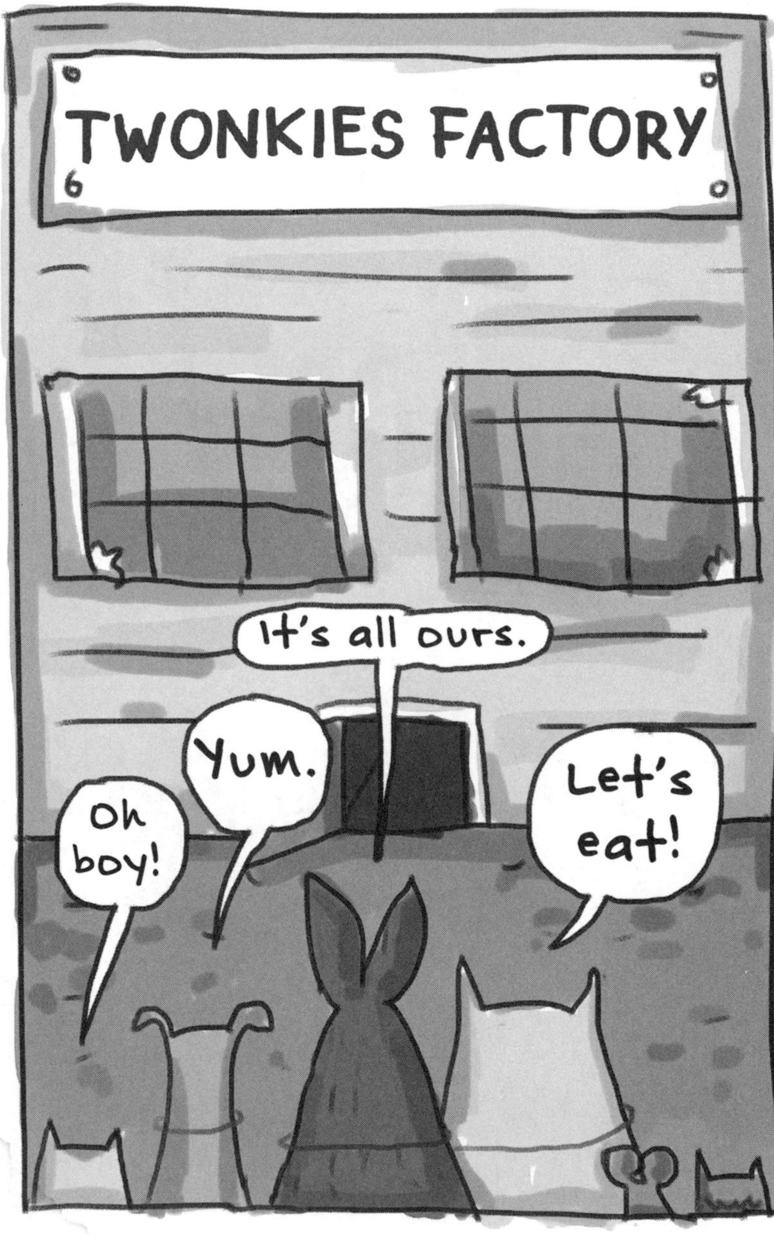
TWONKIES FACTORY
It's all ours.
Oh boy!
Yum.
Let's eat!

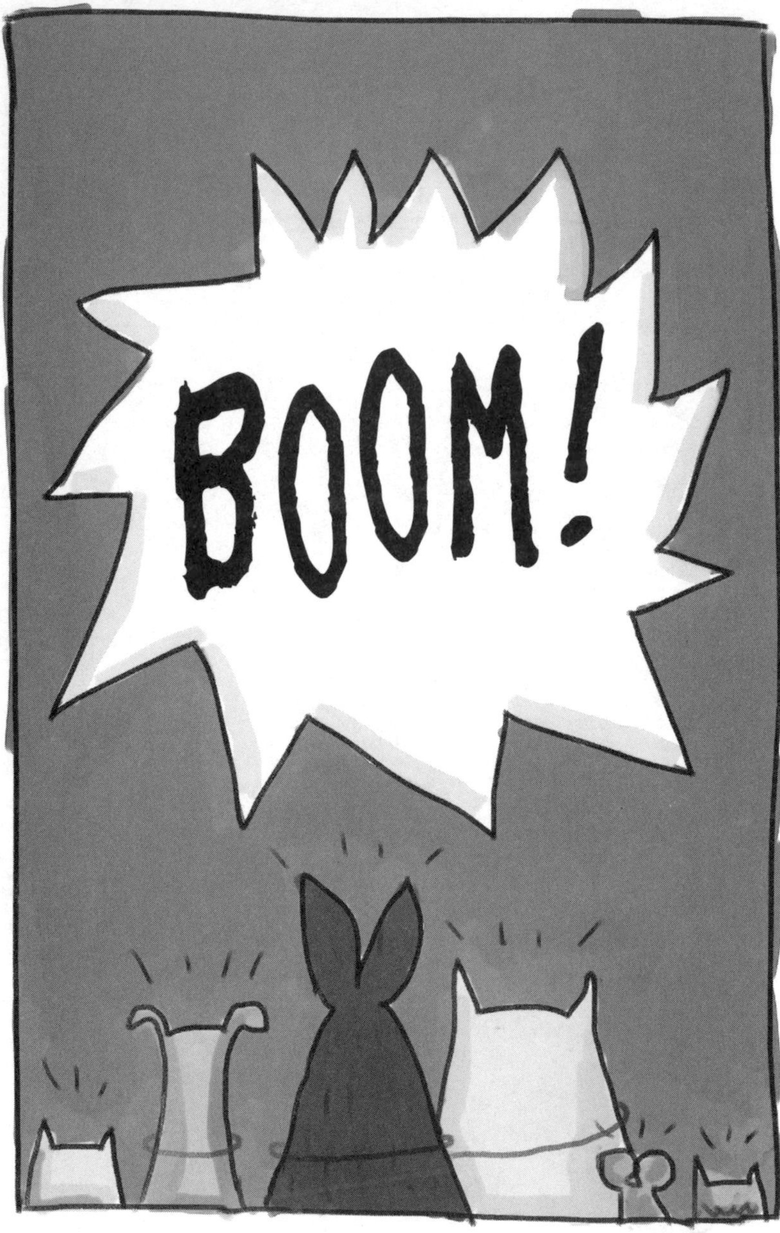
BOOM!

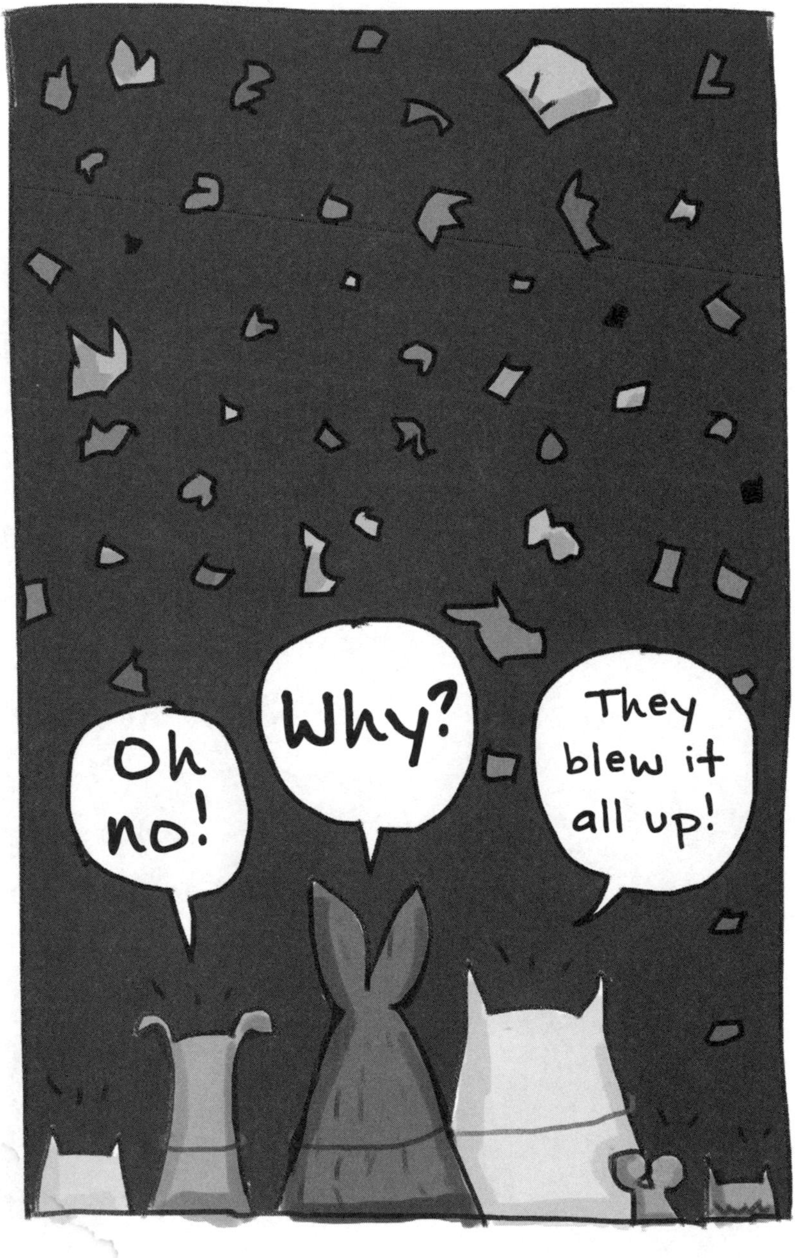
Oh no!
Why?
They blew it all up!

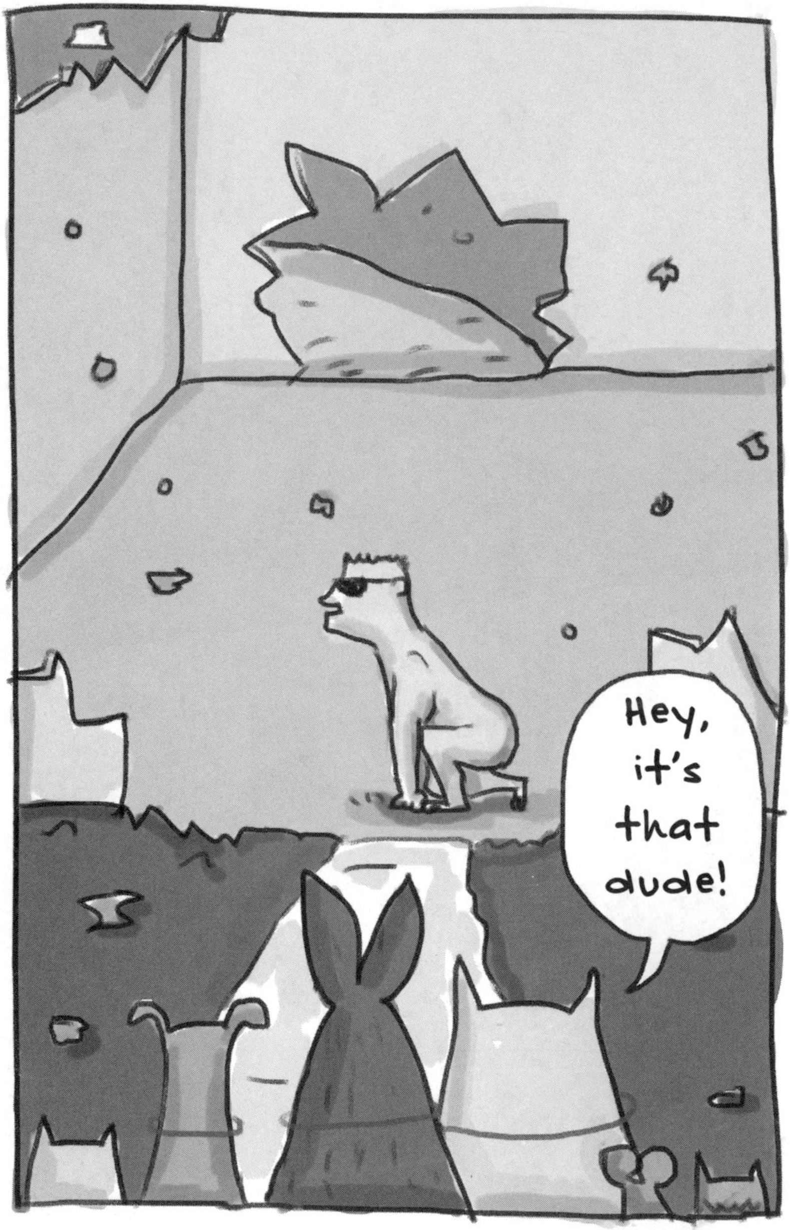
Hey, it's that dude!

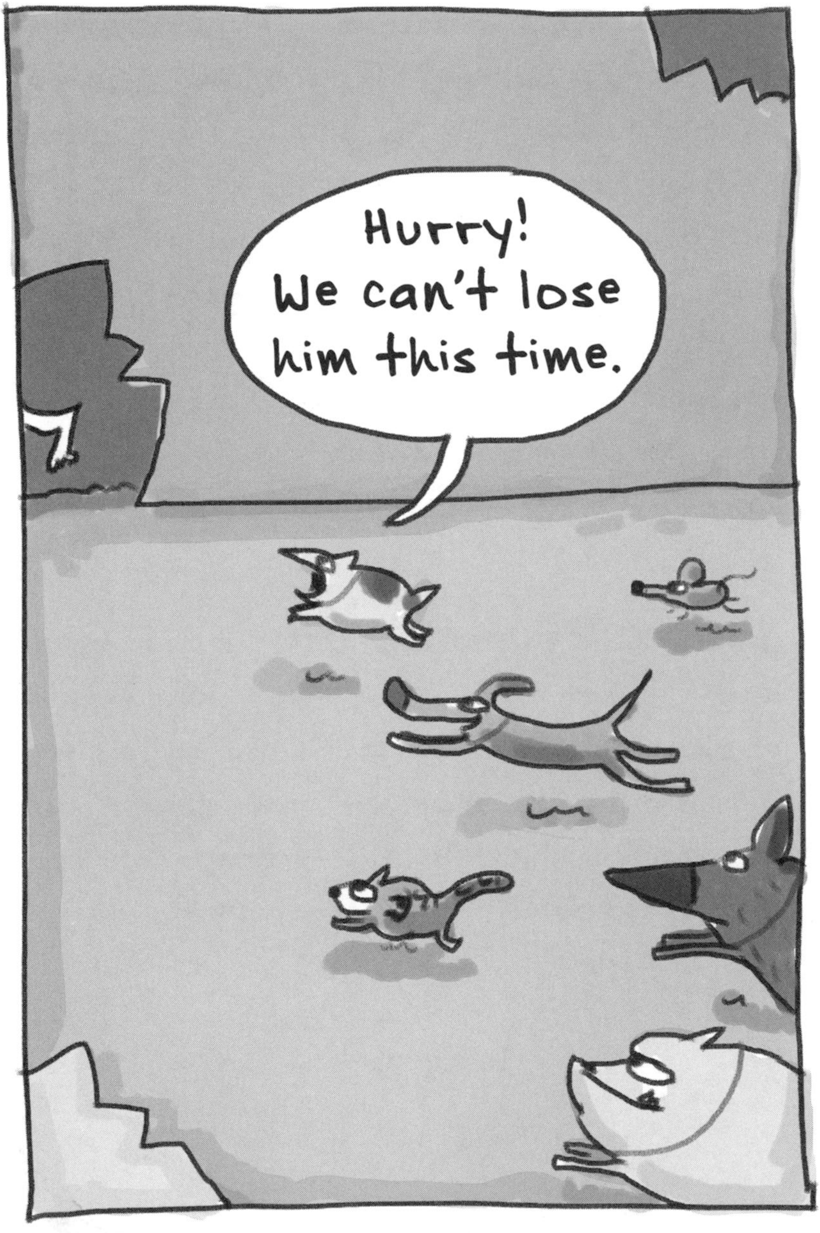
Hurry! We can't lose him this time.

James Proimos III attended St. Mary's College of Maryland, where he obtained a BA in psychology. When not writing graphic novels, he takes on gigs as a quality control specialist in the video game industry. He currently lives in Maryland with his wife and goofy rescued mutt, as well as a housemate and that housemate's spunky Jack Russell mix.

James Proimos Jr. has written and illustrated numerous children's books, including the critically acclaimed picture book Year of the Jungle by Suzanne Collins. He's a former writer and creator for television, and a dad.